PRAISE FOR THE N(OF KIM KARR

The 27 Club

"Not afraid to take chances with her writing, Kim Karr weaves an epic tale of family, love, and growth."   —Heroes and Heartbreakers

"It's truly unique and it touched my heart."
                    —*New York Times* bestselling author Katy Evans

THE CONNECTIONS SERIES

Frayed

"Angst-filled and compulsively readable. . . . Karr's world is filled with imperfect yet relatable characters, a familiar but well-written story, and hotter-than-hot sex scenes."   —*Publishers Weekly*

"Filled with passion, heart, and emotion. . . . Kim Karr did an amazing job with this story."   —Debbie's Book Bag

"This series is absolutely amazing: from the rich and colorful cast of characters, to the crazy and surprising plot twists, and the all-consuming blazing-hot passion. . . . [Karr] is at the very top of my autobuy list." —A Bookish Escape

"Kim Karr is an amazing storyteller. . . . [*Frayed*] is dramatic, intense, and realistic."   —The Reading Cafe

continued . . .

Mended

"Kim Karr is one of my few autobuys! Romantic, sexy, and downright gripping! I read it in one sitting because I just couldn't put it down!"

—*New York Times* bestselling author Vi Keeland

"Prepare to have your heart stolen by another Wilde brother. Fans of the first two titles in the series will surely fall in love with Xander Wilde and *Mended* . . . scorching hot."

—*Romantic Times*

"A stunning new romance that has it all . . . tension, heartbreak, passion, and love. . . . [*Mended*] showcases the best aspects of what these stories can give us emotionally."

—Harlequin Junkie

"Incredibly sweet. [Xander and Ivy] are a great couple."

—Book Binge

Torn

"I was riveted from the first line and couldn't put it down until the last word was read."

—*New York Times* bestselling author A. L. Jackson

"After an edge-of-your-seat cliff-hanger, Kim Karr returns to beloved characters Dahlia and River. . . . Their passion is intense."

—Fresh Fiction

"The story is fabulous, the characters are rich and full of emotion, and the romance, passion, and sexy are wonderfully balanced with the angst and heartbreak."

—Bookish Temptations

Connected

"I was pulled in from the first word and felt every emotion . . . an incredibly emotional, romantic, sexy, and addictive read."
—Samantha Young, *New York Times* bestselling author of *Moonlight on Nightingale Way*

"Emotional, unpredictable, and downright hot."
—K. A. Tucker, author of *Ten Tiny Breaths*

"This book had all my favorite things. This was one of those holy-smokes kind of books!" —Shelly Crane, *New York Times* bestselling author of *Significance*

"It's been two weeks since I finished *Connected* and Dahlia and River are still in my head."
—Bookaholics Blog (5 stars)

"I can't say enough about this book! I LOVED IT! You will be sighing, swooning, and smiling often but you will also be crying, yelling, and you will have your jaw drop to the floor once or twice."
—The Book Enthusiast

"I can't wait for more of [Karr's] books!"
—Aestas Book Blog

"Grabbed my attention and held on to it from beginning to end. . . . The romance, the heat, the angst, the storytelling, and the characters are all captivating and very well balanced."
—Bookish Temptations

"A sexy, emotional, and wonderfully romantic debut. . . . Kim Karr has a fantastic 'voice,' which will only continue to grow and refine."
—Swept Away by Romance

ALSO BY KIM KARR

THE CONNECTIONS SERIES
Connected
Torn
Dazed (Penguin digital novella)
Mended
Blurred (Penguin digital novella)
Frayed

The 27 Club

TOXIC

KIM KARR

NEW AMERICAN LIBRARY

New American Library
Published by the Penguin Group
Penguin Group (USA) LLC, 375 Hudson Street,
New York, New York 10014

USA | Canada | UK | Ireland | Australia | New Zealand | India | South Africa | China
penguin.com
A Penguin Random House Company

First published by New American Library,
a division of Penguin Group (USA) LLC

First Printing, July 2015

 REGISTERED TRADEMARK—MARCA REGISTRADA

LIBRARY OF CONGRESS CATALOGING-IN-PUBLICATION DATA:
Karr, Kim.
Toxic/Kim Karr.
p. cm.
ISBN 978-0-451-47567-1
I. Title.
PS3611.A78464T69 2015
813'.6—dc23   2015007975

Printed in the United States of America
1 3 5 7 9 10 8 6 4 2

Set in Electra LT STD

"I wanted a perfect ending. Now I've learned, the hard way, that some poems don't rhyme, and some stories don't have a clear beginning, middle, and end. Life is about not knowing, having to change, taking the moment and making the best of it, without knowing what's going to happen next. Delicious Ambiguity."

—GILDA RADNER

PROLOGUE

On Pause

July 2014

I had a ring on my finger and no date.

It didn't bother me. But it did bother my fiancé.

He had an old-school mind-set. He believed in the whole *first comes love, then comes marriage, then comes the baby in the baby carriage* thing.

The simple truth was that he was ready to get married and I wasn't quite there. But if someone had asked why not, I wouldn't be able to explain it.

I just didn't know.

I slipped the engagement ring off and held it up to the light.

The stack of wedding magazines on my desk was growing with each passing week and yet, I didn't feel compelled to look through them. I had no clear picture of what I wanted my wedding dress to look like. No preference as to where the honeymoon would take place. And when I thought of my future, I wasn't certain what I saw.

That's what bothered me the most.

What did my future hold?

No matter how many times I asked myself that question, nothing appeared to fill the blank space. I just couldn't see it. Don't get me wrong, though. I loved Dawson. I wanted to be with him. It was everything else that seemed insurmountable.

Cohabitating.

Kids.

House.

Whatever came next.

Then again, maybe it was just the jitters. After all, his marriage proposal had come out of nowhere and truthfully, I never actually said yes.

I opened the door.

And there it sat.

On top of the white fluffy duvet cover was a gleaming red box.

I was surprised—no, shocked—and I felt a little queasy to be honest. Marriage had never come up in conversation.

Suddenly, Dawson dropped to his knee right before me. "Phoebe St. Claire, will you marry me?"

"What?" I asked.

He looked up at me. "I've loved you since the moment I saw you. I know it wasn't the same for you but I know I can make you happy. Give me the chance."

I stared at him as he rose to his feet and walked to the bed. There was no time to think about the most appropriate response. He lifted the box and opened it, showing it to me. Written in gold on the inner lid was the question, WILL YOU MARRY ME?

I think I nodded. I'm not sure. The room was closing in on me and I felt like I was suffocating. I didn't know if I should say yes but knew I loved him.

Then it all happened so fast.

He slid the ring on my finger, kissed me, and snapped a picture. And before I knew it, I was engaged.

He was so excited that he announced it publicly in a tweet that read, "She said YES."

I never actually did.

My thoughts were a jumbled mess and I wasn't making any sense, even to myself. So what if I never actually said the word "yes"? I had agreed to marry him many times since that day. I loved him. He loved me. We were going to have a great life together.

Besides, I was being delusional and my irrationality was purely circumstantial. I had not seen what I thought I saw today. My rapidly beating heart needed to calm itself down because even if I had seen *him*, it's not like that would change anything. That part of my life ended with my lies. It was time to stop this nonsense. There was absolutely no place in my life for any of it.

Just then, the sunlight hit my ring and it sparkled so brilliantly, it was like the universe's way of gently reminding me I was happy, I really did want to marry Dawson.

Smiling, I slipped the ring back on my finger. But even that didn't stop the past from replaying in my mind. Like a movie on rewind, the painful memories would start at the tragic end and make their way back to the beautiful beginning. The torture came with each pause, where I should have told the truth. As my pulse jumped and stuttered over and over, I squeezed my eyes shut and tried to block out the vivid memories.

I knew where it was coming from but I also knew I hadn't actually seen *him* at the restaurant earlier today. It was just wishful thinking. The strange familiarity that stirred in my belly didn't really exist. He was in my subconscious only because today marked five years since I'd last seen him. Since I walked away and he didn't follow.

This craziness had to stop. What happened was a long time ago and I didn't have time for any more regret. Yet still, I couldn't stop myself from staring out the window and remembering how things had been between us.

I'm not sure how much time had passed when my e-mail pinged and I finally snapped out of the daze I had been in. I heaved a heavy sigh and straightened my shoulders. I had work to do. It was probably the reports I had requested from our CFO. I was the newly appointed CEO of The Saint Corporation. Although I held the position willingly it had not really been my choice. When my father was indicted for insider trading, I was named interim head of TSC. While he served his three-year sentence, it was my job to save the hotel chain from liquidation.

There's not a day that passes that I'm not scared I won't be able to accomplish it.

With a half turn, I was at my computer and opening the new file. As the minutes ticked by, I had to force myself to focus on the numbers. I'd been twirling from my desk to the window and back since I'd returned from lunch and I was determined to stop the dawdling, daydreaming, and everything else I had been thinking about that wasn't work related.

In deep concentration, I scanned the northern region first, and then moved on to the southern, before studying the western region. Each spreadsheet looked the same. Occupancy rates were down, expenses were up, and losses were mounting. On top of that, the stock price had dropped yet again.

I was going to be forced to sell more stock to stay afloat.

Feeling frustrated, I exhaled and stared at the downward trending red lines of the quarterly income comparison charts looking for answers that I knew I wasn't going to find there. It wasn't long before the loss markers started to run together and all I could see was a white blur that morphed into another cut from the reel playing in my head.

The bright sun streamed through the kitchen window. I was sitting in a chair at the table eating a bowl of cereal when he swiftly turned me around. He dropped to his knees and his hands parted my thighs. I gasped when his hot, wet mouth found my naked flesh beneath my T-shirt and his tongue lapped my clit.

Stroke.

Lick.

Stroke.

Lick.

My body moved on its own—my head tipping back, my back arching, and my hands gripping the arms of the chair.

Kiss.

Suck.

Kiss.

I couldn't quiet the moans of pleasure that escaped my throat. It felt too good. Then he inserted a finger and I came hard and rode out the waves of pleasure.

"Do you need anything else?"

I blinked and a nervous, "What?" escaped my lips.

My thoughts had wandered again.

Oh God, please tell me I hadn't been moaning out loud.

"I'm leaving for the day. I just wanted to make sure the reports I sent to you were what you were looking for."

I glanced at the spreadsheet. "Yes, Hunter, they are. Thanks for pulling them together so quickly."

"Are you okay?"

I squeezed the bridge of my nose. "I'm fine. It's the numbers that aren't. I want to review them with you tomorrow."

He heaved a sigh. "I thought you might. I already pulled detailed expense reports."

With a click, I closed the reports. "Great. We'll sift through them together. Have a good night."

Hunter gave me a nod. "You too."

As soon as he left, I jumped to my feet. It was time to go. I had to get out of here. I felt like a prisoner in my own skin. I had to escape.

Outside, the hot summer air made it hard to breathe. And for some reason, in every man I passed, I saw *him*.

His handsome face.

His blue eyes.

His long, lean body.

What was wrong with me?

So what if I'd agreed to meet with a wedding planner tonight?

It didn't mean anything other than a friendly conversation about where we should start.

And besides, Dawson was *the one*.

He was not.

I didn't really see him today. He was merely a figment of my imagination. A delusion brought on by stress—and not stress over meeting the wedding planner, or picking a date, or getting married. I wanted those things. I wanted Dawson. He was good for me.

Finally, I arrived at my fiancé's building. Wanting to forgo the social niceties, I hurried past the doorman to catch the elevator before he even noticed I had entered the lobby. In a matter of minutes, the doors dinged and I stepped out into Dawson's spacious penthouse apartment. "Dawson," I called.

When he didn't answer, I climbed the stairs up to his bedroom. The view of the city from the landing was amazing but I didn't stop to admire it. I couldn't afford to let my mind wander anymore.

As I entered through the doorway, he was walking into his room with a towel around his waist and his hair was dripping wet.

"Hey," I said.

Dawson looked surprised. "Hey, I thought we were meeting at Whitney's?"

I shrugged. "I wanted to see you first."

He smiled like he'd just won the lottery. "Good, I was going to call you as soon as I got dressed."

I drank in the sight of his body, muscles well defined from hours spent working out, his skin glistening with beads of water, his shiny hair the color of honey, his eyes like expensive chocolate, and I was overcome with need. I had been having thoughts of sex all day and I needed him.

Right now.

My emotions were a mess and I felt the need to connect with him. Without further thought, I crossed the room, stripping off my clothes as I headed toward his bed. "Dawson," I said in a low voice that didn't sound at all like me.

He hadn't noticed the clothes I'd discarded or my naked body because he had turned to open his drawer. Just as he pulled out a pair of boxers, he twisted at the sound of his name and his eyes went wide. "What are you doing?"

"Come here." I crooked a finger.

"Phoebe, we have to go. We have an appointment at seven."

I ran my hands down my body. "We can be a little late."

He looked at his watch and then at me. "What's gotten into you?"

Dawson liked order. He liked things planned and executed as planned. Spontaneity wasn't part of his DNA. I knew this but I couldn't help myself.

Realizing I had to spell it out, I sat on the edge of the bed and let my thighs hang open. My glistening pussy was all he should need to see to know what I wanted. "Kiss me," I said in a low voice.

For a minute, I thought he was going to put his boxers on. I think he contemplated it but in the end, he let his towel fall and strode toward me. He gave me a little laugh. "I just saw you at lunch, you couldn't have missed me yet. Is something going on . . ."

I stopped listening. I didn't want to talk. In fact, I really wanted him to shut up.

His cock rose as he walked over to me but he wasn't completely erect yet when he reached the bed. He would be soon. I spread my legs wider. I wanted him to drop to his knees and kiss up my thighs, between my thighs, under my thighs. Everywhere. But instead, he looked down and gave himself a few strokes until there was no limpness left. Then he motioned with his head. "Let's move up onto the bed."

I ignored his suggestion and reached around him to grab his tight ass and pull him toward my mouth. I was going to suck him off. Make him scream out my name as I took him all the way to the back of my throat.

There was a quick glance at his watch before he bent down and took my mouth with his. It was a subtle way to stop me. He was obviously in a hurry.

His kiss was soft and gentle and when he pulled back, his knees hit the bed and he scooped me up and moved me to the pillows.

"I love—" he started to say but I put my finger over his mouth and shook my head.

Dawson slid inside me in a matter of moments.

He was moving painfully slowly for my taste.

It wasn't enough. I wanted him to fuck me. I wrapped my legs around him and urged him to move faster. He picked up the pace but it still wasn't enough. I wasn't going to have the release I'd been craving like this. I didn't always orgasm when we made love but today I needed it desperately.

"I want to be on top," I whispered.

His eyes were shut and he opened them. "Okay."

I started the roll and he followed. He slipped out in the process but soon enough I was straddling his hips and guiding his cock inside me. Up I rose, and then down I slammed.

Up.

Down.

Faster and faster.

"Oh fuck," he groaned.

I smiled at him as I took up the pace even more.

Harder.

Faster.

He was getting close. I could read the signs. I put my finger on my clit and applied pressure as I chased the orgasm that I needed to have.

"Let me," he said.

His fingers took over and I leaned back on his legs, trying to let myself go. I focused on the pressure he was applying. On the way he circled me. The speed at which he was doing it. I wanted to free my mind of everything. I wanted to let myself go. But something was holding me back.

"I'm going to come, baby. What about you?"

"Yes. I'm there," I said even though I wasn't.

Dawson stilled my hips and grunted and groaned as he came. When he was done, I collapsed on his chest—my insides still a tangled knotted mess.

Fingers gently pushed the hair from my face. "Will you marry me?"

With a smile, I looked up at him.

Dawson Vanderbilt was the Prince of Camelot, or at least that was the nickname my neighbor, Mrs. Bardot, had given my blond John F. Kennedy Jr. look-alike boyfriend the moment she laid eyes on him.

"How was work?" I asked.

He sat up. "My brother-in-law was named president of Vanderbilt Brokerage of London today, so it was a good day."

Vanderbilt Brokerage was the largest American stock brokerage and securities firm in the US. They had recently expanded into London. The European market might have been new ground for the company, but the Vanderbilt family business had been around for many generations. Dawson's father was still at the helm and Dawson himself was recently not only awarded a seat on the stock exchange but was appointed the head of the acquisitions division.

"Blaine must be thrilled."

He got to his feet and found his boxers. "My sister had some choice words, but thrilled wasn't one of them."

"I thought she wanted to move to—"

He came back over to me and put his palms on the mattress. "I asked you a question."

"Dawson, you've asked me that same question every day since we got engaged. You already know I will."

He leaned a little closer. "Then pick a date."

I ducked under his arm and rose off the bed. "It's not that easy."

"Phoebe, it really is."

I started to tremble and suddenly felt very naked. "I need to prepare," I blurted out.

"Prepare for what?" he asked.

"Combining both of our households." I wasn't sure why I said that.

He walked over to his closet and stepped in. "I was thinking we could reorganize my apartment this weekend."

I started to put my own clothes back on. "I'm moving into your place?"

He peeked his head out the door. "Phoebe, of course you are. Your apartment is too small."

He was right.

"After we're married, we can convert the gym near the master into a nursery."

I froze. "A nursery?"

Dawson stepped out of the closet completely dressed. "Yeah, for a baby."

My fingers shook as I buttoned my blouse. "I know what a nursery is but I'm nowhere near ready to have children."

His eyes almost sparkled. "You say that now, but all women quit their jobs and have babies eventually."

My jaw dropped. "You said you were fine with me working. I want my career."

"I am fine with it. I know how important TSC is to you but your father will be back."

"In two and a half years," I clarified.

He ran a hand through his hair. "Baby, let's just take things as they come."

I stared at him. "I'm not going to end up like my mother—an unhappy wife who, before my father's legal troubles, filled her social calendar and fucked around on the side to fulfill her other needs."

He took a step closer. "That won't happen."

He was wrong.

I started to feel like I was suffocating.

"Phoebe, don't shut down." His voice had a hard edge to it.

"I'm not shutting down," I replied in a whisper.

I was.

His chin bobbed up and down. "You shut down every time I bring up picking a date."

I stepped into my shoes. "That's not true."

Dawson sighed in exasperation. "It is. That's what I was going to call you about. Before we go to meet Whitney, I want you to pick a date."

"Right now?" I asked, raising my voice.

He stepped closer to me and lifted my chin. Then in a firm voice, he said, "Yes. Right now."

My mouth dropped. He wasn't normally so assertive with me. Others yes, but not me. Something about the command in his tone turned me on and I wondered if we could try the bed thing again.

He stared at me, silently demanding an answer.

I did love him. I did want to marry him. I could do this for him. I mean how hard was it to pick a date. "October fifteenth."

"October, like in four months?"

"Yes, this October."

He laughed. "We can't get the Plaza on such short notice."

"I was thinking someplace different. There's this nineteenth-century metal factory called the Foundry. It has old exposed brick and modern steel railings. I think it would be perfect."

"Come on, Phoebe, you know everyone in my family gets married at the Plaza."

I frowned. "But you can be the one to change that."

He shook his head. "You know I can't but let me see what I can do."

I nodded because I was unable to speak. Suddenly I felt like I couldn't breathe.

"You're sure?"

I nodded again but the truth was, I wasn't.

And I wished I could just put our wedding plans on pause.

CHAPTER 1

Familiar Faces

October 2014

My mother taught me many things . . .

To stand up straight.

To be thankful for what I had.

To never talk to strangers.

And to always answer when spoken to.

I didn't always listen.

"I miss you." The text had arrived early this morning and I hadn't been able to reply. I didn't know what to say but I knew why Dawson had sent it.

It was October fifteenth.

Our wedding day.

Or it was supposed to have been anyway.

The rain was steadily falling as Lily and I left the movie theater and quickly made our way to the waiting car.

As soon as I got in, I collapsed in the smooth leather seat and looked next to me. "Thank you."

"For what?"

"For always being there for me."

"That's what best friends are for." She smiled.

And that's what she was. Lily Monroe had been my best friend for as long as I could remember. And like me, she was in a strange place.

"Has he called yet?" I asked, uncertain if I should bring it up.

Lily shook her head.

"You should just call him."

She shot me an *if looks could kill* glare. "No, I will not. And we're not talking about him. As far as I'm concerned, Preston Tyler is dead."

Okay then.

I knew when to shut up.

Lily and Preston were always breaking up and getting back together but this was the longest they had been apart in the three years they had been a couple. The breakup was going on nearly four weeks.

Lily opened her purse. "Here," she said as she unscrewed a small bottle of wine. It was the kind you get when you're flying. A glass for one.

I took it and gave her a smile and when she pulled out a second, I had to laugh. "Always prepared."

"You know it," she said, raising her hand. "To rainy days."

"And rainy nights." I clinked her bottle.

"To new beginnings."

"And old endings," I said, and then I drank the wine.

All of it.

I needed it.

After a final gulp, I let my forehead fall to the window. The sound of faint raindrops that drizzled down it as I stared out into the night triggered something inside me—that lonely ache that I couldn't seem to ever shake. And for the first time since I had woken up that morning, I allowed a melancholy wave of sorrow to wash over me.

I'd second-guessed my decision to end things with Dawson every day. So when I woke up this morning, I thought I'd be sadder than I had been.

But I wasn't sad at all.

I was relieved.

I was ready for the shadow that had been looming over me since I broke off the engagement to be gone. Even after the wedding was canceled, the countdown to the big day was still there. Just because two people ceased to exist as a unit, it didn't mean you no longer felt the other person's presence in your life.

And Dawson Vanderbilt, even with his gallant stand-up and let's be friends attitude, had felt like a constant mark of failure in my life.

The seemingly perfect man, a wedding planned with all the trimmings, and I still couldn't go through with it. I knew the chemistry wasn't there to sustain a life of happiness together.

I loved him, yet the spark I wanted to feel each time I saw him and the leg I wanted to kick back with a pointed toe when he kissed me—neither ever came.

My phone rang and glancing at the screen, I rolled my eyes.

"Your mother again?" Lily asked.

I nodded. "She's called me every hour since I left her at lunch. She says she's checking on me but I can't help but feel like it's more. Like she's punishing me for not going through with the wedding by reminding me of all the things we would have been doing today."

"She means well, you know she does."

"I suppose," I said as I glanced again at the ringing phone.

"Give it to me."

I looked at Lily questioningly.

"Give me your phone."

She powered it off. "Everyone you need to talk to will be right inside there." She pointed to the large brick building we were coming up on in the Meatpacking District.

I gave her a weak smile and slipped my phone in my purse.

When the car slowed, Lily put her hand on my leg. "You sure you're up to this? We could just go back to my place and watch another movie."

I flashed her a huge grin, letting my pearly whites show as the black Escalade pulled up to the curb. "Are you kidding?" I chuckled. "And miss the funeral tonight?"

She giggled. "Speaking of, did you see Danny's tweet?"

I shook my head.

She pulled out her phone, tapped a few buttons, and showed me. "May our ideals RIP. #Bestfuckingfriends #Somethingsshouldneverdie."

"I really have missed him," I sighed.

"Me too but at least his social media obsession keeps us up to date with his daily life," Lily replied with a wink.

"That's true."

"Last chance," she said.

For one moment, I thought about backing out but I plastered a smile on my face instead. "I'm fine. Now let's go have some fun."

The door opened and a big black umbrella was held above it. I placed my hand on Hugh's shoulder. "I'll take a cab home, so don't wait up for my call."

Hugh had been our family's driver since I was eight years old.

"Miss Phoebe," he said in his heavy English accent. "You know your father insists I see to it that you make it home safely."

With one foot out the door, I tried not to laugh at the irony that even from his jail cell, my father still felt the need to watch over me. "I promise I will."

He shook his head with a heavy sigh, conceding quickly before an argument arose that he knew he'd never win.

I gave him a little squeeze before dropping my other foot to the ground. "Have a good night."

As of that morning, Hugh's duties had been transferred from our family's personal driver to a driver for the Saint Hotel. He'd still drive my mother as well, of course. Poppy had all but refused to cut back and I knew losing her driver wouldn't sit well. Soon enough she would be feeling the repercussions of not doing as I had suggested. The Hamptons house went on the market last year and sold right away so that kept her bank account full over the past year. But with no money coming in from The Saint Corporation, I estimated within a year she'd have nothing left.

The trust fund I had access to was also almost empty. My grandfather had divided the money in half—I got the first half when I turned twenty-one and the second when I turn thirty-one, which was still five years away. Most of what I had was used for my father's legal defense when all of his and my mother's assets were frozen. I was surprised that my father dragged the proceedings out as long as he did. I knew he was guilty. Everyone knew he was guilty. He'd been charged once before though, when I was little, and had gotten off. I think that's why he refused to plead guilty. But this time it cost him—no, us—a fortune. And he wasn't acquitted as he was over twenty years ago. I had never thought of my father as selfish, but I did now. After everything, in the end, to receive a lighter sentence, he finally did plead guilty.

By then the St. Claire fortune had been nearly depleted. My parents had been living beyond their means for years anyway, so it didn't take much to empty them once their accounts had been released.

I had to turn the company around. If not we were not only going to be penniless, we would be homeless. My apartment was a rental, with a steep rent. My lease would be up next month and I planned to move out of the Park Avenue apartment my mother had insisted on when I went to grad school. But my mother would never leave her home on East Seventy-sixth Street until she was forced to. And a small part of me didn't want her to. It was my childhood home after all. But the reasonable side of me knew that even after the second mortgage was paid off, the five-story home would sell for enough that she'd never have to worry about money.

And then I wouldn't have to worry about her.

The open velvet rope was only a few feet away but it seemed so much farther. I grabbed on to Lily's arm to steady myself. I was feeling slightly tipsy from the wine and my mind was running in a million different directions.

My mother.

My father.

My job.

I took a deep breath.

The cool air felt good in my lungs. It helped to shift my mind away from my problems. I looked at Lily; she was worried about me, I could tell. But I knew I'd be fine. Today I was allowed to be down but tomorrow I would pick myself back up. Still, I wanted to ease her mind. With thoughts of the flick we had just watched, more specifically of the very hot, very sexy Captain America, slamming into my head, I decided to do something to convince Lily I was okay.

So I held my phone to my ear in mock conversation and spoke loud enough for her to hear. "Hello, Marvel Studios, I really want to play the Black Widow in the next *Captain America* movie."

She looped her arm through mine and her dirty-sounding chuckle was loud. "Gorgeous, all legs, and sexy vixen with a husky voice—yeah, I'd say that part works for you."

Flashing a smile at the bouncer, I stopped. "We're Danny Capshaw's guests, Phoebe St. Claire and Lily Monroe."

He glanced down at his clipboard and nodded for us to pass.

Danny belonged to some entertainment circuit that had come to the city last year, called Jet Set. It was the hottest new thing—membership not only allowed exclusive weekend access into some of the city's hottest clubs, it was the only way to gain VIP status. It was brilliant. Nothing the rich and famous valued more than exclusivity. And they were more than willing to pay—a lot. Membership fees were ridiculously high.

The soles of my high heels clicked on the red-and-white-checked floor, and as soon as we entered the club, my vision blurred as the pink walls coated everything in my sight with a slight blush. I looked over to Lily. "By the way, I was thinking more like a pistol-toting badass, but I'll take sexpot."

Right in front of a fifteen-foot Rorschach print by Andy Warhol, Lily snorted, "You'd have to remove the cobwebs from your vagina to even remotely gain that title."

"It hasn't been that long."

She rolled her eyes.

"What? It hasn't. Just because when you and Preston are on, you do it morning, noon, and night doesn't mean the rest of us do."

She shrugged. "I can't help it if I have an overactive libido."

I had to laugh.

"And besides, most younger couples do it more than once a week."

"Dawson and I did it more than that but even if we didn't, I'm sure we'd be considered way more normal than you and Preston."

With a tug of my hand, Lily led me toward our table. "Let's see what everyone else has to say about it."

"Oh God, let's not."

Everyone else was our four best friends. We had pledged growing up we wouldn't turn into our parents but as of that very morning the last of us entered the ranks. Now, each and every one of us had joined our prospective family businesses. Making it official, we'd broken the vow. And now we were doing the only thing we could—gathering together to bury it.

Morbid yet true.

Making our way through the crowd, I noticed the way the glass shelves that towered over the bar seemed to shimmer with the aged scotches and exotic liquors. It was a Saturday night, and like most Saturday nights in every nightclub all around the world, the patrons were out to celebrate. But unlike everyone else, we were coming together to mourn the death of our young ideals.

Coincidence the burial was taking place on the same day as my canceled wedding?

I hardly thought so.

It had to have been a sign that it was time to put them both to rest.

The Rose Bar was the newest addition to Jet Set. Danny met the owner of

Jet Set last year while he was partying in a club in Miami. Under its new management, the Rose Bar had been touted as one of America's swankiest clubs. It even had a fleet of white cars, including Hummers, Lamborghinis, Ferraris, and Porsches, used to pick up and drop off Jet Set members.

The club was packed and brimming with wealthy men and women, some of whom I was sure would turn up on Page Six. Because the men and women inside weren't just anyones, we were all someones—the great-granddaughter of Eisenhower, the great-nephew of Ford, a great-cousin of Kennedy. No one needed to know how many greats were before our names—it was irrelevant. The bloodlines were all that ever mattered.

I rolled my eyes at the thought and draped my leather jacket over my arm. My little black dress fell a few inches above my knees and the vertical lines of crystals gave it some shape. I preferred comfort to style in a way that seemed to separate me from my peers whose motto was all fashion.

Lily and I passed a brilliant red billiards table and a loud cackle of laughter caused me to look up. At the center booth, in the middle of the VIP section sat a bunch of guys. Even as Lily continued to pull me along, my eyes stayed locked where they were, as if some kind of magnetic force wouldn't allow my gaze to shift.

The guys in the booth toasted one another and then slammed back their drinks, laughing boisterously. However, when a group of scantily clad women walked by their table, they all stopped talking. The women eyed the guys as languorously as they possibly could, hoping for an invitation to join them, I was sure. The guys stared back with equal vigor.

I knew those guys.

I dropped Lily's hand and walked closer. Standing at the edge of the stairs, I recognized a few of the girls' faces from grad school at Stern. My eyes redirected to the horseshoe of men in the booth, also from Stern. Lars Jefferson was the bookend to the group. In grad school he was always the loudest, most obnoxious, and most arrogant guy on campus. He held his elite social status as a pass—a pass to do and say anything he wanted. Unfortunately, he was also Dawson's best friend.

I never could stand him.

He leaned forward and that's when I saw the blond hair I'd have known anywhere.

Dawson.

I froze, glued to the spot I was standing in.

It had been three months since I'd broken up with Dawson. Six weeks after we set the date. The day I was supposed to move in with him. Now I couldn't help but stare. Of all the places to run into him, I never thought I'd see him here.

Lars stared at the women. He took his time choosing the girl he wanted and then beckoned her with his smile. I watched as it went down, needing to see if my ex-fiancé did the same. Lars tipped his chin and sure enough the woman beamed with glee. Dawson just sat there while a few of the other guys followed Lars' lead.

The girl Lars showed interest in brushed her jet-black bangs away from her face, patted her hips with her hands, and walked slowly to the table. I was certain she must have known who he was and probably also knew he was involved with someone. From the white-toothed smile Lars gave her as she walked over, she must have been confident that didn't matter.

"Hi," she said to him.

I was good at lipreading. I'd spent a great deal of time watching people. No, I'd studied couples' interactions. It was an unhealthy habit I had picked up when I was lost. But it was Dawson who had helped me stop. It was Dawson who helped me live again. It was Dawson with that group of men looking to fuck any girl they could. And it was Dawson who I had let go.

Ice formed in my belly.

Lars ran his eyes up and down the girl's body, as if he was trying to assess her dress size. Then he gave Dawson a sideways look. Dawson shrugged. If it was because he wasn't interested or didn't care, I couldn't tell. But then Dawson shifted his eyes toward a pretty blonde who walked by and Lars did the same. I had to assume Lars maybe just wanted what Dawson was interested in.

Prick.

Hand on hip, the woman did a runway turn, like a schoolgirl in front of her bedroom mirror, and started to walk toward them again. When she passed, Dawson nudged Lars. Comically, Lars got up and chased her.

My eyes settled on Dawson. There were so many guys in the club and they were just as handsome as the ones at that center table, but none of them were as eligible as those bachelors sitting together. None of them had ever been married, each was under thirty years old, and surprisingly, each was very gainfully employed. They were New York City's biggest catches and every Eloise could only hope to land one of them.

Why had I been the exception?

"Stop shooting daggers his way. He's not doing anything wrong," Lily barked at me.

I blinked a few times, suddenly realizing I was doing just what she said I was. The shock I felt that Dawson would join that crowd looking for a meaningless hookup was quickly replaced by hurt.

Over the thumping bass of the music, Lily said, "Come on. You're staring."

I gaped at her. "I'm not staring," I snapped.

She took my hand. "Hey, are you okay?"

I nodded.

"Do you remember why you broke up with him?" she asked.

I nodded again.

"Then let's go."

I didn't move. "I just feel a little confused right now."

Her grip around my fingers tightened. "I know. And you know I love you and I'm only looking out for you when I remind you again that you broke up with him for a reason, and a good one. So quit looking like you wish you were still together."

My eyes focused on my best friend. "I don't regret the breakup."

She dropped her hold on my hand and moved to stand in front of me, blatantly blocking my view. "I know you don't and you shouldn't. He wasn't right for you."

I pursed my lips. "I wasn't right for him."

Her face filled with concern. "You weren't right for each other. So why the sad face?"

I bit my lip in contemplation. "This is the first time I've seen him since he brought over my stuff. He looks happy."

She grabbed my hand and squeezed it. "Good. Now you can stop feeling guilty."

I nodded.

I wished it was that easy.

She turned on her heels. "Come on, tonight's the last night we'll all be together for a long time."

With a genuine smile forming on my lips, I shifted my eyes to find our friends. Jamie was lounging in a booth on the other side of the VIP section. The neon lights from the disco ball above the dance floor flickered all around him as he took a large gulp of his scotch, maybe trying to wash down the bad taste of the last foreclosure he had to make that put someone on the street.

Emmy was filming him with a video camera, probably wishing she could film the two of them together. When we were younger, she had aspirations of going to Hollywood and being an actress. She settled on home movie production for the time being and brought her video camera everywhere. Her parents held her trust fund over her head to keep her in New York. Soon though, when she turned thirty, she would have complete ownership and then, we were sure, she'd be gone.

Logan was in a deep discussion over in the corner of the bar, about what was anyone's guess—he never discussed his job or his life. Although a good friend, I knew very little about him. He was the quiet, secretive one.

A lot like me.

But his reasons for remaining quiet were different from mine—mine were internal, the way I felt about myself and this world of ours. His were more external. He'd grown up in two very different worlds and I think he struggled with which one he belonged in.

Danny made me laugh. He was dancing with some guy I'd never seen before. Throwing his hands around like a rapper, more than likely mourning the loss of his freedom. Always the happy-go-lucky one in the group, he'd recently joined the ranks of the employed, sitting beside his father and learning the ropes of the gaming industry that had made his great-great-grandfather billions. Of all of us he had held out the longest. Went on sabbatical after grad school to find himself but when he came back he found himself all right, right beside his tycoon father being groomed to run the family-owned business.

These people gathered here tonight were like my family. We grew up together, went to the same parties, to the same schools, and once upon a time we all hated the life that having money brought. Those days were long over. We'd tried our best to hold on to them, but life took over and crushed those ideals. We had all decided further education was the quickest and easiest way to avoid the family binds that awaited us. Me, it wasn't the business I was avoiding. I just didn't care what path I took and where it led. But none of it had mattered because when we graduated, whether it was with an MBA, law degree, or other certification, the family calling was inevitable.

Lily Monroe, textile heiress, was learning the apparel business that had been started by her great-grandfather. She loved to shop, knew clothing well, what fashions worked and what didn't. She would make a great figurehead for the House of Monroe someday, but running the company didn't interest her. Her goals were all short-term. She had become the true socialite of the group and hated working more than any of us. Her passion was ballet and what she wanted more than anything was to be a ballerina. But a knee injury in her freshman year at Juilliard changed all that, and as time passed, Lily's dream had too. I prayed Lily would never have to take over the family business like I had, and so did she.

Logan McPherson was the grandson of a hedge fund manager and philanthropist worth an estimated twenty billion dollars. His grandfather was one of the wealthiest men in the city, but Logan never seemed to care and he never discussed money. He was an attorney who spent most of his time in Boston. I knew he was licensed in both states but wasn't sure if he was practicing in either. No one knew much about his work.

Emmy Lane, publishing heiress, refused to learn what it would take to run a long list of publications owned by her family and because of her resistance, her parents were not on board with her plan to relocate to LA. She hadn't gotten the big break she was waiting for but she still continued to audition for parts here in the city. Lane Publishing might have been her family legacy but her passion was acting and she still hoped someday she would be a star.

James Ashton, Harvard graduate and real estate heir, acquired his real estate license shortly after grad school and learned quickly how to wheel and deal with the bigwigs.

And Danny, poor Danny just recently settled into his destiny, marking day one of the rest of his life. Danny had choices though. His father was a gaming heir from very old money and his mother was of the European "fast set." Her family had founded Fiat and led a glamorous life that included elaborate parties, streamlined yachts, fast cars, and luxurious villas. Although Fiat was no longer family owned, he could have joined the board. In the end, he opted for the gaming industry. Churchill Downs was where his training would begin and he'd be based in Kentucky for the next year. He had mixed emotions about leaving the city but since he'd been back and forth for the last two years, what was one more? Well, that's what he said anyway.

And then there was me. Phoebe St. Claire—heiress to a hotel empire that was crumbling before my eyes.

My great-grandfather bought his first hotel at the height of the oil boom. His father disapproved of the investment but the hotel broke all records and soon my great-grandfather expanded throughout the country, adding hotel after hotel. Just before his death The Saint Corporation, known as TSC, expanded internationally to be the first international hotel chain promulgating a certain worldwide standard for hotel accommodations everywhere. Through the years, the international division was sold off, and under my father's reign, all that remained were the US operations. As my father's only child, I always knew I was next in line to run what was left of the hotel empire. It simply happened sooner than I thought. The circumstances only compounded the financial distress of the already vulnerable company.

With a whistle, Jamie held up a bottle of Piper-Heidsieck champagne. Danny and Logan headed toward him and Emmy without any further prompting. Together, Lily and I climbed the steps up to the booth.

Jamie stood and pulled me close to him. "You doing okay today?"

I put my finger to his lips. "We'll talk later."

"Dawson's here."

"I know," I said, and glanced over my shoulder toward his table.

If Lily had always been my very best girlfriend, Jamie held the spot as my very best boyfriend. In fact, I think I was always more open with him than I was with Lily. We just had an ease between us.

"My man," Jamie said, turning to Danny. "How was your first day on the job?"

"Fucking sucked. But I expected worse."

I turned around and hugged him. "Something tells me you loved it."

Shoulders lifting he said, "I'll let you know after a month in Kentucky when I'm not under my father's watchful eye."

"Phoebe, you made it." Emmy greeted me with a hug and Logan joined in.

I purposely moved myself to the other side of the booth so my back was to the center of the room. Nothing good would come of me staring at Dawson all night.

Once we all sat down, Jamie passed glasses to each of us, and then raised his. "Today, we have gathered to mourn the loss of our youth. We were once young, wild, and free but all that remains now is for us to get even wilder. So let's get fucking drunk."

"Cheers," we all said in unison as we clinked our glasses.

An hour later, and after too many bottles of champagne and wine, for what had to have been the twentieth time of the night, we brought our hands to the center of the table. The six of us shared a bond that could not be broken by any-one, and we all knew it. And this time, as our flutes clinked, we said together at the top of our lungs, "Friends forever," and pressed our glasses to our foreheads.

It was a private signal between us. We'd seen each other through so much; no words could describe what we felt for one another. And no one knew any of us like we knew one another. Through thick and thin, united we stood.

Dramatic—yes.

Real—absolutely.

After we finished our toast, I stood on wobbly legs. "Excuse me, I have to use the restroom."

"Do you want me to come with you?" Emmy asked.

She was nestled close to Jamie and seemed pretty happy right where she was. Some things never changed. "No, you stay put."

I looked down at my watch. It was only twelve ten, or maybe it was two. Funny, I couldn't tell which was the big hand and which was the little one.

The stairs nearest to our booth offered me the chance to glance toward Dawson. As I took the step, I had a strange feeling someone was watching me. A silver zipper on a distressed leather jacket caught the reflection of one of the beams of light flaring down from the twirling disco ball. The leather stood out in a sea of fine fabric suits and sequin dresses but then faded into the crowd. For a moment, a sense of familiarity stirred in my belly. But I pushed the feel-ing aside and just thought—too much alcohol.

The restrooms were near the back—I'd been here before it changed own-ers and I remembered. Or I thought I did. I tried to peer through the crowd to locate the bathrooms but the place was way too big to see around the bar or the dance floor.

"Hello, gorgeous. Long time no see. I was just coming to say hi." Lars leaned down and kissed me right on the mouth.

I quickly stepped back, surprised by his close proximity and repelled by the feel of his lips on mine.

He shoved a glass of wine into my hand. "I bought you a drink. Thought we could celebrate . . . you know, moving on."

I stepped back again.

And when I did, Lars' eyes widened and his grin was wicked. "Whoa, you look sexy as hell. Did you start celebrating without me?"

I stood as straight as I could, trying to shake off the feeling of bugs crawling all over my body from the prickle of his stare. "No! I'm here to celebrate Danny's new job." That wasn't really the truth, but I wasn't about to explain to Lars.

"Well, fuck me upside down, but, Phoebe, it looks like you want to do more than celebrate."

I considered his comment. My dress was shorter than I'd normally have worn, and the neckline much lower than I'd ever worn. But Lily had bought it specifically for me, for my unwedding day as she called it, and dropped it off that morning. How could I have refused her?

He lifted my chin. "You changed your hair too."

"I cut it."

After I broke up with Dawson I needed a change, so I cut my long tresses to just above my shoulders and darkened them a bit at the same time. My once long, wavy, golden blond hair was shorter, darker, and straighter.

My mother hated it. She said it looked like a bob and she detested bobs. I happened to love it. The whole change made me feel lighter, freer.

Lars tugged on the ends of my hair. "You changed the color too. It looks sultry." He licked his lips. "You look sexy as fuck."

I jerked my head back and just stared at him. Unsure where he was going with this and not really caring, I just wanted to escape his scrutiny.

"You've put some weight on too. Not so skinny anymore."

I shrugged. I couldn't control my weight. If I lost my appetite for even a day, I looked unhealthily skinny. Everyone thought it was great to have such a high metabolism. But it wasn't. I had to work at maintaining a healthy weight or my frame looked boylike.

"Has Dawson seen you yet?"

Disbelief clouded my narrowing eyes at the nerve of him. Like my ex-fiancé seeing me looking different would change anything about our relationship?

My vision began to blur at that point and I knew I had had way too much to drink.

Lars' mouth was at my ear before I could move away. "Your outfit makes it look like you have curves in all the right places though, don't worry."

I thought I might vomit.

Was he for real?

Words flew out of my mouth at lightning speed. "You're such a dick. Go find some other woman to harass who's into your kind of foreplay."

An evil grin formed on his lips. "A dirty mouth too, just the way I like them."

"You like them any way you can get them," I spat back.

Bile rose in my throat and I wasn't sure if it was his attention or the alcohol causing the sick feeling.

"Feisty." He grinned. "What was Dawson thinking letting you go? I bet you're an animal in the sack."

"Get lost," I told him and turned to walk away.

He grabbed my wrist. "Now that you're all worked up, what do you say we get out of here? I won't tell Dawson."

I tried to free myself of his grip but he wouldn't let go.

Someone stepped between us. The distressed leather was the first thing my eyes were focused on when my skin started to tingle with a sense of familiarity. The tingling quickly turned into trembling as my gaze lifted and I saw the bluest of blue eyes.

They were soft, concerned, knowing.

They were the eyes of my past.

It was *him*.

I was surprised.

I was shocked.

I was mesmerized.

My body started to tremble even more and I downed the glass of wine I had been holding to help calm my nerves.

Still, I couldn't stop staring. He looked the same. No, he looked better, if that was possible. His hair was shorter but his devastating good looks were even more striking.

This time I knew he was real—he wasn't a figment of my imagination. Just that one look into his eyes and all the hurt was forgotten. It was as if the last five years had never happened.

I lost myself in his eyes and I couldn't stop myself from going back to when we'd first met.

It was the day I came alive.

CHAPTER 2

Just Kiss Me

June 2009

It was my twenty-first birthday.

Under the warm night sky, I watched as guests in black tie and fancy dresses pulled up to the country club.

Most of the invited guests were decades older than I.

But I'd expected that.

I said hello and smiled like I knew I should.

I was a St. Claire after all.

Once everyone had arrived, my mother looked over at me. "Come on. Let's go in."

Together with my mother and father, I entered the large white tent filled with gorgeous flowers that scented the air. My father grabbed two flutes of champagne from a tray and handed one to me and one to my mother. I smiled at him and they looked around. They had gone all out this year. Waiters carried trays of caviar, smoked salmon, and other various delicacies. There was a sushi bar at one end and a cake the size of one of the tables at the other.

My friends were sitting together at a table and I made my way over to them. For the next few hours we talked. And drank. And then danced.

At midnight my parents joined hands and made a toast—they were such a united front.

"You'll always be our little girl no matter how old you are," they both said.

The toast went on and on about how special I was and how bright my future looked. They had it all mapped out. I couldn't help but cry. However, I wasn't sure if I was crying over their words or about their words.

I felt like I was suffocating.

What they wished for me wasn't how I saw my future. The problem was, at twenty-one, I didn't know what I was going to do.

Forced to always do what they wanted, I began to wonder if even with a college degree and a trust fund, that would ever change. Feeling a bit drunk and overwhelmed with so many and so few choices at the same time, I needed some time alone and snuck off toward the beach path.

I ran toward the ocean and twirled in the sand as the wind blew around me. Once I started to feel dizzy from twirling, I still wasn't ready to head back to the party, so I took the path that would lead me to the large Olympic-sized pool. I tugged my sandals off with thoughts of putting my feet in the water to rinse the mud and sand away. As I approached the pool, I noticed how it glowed like it was lit by small pale fires. Lost in the enchantment of it, the sudden movement beneath the surface startled me.

A fair-haired boy emerged from the water. He pulled himself up and out so quickly that I was momentarily stunned.

He drank me in with his eyes.

The way he looked at me made me shiver. No one had ever looked at me like that before.

I found myself gazing into his intense eyes.

He was utterly beautiful. His bare chest was sculpted but not overly bulky like Danny or Jamie. They worked out every day pumping obnoxious amounts of iron to look the way they did. In contrast, the boy standing before me had a swimmer's build—long and lean and breathtaking.

He stood stoicly and a cautious look crossed his face. That long and lean body was in a pair of bright green neon swim trunks.

Right away I could tell he didn't care what anyone thought about him.

I loved the idea of that.

So I smiled at him.

He shook his head and his hair fell into his eyes.

I wanted to reach out and push it away. It wasn't long, but it wasn't short. It was perfect.

"Hey," he said, grabbing a towel off the ground.

It didn't belong to the club. It was small, beige, and a bit worn—not the large hunter-green fluffy ones monogrammed in white I'd always gotten when I used to come here to swim as a kid.

"Hey," I said back, swinging my sandals nervously.

He grabbed a pair of jeans that lay next to where the towel had been and walked right by me.

I turned to watch him as he strode into one of the cabanas and dropped his trunks. I froze and squeezed my eyes shut, thinking I shouldn't be watching him but then opened them quickly when I couldn't resist maybe catching a glimpse.

"Didn't your parents ever tell you it isn't polite to stare?" His voice was low and sexy, and it tugged me out of my own head.

I put my hands on my hips. "Didn't your parents ever teach you not to undress in mixed company?"

He pulled his jeans on and laughed. "My mother might have mentioned that once or twice but I've never been good at following the rules."

And it didn't escape my notice that he didn't put any underwear on first.

Hot. Totally and completely hot.

I didn't see anything I shouldn't have seen, it was too dark, but something inside me electrified at the thought of seeing him naked and I stepped closer. That's when I noticed the scuffed-up black work boots on one of the lounges with a T-shirt thrown next to them.

I raised a brow. "Is this your changing room?"

He laughed again but this time added a smile and put his hands up. "Okay, you caught me. I better get out of here before anyone else does."

He was adorable and charming and my heart skipped a beat or two.

Then I stepped even closer and entered the cabana entrance, effectively blocking his way. "Why? You're not doing anything wrong."

He shrugged but he didn't try to move around me. "I usually swim in the ocean but when the water is too rough, like tonight, I come here."

I bit my lip in contemplation before speaking. "Does it really matter if you get caught?"

He crossed his arms over his bare chest. "Let's say it's not just the swimming. It's more that I've been caught doing a few too many things that I shouldn't have been doing in the past."

A bad boy.

The thought made my pulse thunder. "So you're not a member at this club?"

He cleared his throat and shifted from foot to foot. "No," he laughed but his laugh was anything but genuine. "Are you?"

I hesitated as I considered my answer. "No, I was just walking the beach and wanted to rinse my feet. I'm Phoebe," I said, extending my hand. Technically, I wasn't lying. I wasn't a member, my parents were. I hadn't even been here in years. And I was out for a walk.

Amusement danced in his blue eyes. "Jeremy," he said back.

When I chewed on my lower lip, I noticed how his eyes focused on it. Mine focused on the entirety of his mouth—his strong, firm jaw, his sensuous lips, and his tongue that had snuck out to lick his lips.

I felt compelled to speak but wouldn't have minded if all we had done was stare. "Is this your first summer in the Hamptons?" I asked because I'd never seen him before.

He shook his head. "I've been coming here ever since I was born. My mother is a caterer in the city. She moves her business here every summer." He bobbed his head toward the main building. "She works out of the club."

I twisted the butterfly ring I always wore on my right hand. "And your dad?"

He flinched. "He went away a long time ago."

"I'm sorry."

He shrugged. "Don't be."

I knew I had to change the subject or he'd leave. "So tell me, what do you do during the day that you have to swim at night?"

A breeze flapped the canvas and he looked around before he answered. "Odds and ends type jobs. I've been working here since I was fourteen. Management lets me use the pool at night unless there's an event going on like tonight."

I gave him a questioning look.

"Don't want to disturb the paying guests, you know."

I rolled my eyes. "The party isn't even taking place over here."

"But tonight it's the almighty St. Claires and we wouldn't want to ruffle Chandler's feathers. Bad things happen to those that do."

I was momentarily stunned at the way he spoke about my family and my father. "What . . . what do you mean?" I couldn't help the way it came out.

He shrugged. "Nothing. Just a generality about blue bloods. Never mind."

"No really, what do you mean? I'm curious."

He hesitated before he spoke. "I'm one of his victims."

I started to get nervous. What did he mean?

He shoved his hands in his pockets, and then smirked. "I might have taken his car for a joyride last summer when I was a valet."

The face he made was full of mischief—it was adorable actually—but my mouth still dropped. My father probably loved only my mother and me more than his bright red vintage Ferrari. It was his baby. "What happened when he found out?"

"Let's just say it wasn't pretty. He was irate and wanted me gone. I would have been fired if it weren't for my mother's intervention. But I've been banned from being anywhere near the guests. This summer I get to clean the pool, wash the dishes, stock the bar, you know, like I said, odds and ends."

"Oh, I'm so sorry."

Jeremy grinned again and with a shrug said, "I need the money, so I'll do what I have to do." And then he winked at me. "And I'm trying to stay clear of trouble."

My cheeks blazed and I dropped my stare. I was looking down at his bare toes, and I even found those sexy.

He must have known I was staring at his feet because he cleared his throat. But I didn't care.

I lifted my gaze and coyly said, "I thought you didn't follow the rules."

He smiled a big, wide sexy grin that made my stomach flutter. "I don't make a habit of it. But seriously, my manager here is friends with the manager of Southe Pointe and he's arranged for me to get an interview there."

"Why do you want to work there?" I was curious. He seemed to know what he wanted. Whereas me, I had no clue.

He picked up his boots and dropped them to the ground, shoving his feet in them. "I want to open my own nightclub and working there will be great experience."

"You do?"

He gave me a slight nod and pulled a pack of cigarettes from his jeans pocket. "Yeah, someday. But not here. I'm thinking Miami."

I sat down on the lounge chair, interested in hearing more. "Why Miami?"

With an unlit cigarette dangling from his mouth, he took a seat in the chair next to mine. "My grandmother lives there and my mother and I have spent every Christmas there. I love the beach. And I think it would be a great place to open a club like the one here. What about you?"

I pointed to his mouth. "You can light that, it doesn't bother me."

He flashed me a heated grin. "I'm trying to quit. It's a slow, hard process but I'm almost there."

Something about his tone had my insides melting.

He tucked the cigarette behind his ear. "You didn't answer my question."

I laughed, not genuinely at all. "I know. My answer isn't so clear cut. I graduated from college last month and still have no idea what I want to do. I'm thinking about moving to Chicago or LA, but my father wants me to go to grad school in the city. I haven't decided yet."

His thoughts seemed to wander for a few short moments but then he pulled himself out of wherever he'd gone. "Why Chicago or LA?"

"I think it will be easy to get a job in either of those places."

"Did you apply to grad schools yet?"

"Yes, Stern, but I don't really want to stay in the city."

He leaned back in his chair. "You don't like the city?"

I pulled my knees close to me. "I love it. I just want to get away from my parents."

"Ahhh . . . got you. Looks like we're both stuck in limbo."

I laughed again. "I don't think you are."

He sighed. "I graduated from NYU last month thinking I would be starting graduate school at Stanford in the fall. They have the best Entertainment Management program in the country. I thought I was a shoo-in for one of their scholarships, but it never came through and I didn't apply anywhere else, so I have to decide if I should go elsewhere or just get out there and start my life."

The passion in his voice made me envious and I tried to think what I was passionate about. When I couldn't come up with anything, I refocused on him. "Well, working at Southe Pointe seems like a great start."

"Yeah, right now that's my only choice."

I could tell his limitations irritated him. "You could take out student loans. Couldn't you?"

He thrust a hand through his hair. "I'd rather not. Why don't you want to go to grad school?"

That was a good question. I shrugged. "Because my father wants me to."

He eyed me. "If that's the only reason, maybe you should go. The job market out there is tough and the more you have to offer, the better the job you'll get."

"Yes, you're right. I just don't know if it's right for me."

He seemed genuinely annoyed with me. "Well. I guess you'll make the right choice. I gotta go. Can I walk you somewhere?"

I didn't want him to go.

He stood and extended his hand. "You shouldn't be out here wandering around alone."

I took his hand and rose to my feet. Electricity zapped through me as I did and I shivered under the intensity of his gaze. "Why?"

He must have felt it too because he dropped his hold on me and started gathering the things he had piled all together on a lounge. "You never know what kind of trouble you might run into."

"Maybe I like trouble." I knew I was flirting but I couldn't help myself.

It was so unlike me.

That earned me a glance—amusement once again danced in his eyes.

I stepped closer to stop him. I had an urge to kiss him but I held back and watched the water drip down from his hair to his smooth chest. I wanted to lick it off but bit my lip harder to resist that urge as well.

He tilted his head. "There's something different about you."

"What do you mean?" My voice was breathy but I couldn't help it. He was so close. He smelled like chlorine and something unidentifiable. For some reason I felt incredibly turned on by the scent.

He shrugged. "You don't look right through me like most of the people I've met here."

His words made my heart ache. I knew what he was talking about. I'd even seen my friends do it—treat those who should have been peers, like they were beneath them.

Before I could find the right words, he spoke again. "So tell me, what brings you here this summer?"

Voices drew our attention over my shoulder and I lost my opportunity to tell him the truth—that I too had been coming here since I was born.

That I was a St. Claire.

Jeremy grabbed his things and pulled me back behind the lounges. "I'm

serious—I can't get caught here. If I do, I'll lose the opportunity for the Southe
Pointe hookup."

I nodded in understanding and huddled with him. The canvas cloth of the
cabana brushed my bare back as I sat on the concrete in my *I'm trying to be a
rebel* dressy shorts and set my shoes next to me. His body followed mine and I
shivered.

As he sat down—flesh to flesh—our arms touched.

The contact was unlike anything I'd ever felt. There was something about
him. I wanted to know more. I wanted more of him.

Two silhouettes walked hand in hand down the same path that I had taken
to get here. As they got closer, I froze for the second time that night. One
woman and one man—my mother and the club's tennis pro. He kissed her and
there was no mistaking he had done it before. As he fumbled in his pockets for
his keys to the office, I cringed and felt like I might throw up. They kissed
again and he practically pulled her clothes off before he even opened the door.

My world turned on its axis—my mother was cheating on my father.

"Don't be shocked. It happens all the time," Jeremy said.

I blinked, swallowed, blinked again.

"The tennis pro has a slew of women he fucks on a regular basis."

Bile rose up my throat. He didn't know that woman was my mother. I had
to get out of there. I stood up and ran as fast as I could to the beach.

"Hey, what's the matter?" Jeremy called. He was on my heels.

"I have to go," I managed to squeal over my shoulder.

My feet hit the soft ground and sand sifted through my toes. I made it just
beyond the dunes before Jeremy caught up with me.

When he took hold of my wrist and tugged on it, I lost my footing and we
both fell onto the sand. His hard body covered mine and those blue eyes sparkled in the moonlight as he looked at me. It was like he could really see me.
Like no one else ever had. "Why are you running?"

I could barely breathe with him above me. "You said you had to go."

He shook his head slowly. "I don't."

Butterflies played in my belly.

"You're beautiful. You know that?" His voice was strong, warm, certain.

And as the words left his mouth, I believed him. It wasn't a line he was
using. And for the first time, a guy made me feel like I really was beautiful.

Not my clothes.

Not my house.

Me.

Just me.

I didn't say anything to him but a strange pulsing between my thighs encouraged me to rock my hips into his.

He groaned when I did, and the sound he made caused my body to come alive. I stroked my hands along the lean muscles of his back, digging my fingers into his flesh. When he plucked the flower from my hair and handed it to me, I was completely charmed. "Spend the night with me," he said.

Yet, I couldn't answer him.

Instead, I stared at his mouth.

His lips quirked up as he leaned down and brushed his lips over mine.

He didn't kiss me though.

With his eyes already locked on mine, we both lost ourselves in that moment, in each other. I couldn't see anything but him. I didn't hear anything but his breath. I could feel only his body against mine.

We were covered in sand.

I didn't care.

I lifted my head as he lowered his and our lips met in the middle. Lush. Soft. Sensual. He kissed me soft and slow and he kissed me hard and fast. He kissed and kissed me.

I liked the feel of his lips.

I really liked the taste of his mouth.

And I loved the feeling of his body pressed against mine.

I started to tremble in delight as his mouth devoured mine.

He took all my air away.

I didn't care—I didn't need to breathe.

The kiss was sensual and delivered with a fierceness I wanted to eat up.

I could have kissed him all night.

I ran my hands through his wet hair. It was soft and I tugged on it a little. He groaned once again and the sound cascaded through me like an instant shot of arousal. His hands roamed my body and mine searched his with equal curiosity.

He pulled back. "We don't have to do anything. Just say you'll stay with me."

I forgot I hadn't answered him.

I lifted my gaze and locked it on his. "Yes," I whispered.

He continued to stare at me with eyes that were full of intensity.

"Now kiss me. Just kiss me," I whispered.

He did, and then he extended his hand. "Follow me."

His motorcycle was parked around back and as I hopped on, I looked around and prayed no one saw me.

The building was long and rectangular. Made of brick. There were about a dozen windows but no doors. He led me around to the side and pulled out a key card. He slid it down and instantly a green light illuminated. The corridor was empty. I ran barefoot down the worn carpet with no idea where I was going. I could hear him stalking behind me. When I got to the end, I stopped and turned around. I had no place else to go. I was trapped. He took one step forward. I took one back.

My heart thumped in my chest.

He took another step and grabbed for my hands. Step by step we went, him forward, me back. We moved like that—a predator and his prey, until my spine made contact with a door. He was close. So close. He took one last step and his expression shifted from amusement to something more lustful, darker. We were chest to chest, hip to hip and when he pressed into me, his cock nudged my lower belly.

I gasped, trying to catch my breath.

Suddenly, his fingers encircled my wrists and he lifted my arms above my head. I blinked, realizing I was pinned to the door. I was his prisoner, held captive by his hands, his mouth, and his body.

But freedom from this type of captivity wasn't anything I wished to be granted.

He kissed my open mouth, light flicks of his tongue wisped against mine. Sparks ignited and I swear my leg kicked up all on its own. I urged him for more, pushing my body so far into his we could have been one.

Breathing hard, he let me go and stepped back. "You sure about this?"

"Yes." My voice was nothing more than a rasp.

He unlocked his door but before he opened it, he swooped down and took my mouth with a bruising force. He wanted me. I wanted him. We'd only just met but there was no reason to wait.

I reached behind and turned the knob. We both stumbled inside the small apartment, a tangle of arms and legs. In a fit of laughter, we stared at each other. When he slammed the door, my pulse raced.

We were alone.

In another swooping movement, he lifted me and my legs automatically wrapped around his waist at the same time my arms encircled his neck.

He had one hand inside the waistband of my dressy shorts and the other beneath my flowy top. He knew what he wanted and how to get it.

I liked that about him.

"No one's here?"

He shook his head, just once, and then took my mouth again.

I pulled back. "Your mother won't be coming home?"

He set me down. "She's out of town."

"It's okay that—" I was nervous and babbling.

He cut me off. "Kiss me." His voice was rough.

My toes curled and our breaths mingled. I placed my lips on his—he tasted of salt and sand and I wanted to eat him up. I licked up his throat, across his strong jaw, and back down. I unfurled my legs from his waist and set my feet on the floor for balance.

As soon as I did, his hands wandered. The tips of his fingers brushing the lacey fabric of my bra and then gliding down to my shorts. After a beat, he took my head in his palms and his lips made their way down my throat. "Is this okay?"

I threw my head back. "Yes."

He kissed over my bare shoulder. "This?"

I closed my eyes. "Yes."

This time, he pulled me forward, while he moved backward. Down a hallway. Through a door. We moved until his lips were no longer on my skin. Then I opened my eyes and looked down to see him sitting on a bed. If I had any second doubts, they were obliterated when my eyes met his intense blue ones—I wanted him.

All of him.

Every single bit.

His hands smoothed down my sides and when they went back up, they were under the flimsy silk of my camisole top. His fingertips dipped under the lace of my bra and my nipples peaked against them.

I shivered.

I think he did too.

"Is this okay?" he asked.

I nodded, unable to speak. I wanted to scream—anything is okay. Everything is okay. We'd spent enough time roaming each other's bodies. I wanted more. I wasn't in the habit of sleeping with a guy I'd only just met. But he wasn't just any guy. I couldn't explain it. I needed him inside me.

I was no longer drunk, but I was intoxicated—on him. Convinced of the fact that it didn't matter who I was, I didn't stop.

It was just him.

And me.

Two people who wanted each other.

"Take your top off. I want to see you," he growled.

I didn't stop there. I took my bra off too.

The hissing sound he made was reward enough but the way his palms moved to expertly cup my breasts, kneading and caressing them, drove me out of my mind. Then he pulled my body to his mouth and I went insane. His tongue licked around one of my nipples, while his fingers rolled the other one into a stiff peak. When he switched sides, he sucked on the nipple he'd just touched and the stimulation was so much I couldn't help but moan.

"Take your shorts off," he demanded around his ministrations to my breasts.

He sat on the bed while I stood before him. I would have knelt before him if I had the courage. That's how much I wanted him.

I stepped back and looked at him. His eyes were half-lidded and his expression was something new. I could see how much he wanted me. No one had ever looked at me like that before. I was always the tall, gawky one, with a boylike figure. But I could see that wasn't what he saw.

With trembling fingers, I stripped out of my shorts and stood before him wearing only a tiny triangle of white lace.

"You're so fucking beautiful."

My pulse raced. I believed him.

He leaned forward and grabbed my ass. His fingers caressed along the outline of my thong and then up the middle and back down. Over and over. All the while his tongue traced around the triangle that was now completely wet. I'd never let a man put his face where his was. I had never wanted to. Oral sex was an exchange and I never felt like giving, so I never asked to receive.

"Take your panties off, I want to make you feel good." His voice grew hoarse.

I knew he could.

"I want to lick you, suck you between my lips, taste you, eat you until you scream."

My breath caught on his words.

His mouth was already on my clit and it felt so good. I couldn't imagine what it was going to feel like with no barriers.

I wanted to know.

I slid my panties down and stepped out of them. As soon as I did, his mouth was on my bare flesh and his tongue was circling my clit. Over and over he licked and sucked me until I arched in ecstasy and cried out as the sensations took over. I had to remind myself to breathe. I grabbed his head to stop my knees from buckling beneath me but then he inserted a finger inside me and I knew it must have been him holding me up because my body was a tingling mess.

"You're so tight. So wet," he groaned.

I closed my eyes and lost myself in his voice. It happened before I knew what it was. My toes curled as pleasure ripped through me. I thought it was so cliché when a woman said she saw stars. But I saw stars, the moon, and every planet in the solar system. I never wanted the amazing feelings to end. When I finally stopped moaning and floated down to earth, he pulled his face away from my pussy.

I missed his warm breath there immediately.

He pulled me onto the bed and up toward the pillows. Before we settled, I reached for his shirt. He shook his head. "This was about you. I don't want you to feel pressured."

"I don't. I want to make you feel good."

The bright gleam in his eyes told me he wanted that too. "Take your shirt off," I told him and had no idea where my commanding tone came from.

He laughed and I thought he wasn't going to do as I'd asked, but then he did.

He stretched so we were facing each other and I ran my fingers down his smooth chest, tracing every line and muscle. When I reached the top of his jeans, I looked at him.

His face was filled with desire.

"Take your—" I started to say but stalled. I took a deep breath. "Can you take your pants off?" My voice was void of any forcefulness.

His eyes sparkled with amusement and when he did what I'd asked, his cock sprung free. He was long and hard and beautiful. I couldn't wait to touch him. I had him in my hands and was stroking him before he had even lain back down.

He covered my hands with his.

"What?" I asked.

"Let me show you."

I should have been embarrassed but I wasn't.

His hand moved mine slower, up and down his erection in smooth even strokes. I wouldn't have ever thought I could be so turned on but my sex clenched as my palms rubbed over his silky smooth shaft.

He reached over to the bedside table and pulled out a condom. "Fuck me," he said to me as he ripped it open.

I couldn't wait.

As soon as he put the condom on, he pulled me on top of him. I was on my knees and stared down at him. At his flat belly that was tight with muscles. At his strong arms. At his face. At him.

Just him.

He positioned himself with ease and I lowered myself down.

He filled me and it felt so good. His hands were on my hips and he guided me. Moving me up and down—slowly at first, then faster, much faster. His hips were surging forward. He was groaning. My lower belly coiled with tension and my thighs began to vibrate.

He was fucking me hard and I knew without a doubt that I was going to come again. As he thrust deeper, I placed his fingers back on me and it wasn't long before I was coming again. I thought I'd come before this night but if this was what an orgasm was—I knew I never had.

I screamed out—loudly.

"Fuck," he hissed as he stilled his body.

I collapsed on his chest and he pulled me tight. For a few moments, his fingers rubbed shapes on my back. Nondescript. But shapes nonetheless. Soon, too soon, he shifted and rolled me to my back as he stood to dispose of the condom.

"Are you thirsty?" he asked.

I shook my head no.

He lowered himself back down and his head landed on the pillow next to mine. He was so close to me I could see the blue glimmering in his eyes from the faint light illuminating the room.

After a few minutes, I moved even closer so that we were on the same pillow. "I can't believe we just did that."

He looked concerned. "Do you regret it?"

"No, not at all," I sighed dreamily.

"Then what?"

I hesitated. "It's just . . . I don't even know you. We're strangers."

He shook his head. "We're not though. You know more about me than most people."

I blew a piece of hair out of my eyes. "I doubt that."

"It's true. But what do you want to know?"

I squirmed under his intense gaze. "Everything."

He grinned. "Just kiss me."

CHAPTER 3

My Name

"Get your hands off her," Jeremy growled in the most ferocious way.

His voice was deeper, but I would have known it anywhere.

"What's it to you?" Lars spat.

It all happened so fast. Jeremy forcefully grabbed Lars' arm and yanked it off me and then he spun around to face Lars. "Get lost, asshole."

"Fuck you." Lars seethed, but after a few seconds of staring, he stomped away.

Jeremy turned back around to face me. "Are you okay?"

I nodded. Even though I was shaking, I reached my hand out to touch his face but stopped myself just in time. "Jeremy," I gasped.

"Phoebe." His voice broke on my name.

My breath caught and my pulse thundered from the sound of his voice saying my name. Blood swooshed in my ears as I tried to flush my past out of the present. He was still eye-wateringly handsome. His heart-pounding physique, his scent, and the intensity of his stare that always seduced me—it was all there.

I'd loved him once, even though I'd never told him I did.

And as I looked at him, everything I'd ever felt for him came rushing back. In a moment of extreme clarity, I realized he was the one I was measuring my relationship with Dawson against and what I'd had with him never could compare to what I'd shared with Dawson.

What Jeremy and I had was epic.

Jeremy was the reason I couldn't commit—I was searching for what I'd had with him before I lost him.

I stood paralyzed as everything that he once was to me came rushing back.

Out of nowhere, Lars was striding back toward us but Jamie stepped in front of him and threw a punch to his jaw.

"What the fuck!" Lars yelled.

"Learn to keep your hands to yourself," Jamie muttered and started toward me.

"Hey, douche bag," Lars called to him.

Jamie turned around and Lars shoved him so hard, he went flying backward and into a waitress carrying a tray full of drinks.

All of our heads snapped to the sound of glass shattering, and in the chaos Lars slipped away.

Jeremy went after him.

"Fucking hell," Jamie muttered from the floor.

I snapped out of it and raced toward him. "Jamie, are you okay?"

He was on the ground covered in food and drinks. He rubbed the back of his head and then tried to sit up but fell back down. I thought I saw red but I think it was a Bloody Mary. He tried to sit up again. It wasn't until the third attempt that he managed to do so.

I felt dizzy as I bent down. The room started to fade in and out. "Whoa," Jamie said, steadying me. "Don't worry about me. Go sit down."

Out of the corner of my eye, I saw Dawson standing close by but he kept his distance. "I'm fine."

A hand gripped my arm and brought me to my feet. I could feel the current course through me the minute Jeremy touched me.

"Here, drink this," he said, handing me a glass of water.

"Thank you."

He moved quickly, extending a hand and helping Jamie to his feet. "You okay, man?"

I watched him and wondered if that was going to be it for our communication tonight. I downed the water, knowing I'd drunk way too much alcohol.

As Jamie shook his limbs, loose pieces of glass dropped to the pool of mixed liquors that puddled at his feet. "Yeah, I think so. Did you find that asshole?"

Jeremy shook his head. "He took off. I'm not sure in which direction."

"Fuck him," Jamie cursed and then turned toward the waitress who was staring at us in disbelief. At least she was completely unmarred by any of the spillage. "I am so sorry. Let me cover this," Jamie said, reaching into his wallet.

The cocktail waitress refused his money and stood in some kind of shock for a beat before Jeremy whispered something in her ear.

She nodded and then looked at me. "Come on. It looks like you need to sit down."

I did need to sit down. My head was spinning and my vision was blurring. But I didn't want to leave Jeremy's side. Which must have been obvious.

"Go on," he said in that husky voice I had always loved.

I shook my head no.

He stepped toward me. Not too close but close enough that my body hummed from his proximity. "Go with Shelly, Phoebe St. Claire. We'll talk later," he whispered in my ear.

Even his breath was familiar.

Everything about him made me swoon.

He stepped back just as quickly as he had approached. When he did, the room started to spin but what kept me grounded was one simple fact—he knew who I really was.

And he was talking to me.

Shelly took my arm.

But I worried that once I turned my back—I'd never see him again.

It wasn't that unlikely.

After all, it had happened before.

CHAPTER 4

Follow Me

July 2009

He was a bad boy.

A boy my mother would never approve of.

He smoked. He rode a motorcycle. He swore. He talked dirty. He went commando. He did what he wanted, when he wanted. But I could see he was trying to mature—"evolve" is what he called it.

There was nothing at all I didn't like about him, but I didn't tell him that. I preferred standing strong beside him, trying to counter his commands with even more authoritative ones. He said it was cute. I didn't care if he didn't see me as fierce, I felt like I was. When I was with him, I was someone else. Someone I liked. Someone I wanted to be. I was strong for the first time in my life.

Spend the night with me turned into spend the week together, which turned into me practically moving in with him. His mother had gone to Miami and had to stay there. Sadly, his grandmother was dying.

Jeremy worked two jobs. The days were long when he worked. But the nights he worked were even longer. During those times, I stayed at the house with my friends. At first things were calm there—we lay on the beach, hung out, and the guys drank.

But it had been only three weeks since we'd arrived, and things were getting out of hand. Chaos had ensued on a nightly basis—parties, drugs, lots of drugs, alcohol, limos, lobsters, caviar, champagne, anyone and everyone who was in the Hamptons for the summer stopping by. It was crazy, but I didn't care about that kind of crazy.

I had my own crazy going on.

My friends and I had rented a house together for the summer. The house wasn't crazy big like any of our parents' homes in the Hamptons. It wasn't in the epicenter of town. But it was available. It belonged to my college roommate's father. The Charlestons had purchased a new house a block or so away and Mr. Charleston wanted to do some repairs before he put it on the market. He rented it to us with the contingency that he could work on it while we stayed there.

I loved the place.

I was the only one.

Standing in front of the television screen, I strapped the plastic guitar across my chest and assumed my best rocker stance. My fingers twitched slightly on the fret buttons in anticipation as the camera zoomed down to my on-screen avatar and I listened for the first beats of the song to start up.

"Since when do you play Guitar Hero?"

"You're back," I said and looked over. "Oh my God, what happened to you?" Logan had a jagged cut under his eye that had a butterfly bandage on it.

He shrugged. "Nothing really. A small fight. I'm fine."

"You were in Boston again?"

He nodded.

I could tell he didn't want to talk about it. "Do you want to play?"

He picked up the second guitar. "You mean, do I want to kick your ass? Hell yeah."

Jamie leaned against the door frame, staring at me curiously. "What's gotten into you? Poker the other night. A game of pool last week, and now this? Who are you and what have you done with the real Phoebe St. Claire?"

"She's branching out," Logan offered.

"Jeremy taught me," I added.

"When are you bringing this dude over? I need to thank him for bringing my friend out of her shell, breaking through her reserve."

"You know I can't invite him over here."

"No, I don't know that. Give up the game and tell him who you are."

"Jamie, it's not a game. And you don't understand."

The music kicked in and the screen displayed the note chart. I focused on the bottom of it. More specifically, on the target line with the five color-coded discs that corresponded to the top-down order of fret buttons on the controller. Still, I couldn't catch the beat. I had lost my concentration.

"Here, give it to me," Jamie said.

I handed him the guitar.

He strapped it on and started playing. Right away, the color-coded gems slid along the fret lines toward the target line with ease. He hit the matching fret buttons and strum bar at the same time the gems hit the target line. He was good. Almost as good as Jeremy.

When a small flame burst above the gems on the screen, he yelled, "Fuck, yes."

His score was ridiculously high when he finished. He turned to Logan. "Just call me master."

Logan took his stance. "Fuck that, you know I'm the master."

Jamie rolled his eyes and then turned to me. "The key to scoring is timing. It really helps if you know the song so playing the Sex Pistols when you listen to top forty isn't going to help you. And then there are the HOPOs."

"The what?" Jeremy had yet to mention them.

"HOPOs: hammer on and pull-off notes. It's Guitar Hero lexicon."

"That's too much information." I turned to watch Logan, who was going to town on "Free Bird." Another classic rock song. I got it now and Britney would be my strategy the next time Jeremy and I played.

Logan jammed out the last of the song with his fingers moving so fast I was in awe. When he finished, he gave Jamie his classic head bob and waved the guitar in the air. "Who owned who?"

Jamie pouted. "Rematch."

"Hey, I hate to leave you both but I have to get ready. Jeremy is picking me up in thirty minutes."

Jamie gave me a narrow-eyed glance. "Let him at least come in past the door this time."

"I have. But no one ever notices."

"We've talked a few times," Logan vouched for me.

"See," I said to Jamie and left it at that.

I ran up the stairs to get changed. Lily had taken off for St. Bart's yesterday with some guy she met at a party but left most of her wardrobe behind for me. I rifled through her closet and found a simple white dress with an empire waist. Jeremy was picking me up in his mother's car instead of his motorcycle so I could actually wear a dress. Tonight he wanted me to get to know his best friend, Kat. Kat was a petite girl. She had jet-black hair and bangs and looked like a kewpie doll.

I really didn't like her but my reason was stupid—she knew Jeremy so well and he called her Kit-Kat.

I was jealous.

I knew I shouldn't have been. Jeremy spent all his free time with me. When he wasn't working, he taught me how to drive, to play pool, to master Guitar Hero, how to have fun, how to be spontaneous—he taught me how to live.

In the past three weeks, we'd explored parts of the Hamptons I'd never been to—we walked Hedge's Harper, strolled along the Long Wharf, and flew kites on Peter's Pond.

He also let his rebel side slip out every now and then. When he did, we followed our own version of crazy, like swim naked in the ocean at three a.m., eat eggs on top of leftover pizza for breakfast, drive his motorcycle to Montauk to watch the sunrise, have sex whenever the moment struck. We didn't care where we were—we found places.

He was crazy.

I was crazy with him.

I loved it.

I loved him.

But I hadn't said the words out loud.

Neither had he.

I shook away my jealousy about Kat and slipped the dress on. When I did, I had to laugh. The simple white dress had a deep plunging neckline. So Lily. I went to take it off but took one more glance at myself in the mirror. I liked what I saw. I twirled around and looked again. I never liked to look in the mirror. What had changed?

But I knew what it was. I was more confident about who I was. I felt like a butterfly that had just emerged from her cocoon. When the thought gave me a burst of confidence, I decided to keep the dress on. I grabbed a necklace and my flat gold sandals and headed down the stairs.

As I was leaving, I took hold of the doorknob and looked back. Both men were gazing at me. "What?"

"You look hot," Jamie said.

Logan cleared his throat. "Second that."

My smile was huge. "Thanks guys." I ran over and hugged them and then rushed out to the driveway.

Jeremy was just pulling up as my sandals hit the plush green grass. I liked to walk under the large elm trees that lined the driveway instead of on the gravel. He stopped the car and hopped out. And so did Kat. She had been sitting in the front seat. Since I wasn't expecting her to be with him, jealousy ran through my veins before I could stop it.

She ran toward me and threw her arms around me. "Phoebe, I'm glad to finally meet you."

I blinked in shock at how nice she was and the smile I gave her in greeting was genuine. "Hi, Kat, it's nice to meet you too."

Jeremy slid his hands on my hips and pulled me back. "Don't I get a hi?"

I turned and wrapped my arms around him. "Hi, sexy."

He grinned. "Sexy, huh? I'm looking at sexy."

I pressed myself into him, something I normally wouldn't have done in front of people but I had to make my mark. I was surprised when he slid his tongue into my mouth in a deep kiss.

I leaned back. "I missed you."

The look he gave me sent shivers through my body. "Ready?"

I walked around to the front of the car at the same time Kat did. "I'll sit in the back," she offered.

How could I not like her—she was just too nice.

We rode into town and talked. It made me feel nervous—a different kind of nervous.

"So, who's staying with you?" she asked.

"There were five of my friends, but one took off."

"Six girls under one roof?"

"No. Three of my friends are guys."

"Oh." Out of the corner of my eye, I saw her slide Jeremy a look. I'd never thought about it but he seemed okay with it. He knew who lived in the house and didn't seem to mind.

After that, she changed the subject. *Thank God.*

"How was work today?" Kat asked Jeremy.

He thumped his hands against the steering wheel, listening to the music and talking. "I can't complain."

She leaned forward. "What about you, Phoebe? You don't have to work this summer?"

I shook my head. "My father's friend owns the house and gave us a good deal. And besides, I'm splitting the rent with five of my friends."

"Still, that couldn't have been cheap."

"My parents gave it to me for a graduation gift."

"Nice," she said and leaned back.

"How's the catering going?" Jeremy asked her.

I was relieved for his unintentional intervention.

By the time we got to the restaurant, Kat was telling Jeremy about some of the catering jobs she and her mother had done. Kat and her mother were running Jeremy's mother's business for her for the summer.

We parked across the street from the pizzeria and he held my hand as we crossed. Kat hurried beside him and he put his hand on the small of her back to keep her in step. When he held the door open for us to go inside, she went first. I followed and he brushed his body against mine as we entered the restaurant together.

"Let's find a table," he said, rubbing his stomach. "I'm starving."

I looked around. I'd never been to this restaurant. "How's the food?"

It was an innocent question.

"The best pizza in the world. You've never been here?" Kat asked.

"No, but I love pizza."

"Really, everyone on a budget comes here."

I smacked my lips together. "Never been."

Jeremy held his arm out toward a booth in the corner and I slid in first. He sat next to me and Kat sat across from him.

She smiled as she handed me a menu.

I felt like she knew who I was. I couldn't shake the concern.

Guilt sucked.

"We got a call to do a job at the St. Claires' Saturday night," she said to Jeremy.

I froze.

Did she know?

Jeremy stiffened. "I hope you told them to fuck off."

Panic rose in my gut. He seemed to hate my father so much.

Kat laughed. "Didn't have to. We were already booked and without your mom, one job a night is all we can manage."

My eyes dropped to the menu. I was afraid the fear in them was evident. I had to tell him the truth soon but he hated anyone with money so much. How could I make him understand?

"Phoebe," Kat said. "Did you hear me?"

"No, sorry."

"I'm glad you eat."

"What do you mean?"

Jeremy even looked at her sideways.

"You're so skinny. Most of the time, girls as skinny as you never eat."

Now I knew for certain her niceness was an act.

"Actually, I've struggled with being too skinny my whole life and I've hated it."

"Come on, no girl hates being too thin."

I shrugged. "I do."

Jeremy slipped his arm around me. His lips grazed my ears. "I think you're sexy as hell."

I turned to him and kissed him. I wanted to tell Kit-Kat that I'd gained weight in college but decided to take the higher road.

She seemed to drop it.

Jeremy played with the hem of my dress and I concentrated on him and his touch.

We ordered and ate and the rest of the dinner conversation was actually pleasant.

Nice.

"I'll be right back," Kat said after we'd finished eating.

Once she'd walked away, Jeremy turned toward me and pressed me against the wall. "I can't wait to fuck you."

It came out of nowhere, but then again it usually did.

Still, I felt the same.

His hands slipped under the hem of my dress. "Fuck, you're so wet."

"I already told you, I missed you today."

His lips grazed my jaw. "Yeah, but you didn't tell me how much."

Pleasure had immobilized me as he kissed my mouth—lip to lip.

His mouth tasted faintly like beer and garlic. Delicious. "Tell me what you want me to do to you first."

"Whatever you want," I breathed.

"Tell me you want me to eat you."

My shock at the words he used had long ago dissipated. He spoke only the truth. I'd almost forgotten we were in a public place, I was so fixated on his mouth. What he was saying. How he was describing what he wanted me to say. He did that to me all the time.

"Tell me."

I almost repeated everything out loud. "Yes, that. All of that."

He pulled back and took my lip with him. "Soon," he whispered. I was surprised he gave up trying to get me to talk dirty. He liked it when I told him what I wanted.

"I'm ready if you are." Kat had sat back down.

How long had she been there?

Jeremy eyed me, and then grabbed the bill. "We're ready."

I tried to pay my share, but he refused to let me. He always refused.

I hated that he worked so hard for what he had and I'd just come into a trust fund with millions in it. I wanted to share with him what I had. Pay for him to go to grad school. But I knew he'd never accept a dime from anyone. That was just how he was—proud.

On the drive home, Kat and Jeremy mostly talked. It was a relief. He stroked his thumb back and forth over my hand while I closed my eyes and pretended everything was going to be okay.

But I knew that wasn't true.

How could it be?

Kat was suspicious.

Jeremy didn't have a clue.

I was a liar.

And I knew I was going to stay that way.

Another three weeks passed.

Everything was blissful.

But I had yet to tell him the truth.

What Jeremy and I were having was a great love affair.

That's what Lily called it anyway. She called me almost every day for up-dates. She wanted sex updates more than anything else. She couldn't have been happier for me. She was even more happy that I had come to know what a real orgasm was. And she was right; I hadn't known what I was missing.

But what she didn't understand was the guilt I felt that my new relationship was built on a lie. For almost two months now, I had been pretending to be Phoebe Saint. A girl from the city. No one special. Average. No one anyone particularly cared about except Jeremy.

And that was all true, except for two things—my name and my money.

The lie had grown gargantuan. I had told him my father was a manager, which he was. I just didn't tell him my father was the man he hated.

My friends pleaded with me to tell him the truth. They could see how much I cared about him. But they were so lost in their own adventures—mine wasn't much of a blip on their radar. With Lily gone, I was mostly on my own. Emmy was high now most of the time, Danny was being Danny and just having fun, and Logan, like me, wasn't around much. Something was going on with his father that had caused him to have to go to Boston a few times. All I knew was each time he came back he had enough coke with him to make both Emmy and Jamie happy.

I, on the other hand, wasn't pleased with the drug use at all but since Jamie wasn't exactly happy with me, he wasn't listening to what I had to say. He didn't like where my relationship with Jeremy was headed, which according to him was nowhere since I refused to tell him the truth.

It wasn't that I refused.

I just couldn't.

Jeremy and I spent little time in town. We'd ventured into South Hampton itself only once or twice, so it wasn't hard to avoid seeing my parents.

At least I didn't have that to worry about. I couldn't even think about whether my father would find out about my mother's affair and leave her. Regardless of everything, my father and I were her life. I couldn't accept what she'd done. I didn't understand it. I despised cheaters. So I chose not to think about it.

Instead I spent my time with Jeremy—happy. Time passed quickly.

It was a sunny afternoon and I was sitting out on the back porch when I clicked SCHEDULE on the Department of Motor Vehicles Web site. Signing up to take my driver's test was so easy, so real, I couldn't contain myself.

I shot up and ran in the house. "Jamie," I yelled.

He came into the kitchen looking like shit. "What the fuck? Is the house on fire?"

"I need a ride to the club."

He ran his hand through his hair. "Why now?"

"I have some good news I can't wait to share."

"And that would be?"

"I scheduled my test to get my license."

Jamie never said no. "You better fucking love me because you know if you were anyone else you'd have to blow me first."

I was used to his crassness. Jeremy would probably kick his ass just for saying it to me, but I knew if they'd spent any real time together, they'd be friends. They were a lot alike.

Emmy walked in. "Can I tag along?"

She must have been listening.

Her bleached waves of hair fell all the way to the points of her pelvic bones, which protruded even more in her skimpy bikini.

"Sure," I said.

"Sorry," Jamie said, sweeping her with his eyes. "I have some things to do afterward."

Emmy pursed her lips. "I bet you do."

Jamie sighed heavily and turned and walked outside.

I stayed behind. I didn't care if she came but obviously Jamie did. I wondered what was going on but I knew better than to ask him.

"Are you okay?" I asked Emmy instead.

Her head shot up and I noticed her face was pale, there were dark circles under her eyes, and her cheeks were hollow. "Couldn't be better."

"Well, if you need to talk—"

"You won't be around," she said fiercely and walked out the back door, slamming it behind her.

We hadn't been getting along for a while.

I didn't follow her. Instead, I went the other way—toward Jamie.

He stood on the broken front porch step with his hands in his pockets. "Ready?"

I nodded. "Emmy's not eating again." I didn't have to ask her, I could tell.

"Yeah, I know."

"Did you tell her parents?"

"Fuck no, they'd just lock her away again."

We took our time walking to his car. "She needs to quit the coke."

He nodded.

"And so do you."

He looked like crap as well. "I know."

I wasn't going to lecture him. He knew it was time to quit. "What are we going to do about Emmy?"

"We? We aren't going to do shit. She'll freak if she thinks you're in on anything."

I looked at him knowingly.

"I'm going to stop by her sister's after I drop you off."

"Is that why she's mad at you?"

His laugh was bitter. "No, she doesn't have a fucking clue. She's mad because I fucked some redhead model last night and I wouldn't let her join us."

"So you two broke up again?"

He opened my door. "No. There's no breaking up since I was never with her."

"Yes, you were."

He lifted a brow. "Do you really want to talk about this?"

I pulled the door closed, not only on him but the conversation. We obviously had different definitions of what being with someone meant. Mine was that if you slept with someone consistently, you were with him or her. Same argument we'd had for years, but in his defense, we had agreed it was best not to discuss Emmy.

As soon as he got in the car, he turned to me. "You need to tell your boyfriend the truth, Phoebs."

"What's the matter with you?" I blurted out.

"You," he spit back. "I'm tired of all the bullshit going on here. Emmy's issues. Logan disappearing. Danny hiding who he is. And you too. Just quit the fucking lying to that guy. He doesn't deserve it. Who you are isn't a big deal and you're making it worse by continuing to lie to him. He's going to find out."

The hostility in Jamie's eyes made my guilt instantly flare. "I know," I sighed. "I want to tell him. I've tried to tell him so many times already but I just can't seem to get the words out."

"What is it you're really afraid of?" he asked.

I didn't hesitate in my answer. "You already know. That he'll dump me because of who I am," I confessed again.

He looked at me knowingly.

"He has this chip on his shoulder about people with money."

"So you've said. Did something happen to him?"

"I think it's just from spending every summer of his life in the Hamptons and being subjected to poor behavior."

"I can see that. But he knows you. If he dumps you because of your family, he's not the right one for you anyway."

I shook my head. "You don't understand."

"I do and that's why you need to tell him before it's too late."

"I will . . . soon," I conceded.

Concern flashed in his eyes. "Promise?"

"Promise."

But I couldn't tell Jeremy today. Today was a good day and I didn't want to ruin it.

He had been the one to teach me how to drive, and even though my mother had insisted it wasn't necessary—"After all that's what drivers are for," she'd said on many occasions—I'd finally made my appointment to get my license.

And I was excited to tell him that I had. He had been urging me to do so.

Jamie and I drove in silence the rest of the way.

When I got out of the car, I turned to him. "Thank you, Jamie. I really appreciate it."

He reached for my hand. "You know I'd do anything for you and I don't want to see you get hurt."

"I know." I closed the door and thanked him again for the ride.

The parking lot was empty except for a few cars and Jeremy's motorcycle. It was Monday and the country club was closed but Jeremy was working to prepare for the Fourth of July celebration.

I began at the pool but he wasn't there. I walked around the grounds but there was no sign of him. An hour had passed and I had looked everywhere for him but he was nowhere to be found. I started to search places I'd never been. When I still couldn't find him, I went up front, a place I normally stayed away from.

"Miss St. Claire, how nice to see you. What can I help you with?"

The hairs on my arms rose. I was surprised the receptionist had remembered me but I'm sure part of her job was remembering everybody. "I'm looking for Jeremy McQueen?"

"I'm not sure where he might be or even if he's still working here."

I smiled. "Thank you. Have a good day." I should have known she'd be no help.

I went back outside and finally pulled out my phone to call him. I had wanted to surprise him but it didn't look like that was going to happen.

When he didn't answer, I was ready to give up. I stopped in the restroom before heading back out to call Jamie and shock filled me as I stared through the open door.

The shock turned into betrayal quickly.

There he was—embracing her. Kat. Locked away. Hiding. If he wanted her, why be with me when it was so easy to be with her?

Kit-Kat.

I didn't like their friendship. I didn't. I never could explain why. But seeing the two of them together, like that, I knew why. Jealousy. And valid jealousy at that.

Panic rose in my chest but it turned to something darker very quickly. "I can't believe you. You lying cheat." My words were sharp like glass.

He looked at me. Our eyes locked. He dropped his hold on her. My stomach turned and my throat got tight.

How long had he been touching her like he touched me?

He was as much a liar as I was. How could I have been so naive?

"Phoebe," he said, shocked to see me.

I shook my head, mouth clamped shut with nothing else to say.

He took a tentative step my way.

I flinched and took off, running as fast as I could. I felt sick. Sicker than I'd ever felt.

"Phoebe!" he called.

Without turning around, I wove my way through the hallways.

"Wait up, it's not what you think," he yelled.

I didn't stop. I just kept running right out to the parking lot.

As soon as my feet hit the pavement, he grabbed me and turned me around. I wouldn't look at him. I was trembling. "You are a cheat."

Angry. Upset. Hurt. That was all I could say.

He took my face in his hands. His eyes, his blue eyes, blazed with intensity. "You don't really believe that?"

I couldn't listen. All I could see was the way his hands grasped her face and his thumbs stroked her cheeks, while his lips kissed her forehead. It was the way he always comforted me. It was special to me and he had been doing it to someone else.

"How could you do that?" I shouted and broke free of him.

His thumb kept caressing my cheek. "I'm sorry, okay? But it's not what you think."

"Don't touch me," I said sharply, jerking back.

"Phoebe, you're overreacting. Let me explain."

I couldn't. I was too raw. I looked at him, stared into his eyes and as tears sprung into mine, I whispered, "I have to go."

He reached for me. "Phoebe, don't walk away from me."

I glowered at him.

"Phoebe," he said in a hoarse voice.

I shook my head and threw him a disgusted look. As soon as I did, something changed in him. Just like that, he went hard, cold. I could see he'd disconnected from me—completely.

Feeling myself about to crumble, the thoughts of his betrayal forced my need for self-preservation. I twisted the butterfly ring I wore on my right hand. The one my parents had given me for my eighteenth birthday. It was meant to signify change and transformation into adulthood but right then I felt like that lost child I had always been. I didn't know what to do but somehow I managed to speak. "Please, leave me alone."

Rage seemed to overcome him, his temper taking over. "What do you think, that I was fucking her too?"

I just stared at him. That's exactly what I thought.

He shook his head. "Believe what you want. I thought you knew me better than that."

I'd thought so too. "I will." I walked toward the main road where I dissolved into a weeping mess. I walked for some time, thinking he might have followed me. When I finally had the courage to look back, I saw the long and narrow road. The trees that blew in the wind. The sky that looked especially blue. But the picture was still ugly because he wasn't in it.

I'd turned my back and he hadn't followed me.

CHAPTER 5

Next to Him

Where was I?

The soft, sensuous fabric that enveloped my bare skin felt unfamiliar. My mouth was dry. My stomach uneasy. My head pounded. Against my better judgment, I peeked through one eye and a sea of gray blurred my vision, not the familiar pale blue bedding I was used to. With my fingertips, I caressed the material; soft jersey lay beneath my palms, not the silky satin of my own sheets.

It was not my bed.

On high alert, my eyes flew open and small pieces of the night before swept through my mind.

My wedding day.

The club.

Champagne.

Drinking. A lot of drinking.

My friends.

Dawson.

Lars.

Fucking Lars.

And Jeremy.

Jeremy!

My senses intensified as the rhythmic sound of steady breathing drew my attention. I couldn't move. Finally, I slowly forced myself to turn around and my stomach rolled with the motion.

First I felt relief.

Then horror.

On its heels came nervousness.

A muss of sandy brown hair, messy and wild, rested on the pillow beside me. His bare back was to me, and the familiarity of his long, lean body caused my breath to catch at the sight. I'd have known him anywhere.

There was a time—he was my world.

Yet, in that moment, I had no idea what I was doing with him.

Him!

Faint snapshots of memory of the night before flashed before me. I remembered gazing into his eyes, talking to him, walking away from him, but that was all I could recall.

My heart beat frantically and I wanted to scream, "What am I doing here with you?" but instead I lay frozen and tried to recall how I'd ended up here.

With him!

Squeezing my eyes closed, I focused. But all I saw was a black hole. And I couldn't control my near hysterical reaction. Not when he was the one lying beside me.

I concentrated.

I tried with all my might to remember.

When I couldn't, panic encroached further on me.

My breathing became erratic. My pulse raced. My heart sped up.

I wasn't afraid of him, but I was petrified to see him again—sober. Yet, the magnetic pull that was always there kept me where I was.

It stopped me from running.

I had spent so many days, weeks, months, even years reliving my time with him—embracing the good times, wishing I hadn't lied, wishing I didn't see what I did, wanting so desperately to have reacted differently.

Yet, it never changed the past.

I should have been more confident in us.

This was my chance to make it right.

Through everything, all the heartache, the loneliness, the sadness and sorrow, the one thing I never regretted was meeting him.

Him.

Jeremy McQueen.

He wasn't just any boy—he was "the boy." The one I never should have met, and the one I'd never trade meeting for the world.

Although my experience with him changed my life, for the longest time I wasn't sure if it had made it better or worse. I should have been stronger after him. I should have been more determined to be who I wanted to be. But instead I felt weaker than ever and took the road laid out for me. It wasn't his fault though—it was mine.

My choices.

My weaknesses.

But I was in a good place now. Why I ever wanted to change my life, I couldn't recall anymore. I loved my job, was happy and satisfied with what I had become.

I stared at his tousled sandy brown hair, in what I could only assume was his bed, and started to wonder if what happened that summer so long ago was actually a blessing. After all those years, I still didn't know for certain. All I knew for sure was that after him, I'd never been the same. But I had locked those memories away long ago, rarely letting them out. Thinking about that time was a luxury I couldn't afford—it made me sad, weak, and at times unable to function.

So as I lay here, I couldn't fathom what I was doing with him. Why we would have ended up together at the end of the night. I should have stayed away from him. My nerves started to fray as the memories I had so diligently packed away came rushing back, no doubt elicited not only from his reappearance in my life, but from his close proximity. The twinges in my stomach were relentless.

I had to calm down or I'd never recall any of the events of the previous night that had led me here.

The sound of splashing water from overhead caused my gaze to shift upward. The architecture of the ceiling was a combination of exposed wooden joists and a skylight that blended seamlessly together, offering a beautiful view of the outdoors.

I saw that it was raining outside as I scanned my surroundings. All the walls were painted white and the one across from me was exposed brick. The floors looked like old wooden planks that had been stained a chocolate brown.

With a thump in my chest, I couldn't help but peek over at him again. He was the boy I'd caught a glimpse of in the pool on my twenty-first birthday and in that one moment he had forever changed my life. Meeting him opened my heart. Little did I know then, but his face and body would haunt my dreams for years to come. Now inexplicably I was in bed with him, and I had no idea what had brought us to this point.

He stirred, but didn't wake, for which I was grateful because I wasn't ready to talk to him yet.

I had, however, dared to widen my gaze and the sight of him lying on top of the sheets, all long, muscled limbs, and smooth sun-kissed skin made me yearn to touch him.

Except I knew I shouldn't.

Slowly, I turned over.

This was killing me. I couldn't stare at him so close to me and not touch him. Once I was facing away from him, I stared out a huge industrial window. The neo-Gothic design of the Woolworth Building in the distance gave me a slight sense of direction.

Tribeca.

Sunlight fought to filter through the clouds and I closed my eyes again. When I was young I had a favorite book—*The Velveteen Rabbit*. There was a passage in that book that I often thought about whenever I thought about Jeremy because it seemed so fitting.

"What is REAL?" the Velveteen Rabbit asked the Skin Horse one day. "Does it mean having things that buzz inside you and a stick-out handle?"

"Real isn't how you are made," said the Skin Horse. "It's a thing that happens to you. When a child loves you for a long, long time, not just to play with, but really loves you, then you become Real."

"Does it hurt?" asked the Velveteen Rabbit.

The Skin Horse answered with "sometimes."

I'd have answered differently.

Jeremy made me feel real for the first time in my life. And yes, it had hurt when he left. His absence from my life broke my heart into so many pieces—I never found them all. . . .

Now, he was beside me and I had no idea whether I would only break further.

CHAPTER 6

No Good-byes

July 2009

After leaving him at the country club I walked and walked and walked.

He would come for me.

I waited for it.

He never did.

Finally, I called Jamie and managed to ask him to come back for me. Then I walked some more. The breeze blew in my face, drying my tears. I hadn't even realized a car had pulled in front of me until I almost walked into it. For a brief moment, I thought it was Jeremy in his mother's car.

It wasn't.

"Phoebe, what's the matter?" Jamie's concerned voice just brought on more tears.

I leaned in through the window and cried on his shoulder. Told him what happened.

"It was your first fight. Relax," he said.

I got in the front seat. "No, it was our last fight."

He laughed. "You are being way too dramatic. It's not like you."

I threw my head back. "I love him."

He started the car. "I know. And some time apart won't hurt. Take a small break and then go find him."

"He's with her now."

Jamie shook his head. "You can't believe that. You know he loves you."

I wasn't so sure.

By the time we pulled in the driveway, I was thinking more clearly.

Jamie put his hand on my shoulder. "Come on, party time."

"I can't. I'm not in the mood."

"Your choice."

"What happened when you went to Emmy's sister's by the way?"

"She's coming to get her tomorrow."

I wasn't that surprised. "Wow. So fast."

He opened the door for me and put his finger on his lips. "It's what's best for her."

"I know but I'm sure she's mad at you."

"At all of us," he said.

I sighed.

"But I had to do it. She's a mess," he whispered.

"So are you," I countered.

"And fuck you too."

I grabbed his arm. "I'm sorry."

He sat on the bottom step. "Don't worry about it. I'll be fine. It's you I'm worried about. What are you going to do about Jeremy?"

I sat down beside him. "I owe him the truth. But I think you're right—a cooling period wouldn't hurt. I'll go to him tomorrow."

Jamie squeezed my knee. "Good plan."

"I'm going to lay down for a bit."

"I'm here if you need to talk."

"I know."

I went upstairs and threw myself on my bed. Then I cried until I couldn't cry anymore.

My phone ringing startled me. I lifted on my elbows and realized it was dark, pitch dark. I squinted at my phone. It was three in the morning. I didn't recognize the number but answered anyway.

Because it might be him.

"Hello."

Silence.

"Hello?" I said again.

"Phoebe honey, it's your mother. I need you."

"Mom, what is it? Where are you?"

Through sobs, she said, "I've been arrested."

"What? Why?"

"Can you just come? I can't reach your father."

"Of course. I'll be right there as soon as I can."

I hung up and called a cab.

I arrived at the police station to discover my mother had been arrested for driving while intoxicated and another man was in the car with her.

Once I finally reached my father we spent the morning at the courthouse. As soon as she was released, my father whisked us back to the city. There was no way I could stay behind in the Hamptons. My mother was a wreck. My father had somehow managed to contain the situation and by some miracle, it wasn't plastered all over Page Six.

Yet my mother refused to explain herself. I knew something must have happened to cause her to go off the deep end like that. Drinking and getting drunk in public were just never her thing.

I refused to accept that my mother was a cheating drunk. But since she refused to talk to me, I refused to talk to her about anything else.

As soon as we arrived back in the city, she and my father took to their room. They didn't shout, but I knew they were discussing what had happened, choosing to leave me out of it. I had other things on my mind than trying to eavesdrop. I couldn't hear them anyway. So I went to my room and tried to call Jeremy. He didn't answer. I called over and over but he never picked up.

The next day both of my parents were sitting together at the breakfast table like nothing had happened. I couldn't believe them. Both refused to discuss the issue and after a few days of normalcy when there shouldn't have been, I decided to go back to the Hamptons. When I finally did, I went right to Jeremy's apartment.

It was empty.

My calls continued to go unanswered.

I tried to find him at the club.

"He doesn't work here anymore," I was told.

I went to Southe Pointe.

"He doesn't work here anymore," I was told again.

I looked everywhere but he'd disappeared. When I called him the next day, his phone line had been disconnected.

And I fell apart.

I had found myself in him, and with his absence, I was utterly lost.

I couldn't stop thinking about him. But as the days passed by, I stopped looking for him. It was obvious he didn't want to talk to me.

Maybe he wanted her.

Not me.

He'd left me.

I had to let him go.

Days passed.

I couldn't stop thinking about him.

Weeks passed.

I still couldn't stop thinking about him.

The summer ended.

And he was still on my mind.

With his disappearance, the flame he had lit within me extinguished and my need for freedom and social independence went with it. I tried to remain wild and free. I tried so hard to hold on to that one thing Jeremy had taught me.

But I just couldn't.

I was weak.

And I couldn't stop thinking about him.

The boy I loved and lost.

Him.

The boy I'd never forget.

CHAPTER 7

Not Again

We hadn't even talked yet.

And he was seeping back inside my heart. And I knew it was going to affect me.

After all these years, he was back in my life, lying beside me, and I was afraid to wake him and ask him how he could have left me so easily.

Or why he was back now.

The pain Jeremy had caused me was unbearable; it was why I had banished the thoughts of him from my mind so long ago. But they were back in full force and I couldn't stop the hurt from creeping back into my soul.

The memories were too strong.

The sting of the finality just too sad.

So many years, I had wished for a different ending but you can't change what already happened. Even though there was a time I wanted to believe you could. A time I obsessed about what could have been. But I had managed to pack that painful existence away. And now, just like that, here it was.

The mattress shifted and the movement caused my nerves to twitch. Was he awake?

I needed answers.

My pulse sped up as I cautiously twisted back around.

With a hand flung over his head, he was facing me.

Oh God.

He was always so beautiful.

Still sleeping, his eyes were shut but I didn't need them to be opened to remember. Jeremy's eyes were the bluest of blue. Their color haunted me. And the dark fringe of his lashes still managed to mesmerize me.

With the sheet at his midriff, I allowed myself a glimpse of his bare torso.

I never could resist staring at him.

Smooth skin. Tanned. Long. Lean. Full of hidden strength. My eyes traced the lines of his muscles. His abs were taut. The ridges beneath his ribs pronounced. The definition of the sculpted lines that disappeared beneath the sheet couldn't be denied.

The sight caused riots of butterflies to stir in my belly and panic to rise in my throat.

Had we had sex?

For the first time since waking up, I assessed my own state of undress.

Underwear and bra. Nothing else.

What did it mean?

My gaze lifted to look around me once more. It had been so long since I'd done this. That summer we spent together, I'd lie next to him and watch him sleep all the time. I was a morning person. He was not. I loved to observe the peaceful bliss his body portrayed while he slept. Awake, he was always on the go. Asleep he was quiet, calm, still.

I wondered if he was still the same.

The urge to push his hair off his forehead was so strong my fingers curled in anticipation. I forced myself to clutch the pillow and close my eyes again. But I couldn't keep them closed when Jeremy's sleeping form taunted me. He looked older, more mature, but largely the same. The stubble on his jaw was just how I remembered. Everything about him was just how I remembered.

I quickly considered leaving before he woke up. I considered waking him. In the end, watching was the preferable choice.

Watching and recalling our face-to-face of the previous night.

He knew my name—my real name. I remembered that much.

Suddenly, Jeremy's eyes opened and I slammed mine shut. I wasn't ready to talk to him. My nerves flared. He made a grunting noise that made my eyes flutter open but they closed again at the sight of his gorgeous face staring at me. I had to remember what I said to him, how I got here, and if we . . . well you know. But knowing he was awake made my heart spasm. I really wanted to see him, talk to him, and just be with him.

Finally, I accepted that I had to give up and ask. I just couldn't recall anything after the cocktail waitress took me into the bathroom. The rest of the night was a blank slate. Nothing. It was as if I'd been drugged. At least I knew for certain he knew who I was. The burden of that lie was gone. I'd always wondered if he would have found out who I really was. Would he have read about me in the papers?

He wasn't one to read Page Six. But he had found out—somehow.

Of course, I wished I'd told him the truth so many times. But lying beside him this morning, I never wished for that to be truer than right then.

The mattress creaked and my eyes snapped open.

Jeremy was already out of bed and sauntering toward the bathroom. That walk, I remembered that walk. Back then it was the sexiest walk I'd ever seen. *And it still was.*

He wasn't naked—he was wearing a pair of boxers. He had never worn boxers while he slept when we were together. I stared at him and the memory of our time together momentarily stunned me into silence.

My breathing hitched and I became all too aware of his overpowering presence. "Jeremy?" I finally managed.

"Yeah," he answered, without as much as a backward glance. His tone was distant, uninterested even. As if seeing me was the last thing he wanted to do.

Although I wasn't sure what I expected, his tone definitely took me by surprise. He sounded angry. That I could understand. But the complete disconnect between us shattered the bubble I'd sealed myself in for the past hour or so. What was I thinking would come of this anyway?

"What am I doing here?" I asked in a weak voice.

He twisted around and the heat of his gaze seared me but he said nothing. He just continued to practically strip me naked with that brooding stare.

I swallowed. "Jeremy?" I managed again.

Hot and cold. Fire and ice. That's what I felt when he looked at me. His gaze lazily slid down my body and back up until he finally said, "Is that a rhetorical question?"

I shivered and shook my head no.

Coolly, he narrowed his eyes at me. "You're not seriously going to pretend you don't remember?"

My body went rigid at his bitter tone and I couldn't answer him. I really didn't remember. Blood rushed in my ears as my heartbeat sped out of control. I wanted to move my mouth but instead just sat there with it hanging open and my knuckles turning white from clutching the sheets I had inadvertently pulled up to cover myself.

I was a sorry, sorry mess.

His eyes flickered with some unknown emotion—darkness maybe. And then just like that, he continued striding away from me. He did however stop at the bathroom door, where he proceeded to grab each side of the door frame, flexing the muscles of his defined back, and then he tossed in my direction, "Can I just say, you were a lot more fun than I remember you ever being," before he slammed the door behind him.

Shock pierced me at the callousness of his words. Like I was some one-night stand he'd fucked and now he was done with me. I gasped for air as it all left my lungs. How could he be so cruel? And his eyes. His blue eyes, they were always so intense but today the intensity in his stare was laced with a bitterness that slammed any hopes I might have been building about him right down to the ground.

Tears sprang to my eyes at the animosity I'd just witnessed. I didn't know what I expected but it wasn't what I got. He was cold and distant. Arrogant. Rude. An utter asshole. Not at all the charming, although at times brooding, but still always endearing Jeremy I remembered.

With my heart clipped, I scanned the room for my clothes. His were scattered on the floor in piles, as if he stripped while walking.

We used to do that all the time as we headed to bed.

Oh God!

But my clothes weren't beside his as they had been that summer. Instead, they were on his dresser. My dress was folded neatly, my shoes and purse beside it.

Confusion wreaked havoc in my mind. Suddenly feeling sick, I had to get out of there before he came back in the room and destroyed me even further by throwing me out.

In a mad dash, I grabbed my dress and tossed it over my head. Shoving my feet into my heels, I reached for my purse and scurried into the hallway. A flight of stairs led upstairs and another flight led down.

I decided on the descending set, which landed me right in front of the door.

With trembling fingers, I unlocked it. His motorcycle was outside along with a bicycle beside it. I hurried past them both and found the elevator. In a matter of minutes, I was exiting his building and walking out into the cool October morning.

Leaving him behind—again.

Even as I dashed out of his apartment, my mind was still enraptured by him. I knew it shouldn't have been but I couldn't fight it. Against my will, I began to wonder how long he'd lived there.

I'd tried to find him once when I thought he lived in Brooklyn.

But I never tried again after that day.

The pain, like today, was just too great.

CHAPTER 8

The Brooklyn Bridge

December 2009

Whatever.

That was pretty much my newfound attitude about life.

The best-laid plans are those made by someone else became my philosophy. I went back to the city with nothing but a hole in my heart and a tainted memory of what Jeremy and I had once shared.

My parents were oblivious to my despair. They were dealing with their own set of issues. Not only had my mother been cheating on my father, but my father was cheating on my mother as well. That's why we couldn't reach him the night of Poppy's arrest—he was with another woman.

It wasn't like my mother to drink so much, and it certainly wasn't like her to drive. She rarely ever did. But she wouldn't tell me what caused her misguided behavior and I wasn't strong enough to push.

The less I knew the better.

I didn't even know what I wanted anymore.

All I knew was that I was alone and I didn't want to be—I wanted him back.

As the months passed, I got into a routine. I went to school at Stern because leaving New York now seemed unfathomable. I was always a good student and that hadn't changed, but my behavior had.

I drank.

A lot.

I was lost again.

I was acting reckless.

Plagued by self-doubt. Ripped open by endless questions. My mind wouldn't rest.

Had Jeremy been seeing Kat the entire time he had been seeing me? Had I somehow pushed them together and they ran away? Had he deceived me throughout our entire relationship like I had him? If so, why?

But that was one question I couldn't answer.

So instead, I tried to answer another. Were the feelings ever real? I needed to know. I became obsessed with studying people—their interactions. I wanted to see if their feelings for each other were genuine. Gauge them against what we shared. How we acted.

I was a loner at grad school. I felt so burned by Jeremy that I didn't bother to make friends. I was too broken. Jamie was back at Harvard pursuing his advanced education degree in Real Estate. Logan went to law school in Boston. Emmy had gone back to California to try her hand at acting. And Danny had taken off to see the world. If it wasn't for Lily, I would have been truly alone. But her life had also changed. She had a different agenda than me. She wanted to get married. And her social scene was no longer mine, so we rarely went out.

Time passed and it was Christmas break before I knew it. I was staying at my parents' town house on East Seventy-sixth Street. It had been six months and Jeremy was still on my mind. I couldn't stop thinking about him.

It was unhealthy and I knew it.

I didn't care.

There was a knock on my bedroom door.

"Come in," I called.

The door opened. "Merry Christmas, honey," my mother said. "We'll be leaving for brunch in an hour and I thought you might want to open your presents before we go."

I rolled over. "Mom, I'm a little old for Christmas morning."

She surprised me when she sat beside me on my bed and combed the hair from my eyes. "What's wrong, Phoebe?"

I smiled at her. She looked happy today and I didn't want to ruin it. I knew she was struggling through life just like me. "Nothing, I'm just tired. I'll get up now and be down soon."

She kissed me on the forehead. "Your father and I will be waiting."

After she left, I sat up on my bed and put my head in my hands. I had to try to do something. Out of reflex more than thought, I grabbed my laptop and opened it up. My fingers hovered over the keyboard. I was scared. I had yet to find the courage to type his name, but today I did. I knew he lived in Brooklyn but I had never asked anything more. I wished I had. Google gave me his address and I wrote it down, tucking it away for a day when another bout of courage struck.

Feeling slightly better, I hopped out of bed and got ready to celebrate Christmas.

A week passed after Christmas before I felt like I could do it. The strength came out of nowhere, but I harnessed it and picked up the phone.

"Hello?" An English accent came over the line.

"Hugh, I was hoping you could do me a favor?"

"You know I will help you if I can, Phoebe."

"I need a ride to Brooklyn, but I don't want you to tell my parents."

"I can do that," he said. "When?"

"Now?" I asked.

"I just dropped your father off, so I'll be there shortly. And by the way, Happy New Year."

"Happy New Year," I said, realizing it was New Year's Eve.

I hung up and searched my closet for something to wear. I wanted to look nice, but not too nice. I settled on a pair of jeans and a creamy cashmere sweater with a pair of tan boots. I blew my hair straight and then pulled it back. That was how I always wore it in the summer. I wanted to look the same.

Hugh picked me up within thirty minutes of my call and drove me with no questions asked. I knew he would.

As we drove over the bridge, I started to panic. I looked down between the cables into the East River and my panic deepened. What if Jeremy wasn't there? What if he was? What if he answered the door only to slam it in my face?

I struggled to take a deep breath.

Calm.

I had to stay calm.

I stared at the hundreds and hundreds of love locks on the wire fence where the pedestrian lovers walked and proclaimed their love and wondered how many of those couples who had thrown away the keys to their locks were still together.

I shook the grim thought away.

Soon enough, the Gothic-style architecture was behind me and at last I could breathe again. I stared out the window and watched the snow fall. It didn't melt as soon as it hit the ground. It was building inch upon inch. By the day's end, we'd have snowdrifts. I closed my eyes and dreamed about playing in the snow. I'd always wanted to when I was younger but was rarely ever allowed.

"This is the address you gave me," Hugh said from the front of the Mercedes.

My eyes flew open. I hadn't realized we'd stopped. I looked out the window at the slight mounds of snow that had already accumulated and the trees that lined the street whose leaves had long ago fallen. The brick building in front of me bore the gold numbers 728. It was his address. I'd stared at it all week, so I knew it was without a doubt.

Hugh opened my door and I stepped onto the neat sidewalk that someone had shoveled.

Maybe Jeremy had done that for his mother.

The five stairs to the door seemed like a huge obstacle. Nervousness overtook me as I rang the bell. I had no idea what I was going to say. I just needed to see him. To tell him the truth. To find out the truth about Kat. I wasn't looking for a happy ending. I just needed an ending.

A woman opened the door. She looked at me. "Yes, can I help you?"

"Mrs. McQueen?" I asked. My voice breaking.

"No, I'm sorry. She moved out months ago."

My heart cracked open a little more. "Do you know where she moved to?"

"When I came to look at the place before renting it, the woman mentioned Florida."

My heart sank—he'd moved to Miami to pursue his dream. And left me behind.

The finality rocked me.

"Thank you. Sorry to bother you," I managed.

I walked slowly to the car, the hurt feeling fresh all over again.

I knew then, I had to move on.

It was New Year's Eve. Tomorrow was a new year.

A clean slate. Time to forget him.

But even as I thought the words, I suspected I never would.

CHAPTER 9

Into the Night

Holding back my sobs, I rushed to the corner and hailed a cab, not even caring that I didn't have a jacket or that I looked like I was doing the walk of shame.

Maybe I was.

"Where to?" the cab driver mumbled.

"Upper East Side. Eleven hundred Park Avenue."

I sank into the seat and tried not to be sick during the ride to my apartment building. I couldn't understand why my friends would have let me leave with him, especially considering the state I was in. But the bigger question was what did Jeremy want with me?

Sex?

I found that hard to believe.

Payback?

Maybe.

What about what he did though? Sure, what I did was wrong, but what he did was unforgivable.

He disappeared. He left me. Gave up on us. Just like that!

Yet, I was able to look past that as I lay beside him earlier that morning. Thinking of it now made me feel even sicker. I hung my head between my legs. I tipped it back against the seat. Nothing worked. I was going to throw up—in the cab.

"Pull over," I yelled to the driver.

He did. Just in time.

When he pulled up to the limestone building where my apartment was located, I apologized profusely and quickly paid him. Then, I hopped out, a little too fast. My head was spinning and I took a moment to stand still on the sidewalk. When I felt a little more stable, I made my way to the lobby doors.

"Good morning, Miss St. Claire," Jack, the doorman, greeted me.

"Good morning," I returned.

He opened the door and followed me into the lobby. "Miss St. Claire, I'm sorry to bother you but Mr. Vanderbilt left this for you earlier this morning." He handed me a folded piece of paper.

"Thank you. When was he here?"

"When I first started my shift. It was around five a.m. He went up to your apartment and then came back down and wrote the note. I hope you don't mind I let him up?"

"No, of course not."

I turned around to open the note and read it.

Phoebe,

   I'm worried about you. Do you know what you're doing? Why aren't you answering your phone? Don't shut me out. Call me as soon as you get this.

   I will always love you,
    Dawson

What was he talking about?

Oh God, I couldn't talk to him until I knew what I had done last night.

Had he seen me with Jeremy? If so, what had he seen?

Did it really matter?

That was one question I knew the answer to—yes, it did. No matter what, I respected Dawson and I would never hurt him on purpose.

With a sudden sense of urgency, I knew I had to talk to Jamie. He'd be able to help me. As soon as I pressed the elevator button I pulled my phone out of my purse. It was turned off. Of course it was. I remembered Lily doing it before we got to the club last night.

I turned it on and multiple missed calls and texts flashed across my screen just as the elevator opened to my floor. I ignored them all and tapped Jamie's number. I unlocked the door at the same time I waited for the call to connect. Jamie had to be able to fill in the missing pieces of last night.

Yet, I was worried. I couldn't believe he would ever let me go home with Jeremy in the condition I was in. Jamie was protective. It was beyond odd. Jamie's phone went directly to voice mail. I tried again. Same thing.

In a flurry, I kicked my shoes off and stripped out of my wet clothes. I hadn't even realized it was still raining when I ran out of Jeremy's loft. Throwing on a pair of jeans, a sweater, and some boots, I then brushed my teeth and pulled my hair back. I didn't stop to look in the mirror. What I looked like wasn't important. What I had done and why was what I needed to figure out.

I grabbed an umbrella on my way out the door and hurriedly hit the elevator button. When it opened, I walked directly in and practically mowed down Mrs. Bardot on her way out.

My apartment was one of two on this floor and my neighbor was an amazing seventy-year-old woman who spent a great deal of time in her native country, France.

Bette Bardot was a French-born former actress and fashion model, who now spent her time as an animal rights activist. She was one of the best-known sex symbols of the 1960s and 1970s, and in her day was referred to simply by her initials—BB.

Her once famous blond locks were now gray but still long, and her bombshell body had widened slightly but she was still very attractive.

"Mrs. Bardot, I'm so sorry," I apologized as I stepped back.

Her coffee and bag of bagels were intact, at least. "Bonjour Phoebe, my dear. I'm so very glad to see you made it home safely."

My cheeks flamed in embarrassment. "Whatever do you mean?"

"Oh darling, I returned home on the red-eye late last night and while I was waiting for my luggage to be brought in, I saw you and a very handsome gentleman in a deep conversation in the lobby and a few minutes later, I saw you getting into a white Porsche with him. It only caught my attention because at first I thought he was dropping you off at that late hour, but obviously he was not since you got back in the car with him. Then early this morning, I couldn't sleep, jet lag, you know how that is."

I nodded anxiously.

"So I decided a walk on the treadmill would suit me. On my way down to the gym, I saw that JFK look-alike of yours in the lobby talking to Jack. I overheard him asking if you'd come home. But don't worry I didn't mention a thing. Us girls have to stick together."

"Oh, it's not what you think."

She winked at me. "Of course not, my dear. It never is."

The elevator doors started to close and I stepped inside.

Mrs. Bardot was already walking toward her door waving her hand at me. "*Au revoir.*"

"Have a good day," I called, and then collapsed against the elevator wall.

If Jeremy had brought me back here, how did I not only end up going back to his place, but sleeping beside him in his bed? And what were we in deep conversation about?

Hopefully, the person I was headed to see could shed some light on the situation.

Jamie's place was no more than five blocks away and I practically sprinted the entire way to Fifth Avenue. The green awning flapped in the breeze but the rain had stopped as I entered the lobby.

"He's expecting me," I lied to Harold, the doorman.

Harold smiled at me. "Go on up then."

I figured if Jamie wasn't answering the phone, he wouldn't answer the buzzer either, but me pounding on his door was something he couldn't ignore.

The elevator ride seemed so slow but then I was outside his door knocking before I knew it. There was no answer. I kept knocking, louder and louder with every passing second.

"Shhh . . ." a voice whispered as the door cracked open and Emmy peeked out at me.

"Hi," I said, wondering why she wasn't letting me in.

"Hi," she whispered.

Emmy was always so dramatic. At one time, we had been the closest of friends, but as all things do, our friendship had changed. We still talked, but not as often nor about anything personal. Lily and Emmy, though, they had broken communication off long ago. Yet the three of us still did things together. Our mothers were all friends and the need to keep up appearances for their sakes ran deep in all of us. I'm not really sure why.

I peered at her through the opening. "Can I come in? I really need to talk to Jamie."

She continued to stare at me.

But instead of waiting for a response I pushed the door open.

"Phoebe, James is still asleep," she scolded.

I started for his bedroom in spite of her protest.

She grabbed my arm. "You need to let him sleep. We were in the ER until around five this morning. He took some mild painkillers as soon as we got back and he's out cold."

"ER! What happened?"

She tugged on the hem of his button down. "He's fine. When he fell last night, he hit something sharp and it sliced the back of his scalp open. There was no skull damage but they had to shave his head to make sure all the glass was out and he opted for stitches over staples."

I cringed and flopped into the chair nearest to me. "I had no idea."

"You were pretty out of it and James didn't want to upset you any more than you already were."

I pursed my lips together. "What do you mean?"

"You know, with that guy getting into it with Dawson. James also knew you'd had too much to drink, so Danny and I took him to the hospital and Logan and Lily were supposed to bring you home. But Dawson called me last night looking for you. He said you weren't in your apartment. What happened to you?"

I just looked at her blankly.

"Tell me. I never had a chance to tell him Dawson called. James will be pissed. He doesn't know you didn't make it home. I want to be able to explain. And you look terrible. Are you okay? What happened?"

I sighed and stood up. Too many questions. "Yes, I'm fine. Just confused. Can you ask Jamie to call me when he wakes up?"

The tension in the air seemed palpable, but then she smiled. "Sure, I will. We can all talk then."

I wanted to ask her if she was okay, since she didn't look that great either. But like me, I'm sure she was just exhausted.

She hugged me. "I'll see you tonight, right?"

I looked at her questioningly.

She pulled away. "The Glitter Gala."

"Right." The New York City Ballet. We never missed it—Lily, Emmy, and

ogether until we were ten years old and it was
our mothers when we were young and just
ver, this year it wasn't just us. The six of us
oodbye to Danny.

when I glanced at it, I saw it was Dawson. I
another small hug and kiss on the cheek.

to make. Dawson would have to wait, but
alk to him; he'd know right away that I was
e'd be concerned.
im back.

phone rang again. This time it was Lily.

ou," I answered.
m glad to see you finally decided to answer my call."
d to talk."

ost of last night."

me just how fine I was."

imosas at Sarabeth's and then dress shopping for tonight

to your place?"

sation calls for alcohol and muffins."

eet you for brunch but I'm not shopping today."

ou kidding me? What are you going to wear tonight?"

omething in my closet."

loss."

ant to meet?"

y," she said and hung up.

locks to Sarabeth's passed in a blur. My mind was scat-

was okay. I felt guilty. I felt sick. I felt so confused.

ead and shortly after I arrived, I was escorted to a table.

I slumped in the chair and decided it wa
and read my text messages. There were thr
call him, three hang-ups from Lily, a text fr
hang-ups from James, and a voice message
I hit listen and my jaw dropped when I hea
using Jeremy's phone so I have his numbe

If I could have denied making the call
my own voice. Why would he have given
driven me home, only to bring me back t
when he obviously hated me?

"You look like shit."

My gaze flicked up at Lily in her perfect

She sat down and crossed her legs. "What

"Listen to this." I handed her my phone.

Ten seconds passed before her eyes cut to mi
number."

"Hi, ladies. What can I get you this morning?" t

"Two mimosas, two coffees, and a basket of muff
she looked at me. "Anything else?"

I shook my head no.

"I'll bring your coffees right away," the waitress said

"Why didn't you tell me about Jamie?" I asked Lily.

Lily sat sideways at our small round table and the ti
bootie peeked out from under the white linen. "I didn't
besides, Danny said he was fine."

"I know that now."

She raised a questioning brow.

"I went by to see Jamie just before you called and
told me everything. Did you know he had to have his h

She laughed.

"It's not funny."

"I'm not laughing about James. It's Emmy. How is it
make sure she has a reason to stay close to James? Are th
item?"

myself. We had been in dance t
one of those things we did with
kept doing year after year. Howe
were going together as one final g

My phone started ringing and
ignored the call and gave Emmy
"I have to run."

Lily was next on my list of calls
it was for his own good. I couldn't t
clueless about last night and then he

After I talked to Lily, I'd call h
As I exited the elevator, my p
Perfect.

"I was just about to call y
"Well, hello to you too. I'
I sighed. "Lily, we need
"Yes. We. Do."

"I can't remember n
"Really?"
"Really."

"You seemed fine."
"I need you to tell
She laughed. "M
at Bergdorf's."

"Can I just com
"No. This conve
I groaned. "I'll
She tsked. "Are
"I'm sure I hav
"Okay then, yc
"When do you
"See you in tw
The three sho
tered. I hoped Jan
Lily had calleo

RR

s time to listen to my voice mails
ee from Dawson all asking me to
om her telling me to call her, two
from a number I didn't recognize.
rd my own voice, "Hey, it's just me
. See you. 'Bye."
, I would have, but I couldn't refute
me his phone? Why would he have
his place? Why did I sound happy

orange shift dress.
is it?"

e. "Okay, so you wanted his

he waitress asked.
ns," Lily answered, then

and then disappeared.

of her leopard ankle
nt to upset you. And

my was there. She
shaved?"

always manages to
inally officially an

Then it was my turn to laugh. "Not that I'm aware of, but you know Jamie and I don't discuss her."

"She's been hanging out with him a lot lately."

"I know. She's in between boyfriends again."

"Why does he allow himself to get sucked back into her web?"

"For some reason he feels responsible for her. But I know he's been seeing other people this time. He told me last week about some model that wanted to sniff a line off his—" I stopped there.

She raised a palm. "Please tell me his stomach, his arm, his thigh even. . . ." I shook my head.

She groaned. "That's just disgusting. Where does he find these girls?"

The question was rhetorical but I answered anyway. "They find him."

"He's not using again, is he?" she asked.

"No, of course not. You know he stopped the summer after graduation."

She breathed in a heavy sigh. "That summer was out of control. I'm still sorry I missed being there for you."

I cradled my head in my hands, the heft of all my own issues weighing me down.

"What's going on in that head of yours?" Lily asked. "You left the Rose Bar last night on cloud nine."

I looked up. "I don't remember a thing from last night after Lars shoved Jamie to the ground and the cocktail waitress brought me to the ladies' room."

Lily made a face. "So you said. I just don't get it."

"Me either."

"Do you think someone slipped you a Roofie?"

"At the Rose Bar? I doubt it."

"Never put it past anyone. Did you drink anything after you left our table?"

I thought long and hard until a vision flashed before me. Lars shoving a wineglass in my hand. Me drinking all of it. My mouth dropped. "Oh my God."

"What?"

"Lars. Lars gave me a glass of wine. You don't think he would?" I didn't have to finish.

Lily drew in a breath. "I wouldn't put it past him."

Then I remembered Jeremy handing me a glass of water. "Jeremy gave me water too."

"Do you think he would have done that?"

"No. But I doubt Lars would have either."

She shrugged. "I have to agree."

"Honestly Lily, I think I just had too much to drink."

"Maybe but I have to say that you seemed fine. You were—"

I didn't let her finish. "I was what?"

She shrugged. "Determined."

I gave her a questioning look. "What do you mean?"

"Dawson wanted to take you home, but you insisted on having Jeremy drive you."

Maybe I'd just had too much to drink then.

"What happened with Dawson and Jeremy?" I asked.

"I don't know. I was with you in the restroom when that conversation took place. Honestly, no one was going to talk you out of letting Jeremy bring you home, not even Dawson. So after Dawson left, I talked to Jeremy and so did Logan. He seemed on the up-and-up and promised to get you home safely."

"Well, I guess he did but for some reason I didn't stay. Either way, I woke up in his bed!"

Just then the waitress set our coffees down and I gave her a smile, as my cheeks turned pink for the second time that morning.

"Okay, so you had sex with him. It was obvious you wanted to sleep with him so what's the big deal?"

"What's the big deal? I don't remember it and just to be clear, I don't know if we did it."

"Why didn't you just ask him?"

"Because he acted like a complete asshole this morning and I took off."

"Two mimosas and a basket of muffins," the waitress said cheerily as she set the items on the table.

I smiled at her again as my blush bloomed even brighter.

"Anything else?"

"I think we're good," Lily replied and then redirected her attention to me. "What exactly did he say that made him out to be an asshole?"

"It was the way he looked at me." Well, it was something else too, but I couldn't tell her that—it was just too embarrassing.

"He seemed fine last night. What happened to cause the mood shift?"

I poured cream in my coffee and stirred it. "I have no idea."

"You really don't know if you slept with him?"

"I really don't," I sighed.

"Then you have to call him."

"No way. You don't understand."

"Oh, I think I do. You told me the entire story last night, over and over, in detail I might add."

I sipped my coffee and almost choked. "What did I tell you that you didn't already know?"

"Just that you thought he was your great love." She leaned toward me. "It's not like I wouldn't have liked to know that or anything."

"Lily, I was drunk. Ignore what I said."

"Muffin?" she asked, passing me the basket.

"No! I can't eat. Why are you acting like none of this is a big deal?"

"Because Jeremy McQueen is back in your life." She smiled. "And I think your life is about to get back on track." She added a wink.

I rolled my eyes. "Please don't spin this into one of your tragic love stories."

"Oh, St. Claire, I don't have to spin it into anything. It already is."

"I told you, he isn't interested in me."

She tilted her head. "I'm not so sure."

"Well, even if he was, which he isn't, maybe I'm not interested in him."

She snickered. Actually snickered. "He is the first guy that brought you to orgasm."

I shrugged my shoulders. "So?"

"It has to mean something."

I shook my head. "Focus. I have to call Dawson back."

"So call him back."

"I have no idea what to say to him."

She popped a piece of muffin in her mouth. "Tell him the truth—the man who brought you endless pleasure is back in your life."

"Lily, you're riding my last nerve. Could you please take this seriously?"

She tilted her head. "Phoebe, I am. It's just I don't want you to blow this by focusing on the wrong thing."

Frustrated, I glared at her. "There's nothing to blow."

Just then my phone beeped. I glanced at the screen. It was a text. From him.

Him: You shouldn't have left.

Me: You were an asshole.

Him: I know and I'm sorry. We need to talk.

Me: There's nothing to talk about.

Him: When can I see you?

I wanted to text, "Never." I thought about texting, "Now." But the first seemed too final and the second seemed too needy, so I didn't reply at all. Honestly, I was pissed. Pissed for the way he treated me. Pissed at him for coming back into my life. I'd moved on. And pissed that I was considering putting myself out there again and talking to him.

"Who is it?" Lily asked.

My eyes flicked up. "It's him."

She practically squealed, "Let me see."

I handed her my phone and then attempted to twist my butterfly ring but my finger was so swollen that it wouldn't turn.

I started to cry.

Lily set my phone down and reached across the table. "Hey, I'm sorry. Talk to me."

I took a sip of my mimosa. "He crushed me—again."

"You have to talk to him."

I dabbed at my tears. "No, I don't."

She twisted her lips. "Phoebe. You do."

"He was an asshole," I blurted out. "And I can't."

"Yes, you can. He wants to talk to you. And he's your great love. You have to give him a second chance."

I sniffed and shook my head. "No, I don't."

"Call him. Talk to him. See what's going on. You owe yourself that much."

"What about Dawson?"

Lily reached for another muffin and cut it in half. As she spread apricot preserves on it she said, "You have to talk to him too."

I took the other half of her muffin. "You make it sound so easy."

Lily sighed. "You have to let him go and focus on Jeremy."

"I already let him go and why would I focus on someone as rude as Jeremy McQueen?"

She eyed me. "One person at a time. First, you never really let Dawson go. Tell him in no uncertain terms the two of you are over. Over. Over. Do I have to say it again?"

I shot her a look. "No, I get it."

She narrowed her eyes. "Are you sure?"

I made a face.

Lily bounced right back. "Okay, moving on to Jeremy. So, he was an asswipe. Maybe you did something to set him off. He always was moody. At least talk to him and find out. What do you have to lose?"

I knew her question was rhetorical, so I remained quiet. But I wanted to say a lot. My pride. My mind. My heart. Everything.

She chattered on. "And like I've always said, great loves only transpire through tragedy."

I just looked at her.

Maybe this time she was right.

CHAPTER 10

The Park

The cathedral-like canopy of the elms in the Mall of Central Park was magical and always made me feel so much better. It was my favorite place to be, especially in the fall. This time of year, the leaves' vibrancy provided a colorful path to follow all the way to the Bethesda Terrace. I usually ran the path early in the morning when the dew was thick. Some mornings I would stop and sit by the fountain, just to stare at the angel who held a flower in one hand.

When I was younger, my nanny told me that she represented health and purity. Ever since then, whenever I felt troubled, I'd go to sit by the *Angel of the Waters* and let her try to ease my worries.

I felt the urge to make my way toward her today.

After I left Lily to her shopping, I had to clear my head. As I looked up and down the path, orange and yellow leaves surrounded me but that day, they didn't lift my spirits. In fact, I felt lost again. I didn't know what to do.

I walked and walked but it wasn't at the angel where I ended up. I had wandered and stopped just outside the Delacorte Theater. I blinked when I found myself staring at the *Romeo and Juliet* statue.

Was it a sign? I had to laugh despite my emotional anguish. I found a bench and sat down.

Shifting my gaze from the screen of my phone to the tragic couple, I couldn't decide whom I should call first, but then my phone rang, and I didn't have to decide.

"Hi, Dawson."

"Phoebe, are you okay?"

I took a deep breath. "I'm fine."

"Where are you?" He sounded worried but I knew he would be.

"I'm in the park."

"Can I meet you?"

I looked at the statue that represented great love and knew I couldn't meet him where I was, but I did owe it to him to talk to him in person. "I'll come over."

"When?"

"Now."

"Do you want me to send a car?"

"No, I want to walk. I'll be there soon."

Once we hung up, I glanced at the statue one more time. The pose seemed so simple—two lovers about to kiss. Romeo bent over Juliet with her head thrown back. The simplicity of the sculpture seemed to lend an innocence to the moment captured in time.

My phone beeped and my thoughts scattered. When I glanced down, I saw it was a text from Jeremy.

Him: We need to talk. Where can I meet you?

I ignored his text and looked again at Romeo and Juliet. Dawson and I had shared many innocent moments like that, whereas with Jeremy, passion totally consumed us. I walked away from the statue, continuing to turn back and steal glances until I could no longer see it.

Who was my Romeo? Did I have one?

Dawson lived on East Fifty-fifth Street and I took my time walking there. My feet were starting to throb, and I wished I'd put ballet flats on and not worn heeled boots. What was I thinking?

By the time I reached the elegant lobby of his building, the elevator to the penthouse had never looked so good.

When I walked into the giant space, Dawson was leaning over the counter, reading the paper. Next to him sat a bottle of my favorite pinot grigio, with a glass already poured and sitting on the green marble countertop.

I felt like I hadn't been there in so long. The ten-foot ceilings and glass expanse allowed so much natural light in. And the wide plank bleached oak floors also contributed to the airy feeling. Of course, the place was decorated with the most modern of pieces. Dawson prided himself on the decor. And he should—the place really was beautiful. Yet to me it always felt a little cold. It looked like something that belonged in the Museum of Modern Art, not a place where someone lived.

Dawson grabbed the wineglass and walked toward me. "Are you okay?"

I nodded without speaking.

"Are you sure?"

"Yes," I said, suddenly not sure what else to say.

He dropped his gaze. "Why did you insist on leaving with him?"

I merely shrugged. I didn't know why. I hated to tell him that.

Cordially, he kissed me on the cheek and then handed me the glass. "Come on, let's sit down."

The distressed mocha leather sofa was huge and I sat where I always did—on the end with the footrest. He sat a few cushions to my left.

Concern etched his features. "Phoebe, did you know he was back in town?"

"No, I didn't. But how did you know it was him?"

"The look in your eyes was enough but as soon as his name was mentioned, I knew for certain."

"But who else knew who he was?" I found it hard to believe Jeremy ran in our circuit.

Uncomfortable, Dawson rubbed his hands on his wool slacks. "You know what? This is harder to discuss than I thought it would be."

I nodded. He was right—it was.

"But you're okay?"

"I am."

"And I'm assuming you've talked to him and now you're going to stay away from him?"

"I am," I said again. My conviction sounded weak though.

"He's not good for you. You know that?"

I just looked at him.

"You look so tired."

"I am, I'm exhausted actually."

He pulled my feet onto his lap. "I wanted to call you yesterday, but I wasn't sure if that was a good idea so I texted you instead."

I sipped my wine and met his stare. "I'm sorry I didn't respond. I wasn't sure what to say. I thought about calling you but I wasn't sure about that either."

He unzipped one of my boots. "I get it."

"Dawson." My voice had a warning tone.

"What? I can tell your feet are killing you. But if you'd rather leave them on." He started to zip it back up.

"No, you're right. Go ahead."

He took them both off and set them neatly beside his feet on the floor.

My socks were mix-matched and he laughed at them.

I grinned. "I was in a hurry."

"Clearly," he laughed.

"About yesterday," I said. "It was weird. I kept thinking about you all day." I needed to clarify in what way.

His fingers began to massage my feet and it felt so good. "And?"

"I don't know. The day just felt off." Maybe that was the wrong way to explain.

"It did to me too."

I was leading him down the wrong path. Nothing was coming out of it. I set my wineglass on the end table but had nothing else to add. I should keep my mouth shut.

"Do you still think you made the right decision?"

"Dawson. Nothing's changed. But now I think we can both move on." So much for keeping my mouth shut.

He swallowed and looked at me with sudden scrutiny. "Is this 'time to move on' thing about him?"

I pulled a pillow closer and let my head fall back on the armrest. "I assume you mean Jeremy."

"You know I do."

"No. It has nothing to do with him. It's just time."

Pressure hit my toes and it tickled a little. I wiggled my toes but he braced his arm over my legs. "Relax," he said.

I did.

"You're sure you hadn't seen him before? I mean since we broke up?"

My eyes met his. "No, I haven't. I'd tell you if I did."

"Then why did you insist on him taking you home? You could have talked there."

I sat up. "I don't know. Honestly, I have no idea why I would have done that."

"What do you mean?" He sounded alarmed now.

I hadn't wanted to tell him but knew I had to.

"I don't remember anything after Lars tackled Jamie. I think I had too much to drink. But you have to know, I'd never do anything to hurt you on purpose."

He stopped massaging my foot. "Did he . . . take advantage of you?"

I swallowed, remembering the way my clothes were folded neatly on his dresser, similar to the way Dawson had just set my boots down. "No, I don't think so."

A darkness bloomed across his features. "If he did, we'll press charges."

I squeezed his hand. "Dawson, I'm fine. And besides, it seems I went of my own free will."

"That doesn't matter. If you weren't of sound mind, it would be rape."

"Dawson! No!"

He squared his shoulders "Of course it's your decision."

"Like I said, we didn't sleep together."

"No, you said you didn't know."

"Well, I'm almost certain we didn't."

"Do you want me to take you to a doctor?"

I shook my head.

He nodded. "How did you feel seeing him again?"

I took another sip of my wine. "Can we not talk about this?"

"Did he explain his disappearance that summer?"

So much for not talking about it.

I fell back to my pillow and closed my eyes. "Not that I remember."

"I have someone looking into where he's been, what he's been doing."

My eyes popped open. "Why would you do that?"

"To protect you."

I furrowed my brows. "No, please stop them. I don't want to know. And Jeremy's not going to hurt me."

"I'm not so sure about that."

I looked at him. He had that same strange look in his eyes.

"Well, if you change your mind, the investigator is discreet and fast."

I drew my features together. "I said no. And you didn't say how you knew who Jeremy was."

He just shrugged. "Word gets around."

His stories seemed mismatched. I didn't quite believe him.

But then he started massaging my feet again. "How's this?"

"Mmmm," I moaned and soon began to drift off.

Dawson and I were friends before we became lovers and we always talked about everything but talking about another man with him after all that transpired between us didn't seem appropriate, so I let the conversation go.

My phone ringing in my purse woke me up. A blanket covered me and I tossed it aside as I fumbled to the floor to find it. "Hello?"

"Phoebs, it's me," Jamie said.

I stood up to stretch. "Are you okay?"

"Yeah, I'm fine. A little buzz cut and stitches never hurt anyone."

"I can't believe that happened to you."

"Lars the fucker. He's such an asshole."

"I can't argue that."

"The fucker called and apologized though."

"What did he say?"

Jamie gave a dry laugh. "That he might have had too much to drink and that he was sorry."

"Might? That's an understatement."

"Anyway, how are you?"

Dawson walked in the room with a towel around his neck and his workout clothes on. I mouthed, "It's Jamie."

He bobbed his chin. "Is he okay?"

I nodded.

"I'm fine. Just tired," I told Jamie.

"Where are you?"

"I'm at Dawson's."

"What the fuck?"

I looked at my watch and ignored his comment. "I'm headed home to get ready for tonight."

"What the hell are you doing there?"

"What do you mean?"

"After the scene last night."

I walked over toward the window. "What are you talking about?"

"Come on, Phoebs. You left with Jeremy last night after practically begging him to take you home, and now you're at your ex-fiancé's?"

I cringed at the use of the word beg. "Let's talk tonight."

"I'm not going to make it, but tomorrow I want answers."

"What? Why?"

"I still feel like shit and the ballet isn't a cure-all, that's for damn sure."

I laughed. "Not for you, I know. Lunch tomorrow?"

"You bet. Usual spot at noon."

"I hope you feel better. 'Bye, Jamie."

"And Phoebs, I didn't mean to sound harsh. I'm just worried about you."

"I know." I pressed END and tucked my phone in my pocket.

The city looked so much smaller from up here. I couldn't feel the crispness of the air or see the leaves that showered down from the trees but I could sense the hustle and bustle that never ceased. I loved this city and couldn't believe there was a time I ever thought about leaving.

"Stay here tonight. I'll order sushi and we can watch a movie," Dawson said. I hadn't realized he was still in the room.

I turned to face him. "I can't. I have the Glitter Gala. You know that."

"Do you think you could cancel?"

"Dawson, I can't."

He crossed the room. He was sweaty from his workout and didn't like to touch me before he showered, so he kept his distance. "I miss you."

"Dawson, please don't. Nothing has changed between us."

"You don't know that unless you give us another chance. Things change all the time. Let me at least take you out for dinner this week."

"I thought we agreed to move on."

He looked pained. "No. You did." His voice left no doubt that he wasn't ready to move on.

Saddened, I looked at him. "Dawson, it's for the best."

He shook his head. "Not for me. When we broke up I agreed to give you time. And I'm still going to. I'm not ready to give up on you."

There was nothing else to say. We'd had this conversation so many ways when we broke up and I feared this time would end no differently.

I went to pick up my wineglass and take it to the sink, but it was already gone so instead I sat down and pulled my boots on. "Have you talked to Lars?"

He nodded. "He feels bad."

I assumed Lars didn't tell Dawson about propositioning me and I didn't want to hurt him any more, so I didn't either. I stood up and looked at him. "I'll call you. I have a lot going on at work this week."

"I know," he said apologetically.

"I should have gone into the office today."

"Let me help you."

I shook my head. Pouring more money into my family business wasn't the solution—not long-term anyway.

He took a cautious step forward and kissed me gently on the cheek. "I'll wait for your call."

I felt terrible leaving without making it crystal clear there was no future between us. My feelings toward him hadn't changed. And I knew they wouldn't. Sure, I missed him. But it was my friend I missed. Not my lover. I couldn't even ask him what he and Jeremy argued about because instinctively, I knew it was me. I wasn't afraid of what Dawson might have asked him, but I did fear how Jeremy might have answered him.

My phone rang again as I stepped into the elevator. It was Jeremy's number. I knew it by then. I thought about assigning his name to the number but thought better of it. I should erase all signs of him instead. And with that fact in mind, I ignored his call.

I exited the elevator and ran right into the doorman. "Is Hugh picking you up or do you need a cab?" he asked.

"A cab would be great. Thanks, Sam."

My phone rang again.

I twisted my butterfly ring round and round.

It was him again.

My stomach was jumping as I looked down at my screen in contemplation, but once more, I decided not to answer. This time he left a voice mail. I erased it without listening.

The ride home was short. I should have walked to clear my head but I had little time. Once I was back in my apartment, I didn't have a spare moment. I showered quickly, which was good because I didn't have much time to think that way. It was four thirty. Cocktails were at five thirty and Lily was swinging by to pick me up at five.

My closet was jammed with clothes, yet my mood was dismal and I felt like I had nothing to wear. I stood in my short robe and my most favorite necklace trying to decide on an outfit. My phone rang again and my hands fluttered to the strands of the gorgeous pearl and diamond necklace. It was a replica of the one Holly Golightly wore in *Breakfast at Tiffany's*. My mother had a thing for Audrey Hepburn, which is where I developed my obsession for her as well.

Poppy and I did agree on a few things.

And since she had a thing for Audrey, it went without saying she had a thing for Tiffany's. This necklace was the first piece my father had ever purchased for her. She gave it to me on my sixteenth birthday.

My phone stopped ringing and I forced my mind back to the task at hand. I pulled a number of dresses from their hangers before settling on a long jersey dress with a lace top and solid black skirt. It was simple with a round neckline but it was gathered at the waist with side and back cutouts, which gave it an edge that was perfect for the evening's event.

As I contemplated my shoe choices, the buzzer rang. I hurried over to it, cursing to myself that Lily was early. I knew that since I wasn't dressed, she was going to want to pick out my clothes. For some reason, she liked to dress me. It was her thing.

"Yes," I said through the intercom.

"There's someone here to see you, Miss St. Claire." It was the new doorman. His name escaped me. Jack or Harry would have sent Lily up without buzzing.

"It's all good. Thanks."

I ran to the bathroom to brush my hair and pin it back. I wasn't quite finished when there was a knock on the door.

"Coming," I yelled.

Hurrying back to the door, I pulled it open with bobby pins in my teeth and my robe slightly agape.

A clearing of the throat caught my attention. That was not a sound that Lily would make.

I could feel myself start to tingle as my eyes lifted.

It was him.

Him!

My heart skipped in my chest.

There he stood, tall and imposing.

What was he doing at my door?

I fumbled to close my robe without untying the silk sash, but it was too late, he had already seen my skimpy lingerie.

He drew in a long, slow breath and on the exhale said, "Hello."

A shiver ran down my spine as my gaze wandered from his head to his toes. He wore black. All black. A black leather jacket, black T-shirt, black jeans, and black boots.

He looked incredible.

My sex clenched at the sight before me and it took me a few minutes to remember what had happened earlier that very morning. I straightened in an effort to collect myself and when I did, I asked, "What are you doing here?"

"You wouldn't answer my texts or my calls. So I came over. I needed to apologize for this morning and bring you this."

He lifted his arm. It was only then I noticed my leather jacket draped over it.

With trembling fingers, I reached for it.

His hand was fast as sin and he grabbed mine before I could fully take possession of my jacket.

Electricity jolted through my veins.

"Have dinner with me tonight."

No way. No way. No way!

"I can't. I have plans." I wanted to sound stern but my voice sounded like a squeak.

Damn it.

"Tomorrow then." His tone was demanding.

"I can't, I have to work." That was much better.

"After work then." It was like he wasn't going to take no for an answer.

I almost smiled at his persistency. I almost said yes. "I can't." I wanted to high-five myself because I might have actually succeeded in sounding bored.

But then he stepped closer.

And my pulse started to race.

He smelled so good. I couldn't tear my eyes from him and I couldn't stop my entire body from filling with tension. His eyes seemed to glitter with apology.

Oh God. Did I really think that?

I was just too hyperaware of him.

He flashed me a coaxing smile and I felt every square inch of it right down to my core. "I want to explain my behavior this morning. Have dinner with me. Tomorrow. I'll pick you up at your office at eight."

I stared at him. It was like my body and mind were in a trance—under his spell. I couldn't breathe.

"You owe me that much." The words he spoke didn't match the soft tone he had used.

I blinked and tried to come up with a response. Riddled with confusion all I could do was stare. Did either of us owe the other anything? No, I thought. Yet, I knew I couldn't refuse him.

I was a sad, sad girl—a glutton for punishment when it came to him.

The elevator door opened with a ding and Mrs. Bardot came out with her little terrier, Coco, under her arm. "Hi, darling."

"Hi, Mrs. Bardot," I said back.

She scrutinized Jeremy with a gleam in her eye and Coco barked at him. *Good dog.*

Jeremy nodded his head in her direction. "Good evening, Madame."

Madame?

Her return smile was so wide, I had to roll my eyes.

Mrs. Bardot took her time walking to her apartment, but once her door closed, his eyes were back on me, pinning me, searing me, driving me out of my mind. They were hungry, lustful, full of want, full of need. Nothing like they had been that morning.

I swallowed as my heart beat faster and faster.

He transferred my coat fully to my hands. "Tomorrow then."

I nodded and averted my eyes from his steely gaze.

He was closer now, and his breath tickled my neck.

I looked up at him. He seemed taller than I remembered. "My office is at—"

"I know where it is. You told me."

Wariness crept over me.

He grinned at me. "You really don't remember last night. Do you?"

I flushed, squirming. "I told you I didn't."

He slowly shook his head. "That's a real shame."

Just the very sound of his voice and I became a wet noodle all over again.

I couldn't believe it. I was unable to talk to him, stand up to him, or even look at him without having lustful thoughts. I should have told him to cut the crap. I should have told him that I knew we didn't sleep together. But instead, I did something so much better.

"Good-bye, Jeremy," I said, and then I stepped back and closed the door.

High five!

CHAPTER 11

New Beginnings

"It's never happening."

"Why not?" Lily snorted in amusement.

I pushed myself out of the bamboo chair and placed my napkin beside my plate. "I'll be at the bar."

She wiped tears of hysteria from the corners of her eyes. "If you change your mind, I'm sure he hasn't taken the offer off the table."

I shuddered at the mere thought.

He was Benji Peck and his offer had just made me feel like a prostitute. Benji Peck was the lead choreographer for the evening's performance. Prearranged seating had him sitting beside me during dinner, which was all fine and great until after the main dish was served that is, when he outright propositioned me. The man was blunt and to the point and obviously used to getting his way. His proposition was straightforward enough. He'd take me to the wardrobe trailer to see the Sarah Burton costumes worn in the evening's performance and let me try one on, if I agreed to blow him.

Wrong girl.

He should have extended that invitation to Lily because I had a feeling that she would have accepted.

Self-satisfaction hastened my steps toward the bar as I remembered how Benji's jaw had dropped in shock when I answered politely, "Thank you, but no thank you."

He excused himself to use the restroom shortly after and oddly enough, he never returned.

Oh well.

Looking around, the place astonished me. White paper lanterns hung from tree branches that were strategically placed to dapple the room with glitter. Beige linens downplayed the gleam of crystal that adorned each table surrounding the dance floor. And sparkle seemed to be everywhere.

As I waited for my wine, I studied those in attendance. Some people were here for their love of the arts, others for their love of fashion. It was an eclectic mix.

I had never really understood the elusive draw of the event but it was Lily's favorite night of the year. Sometimes a girl dreams about wearing a stunning couture gown. Sometimes a girl dreams about wearing a radiant tutu. And sometimes that girl is a New York City Ballet dancer and she gets to live both dreams at once, wearing tutus designed by couture houses.

Lily had always wanted that dream for herself but the closest she ever got was coming here to the New York City Ballet's Glitter Gala. I glanced back over to where she now stood. She looked radiant in her figure-hugging, shimmering gold gown. She was petite but held her stature as if she were six feet tall. There's no doubt, she would have been a prima ballerina if things had worked out.

My dream growing up couldn't have been more different. I dreamed of a carefree life, one that didn't include overbearing social circles like the one I was currently observing. But my dream, like Lily's, had long ago dissipated, and over the years, I learned to accept what my life of privilege had to offer.

Which is why, as donations were being made at the black-tie dinner reception on the promenade of the David H. Koch Theater, I felt badly that I was unable to contribute.

As I looked out at the sea of wealth, I not only started to wonder what was next if I couldn't save TSC, but I began to worry about myself.

Sure, I had grown accustomed to the comforts of the Upper East Side—clean sidewalks, the parties, the doorman, drivers, the galas, yet there was more to it. It was the only home I'd ever known. What would my life be like if I no longer lived in this world?

Long ago, I had yearned for an out. However, somewhere along the way, comfort replaced that yearning, and fear was slowly taking the place of comfort. Not fear of losing status or material things, but fear of losing myself again.

Without my job, what would I do?

"Phoebe, there you are."

Oh no, please no.

I slowly looked up from the glass of pinot grigio I had been staring into to see the bright red lips of the event cochair, Avery Lake. Avery had that certain drawl to her voice. You know the one, the one that sounded like Mrs. Howell from *Gilligan's Island*. She might as well have just added the *darling* to the end of her greeting.

I really didn't like her—I had my reasons.

She was, however, dressed in a knockout couture gown I was certain had been custom sewn for her hourglass figure. It was white satin with crystals at the neckline, the waist, and the hem. But then again, she was not only a Rockefeller, but a Von Furstenberg as well, so I'd expect no less. She also just so happened to be the current *it girl* of the social circuit.

I placed an air kiss near one cheek, then the other. "Avery, how nice to see you. It's been so long."

Okay, not long enough.

Avery took my hand and gave it a squeeze as she stretched her mouth in a wide smile. "Your donation this year was extremely generous."

Confused, I didn't know what to say. To make matters worse, I couldn't stop staring at her deep ruby-colored lips.

"A million." She winked. "You really outdid yourself."

My only guess was she had the wrong person.

"And in one lump sum, that was a nice touch."

What was going on? If I'd thought she was kidding, I didn't any longer. She was dead serious. When I tried to respond, my voice froze.

A weird rush of relief came over me when she dropped my hand. I wanted this strange encounter to end.

But then she took a step forward. "Listen, I have to run. I just had to say thank you for your contribution in the midst of your own financial woes. Oh, and I'd love to catch up sometime."

I bit my tongue at the underhanded catty remark in light of the precarious situation I was finding myself in.

Her dress swooshed in her rush but she didn't fail to turn and give me a slight wave.

It took everything within me to make myself wave back in the midst of my humiliation. I was thankful at least she hadn't noticed that I'd almost choked when I tried to say "you're welcome."

There I stood, in the chaos, feeling more alone than ever.

Suddenly, the violinist ceased his playing at the same time the lights grew bright and I knew the announcements were about to be made.

I stiffened. Great. More humiliation.

Yet, as soon as the room silenced, it dawned on me that Dawson must have made the donation in my name, and it must have been real, not a mistake. He was the only one besides Jamie who really understood the true bleakness of my financial situation. I had yet to tell Lily just how bad things were. Anyone around me only knew what he or she read in the papers. Dawson though, he knew it all and he also knew how much I loved to contribute to worthy causes—and the ballet was near and dear to my heart since it was my best friend's dream, once upon a time.

Tears sprang to my eyes at his generosity and how much he cared for me. Was I acting stupid not to be with him? Would I ever find someone who loved me the way he did?

"You look beautiful." As the words rumbled into my ear and a familiar hand gripped my waist, I felt a little flutter in my chest.

It was him.

Him.

That flutter started to radiate into an all-out thump that stretched from my head to my toes and obliterated any possibility of coherent thought.

When his fingers lazily grazed across the bare skin of my arm, my body became a flame and he was the match that lit it.

I was on fire.

I whirled around to see Jeremy McQueen in a tuxedo and my breath caught. He was utterly handsome, never mind strong and confident, and sexy as hell. No matter how badly I wanted to douse the heat between us, in that moment, I knew there was absolutely nothing I could do to stop it.

The thought that I should run raced through me, but the need to get closer overpowered that fleeting thought.

"Jeremy." My voice was low. "What are you doing here?"

His grin was wide and devilish.

There was a time I loved to see that look on him. I knew what it meant then, but what it meant from him these days, I had no idea.

"I'm out supporting the arts, just like you," he answered casually.

I tried to contain my shock. "But you . . . you asked me to go to dinner to-night."

"You weren't so tongue-tied last night," he taunted.

All I could do was stare in astonishment.

What was his game?

When he stepped even closer, and the air practically sizzled between us, I couldn't even speak coherently. He was magnetic and an undeniable energy buzzed between us.

I immediately forgot all about my issues.

"And I would have skipped all of this"—he reached his arms out—"to be with you."

Oh God.

Just then Avery's voice boomed over the microphone. "If I could have your attention, please."

Everyone quieted and I had no choice but to turn around to face her. Jeremy stayed where he was and his hand resumed its position on my bare skin, causing me to inhale sharply.

The flame grew even hotter.

"Tonight has been a raging success thanks to all of your contributions but none greater than that of Jeremy McQueen. Jeremy has asked that I refrain from introducing him publicly. For those of you who haven't had the pleasure of meeting him yet, Jeremy is the entrepreneurial genius behind Jet Set. And since we all know how much we like to play, his donation of five hundred Jet Set lifelong membership cards to our silent auction has been the biggest single source of funding in the history of the Glitter Gala."

I stood there shocked. Jeremy owned Jet Set? He despised anything to do with my world—or at least he had.

Glitter started to swirl in the air of the Lincoln Center as applause rang in my ears, but Jeremy didn't move. Instead, he chose to stay close to me.

"Although I did agree I wouldn't introduce Jeremy, he didn't specify that I couldn't point him out to all of you, so if you want to meet him, just look for the man covered in glitter. Enjoy the night, everyone."

I felt a shift in the air and just like that, Jeremy was gone. Dancers from the night's performance had pulled him away and as they surrounded him they threw handfuls of glitter all over him.

It happened quickly, but I noticed the ballerinas didn't miss a spot on his body. They were practically patting the glitter on him. Jealousy knotted in my belly even though I tried to will it away. He wasn't mine. He could be touched any way and anywhere by anyone.

"Isn't he the guy from the club last night? The one that helped James?" Emmy was standing beside me and I hadn't even noticed.

I nodded, not really knowing to what extent he had helped Jamie.

"How well do you know him?" Emmy asked me.

I didn't respond, but wondered where she was going with the conversation.

"Is there something going on between the two of you?" she prodded.

"No," I said a little too quickly and more than likely not at all convincingly.

"Then you don't mind if I . . . talk to him?"

"That's probably not a good idea," Lily answered for me. Where she came from, I had no idea.

Lily and Emmy had become even more estranged than Emmy and I had over the last few years. I wasn't sure if they were too different or too much alike, but whichever, it had caused them to drift apart.

Emmy probably didn't even realize Jeremy was the guy I had spent the summer with so long ago but even if she had, I doubt she would have cared.

Pouting a little, Emmy asked, "Why is that? He's single. Sure, he's taken Avery out a few times, but rumor has it, they aren't exclusive."

My heart sank. Jealousy bubbling inside it.

Lily glared at her. "How would you know? I thought you and Avery weren't speaking."

"We're not." She gave Lily a fake smile.

I almost rolled my eyes at their exchange. Seriously, years had passed since that summer after college graduation when Avery went after Jamie in Emmy's absence. Since he never really chose either, I'm not sure Emmy should have looked so smug. She hadn't really won. Avery just got tired of waiting around for him and gave up. That's when she set her sights on Dawson.

Emmy beamed and continued gossiping. "Anyway, rumor has it she's not happy that he's been seen with other women and is about to dump him."

Dump him? Were they seeing each other? Did she know I slept in his bed?

Bile rose in my throat. I thought about chugging my wine to get rid of the sour taste, but thought better of it. I had taken only a few sips and that was enough to make me feel like throwing up. And with the news Emmy was sharing, I was starting to feel even sicker.

"Well, it doesn't sound like there's anything going on anyway. Maybe he's interested in someone else. Like I said, he's probably not the kind of guy you want to get involved with," Lily repeated. "And what about James?"

Emmy was loosening the straps that held her dress up to expose more of her cleavage. No longer the waif-thin anorexic, she had cut her hair, dyed it platinum, and gotten breast implants. She was a Marilyn Monroe carbon copy, just thinner. "James will never commit to me, you know that," she said honestly.

It was the first time I heard her admit it. I was glad she at least knew the score. "I'm sorry." It was all I could say.

"No worries. I think Mr. Tall, Hot, and Dangerous is just the change of pace I'm looking for. There's something smoldering and brooding about him. You know?"

The thought of Jeremy with anyone else, especially someone I knew, felt like poison shooting through my veins. But somehow I managed to stand stoic.

Lily's face, however, turned red and she was about to lose her cool. I placed my hand on her shoulder in a calming manner but it was too late. "How do you know anything about him?" she bit out.

With a huff, Emmy answered, "Theo told me he ran a bunch of clubs in Miami before he moved here last year and expanded Jet Set to include New York."

Emmy and Theo, Avery's brother, were close. And I was certain if it weren't for the fact that Theo had his sights on Danny, she would have been happy with him.

With a bright red face, Lily just stared openmouthed at Emmy.

I felt even sicker. He'd actually been here a year and he never even tried to contact me.

Eyes bright, Emmy kept going. "Can you imagine how much fun he must be?" She wasn't really asking. She acted like she already knew.

Having had enough, Lily huffed, "Emmy, do you have any idea who he is?"

Emmy looked bored. "I just told you."

"No, I don't mean what he does," she said through gritted teeth.

I wanted to kick her. To tell her to shut up. But instead my eyes were scanning the room for him.

Emmy looked confused.

I felt uneasy.

"He's the guy Phoebe spent the summer after college graduation with."

Shocked, realization dawned on Emmy but that wasn't all. She paled and some emotion seemed to plague her. What it was, I had no idea. All I knew was every ounce of color drained from her face and she meekly said, "Excuse me please. I have to go. I forgot that I told James I'd stop by to check on him."

And just like that, she was gone.

"I told her." Lily looked so proud.

I felt like there was more to her sudden departure. I even thought maybe she would seek out Jeremy to take him with her, but then I saw him working the room with a confidence that commanded attention. Every time I stole a glance his way, he caught me. After a while, I gave up wanting to talk to him— there were too many women surrounding him and he appeared happily entertained by their presence.

Not quite an hour had passed after Emmy's sudden departure and I was feeling utterly exhausted. I turned to Lily. "I'm going to go home."

She looked concerned. "Are you sure?"

"Yes, I have a long week ahead of me and I have some sleep to catch up on."

"Let me call my driver to take you home."

"No, I'll catch a cab."

"Are you sure?" she asked again.

"Yes. Honestly, it will be faster."

She hugged me. "Call me."

"I will," I told her, and then made my way to the coatroom.

The coat check took my ticket and I rested my palms on the counter while I waited.

"Are you leaving so soon?" His voice was smooth behind me.

My body was tingling at his nearness and I really couldn't take any more of his flirting. I squeezed my fingers into fists and let my anger consume me.

"Here you are, ma'am." The coat check interrupted my fury and I fumbled in my purse for some money.

"Here you go," Jeremy said, handing her a twenty and taking my coat.

I slowly turned around to tell him I'd had enough but when I did, I looked straight into his eyes. They looked so blue that my knees weakened and I felt tongue-tied. My anger fled as quickly as it had built up. Shaking it off, I grabbed for my coat. I had to get out of here.

"Allow me," he offered. He held my coat out and I twisted so he could help me into it.

He reached around to button my black lace trench and my body liquefied at his touch. He was hard and lean and arousal shot through me the moment his body connected with mine.

"Let me see you home?" he whispered in my ear.

My pulse was racing. "That's not a good idea."

"It's a ride. What about that isn't a good idea?"

I twisted back and stared at him. I wanted to say no. I knew I should say no . . . except I couldn't. "Okay. But only because I want to talk to you."

He smiled with such charisma that he almost won me over then and there. "This way." His smile turned brighter.

I melted all over again.

The way he took my hand, his hand, and the way he led me—it felt too familiar. We arrived at the elevators and he pressed the button for the garage, not the street.

I looked at him questioningly, wondering why.

"I drove myself," he said.

The look I'd given him had nothing to do with the elevator. I swear I could see a trace of red lipstick on his lips and I knew just whose lips had been there.

Molten lava flowed through my veins. I sucked in a breath and once we were in the elevator, I stared at the floor so I didn't have to see it. I kept it up until I felt him blowing on my cheek and my eyes darted up in surprise.

"You had glitter on your face." He shrugged.

"You're covered in it," I said with a smirk and took the opportunity to wipe my fingers across his lips. "There, I got that."

He didn't need to know *that* was lipstick and not glitter.

The dark fringe of lashes lowered as his lids fluttered. "Thank you," he said in a rumbling tone.

"You're welcome," I said, satisfied it was gone.

He glanced down at his glitter-clad tux. "Looks like I can throw this away."
Damn, he looked so good in that tux.

"Depends," I said.

He raised a brow. "On what?"

"If you want to remember all of those beautiful women touching you."

Grinning, he looked down at the tux again and then over to me. "Nah, what's the purpose if you don't know them intimately."

A weird rush of relief came over me.

We stared at each other, drawn together like two magnets that couldn't defy the laws of science.

"I was offered the chance of a lifetime tonight," I blurted out of pure nervousness.

He made an impressed face. "Oh yeah, do tell."

Realizing what I'd said, I regretted it instantly. "No, I can't. Forget I said anything."

Curiosity filled his features.

Nervously, I tucked a stray piece of hair behind my ear.

Jeremy had the same idea and our hands grazed each other's at the same moment that our eyes locked, and oddly enough, in that moment, there was nothing between us but honesty. I could see him as clearly as I ever had. The high-strung young guy I had fallen in love with had grown into a magnificent man.

I instantly dropped my hand.

"You don't have to be nervous," he said, his words echoing my thoughts.

"I'm not," I lied.

"Yes, you are. You're twisting your ring. You always did that when you were nervous."

I glanced down and sure enough, I was.

When the elevator door opened, Benji Peck stood there before us with a woman on one arm and a costume bag on the other.

As soon as we got out and the doors closed behind me, I burst out in laughter.

Jeremy eyed me. "What am I missing?"

"Him." I jerked my head toward the elevator.

"Him, what?"

"He wanted me to blow him in exchange for a chance to try on one of tonight's performance pieces. Honestly, I didn't think anyone would take him up on that but I guess I was wrong."

Jeremy glowered at me. "He what?"

I swooshed a hand at him, still giggling. "Come on, it's funny."

"What was his name?" Jeremy asked sternly.

I shrugged as if I didn't remember.

He was taking this way too seriously.

Abruptly, he lurched forward and took my hand again. He led me through the garage in silence and stopped in front of a very pretty white Porsche.

"Nice car," I commented.

"I want to know his name," he said tersely.

I patted the hood of the pretty car. "Jeremy, it's not important."

His gaze drifted from my hand to my face and his demeanor softened. "I drove it for you."

I gave him a questioning look.

"Sorry, I keep forgetting you can't remember last night. When I took you to the garage that houses the Rose Bar's fleet, you picked it out. You said you always wanted to drive a Porsche."

My jaw almost hit the floor. "Really, I said that?"

He nodded as he opened my door.

"I don't drive."

Light flared in his eyes. "You know how to drive, you just don't have your license."

He remembered.

"True," I laughed. "But it's been a while."

Once, long ago, I'd scheduled my driver's license test, but I never took it. I shook off the memory and got in.

He looked at me and when I smiled at him, he closed my door. Once he was in and buckled up, the car purred to life. He gave me a grin and then accelerated so fast out of the underground garage, I had to hold on to the door. Rather than fear, adrenaline raced through my veins as he took the curves with such competency.

Jeremy pulled onto Broadway and instead of heading north, the shortest way to my apartment building, he went south.

"Where are we going?"

"You'll see." He grinned.

I started to protest but then he pulled over at the entrance to Central Park and got out of the car. He came around to my door, opened it, and said, "You're up. I'm shotgun."

I shook my head. "No way."

"Last night you said you wanted to drive this car. You weren't in any condition to drive then, but you are now."

"Jeremy," I protested. "I haven't driven in years."

He took my hand and tugged me out of the car.

His touch seared me.

"Then it's time."

We were standing so close and I looked up at him, my heart thumping with excitement. "Tell me what happened last night and this morning first."

He groaned. "This is supposed to be fun, not serious."

"Please, I have to know."

He caged me, his hard body colliding with mine. "Drive us through the park and then I'll tell you."

The heat that surged when he looked into my eyes was something I remembered all too well. But once I realized he wasn't making a move on me, that he was slipping into the passenger seat, I sat behind the wheel of the Porsche 911.

"Zero to sixty in two point six seconds. Give it a try."

My hands shook as I gripped the leather. "I'm illegal. My permit isn't valid anymore."

He shrugged. "So, I'll spend a night with you in jail if we get caught. The trick is not to get caught. Unless . . ." He let the word trail off and just smirked.

The adrenaline and excitement mixed as they flowed through my veins. But it wasn't from the prospect of driving Jeremy's car. It was because he was sitting next to me. I put the car in drive and thought I had pressed down on the accelerator only lightly, but the car jerked forward—fast. Faster than I meant and I slammed on the brake.

I looked over at him. "Sorry."

"Keep going." He was calm and patient. But then again, he always was.

I tried again, and again I accelerated too fast and slammed on the brake.

"You're using two feet, aren't you?"

I looked down at my jewel-encrusted Manolos. "Yes, but my heels keep sticking to the mat, so I have to."

"Take them off."

The tone of his command was sensual and gave me goose bumps. I couldn't help that I wanted to do what he told me to.

"There you go," he encouraged as I drove through Central Park.

I was shaking and nervous and stopped as soon as I reached the exit.

"Why'd you stop?"

"I'm not driving on the streets of Manhattan."

He laughed. "Not yet anyway. Next time we'll take the Alfa Romeo on the Turnpike."

A memory flashed through my mind of the night before. A garage next to the club filled with a fleet of white cars and Jeremy telling me to pick the one I wanted to ride in. "This one," I'd said and pointed to the Alfa Romeo. "No. That one," I countered, pointing to the Porsche.

My door opened and the memory was gone.

He reached for my hand. "You did great."

"I don't know about that, but it was fun," I conceded.

The traffic was light around us. Grabbing my shoes, he walked me around to the passenger side but didn't open the door. Instead he bent down. "Lift your foot."

His touch as he slid on first one shoe and then the other intoxicated me. He watched me intently to gauge my reaction.

I shivered at the intensity I saw in his eyes.

The night was dark and a little chilly through the lace of my coat, but I could see him and felt warm from the heat of his stare.

I must have shivered though because when he stood, he took his glitter-covered jacket off and wrapped it around me. Then he leaned against the car and crossed his arms. "So, about last night." He grinned.

I swallowed, unsure of what he was going to say. *Did I want to know?*

His head dropped but his eyes lifted.

He looked adorable.

"It's a real bummer you don't remember because . . ." He let the words hang in the air.

Fed up, I told him how I felt. "Jeremy, can you stop playing this game you're playing. I know we didn't sleep together."

He shook his head and reached back, flattening his palms to the hood of the car. "I never said we did." He became more serious. "But, by the end of the night, we did agree to leave the past in the past."

My doubt must have registered on my face. I wasn't certain what he had said was even a possibility.

Jeremy arched his back in a stretchlike motion and I couldn't deny the wanton feeling that stripped me of any common sense. "You lied to me about who you were and when I found out, I left without a second thought."

My heart started to slam into my rib cage but somehow I managed to contain my emotion from spilling out. *So that was why.* I had already suspected as much but he made it sound so heartless.

"Hey," he said, drawing my gaze back to his. "I think we can say, it's a draw as to whose wrongdoing outdid whose."

To my own surprise, I nodded in agreement.

He wasn't finished. "I was an immature ass. I was a different person then. And so were you. You were an Upper East Sider who lied about who she was and I had a chip on my shoulder. We were doomed no matter what."

My heart fell but he was right. It would have never worked. I took a hesitant step and leaned against the car, next to him. "If we agreed to let the past stay where it was, then why were you an asshole this morning?"

He cringed. "Last night, after I brought you home, you wanted to see where I lived, so I brought you to my place. On the way, you started to fall asleep, but before you did you promised that in the morning things wouldn't be weird between us."

It was my turn to cringe because things certainly were weird.

Remorse flickered in his eyes. "When I woke up and you pretended to be asleep, it ticked me off. It was like you were playing games and it triggered something I thought I had come to grips with. And then I thought you were lying about not remembering anything and that really pissed me off. So yeah, I was an ass. But even so, you shouldn't have left like that."

Sensing that he was waiting for me to respond, I said, "I know. I'm sorry. This whole thing was just so strange. I didn't know what else to do."

We had drifted nearer to each other and when I turned my head to look at him, he was already looking at me. With our bodies so close, the air so charged between us, I thought sparks should be flying. His face seemed to inch even closer; his lips were dangerously close to mine. I was afraid to move. I wanted this closeness and it was evident he did too, but we were both hesitant.

Just then, a car drove by and slowed, honking its horn and flashing its lights.

Jeremy jerked and stood up straight. The spell was broken. "Come on, we should get going."

We both got into his car and drove to my apartment in silence. I was lost in memories of the past and I thought he might be too. When we arrived in front of my building, he pulled up in the loading area. He left his car running as he walked me to the door. Some of my hair had fallen loose and he tucked it behind my ear.

"I'll see you tomorrow night," he said.

I turned, surprised he wasn't even going to wait to see if I invited him up. I hadn't decided yet, but I was edging toward it.

Harry was holding the door open but I didn't walk through it.

"You should go," Jeremy said, taking a step toward me.

"Yes, I should," I responded, taking a step forward.

Again, his lips were dangerously close to mine—all I'd have to do was raise myself on my toes and lean in.

I didn't.

Jeremy didn't lean forward either. Instead, the sensation of his words whispered across my neck. It wasn't the cool night. I knew this because his breath was warm. "Good night, Phoebe St. Claire."

I had closed my eyes and when I opened them, he was walking away.

"Jeremy," I called.

He turned around and walked backward. "If you want me to sleep over, tonight's not a good night. I didn't bring my overnight bag."

I had to laugh at that. I guess that's what we'd had last night—a sleepover.

"But on second thought, since I've already seen what you're wearing beneath that dress, I could be talked into it."

I had to laugh again.

He pushed his hands in his pockets. "I guess that wasn't what you were going to ask. But I had to try."

"No, it wasn't." I smiled at him though, and my heart beat so frantically that I considered it for a moment, but then I scolded myself for the thought. "Do you think we should just leave well enough alone?"

He stopped and scrubbed his jaw. "If you're asking if that's what I think? No. But I think the question was more rhetorical. Maybe meant for yourself. And I can't answer that for you. But I will be in the bar at the Saint tomorrow night at eight. If you want to see me again, meet me there. If not, that doesn't mean I'm giving up."

With that he turned back around and sauntered with his sexy as hell walk to his car. I noticed I was still wearing his jacket and when some of the glitter fell from it, it made me sad. I grew even sadder when I watched him drive away, going zero to sixty in the two point six seconds as he'd promised.

CHAPTER 12

Another Ending?

I was never any good at making decisions.

Making decisions to do with my life, that is. I always went back and forth, wondering if I had made the right choice. Always second-guessing myself.

So it was no surprise that at work the next day, I was struggling with what to do about Jeremy. There were so many unanswered questions—but did I really need to know the answers?

My life was already so complicated; my job was of utmost importance since the fate of TSC was in my hands. I had to keep a clear head. I couldn't afford to lose myself in him. And when it came to Jeremy McQueen, I didn't think there was any compromise.

I tried to push thoughts of him aside—which was nearly impossible.

I thought I'd start with thanking Dawson for making the donation for me last night. Normally, I would have just called him. Neither of us had spent much time texting each other over the course of our relationship, but I knew if I called him, he'd want to meet and I'd feel guilty if I didn't concede.

Me: Thank you so much for last night.

Dawson: It was nothing. I'd do anything for you. Let me know when you have time for dinner this week.

Me: I will, promise.

With that done, my mind started to wander. I looked down. The reports on my desk were waiting for me and I dug in. The weekly update meeting with the regional managers had taken place first thing that morning and the good news was there was a slight rise in occupancy, but the rise had come from rate deductions, so the result to profit was flat.

There had to be a way to bring people back to the Saint. There was a market out there for luxury hotels, my great-grandfather had seen it, and my grandfather had captured it, but under my father's reign, we had lost our flagship status.

I had to regain it.

My mind kept wandering back to Jeremy as I beat myself raw trying to come up with a solution that didn't include dropping our elite status.

But the time had come to consider it.

My phone beeped with a message and I assumed it was Dawson. When I glanced down, my heart skipped a beat. It wasn't Dawson.

It was *him*.

As if he knew I was thinking about him, Jeremy was messaging me.

Him: Did I tell you how sexy you looked in whatever that was you were wearing under your robe last night? I really hope to see it sometime.

Me: You weren't supposed to see that.

Him: That makes seeing you in your underwear twice and having you sleep in my bed once within twenty-four hours of laying eyes on you again. If I were a betting man, and you know I am, I'd say I'll be seeing you tonight.

I shouldn't have answered his first text, and I wasn't about to respond to his second. For some reason, I was drawn to him like a bee to honey and I knew he was right, no matter how many times I told myself I wasn't going to show up in the bar at the Saint that night, I knew I would be there.

A knock at my door startled me. "Come in," I called.

"Phoebe," Hunter said in his *I've got bad news* tone. Hunter was the new Chief Financial Officer for TSC and he had a stack of papers in his hands. I had let the previous CFO go and hired Hunter when I took over. He was also Logan's uncle, so I trusted him.

I looked at him gravely. "Sit down. What's going on?"

"I decided I should go through the company's financials myself. If we do have to file Chapter Eleven, there will be an audit and I don't want any surprises." He paused to look at me.

"Go ahead, what is it?"

He sighed. "I came across the expenses for your father's apartments. And since they haven't been used in more than two years, I thought perhaps there would be a more efficient alternate use for them. They're prime real estate and I think they could rent for top dollar. It's not that much, but every little bit helps."

My heart sank. "Apartments?"

He nodded. "You didn't know?"

"No. Where are they?" I asked in shock.

"Here, Miami, Las Vegas, and LA."

"In the hotels?"

"All but one. The holding in Miami is a condo."

"Why would he have those?" I asked.

"Phoebe, that's not a question for me to answer, you'd have to ask your father."

No, I didn't have to. I could guess. The other cities, I could almost understand, although he could just take a room as I had been doing when I visited. But my father, like my mother, was extravagant.

"Which hotel location here?" I asked.

We had two hotels in the city—the one where our offices were, located on East Fifty-seventh, and the other in Times Square.

"The Times Square location."

I just stared at him.

He kept talking. "We could easily rent each of the penthouse apartments. I was hoping to get twenty thousand a month from each. We could use the income as your mother's allowance. As for the condo, I'm looking into it further to find out the details."

Penthouses! My father kept penthouses in the plural.

I wanted to laugh. My mother had been using company funds for whatever she wanted for as long as I could remember. I recently had to tell her she could no longer do that. She wasn't happy, but seemed to understand. But she was never going to allow me to put her on an allowance. And especially not with the income used from her husband's fuckpads. In good conscience, I couldn't even ask her to do that.

Just the thought made me cringe.

Her draws on the funds though, would need to be managed somehow.

"Do it. Rent them," I told Hunter in a split-second decision. Fuck my father. I was going to be moving out of my apartment soon with nowhere to go in sight, so he could give up his penthouse apartments while he was serving his time. And as for my mother, I wouldn't tell her where the money came from.

"Do you want to talk to your father about this first?" Hunter asked.

"That won't be necessary. Have them cleaned out and donate everything. As for the condo, let me know when you find out the details."

"I will."

"Thanks, but don't waste too much time on it."

Hunter nodded and slipped an envelope on the desk. "Here are the keys to the apartments. I'll start getting them all ready next month. You might want to make sure there's nothing of value in them first though."

"Hunter."

He looked at me sadly.

"Please don't mention this to my mother."

"I would never. I even hated to bring it to your attention but right now, business is what matters."

"Thank you."

Hunter McPherson was a good man with a big heart and I could see what was happening to TSC was killing him. He stood and started for the door, then turned back. "Phoebe, the company is drowning fast. We can't keep making up our losses by selling more shares of stock."

Worried, I asked him, "We still have controlling shares. Right?"

He nodded. "But every quarter that passes our position weakens. We're getting more and more vulnerable. Are you sure you don't want to file for bankruptcy before it's too late?"

I swallowed the lump in my throat. "I'm sure."

I was determined to save TSC. I had to. If not, I was going to not only lose everything, but also lose myself in the process. I just knew it.

I swirled in my chair and looked out into the park. TSC's offices occupied the two top floors of the hotel and the view was breathtaking. How many hours had I spent staring out this window?

I sighed and tucked the envelope Hunter had given me in my top drawer. Then I gathered my things and headed out to meet Jamie for lunch. It was a beautiful day and the walk would be invigorating.

Jamie was already at the Rouge Tomate cart in Central Park when I spotted him. He was ordering our lunch. I smiled at him and couldn't help but think it would probably be our last lunch outdoors until spring.

"Hey, nice hair," I said, rubbing my hand over his bare head.

Jamie turned to me and kissed me, on the lips like he always did. "You know, I kind of like it. I might just keep it this way."

"If anyone can pull it off, you can."

His eyes roamed over me. "You look amazing. Aren't you working today?"

"I am." I tried to act surprised about his question. To not give away that I had dressed especially nice for any particular reason.

He narrowed his eyes at me.

I shrugged. "I wanted to look nice for you."

I had on one of my favorite fall dresses. It was a black-and-red tulip jacquard with a fitted bodice and a V-neckline, three-quarter-length sleeves, and a short, flared A-line skirt.

"Bullshit."

I tried to look appalled.

He let it go. "Here, a shroom burger, green juice, and chocolate banana cookie."

I took the box of food. "Where to?"

"William Shakespeare; I can't deny you your favorite view when you have so much to share."

"Let me see your head first." I turned him around.

"It's not that bad."

"Jamie, it looks terrible."

"Scalp wounds look worse than they are. But enough stalling, spill it."

I looped my arm through his and we walked with our box lunches in hand. "I spent the night at Jeremy's place and don't remember anything. When I woke up, he acted like a complete ass and I took off. Then he showed up at my place last night to return my coat, asked me out, I said no, but somehow agreed to maybe go out with him tonight, and then he showed up at the gala and drove me home."

Jamie stopped in his tracks. "Did you fuck him?"

I shoved his shoulder. "No, I didn't sleep with him."

He raised his brows. "But you want to."

"What? I didn't say that."

He started walking again. "You didn't have to, I can hear it in your voice."

I found an empty bench for us. "Let's just eat here."

"You sure?"

"Yes, now just tell me what to do."

He laughed. "Like you'd listen. But for shits and giggles what is it you need advice about?"

I sighed. "Dawson was worried, so I went to see him yesterday and when I told him it was time to move on, he told me he wasn't ready."

Jamie sat beside me. "I thought we were talking about Jeremy?"

"What's with all the focus on Jeremy?"

Jamie turned to face me. "Phoebs, you broke it off with Dawson for a reason. Letting guilt attack you isn't going to change any of those reasons. Leave well enough alone and stay away from him. Besides, the love of your life is back."

"I never said he was the love of my life."

"Come on, just admit it."

"Okay, so I haven't forgotten him but I can't shake the fact that he's been here for a year and never bothered to contact me."

"You can't. Really? Because even I get it. Years ago you lied to him and he left. When he moved back, I doubted looking you up was first on his list."

My mouth dropped. "How do you know for sure that's why he left?"

"I talked to him yesterday."

The smell wafted from our burgers as we both unwrapped them. "Why?"

"He called to check on me. After all, I got hurt in his club."

"What did he say?"

Jamie's smile grew devilish and he ran a finger down the middle of my chest. "Admit you wore this for him and I'll tell you."

"I did no such thing."

He sipped his lemonade. "You never show cleavage at work."

I looked down. "I don't have any cleavage to bare, or I would."

He almost spit a piece of his burger out. "You know what I mean."

"Okay, so I might have dressed up for work on the odd chance I decide to meet him later."

He took his time chewing and I tried not to get annoyed. "We played racquetball together yesterday."

My eyes popped. "Racquetball? In your condition."

He rolled his eyes. "It's a cut, it's not like I was dying."

"Emmy made it seem like you were. She was at your apartment, in your shirt I might add, when I stopped by."

He looked surprised.

"She didn't tell you I stopped by?"

"No, but I told her yesterday this thing between us had to end."

That must have been why Emmy told me what she did about Jamie. "Really. What brought this on?"

He looked almost pained.

"Jamie?"

He took a deep breath. "I just don't think I was doing her any good by always being there for her when she needed someone. I thought maybe I loved her in some way but Friday night I realized that wasn't it at all. I mean if I did really love her, I would want to commit, I would care when she was with someone else, I would feel guilty when I was with someone else, but I never felt any of those things. So it was time."

I leaned in to hug him.

He let me but then shrugged it off. "Whatever. Anyway, back on track. Like I said, Jeremy wanted to make sure I was okay and I wanted to make sure he had done the right thing by you."

"I hadn't even talked to you. How did you know?"

He raised a brow. "Logan told me. Can I finish now?" He was getting annoyed.

"Yes," I answered, trying not to laugh at him.

"So when Jeremy called, I asked him to meet me and he did."

I wiped my mouth. "When exactly was this?"

"I had just left him to swim at the club when I called you yesterday but you were with Dawson so I didn't want to get into it."

"Go on."

"You sure you want to hear this?"

I nodded. I was resolved. How much worse could it be?

"It's not like we didn't already know in some way but he told me he had gone to the house we rented that summer the day after you and he had gotten into that argument and that's when he found out who you really were."

"Mr. Charleston must have accidentally let it slip."

"There was more to it though. He said something about a scholarship coming through and he had to leave quickly."

"A scholarship? Really. To Stanford?"

"I have no fucking clue. You need to ask him for the details."

So Jamie had been right all along. I should have just told him from the beginning.

Jamie shrugged. "It's in the past, Phoebs. You need to focus on what you want now and be honest with yourself."

"What do you mean?"

"Was going to see Dawson yesterday a way to keep you away from Jeremy? Because I have to be honest—it's not fair to Dawson."

I wrapped up the rest of my burger and shoved it back in the box. "No, that's just stupid."

He gulped all of his lemonade. "I don't think it is."

"I went to see Dawson because I owed it to him."

"That's what I mean. You don't owe him anything. The best thing you can do for him is to stay away from him."

I sighed and bit my cookie. "I know."

"Good. Now that's settled. Are you going to give Jeremy a chance?"

"I don't even know if that's an option. But if it is, I can't lose myself in him again. I have to get TSC back on its feet."

"You can have a life and work, you know."

I sighed again. "What else did he say?"

Jamie tossed all his wrappers in the box and set it beside him. "We talked mostly about Jet Set and how he accomplished what he had in such a short period of time."

I was curious. "How did he?"

"You know it's funny but what you had told me about him made perfect sense. He never wanted to be around people like us until he realized we might just benefit him."

"That doesn't sound very nice."

Jamie shrugged. "Business, Phoebs. We all make compromises. Anyway, he said one day it occurred to him that it was the people he had stayed away from who would pay anything for almost anything. The harder it is to obtain, the more they'd pay, is what he said."

"He isn't wrong."

"Isn't that the truth? So anyway, he told me he was in Miami, and found it wasn't much different from New York when it came to spending money. He decided to open a club where access had privileges only membership could buy."

I was only half listening to Jamie as my brain was working faster and faster. If Jeremy had been successful with exclusive access clubs at street level, what would happen if those exclusive access clubs . . .

I jumped up. "I have to go. I have an idea." I kissed him good-bye and started walking. "I'll call you later."

"What the hell, Phoebs? I was still talking."

"You're brilliant," I called back.

"I'll clean up." I could hear his laughter.

"I love you," I yelled.

I cursed the high heels I'd worn that prevented me from walking faster back to my office. I was going to meet Jeremy that night all right, just not for the reason he thought—or at least that's what I told myself.

My phone rang as I hurried out of the park and I smiled. "Lily, I was going to call you. Sorry I bailed last night."

"That's why I'm calling. Preston and I are on our way to Paris for Fashion Week."

"Preston? He called you? Tell me everything."

"Actually, I called him. After you left I was talking to Avery and she told me Preston was doing terrible without me."

Avery and Preston were cousins through the Von Furstenberg side so it made sense that Avery would know this.

I stopped at a light. "And?"

"When I called him he told me to come with him and I said yes."

"Did you talk about your issues?"

"No, we'll do that while we're gone."

The light turned and I started walking. "Are you sure that's a good idea?"

"Come on, St. Claire, not everything has to be cleared up to be with the one you love. We'll talk about things as they unfold. But I have to hurry. I have to pack and meet him at JFK in two hours."

The person in front of me came to an abrupt stop and I practically ran into him. "How long will you be gone?"

"That's up in the air."

I was almost to the Saint and started to walk faster. "Well, have fun, I'll miss you. Send me pics and don't forget to call."

"I will. Oh and Phoebe, one more thing."

"What?" I asked as I entered the lobby.

"She's after Jeremy."

"Who?"

"Avery. She wants him. I was able to talk Emmy down but there was no talking Avery down. She wants him."

"What did you say to her?"

"Nothing. She did all the talking."

"Well, he's free to make his own decisions. And I'm not even sure he's interested in me and more important, I'm not sure I'm interested in him."

She scoffed. She actually scoffed. "For once in your adult life, follow your heart, St. Claire. I have to go."

Tears sprang to my eyes. "Go, Lily, go to your Romeo."

"I love you," she said just before she hung up.

I hope you get your happy ending, I thought as I dropped into a seat in the lobby of my hotel alone.

CHAPTER 13

A Date

By the time eight o'clock rolled around, I didn't know which I was more nervous about—seeing him, talking to him, or wondering if he would even show up.

I started down to the bar in plenty of time. I stopped at the restroom to check myself in the mirror and then made my way through the lobby, where I was unexpectedly detained. The desk manager stopped me to ask a question and it was eight oh six before I actually walked through the entrance to the bar.

The Saint's bar was the same in each hotel location. It was my grandfather's vision and he designed the bars to his specifications. He also loved whiskey; therefore, he made sure to make whiskey the draw. Guests at the Saint could choose from one of the most complete selections of whiskey anywhere in the city they were in. They could count on that.

The thirty-five-foot-long mahogany bar was solidly constructed with beautiful leather panels in the front and was backlit. The structure served as the room's focal point. High-top tables extended the bar experience, while the clusters of casual lounge seating were perfect for unwinding with large groups of friends. It was edgy, comfortable, and as I looked around for Jeremy through the few patrons scattered around the beautiful space, I determined, it was no longer a draw.

I also determined Jeremy wasn't there.

My nerves were frayed as I frantically scanned the room for his leather jacket and didn't see it in the vast emptiness that surrounded me.

I stood motionless, no, I stood there crushed.

Soon my eyes landed on a white shirt at the bar.

It was him.

Him.

It was his muss of sandy hair, messy but gorgeous, that gave him away.

My heart beat frantically.

Running into him was one thing, but meeting him, on purpose, was something completely different.

And he showed up. He was there.

I slowly started to walk toward him. My knees were weak and with each step I took, an ache began to build between my thighs. I noticed him look down at his watch and then he turned to look around. I was about ten feet away from him when he did.

He was nervous that I wasn't going to show.

His eyes met mine, and I could see the fire in them. It was a reflection of my own burning desire.

Suddenly, I was breathless and I had to slow my pace to find my footing.

His gaze drifted from my eyes to my breasts, and my nipples tightened from just the look he was giving me.

I knew then I was in trouble.

He was trouble.

"Hi," he mouthed.

"Hi," I mouthed back.

His blue eyes twinkled as he stood up to greet me. "Wow. Just wow."

I smiled at him.

"You look amazing," he added in a low, controlled tone.

I was not so controlled. I was secretly jumping for joy. I had taken more time to get ready this morning than I had for anything in a very long time. I didn't want to admit it, but I wanted to look especially nice for him.

"Thank you." I felt my cheeks start to burn and I willed the blush away.

His gaze roamed over my face. "I'm the one who should be thanking you."

Self-conscious, I averted my stare and nodded a hello to the bartender. He was gawking at me too, probably from the fact that I was obviously nervous—I was usually so collected at work.

Jeremy didn't kiss me hello, he didn't shake my hand, but he did look at me with a yearning that made that ache that was already building between my legs almost painful. "Do you want to grab a drink here before we go to dinner?" he asked.

I looked at his half-empty glass of whiskey and wondered how long he'd been here. He seemed more nervous than I'd ever seen him and I reveled in the fact that he felt the same way I did. "Finish yours and we'll go."

He twisted to push his glass aside. "I'm good."

Relaxing slightly, I leaned a hip against the stool beside his. "No, don't waste it. I can wait."

Jeremy glanced around. "Not exactly hopping in here, is it?"

Somehow, this didn't deflate me. "In my grandfather's day, the whiskey bar was a sought-out commodity."

He leaned very, very, very close. "That wasn't meant to be an insult. It's just I'm in clubs every night and I know the amount of money spent to keep them up and running. I can't imagine even selling the high-priced liquor helps cover costs."

"I didn't take it that way at all," I said, nonplussed.

Pure desire—that's what was racing through my mind as he was talking to me about the very thing I most wanted to talk to him about. Not insults, or criticisms, or even suggestions for improvement. Although, I did hope those would come if we talked business.

Jeremy studied me. "Are you okay?"

Dazed, I pushed away from the stool. "I'm fine. Let's go eat. I'm starving."

Staying at work and continuing to unravel in his presence was not something I wanted to do.

He looked at me with those intense blue eyes and that soft smirking expression before placing some money on the bar. Then he casually took my hand. I tried not to read anything into it. He had done it the night before as well and never even tried to kiss me good night. A fleeting thought entered my mind—what if he was truly interested in Avery? I pushed it away. It wasn't my business.

I had no idea what we were, other than former lovers reunited in what might possibly be a business venture if he said yes to the offer I was about to make him.

Oblivious to what I had in mind, Jeremy tugged his leather jacket on. Then he took my cape from my arm and slipped it around my shoulders. I didn't turn, and when his hard, lean body pressed against mine, my breath caught, and his did as well.

"Ready?" His voice was ragged and it was so sexy.

I nodded, not quite ready to speak until all of my senses had recovered from the sensual contact.

He moved with confidence, a man who knew what he was doing. He led me out of the bar, through the lobby, and out onto the streets of New York City. I assumed he had valeted his car, but when he walked past the valet stand and headed to the corner, I then wondered what he was doing.

Soon I knew.

But then, contemplation seemed to stall his feet. Jeremy had dropped his hold on me and stopped at the top of the subway station, looking down at my high heels as if assessing their ability to withstand the stairs.

I laughed. "I can walk down these stairs."

"Maybe that's not what I was thinking about when I glanced at them." He grinned.

My pulse raced as I considered what else he might have been thinking about.

When he raised a brow, I knew what it was. A long time ago, when we were together, we'd had a conversation about the possibility of me wearing *fuck-me heels* during . . .

Oh God.

Jeremy cleared his throat and the sound pulled me from my lustful thoughts. With flushed cheeks, I blinked away the memories and slowly glanced up to see his handsome face. "Have you ever ridden on the subway?" he asked, perhaps a bit cautiously.

"Yes," I answered indignantly.

"Oh yeah, when was the last time?" he challenged.

I pursed my lips together. "I think I was eight and my girlfriend's grandma took us to Queens."

He laughed—loudly—and pointed his finger at me. "I knew it."

People were rushing to get by us and when someone pushed past me from behind, Jeremy reached to steady me and never let go.

Unconsciously, I found myself stopping and staring up into his blue eyes.

Registering that he had my full attention, Jeremy traced my face. "You look the same, you know. Your hair is different. But you still look the same."

"So do you," I said breathlessly.

His mouth was so close; I thought he might kiss me in that moment.

I wanted him to.

Instead though, he pulled away and pointed to the subway. "I hope you don't mind, but this really is the fastest way to get to where we are going this time of night."

With tension coiling in my belly, I tried to act nonplussed. "I don't mind at all. I'm just surprised you didn't drive."

"To be honest, I wanted to be able to drink if I had to."

I raised a brow.

"If you didn't show, I was going to have to get shitfaced."

Hiding my smile, I responded poignantly, "But you said you knew I would show."

He looked down and shoved his hands in his pockets. "Yeah, about that. I might have been a little overconfident."

I liked seeing him raw. It made everything between us feel more real.

Feeling triumphant, I felt I should even the playing field. "Sorry I was late. Someone stopped me on the way."

"It's fine. Hey, if you'd rather take a taxi, I'm cool with that."

"No, the subway will be fun. Where are we going?"

He took my hand and led me down the stairs. "A restaurant I'm thinking about adding to Jet Set's portfolio."

"I didn't know Jet Set membership included restaurants."

He didn't stop to purchase a metro card. "It doesn't yet, but my business plan includes varying phases of horizontal integration."

This intrigued me. "Integration into what types of businesses?"

Jeremy abruptly halted before the turnstile.

Luckily, I didn't plow into him.

Indicating with a bob of his head I should walk through it, he swiped his card for me. "Anything in the entertainment field."

I could feel his stare on me when I passed through. "Anything?" I asked.

As he swiped his card again, I watched the way the metal bar pushed against his hip bones. He caught me staring.

I didn't care.

With a smirk, he repeated, "Anything."

"Like wax museums, baseball teams, and racetracks?" I asked curiously.

He smirked. "I'll pass on Madame Tussauds but I certainly wouldn't pass up either of the other two. I was thinking more like burlesques clubs, small private charters, even hotels."

"Hotels?"

"Sure, why not?"

Interesting.

We stood on the platform and he pushed my hair away from my face as a train whizzed by in the opposite direction. "You're still the same," he whispered.

"You already told me that."

"No, I mean who you are. You haven't changed."

My stomach knotted as he tried to figure out if the girl he knew so long ago was real or made up. I had heard it in his voice when we'd spoken a few times and just then, I knew for certain, it was what he was thinking. I took his hand before I spoke. "Jeremy, that girl you spent the summer with, she was me. The only thing that wasn't real was my last name. The things we talked about were all true. I did go to an all-girls school, I did live in the city, and my parents were overprotective. My dreams for the future were real. I was real." I squeezed his hand. "And what I felt for you was real."

The train came screeching to a halt and people pushed and shoved to board. We stayed where we were. Neither one of us moved. He stepped closer. "That summer, when your friend overheard me asking the guy who owned the house where you were, she told me I had your name wrong and then clarified what she thought I had mixed up. The thing was, I had talked about your father and you never said anything. I knew there wasn't any mix-up. And I couldn't help but assume everything you had told me was a lie."

"My friend?"

"Yeah, the super-skinny one with the long blond hair. I went looking for you the morning after our fight and she happened to come outside. A driver was loading her bags in a town car and she was waiting for him to finish."

I took a deep breath. Emmy. That was why she left so quickly from the Gala last night, she'd figured it out. But she wasn't the issue. I was. Me and my lies. "I did lie about something else."

Jeremy's body tensed.

"My friends and I weren't fixing up the house. The man who owned it was my father's business associate and he had agreed to rent it to us for the summer while he made repairs."

Remorse swallowed us both whole. Jeremy's forehead fell to mine and he stayed quiet for the longest time. "We've both done things we're not proud of, but the other night when we agreed to leave the past in the past, I was willing to do that. I know you don't remember that conversation, but if you think you can do that, I'd like to see what comes next."

Next?

My body started to tremble. I wanted to kiss him, but we were nowhere near ready for that. With my forehead still against his, I closed my eyes. "I would really like to do that. In fact, I have a proposition for you."

Another train pulled into the station. Jeremy looked at me with a devilish grin and laughed. Free and easy.

I loved the sound.

He took my hand and pulled me toward the subway car. "Come on. This I'm dying to hear."

I followed quickly and we stepped on board. There was no place to sit, so Jeremy took my hand in his and I gripped the horizontal bar. The doors closed and once we were both secure, he tilted his head to the side. "So tell me about this proposition of yours."

Sex oozed from his tone and arousal shot through my body. I wanted him. I wanted him more than I had ever wanted anyone in my life. If we had been anywhere else at that moment, anywhere with a hint of privacy, I would have thrown myself at him. That's how much I wanted him.

"Wipe that smirk off your face first. This is about business, not pleasure," I chided.

"Damn," he mouthed and even mouthing the word, it was hot.

The train started to slow and my footing faltered. Jeremy's tight grip on me saved me from falling onto an older woman's lap. He took the opportunity to pull me closer, and I had to tip my chin to talk to him. He was always tall but he seemed taller. I was five eight and in my four-inch heels that made me six feet. He had to be six two. "Can I be honest with you?"

Jeremy's hand slid slightly from my waist and rested partially on my derriere. "I hope moving forward that's all you'll ever be."

The train stopped and the woman I was standing near stood and took her bag, which had occupied the seat beside her.

Jeremy nodded his head in the direction of the empty seats. I sat down and he sat beside me. We were no longer touching, which was good because what I had to say was really hard for me to talk about and I didn't need the distraction of what his touch did to me.

I dropped my gaze to the ground. "My father is in the Federal Prison Camp at Morgantown. He'll be there for at least another year. When he was first arrested, he resigned as CEO of the Saint Corporation and appointed me to take his place. He stayed on as director and thought he would still be able to make all the decisions. But his decisions were further driving profits down, so I've had to refuse most of his recent advice. The problem is I can't seem to turn the company around. Every quarter profits are continuing to slide."

His hand went to my chin and he lifted it. "I know all about TSC's financial situation and yours too. What I didn't already know, you told me."

"Oh, the night I can't remember. . . ."

He nodded. "Yes, but go on."

With a deep exhale I continued, "Things are at a point now where if I don't turn them around, I won't be able to and I'll be forced to give up the company."

"Would that really be that bad?"

Surprised by his candor, I took a moment before responding. "TSC is my family legacy. I have to fight for it."

Somber, he gave me a nod and we sat in silence.

The train came to a stop and started again before I spoke. "I was thinking about what you've done with Jet Set and it dawned on me the Saint doesn't capitalize on entertainment at all."

He gave a huff of laughter. "Are you thinking about expanding into wax museums?"

I tilted my head in contemplation. "Red velvet ropes and a long queue are just what I need."

He twisted his lip. "Something tells me piles of corpses will be bad for business."

A spell of laughter had me drawing in a calming breath. "You have a point."

My entire focus was on him and I never noticed when the train stopped again until Jeremy stood and took my hand. "Come on, this is our stop."

We exited the subway and climbed the stairs. Outside it was chilly and the wind whipped my hair. I knotted it and tucked it inside my jacket to keep it out of my face. New York City is enormous but familiar landmarks will always tell you where you are. And as soon as I set foot on the street, I knew I was in the Village. After all, I'd gone to grad school down here. And if I hadn't known where I was, and the winding cobblestone streets hadn't given it away, the minute we turned on Bleecker Street would have.

It dawned on me that we were much closer to one of Jeremy's clubs and his loft than my hotel. "You didn't have to pick me up. I could have met you here."

He shook his head. "I asked you out." His face and his tone said, duh what are you, dumb?

It made me laugh.

"What?" he asked.

"Nothing," I said as I walked beside him.

Bemusement danced across his face. "Go on. I'm still waiting to be propositioned."

I bumped his body, and my entire body tightened. I'd forgotten fun between us had always led to heat. Desire made it hard to concentrate, but I somehow managed. "I already told you, I meant in the business sense."

He took my hand and tugged me under the awning of a gourmet cheese shop. It allowed us to stop but not get mowed over by those walking behind us. The store was closed for the day, but the interior lights shone on the intensity in his eyes. I found myself wading in, not wanting to jump in those liquid blue pools. Realization dawned; I wanted to lose myself in him. That's when I knew; I was failing miserably at separating business from pleasure.

"Yes," he said.

One simple word.

My breathing quickened as my gaze shifted from his eyes to his mouth. *Had I heard him right?*

"Yes," he repeated again.

I found it hard to stand. My knees had gone weak and I leaned against the glass for support. The coolness knocked some sense into me and as I shook myself out of the lustful haze I was in, I forced myself to focus. "You don't even know what I'm asking you."

Wickedness now gleamed in his eyes.

That was not helping.

He stepped closer. "You want my help and if it means I get to spend time with you, then yes."

Now flustered, I couldn't steer the conversation. "You have to stop this, I'm serious."

He caged me in. His palms pressed flat against the glass that my own palms were already pressed against. "So am I. Just tell me what it is, and I'll do it."

I lost my words. He was too close for me to focus. Was I going to be able to do this? To work with him? Yes, but I had to find balance. I had to find the strength to not get lost in this man.

In him.

Heady, I ducked out from under his arm.

He instantly turned to face me.

Extricated from his embrace, I felt like I finally had my wits about me. "I want you to consult with me on developing a plan for exclusive access nightclubs at the Saint."

There I said it.

Jeremy leaned back and raised an interested brow.

Gaining my stride, I further explained. "The nightclubs would only be accessible to those staying at the hotel."

He tilted his head. He seemed to be considering my suggestion.

"You hate the idea."

"Sinners." One word. That's all he said.

I looked at him questioningly.

Jeremy was amused. "The name of the nightclubs. Call it Sinners."

My insides lit up. "I love it. How'd you come up with it so fast?"

His eyes twinkled and I caught a glimpse of that bad boy from long ago. "What else could be more perfect than adding a little sin where there's a saint."

"Nothing," I mused. *It was the perfect name.*

"Come on, walk with me."

I watched as he pushed himself off the glass and I repressed any thoughts about his body.

He, on the other hand, went right into business mode. "At first you'd have to offer limited exclusivity though. Weekends only for club members or something like that. Exclusive access takes time to build up to. You have to have a solid base before shutting everyone out."

Impressed, I bit my lip. "Like you do with the clubs?"

He nodded. "I'm working on minimizing nonmembership nights. But it takes time. You have to build your membership first."

"What else are you thinking?"

He grinned wickedly. "A lot."

I smiled. "Go on. Remember, we're talking business."

He turned and walked backward. "I remember."

I gave a huff of resigned laughter. This was going to be a challenge but I was up to it.

Thirty seconds later, he'd sped off a laundry list of ideas that sounded more than doable, they sounded brilliant. "Once design is complete, the key is the launch," he said. "Have your friends be there every night of opening week. Call everyone you know to come. The press too. You have to make people think the place is inaccessible and then I promise you, it will be."

Right in the middle of the sidewalk, I lunged myself at him and wrapped my arms around his neck. "Thank you."

"For what?" he chuckled.

"For believing in my idea."

His palms braced my back and he pressed his lean, hard body into mine. Our breathing was heavy. His lips were so close to mine but still he didn't kiss me. I wasn't sure he wanted to.

Was I misreading the signs?

I pulled away and cleared my throat. "I'm sorry about that."

"Don't be." He grinned deviously.

We started walking again.

"Tell me more," he asked.

I let what had happened go so I could focus. "I spent the afternoon with TSC's CFO. We have three vacant penthouse apartments in key cities. I'd like to start with those and then add to other cities if the project proves successful."

We were almost to the Bowery when he bobbed his head. "This is it."

My jaw dropped. "You're purchasing La Rosetta?"

He opened the ornate door. "Possibly. It's still up in the air."

I'd been here a few times. The interior was simple, uncomplicated, and the ambiance had a sensual appeal about it. That, along with the raved-about food, made it a perfect draw. It was nearly impossible to get a reservation.

Jeremy approached the hostess and as she gushed over him, I watched the boy I had once known, except he was no longer a boy, he was a dashing, charming, confident man. Not that he wasn't always that way—he was just more refined now. He had a certain kind of smoothness to him and it became very apparent, he knew it, and used it to get what he wanted.

I was impressed.

My mind wandered to the thought of Sinners. I hoped it would be TSC's saving grace. It had to be. Hunter and I spent the day working on financial models, calculating what it would take to turn the business around. The bottom line was, it would take filling the hotels to capacity and my hope was that the elusive draw of an exciting new club would do that.

My phone beeped and I pulled it from my purse. It was a text from Lily with a link to Page Six. The text read:

> Lily: *If you want him, you better go after him because like I told you, she's pursuing him. She sent the photos in herself. Preston told me.*

> Me: *I'm with him right now.*

> Lily: *That's my girl.*

> Me: *It's not like that.*

> Lily: *I'm not even going to ask.*

I clicked on the link. It took me to the Sightings section of Page Six. I fumed at my screen. What the hell was going on? Right in front of me were two photos side by side of Jeremy and he wasn't alone. One was of Jeremy and Avery sitting next to each other, deep in conversation at the Rose Bar. They looked at ease; maybe I even saw a glimpse of intimacy if I looked hard enough. I had no idea when that one was taken. The other was an even more intimate picture of Jeremy and Avery dancing at the Glitter Gala. He was covered in glitter, so there was no doubt it was taken the previous night. Avery was gazing up at him in adoration with those feline eyes of hers. The caption read: *Avery Lake getting cozy with enigmatic entrepreneur Jeremy McQueen.*

Cozy!

I felt like someone had driven a spike through my heart.

"Anything good?" Jeremy asked as he turned around.

Somehow I managed to remain calm and shoved my phone in my bag. "No, not at all."

"Your table is ready."

Jeremy held out his arm and I, in turn, blew out a deep breath, and looped mine through.

As we walked though, insecurity nagged at me.

I knew I couldn't afford to let it in—I had too much to accomplish.

CHAPTER 14

The Start of Something New

Jeremy McQueen did not do romance.

Or at least the twenty-one-year-old Jeremy McQueen I had known didn't. The closest he ever came was giving me my own flower from my hair.

Yet, as we were led up the stairs, the atmosphere in the restaurant changed from trendy to romantic. Rose petals led the way to a private dining room and in the middle of the large space, sat a single elegant table set for two. Sensual blues music played softly throughout the room, peonies graced the table, and candles were scattered everywhere.

The room was beautiful and I couldn't help but look up at him in awe. "Who are you?"

He wore a cocky grin. "The guy that's going to sweep you off your feet."

I bit my lip. "What if I don't want to be swept off my feet?"

He shrugged nonchalantly. "I can always toss you over my shoulder and carry you."

I laughed. "No, really, who are you?"

With a chuckle, he answered, "Phoebe, I'm the same guy I always was, just a little older and wiser."

I glanced around again. "It's perfect."

But Jeremy was wrong—he wasn't the same. I didn't know how it was possible, but he was better. He was so much more confident and at ease with himself. He'd let something go. The chip on his shoulder was gone. The hot bad boy had become an insanely sensual man that I couldn't help but want. Right here, in this room.

Change can be both good and bad though.

The old Jeremy would have taken me right there in the lustful haze that was so evident between us. The new Jeremy was more reserved, a businessman with a goal.

Yet I still wondered if that bad boy wasn't in there. Was he seeing Avery Lake while pursuing me?

His mouth was at my ear, and the heat between us jarred me from my thoughts. "When you plan to double the owner's income, there's little he'll refuse to do for you."

My heart beat wildly. My body began to ache insanely for the man beside me.

As he pulled out my chair, I knew beyond a doubt, he was what I yearned for in my life.

Before I could say anything, Jeremy sat down and the sommelier was at our table in an instant. He handed Jeremy the wine list. "Good evening," he said. "We have some astounding autumn wines available. The Barolo and Barbaresco wines are our best selling this month. Might I interest you in a bottle?"

Jeremy glanced at me. "I think the lady prefers white. What do you recommend?"

The wine steward quickly flipped through the pages of the menu. "Here you are sir, the drier ones to the left, the fruitier ones to the right."

Jeremy's eyes scanned the right side.

How did he know what I liked? I didn't drink wine when I was twenty-one. That was for sure.

Jeremy looked up. "We'll have a bottle of the Vespa Bianco 2006."

"Excellent choice. One of the best we have."

As the wine steward walked away, I looked at Jeremy. "How did you know I prefer white wine?"

"You ordered a pinot grigio at my club, and then I saw you drinking it again last night."

"You were watching me last night?"

"If by watching, you mean observing, yes. If by watching, you mean stalking, not exactly, but close enough."

I couldn't help but smile. That photo of him and Avery was taken in a short window somewhere between when he had been painted in glitter and when I had chosen to leave and he was suddenly behind me. He must have been watching me, just as I had been watching him. I knew our eyes had collided many times, but I wasn't sure if it was coincidence.

Now, I knew it wasn't.

I felt something strange in my chest as the realization dawned. It was as if a few missing pieces of my heart floated from him to me to find their long-forgotten place. I couldn't explain it but the fact that he was paying attention to me, when I didn't think he was, did something to me.

I was being way too emotional. I reined it in as best I could and redirected the conversation back to business. "Well, that explains how you knew I was leaving. Now tell me about your plans for this place."

He studied me. "Right. Back to business."

His stare wasn't that of a guy trying to get into a girl's pants. It was more invasive. It was as if he was trying to figure me out. I guess he probably was. I knew I was flipping from hot to cold with him but it wasn't on purpose. Something inside me was telling me to tread carefully, and I was trying really hard to listen. What he told me about the way he had acted the morning I woke up next to him made sense, but still I felt the explanation wasn't completely on the up-and-up. It was nagging at me yet I couldn't explain the unease I felt. But I couldn't ask him about it because I didn't understand it myself; I had to let it go.

The waiter approached the table. "We're going to prepare a sampling of our best dishes for the two of you this evening. But before we begin, I wanted to make certain there was nothing you were allergic to or didn't care for."

Again Jeremy's intense blue eyes were on me. "Do you still avoid red meat?"

I was amazed. "I do."

There was no specific reason I didn't eat red meat. It started when I was younger and my mother insisted I eat it for the iron.

There was a time in my life, I think I was almost twelve, when I rebelled against everything my mother wanted me to do. If she told me to walk, I ran. If she told me to wear a dress, I wore pants. When she told me to come straight home from school, I stopped along the way. If she told me not to get dirty in the park, I rolled in the mud.

It was a phase and it was gone soon enough like so many other childhood phases. And even though I had let most of the things go from back then, avoiding red meat had stuck with me.

The waiter made a note and then looked up. "For you too, sir?"

He nodded. "Yes, let's make it simple."

The waiter left the table. "You said you had penthouses in three cities? Which ones?" Jeremy asked.

I sat up straight. "Hey, wait. I want to know about this place."

"All in good time." The look he shot me was wicked.

Excited to discuss the new TSC project, I didn't protest. "Well, Sinners . . ." I smiled when I said it.

His return smile was gorgeous. It helped ease the tension I was feeling.

"They're in New York, Las Vegas, and LA. I was hoping to open them all around the same time."

Jeremy tapped the table as if counting. "If we can expedite the permits, a New Year's Eve opening would be an excellent way to announce things. You could hire a press correspondent to report from each location."

"We could do a ball drop in the middle of the dance floor," I added excitedly.

He smirked at me. "You got this. So tell me what you need me for?"

Crushing my need to want to respond with something completely inappropriate, I concentrated on the business at hand. "To help design the concept to take to investors. I need financial backing for start-up and then eventually for rollout to the other fifty US locations. TSC's financial position is weak. I know I won't get it without a solid business plan. You've done this before. You know what's needed. And I assume you have the contacts."

He looked at me but he didn't say anything. Maybe I was asking too much.

"Jeremy, I realize you have a business of your own to run, so if you don't think you have the time, I completely understand."

"I already said yes. I'm just trying to understand what you're looking for. That's all."

The wine steward reappeared with a rolling ice bucket beside him and he went to work removing the cork from the bottle.

Jeremy's gaze was on me though, not the sommelier, and I couldn't stop the butterflies that were swarming in my stomach. His stare was hot, intense, hungry; it seemed to be fueled by our business conversation. My stare reflected his with equal vigor.

The steward poured a small amount of the wine in the glass that was already placed in front of Jeremy.

Jeremy swirled, sniffed, and then tasted it. I watched as he sampled the wine all the way to the liquid flowing down his throat, and the eroticism of the moment didn't escape me.

I was completely turned on.

He nodded to the steward, who then in turn poured the wine in my glass, and filled Jeremy's before bowing and departing with, "Enjoy your meal, Mr. McQueen and Miss St. Claire."

"Mr. McQueen." I couldn't stop the words from tumbling out of my mouth.

He gave a dry laugh. "Sounds ridiculous."

I raised my glass. "It absolutely does not sound ridiculous. I like the sound of your full name."

His eyes twinkled. "Feel free to call me it anytime."

Mr. McQueen.

He knew what he was doing. We had spent the meal discussing ideas for Sinners and during dessert, he finally told me about his plans to add restaurants, casinos, horse tracks, country clubs, and someday even hotels and airplanes to Jet Set's portfolio. His ability to see the pieces of his plan fit together was astounding and by the time I had finished my cappuccino, I was certain I had made the right choice to hire him as consultant to TSC's new endeavor.

We had yet to discuss how much he was going to charge and when he'd start. "Jeremy," I said. "We need to discuss your consulting fee."

Before he could respond, the waiter approached our table. "I'm sorry to interrupt, Mr. McQueen."

Jeremy looked up. "What is it, Maurice?"

He had learned the waiter's name when he brought out our first course. I liked the sense of ease he had in getting to know those who would soon be helping him build his empire.

"Your car has arrived."

"Thank you."

I narrowed my eyes at him. "You have a driver for the night?"

He disregarded any hostility in my tone. "No, the Rose Bar has a driver and I thought we'd use the service to get home."

I'd forgotten about that perk.

He stood and extended his hand.

I stood as well but I didn't accept his hand. Something struck me as odd. I stepped closer to him and kept my voice down. "Tell me then, why did we take the subway to get here tonight?"

"I told you, I thought it would be the quickest way."

I stepped even closer. I was so close to him, I thought I could almost hear his heart beating. "Are you sure it wasn't to test me? Were you trying to figure out if I was the same girl you remembered? The one who would do anything you asked? Were you trying to make sure I wasn't one of those snobs you used to dislike so much?"

He didn't say anything and he certainly didn't deny it.

"Would you have asked Avery Lake to ride the subway with you here?"

His brow furrowed. "She has nothing to do with this."

"Well, at least you can admit there is a *this*. I hope I passed your test," I said spitefully and turned and walked down the stairs.

Jeremy was on my heels immediately, only stopping to retrieve our coats. I was already to the door by the time he had them in his hands. He caught up with me on the sidewalk and draped my cape around me.

I was mad and the anger made me hot. I didn't need my damn coat.

"We're right here," he said, pointing to a white four-door Jaguar.

"I'll find my own way home," I tossed over my shoulder and kept walking. I considered taking the subway but I wasn't certain which line to take. We had taken the R to get to the Village but that was from midtown.

His hand gripped my arm. "Phoebe, don't walk away from me. You can be as pissed as you want at me, but I took you out tonight and I'm going to see you to your door, whether you like it or not."

"If I don't want to get in that car, you can't make me."

His features hardened. "Don't bet on that."

I knew he wasn't kidding. He'd throw me over his shoulder if he had to; he'd done it before. I knew I'd get in his car but it would be on my terms. I crossed my arms over my chest. "Admit you were testing me."

His eyes grew stormy. "So what if I was. It's not like I don't have good reason."

Damn him, he was right.

I sighed inwardly, questioning if we really could put the past behind us. "Are you done now? Or is there more you want me to do?"

He held his hand out. "The only thing I want right now is for you to get in the car."

I didn't take his hand, but I did get in the car.

The ride to the Upper East Side was quiet. I didn't look at Jeremy and he didn't look at me. When we pulled up in front of my apartment building, I got out quickly and slammed the car door behind me. He opened it and followed me. I pretended he wasn't there. It was childish, but the game he played was childish too and I was still mad.

When we got on the elevator, I was still pretending he wasn't beside me. But it wasn't as easy as the walk into my building. He was standing so insanely close and my body hummed at his proximity. It became impossible to ignore him when his fingers slid under my chin and he lifted it. "I know you're mad at me but I told you I knew you were the same girl you had always been before we got to the restaurant. I was trying to be honest with you."

I rolled my eyes and jerked out of his hold.

He leaned back against the elevator wall. "I'm leaving for Miami early tomorrow morning. I won't be back until late Friday night. I'll e-mail you a list of things we need to accomplish quickly for the club launch but first and foremost we need your property managers to file for construction permits. It's a remodel, so they can file and we can add the plans as an addendum before each county reviews them."

"You're leaving town?" Any remaining anger I was feeling seeped away at the news.

"Yeah, my assistant is running the Miami branch of Jet Set but I have to go back there once a month to sign checks and review operations."

For some reason, my eyes shot to his mouth. That mouth. I wanted it on mine. I couldn't stop the wanton desire from flooding me. I wanted his lips on my body. I wanted a lot from him. None of which made sense right then.

"Why? Are you going to miss me?" he teased.

I shook my head no, but it wasn't at all convincing. The truth was—I *was* going to miss him, but I wasn't sure I should tell him that. "It's just that we haven't finalized our agreement."

He stared at me again as if trying to figure something out.

The elevator doors opened and I quickly walked into the hallway, needing to escape his stare. I could still feel his eyes on me when I stopped in front of my door—and the thought of the yearning I had seen in his eyes made me fumble for my keys.

He was moving closer.

Closer still.

He was directly behind me, but his body wasn't touching mine.

At that moment, I wanted it to be. I wanted so badly to feel his hardness against me.

When he placed both of his palms above my head, my pulse raced. He leaned down to whisper in my ear and his body was even closer.

But still not close enough.

His warm breath tickled my neck as he spoke. "I don't want any money from you. The only thing I want from you in exchange for my help is for you to consider giving us a second chance. I know it's not that simple. But that's what I want."

I pulled my keys out of my purse and turned around. "We can't do business like that. It's not ethical."

He shrugged. "Then my consulting fee is nominal and if you agree to it, I'll take your word that you'll consider my proposal. You don't have to answer me right now. Just think about it."

My heart was beating so fast. "And if I say no? Then you won't help me?"

"I didn't say that. If you say no, we'll renegotiate. But you haven't said no. Have you?"

I shook my head. My lips parted and my breathing picked up speed. Could I agree to something like that when the fate of my family business was on the line? I wasn't sure. "What exactly do you mean by a second chance?"

"I'd like to be able to take you out and have a good time without the past constantly blocking our way. Everything is up for discussion. Just know, ultimately I want you in my bed and not just sleeping beside me."

My body ached for him at the very thought.

I wanted that too—I wish it were that easy.

He closed the distance between us and I could feel the sparks, the heat. "Just think about it."

"Jeremy," I whimpered.

I wanted to protest his demands but I had nothing to argue. Yet, I couldn't say yes. I wasn't sure if the mess that was our past would ever allow for a future.

My lies.

His abandonment.

Could we rebound from that?

My mouth was agape and he covered it with his finger.

His touch seared me.

"Shhh . . ." he whispered. "No more talking about it tonight. Too much has already happened today. I'm going to leave now. I'm not going to ask you if I can come in. And even though I want to, I'm not going to kiss you good night. You and I both know we never could stop at just a kiss. But I want you to know, I really wanted to fuck you on that table tonight and if I weren't in the middle of closing the deal, I would have at least tried."

I bit down on my lower lip to keep from moaning out loud.

The bad boy was still in there.

"The question is, would you have let me?"

I shook my head no but my body was screaming yes, yes I would have. I couldn't argue with it, my body was reacting on its own; it wanted to give him what he said he wanted.

Right here.

Right now.

He gave me a huff of laughter. "Are you sure about that?"

Adamant, I shook my head again.

Jeremy coasted his hands down to my hips. "I think you're lying."

A delicious shiver rippled through me and when he pressed his fingertips into my skin, I sucked in a breath.

I was so obvious.

Jeremy shrugged and stepped back. "I'll be thinking about you while I'm gone, and I hope you'll be thinking about me."

My breathing became erratic and every muscle in my body thrummed under his touch. I'd been thinking about him for days—no, to be honest, I'd been thinking about him for years. There was no doubt; he'd be on my mind.

"Jeremy . . ."

He leaned forward and caged me between his arms. "Yeah," he answered in a strained voice.

Clearly, we were both hot and bothered and we couldn't continue like this.

"We can't let the past go, we have to talk about it or things like what happened tonight will keep coming up."

He took a deep breath and let it out. "You're probably right."

Just then the elevator dinged and Mrs. Bardot sashayed out. Dressed in a long elegant gown, she looked every bit the movie star she once was.

Jeremy pulled back just enough to kiss my forehead. "Good night."

And with that, he nodded toward Mrs. Bardot and headed for the elevator.

I watched his walk.

She watched his walk too.

He was just too sexy.

The doors began to close but he stopped them. "Hey, I have this thing Saturday night I'd like you to come with me to. But you have to promise not to laugh."

I let my anger and fear and anxiety slide off my shoulders. "What is it?"

"A launch party for the new Assassin's Creed."

"The video game?" I asked.

He nodded.

I smiled at him. "I'd love to."

The doors closed and I looked at Mrs. Bardot, who I could tell was sizing us up.

"What does one wear to a video launch party?" I asked.

"Oh darling, come with me. I have just the thing. I wore it to *The Spy Who Loved Me* premiere."

I slipped my shoes off, left them outside my door, and followed Bette Bardot into the larger half of my floor. She had a massive four-bedroom apartment and I'd been witness, on a number of occasions, to her searching through at least two of those bedrooms filled with clothes for a particular dress.

She stopped in the foyer and turned around. "Did I ever tell you about the time I was in love with two men at the same time? One was very much like your own James Dean type."

Except he wasn't really mine, although it seemed he wanted to be.

CHAPTER 15

Finding a Rhythm

"Harder. It has to be harder," I shouted excitedly into the phone.

Ask me anything about Audrey Hepburn and you had better believe I knew the answer. I was being serious. Audrey Hepburn was no laughing matter. I had a closet jammed with little black dresses and a drawer full of her movies.

I might never have seen *Gone With the Wind*, but I had seen every single Audrey Hepburn movie, watched them over and over, owned them, not only on DVD, but Blu-ray as well. I also had digital downloads on my iPad and my laptop.

"Give me a minute," he said.

"You're not allowed to Google questions."

"How the hell else would I know what to ask you?" Jeremy laughed into the phone.

I fell back onto my bed. "That's cheating. I didn't Google the video game questions I asked you last night."

He laughed again. "Yeah, but asking what game you play with a guitar or which game you're a sniper in doesn't require much research."

He had a point.

"You picked the topic, not me," I quipped.

We'd played twenty questions years ago and it was easy to pick it back up. It was also an easy way to get reacquainted.

"Next time I'm picking James Bond."

"I can't wait. I know the man well," I teased.

My smile was wide as I remembered how much he loved James Bond. I'd loved Audrey back then as well, but getting Jeremy McQueen to sit down and watch *Funny Face* just wasn't something I ever tried to tackle—back then anyway.

My phone beeped and Dawson's name flashed across my screen. I hit ignore. I'd call him back. It was Thursday night and just like Tuesday and Wednesday, I was spending the evening on the phone with Jeremy. His texts started right after he left Monday night. He had asked that we leave our past history to face-to-face discussions. I had agreed because he was away and I wanted to talk to him. And to be honest, I liked that he was making an effort to get to know who I had become.

I hadn't agreed to his payment terms but he started working with me on the project anyway. Tuesday afternoon we'd had phone conferences with the three property managers and Wednesday we discussed the draft for the proposal for the club investment with Hunter. We were going to submit to interested parties late the next week. But on Thursday, I hadn't talked to Jeremy all day. So by the time he called me, I was longing to hear his voice.

"You still there?" he asked, his voice taking on a more serious tone.

The playfulness seemingly gone, I tried to recapture it. "You are so watching *Breakfast at Tiffany's* with me when you get back."

He laughed from deep in his throat. "I know it might be hard to believe, but I actually wouldn't mind watching it with you."

The huskiness in his voice made me sit up. "Then you're in for a treat." My voice sounded seductive. I had no idea where that came from.

"Where are you?" he asked.

"Home."

"I know. Where in your apartment are you?"

"On my bed. Where are you?" I asked.

"Give me a minute."

I heard stomping up some stairs and then a door closed.

"On my bed," he said in that same husky tone.

I nearly stopped breathing.

"Are you still there?" he asked again.

"Yes." My voice was raspy.

In a deep, husky voice he said, "Tell me what you're wearing under your clothes."

Arousal overtook my mind and I answered quickly. "A bra and panties."

"Take off your clothes and tell me what they look like."

Flushing from head to toe I managed to say, "Jeremy!"

"Phoebe, I've seen you in your underwear. Christ, I've seen you naked. Just put your phone on speaker, dim the lights, and describe to me the lucky pieces of fabric covering your tits and pussy."

Shock and desire swarmed through me in equal measure.

Memories of his dirty mouth came back in a flash.

I'd loved it so many years before but we were flesh to flesh then. I'd never had phone sex before. Had no idea how to, but I knew I was about to find out. I wasn't going to turn him down. I wanted this.

The sexual tension that had blossomed between us was causing me to go insane. I was touching myself when I woke up in the middle of the night, and then in the shower before work, and last night and the night before after I hung up the phone with him. I'd been masturbating to the thought of him nonstop. Phone sex had to be so much better.

"Give me a minute," I whispered, needing to ease into the more intimate exchange that I knew was coming. I stripped out of my skirt and blouse and all but tore my hose pulling them off. The lights were already dimmed, so that wasn't an issue. I heard his own mattress squeaking and wondered if he had started without me.

My phone beeped again and I looked down. This time it was an incoming call from Jamie. I ignored it. Then, I took a deep breath and a giant leap of faith as I sat on my bed in my underwear.

Just as I was thinking about what I could say, he spoke. "I have to be honest with you," he said.

My heart sank. I didn't like any conversation that started with those words.

With a heavy exhale, he said, "I've been hard all week just thinking about you and I have to admit, my wrist hasn't been worked out this much in a long time."

Picturing his hand, his cock, his hips, and the perfect choreographed movement of all three had me barely cognizant.

"Phoebe?"

"I'm here," I said in the raspiest tone. "Then I'll be honest too. It's possible that I've made myself come more times this week than I have in my entire life."

I wasn't exactly comfortable initiating a kinky conversation. But I could follow his lead.

"Jesus, Phoebe, you can't talk that way to me when I'm not near you."

Something primal erupted within me. "And I want to do it again."

"Fuckkkk."

I moaned at his use of the word *fuck*. It sounded entirely too delicious.

Equally as delicious was his sexy laugh that followed. "So what are we going to do about this dilemma?"

I sank back into my pillows and pictured his face as I spoke—his lips parted and his eyes heavy-lidded. "I'm wearing nothing but my bra and panties and they're both gray," I said. "With thin black lines."

I heard him suck in a breath.

"My panties are skimpy, a thong, and the friction of the fabric is making me so wet."

"Fuck. My boxers are straining. My cock is rock hard just thinking about how sexy they look on you. Now, that I have that image, take them both off and sit down on your bed." His voice was intense and I knew if I could see him, his eyes would be as well.

He too had stripped

I stood up and removed my underwear and then picked the phone up and put it on my pillow while I turned the covers down.

"Are you naked yet?" he asked impatiently.

"I am. Are you?"

There was a pause. "I am now," he answered.

The sound of his voice was so arousing.

"Sit up," he demanded.

"I already am."

"Good. I'm behind you on the bed and I've pushed your hair aside. I'm brushing my lips across the back of your neck . . . you can feel my warm breath right between your shoulder blades. Can you feel it?"

"Yes," I breathed. I was getting wetter with every passing second.

"I'm lightly kissing down your spine and my hands are reaching in front of you to feel your breasts. Make your fingers mine. Circle your nipples until they're hard. Tell me when they are."

I did as he asked and as my fingers became his, my body burned for him.

"Talk to me, Phoebe. You don't have to talk dirty, just describe what I can't see through the phone."

"My nipples are as hard as diamonds," I whimpered as desire raced through every vein in my body. "And I'm wet, really wet. I want you so much."

"Fuck," he groaned.

It was hard to talk to him like I was, but I closed my eyes and let myself feel the moment. "I wish you were here."

"So do I."

He stopped talking then and I wondered if I shouldn't have said that. "Are you still there?"

"Yeah, I am. I'm still behind you. Pinch your nipples between your fingers and roll them, both of them at the same time, until you feel even wetter."

I imagined him on his knees behind me and sighed in lustful splendor. "Your chest is flush to mine, I can feel the heat of your skin next to me."

"I feel you too. You feel so good."

I moaned at the thought of the true flesh-to-flesh contact I was craving.

"Lie back and when you do, I'm going to kneel over you with my knees at your hips." His voice sounded so erotic and the image I had in my head was X-rated.

"My head is on the pillow, my hair fanned out everywhere. And Jeremy, I'm so wet."

"Oh fuck," he mumbled. "Touch me."

"I am. You're beautiful. So hot and thick as I stroke you up and down. Do you feel me?"

I hoped he was touching himself.

He made a shuddering noise and I knew he was. There were another few seconds of silence before he spoke. "I'm going to loosen your hold now, it's still your turn."

I laughed, but not for long.

"I'm kissing my way down your body. Imagine that I'm tracing the outline of that sexy little mole on your left hip with my tongue."

"I love your mouth, you know."

His laugh was wicked. "I know. I remember. Now spread your thighs for me so I can touch you with it. Your pussy needs attention."

My heart was pounding as need became the driving force of my very existence. Need for the man on the other end of the phone line to bring me to orgasm. "They already are," I whispered in a voice that morphed into a moan as my fingers drifted between my open thighs.

"My tongue is circling your clit, my finger stroking you. You're so wet. So ready for me."

"Oh God," I called out into the darkness of my own room.

"My fingers are sliding into you. Phoebe, slide your fingers, first one, then another inside yourself."

I did—more than willingly. My internal muscles clenched. My clit throbbed. I was panting. I was ready for him.

"I'm licking you, stroking you, fingering you, and your body is already tensing under my touch."

My inhibitions were gone and, as the moment became so intimate, I wanted him to feel the same pleasure he was giving me. "Push your hips forward and pretend your fist is my pussy. I'm so wet for you. So ready for you." I was breathless and panting. My words were strangled as I rode the verge of orgasm.

"I'm so fucking hard. I have to be inside you."

"Close your eyes. You are. You're buried deep inside of me." I couldn't believe that popped out of my mouth but I was glad it did.

There were a few seconds of heavy breathing between us and I knew he must have been lost in the moment. "Oh fuck, you feel so good. I'm going to come. Come with me."

I added a little pressure right where I needed it and then let myself fall, tumble down the rabbit hole that was Jeremy McQueen. I didn't care at that moment if I got lost in him. I wanted to. I wanted to bare myself to him and make him mine. I wanted for him to make me his. I wanted for us to own each other.

He groaned my name with his release and the sounds he made were so incredibly erotic.

My insides clenched as warmth flooded me and I closed my eyes and let myself go. Letting go, I cried out shamelessly, loudly at first then softer as my orgasm spun around me. It was intense, it swallowed me up, and I yearned for Jeremy to be beside me.

And then, even though his name was a whisper on my tongue, I saw him in the stars that you couldn't see in the Manhattan skyline. As they came into focus, I knew where they were from. They were the stars at the Hamptons. The ones I'd seen that summer every time he made love to me on the beach.

My body was trembling and I started to cry at the memory. Emotion took hold of me so quickly that I couldn't push it away like I had become so skilled at doing. Tears sprang into my eyes as the ache and emptiness that had been within me for so long reopened. Before I could wipe them away, his voice was calling for my attention.

"Phoebe, talk to me." His voice was strained with alarm.

I wasn't sure how much time had passed. What were we doing here? Was this real or some crazy attempt to recapture a part of our youth that hadn't even ended well?

"Phoebe, hang up the phone."

I stared in disbelief at the voice coming from my pillow. That was it? All he had to say was just hang up? But he hadn't even let me be the one to do that. The line was already dead before I could reach to press END.

It couldn't have been more than fifteen seconds when my phone rang. This time it was a FaceTime call.

I wanted to throw my phone across the room and let it shatter into a million pieces like he had done with my heart—again.

But before my heart could take control of my mind, I picked up my phone. *I was too weak not to.*

I sat up and pressed ACCEPT but I didn't say anything.

"Phoebe," he said, and I saw the intensity of those blue eyes that I knew so well.

I sat naked on my bed and tried to pull myself together.

"Let me see your face."

I wiped any stray tears and then brought the phone closer to me.

He reached out, like he could actually touch me, and stroked his thumbs over my face. Then he kissed my forehead.

I lost it.

I started crying again.

"If you don't talk to me, I can't help you. Tell me what it is," he insisted.

I knew I was overreacting. Yet I needed to talk it out. I took a deep breath. "You know things won't be the same as they were. They can't be. Too much has happened."

He sighed with what sounded like relief. "I know. They'll be better this time."

"What if they're not?"

"It's not possible."

"How do you know that?"

"I just do. I can feel it. What we had before was built on a lie and hang-ups."

I winced.

"I don't mean to make you feel bad. I had issues too. But we're older now, more mature."

He was right.

"Talk to me some more. Tell me what you're thinking."

This time his tone wasn't sensual. He wasn't trying to seduce me but rather, he was trying to understand me. I lay down on my side and propped the phone on the pillow next to me as I tried to form words in my head that might explain how I was feeling.

"I'm sorry," he whispered.

"For what," I whispered back.

"For pushing you when you weren't ready. You told me that the other night. I should have listened. It's just that I felt like we talked about everything already, I really hoped we could move past the bad stuff. I can see now, that wasn't a good idea."

"Right, the night I don't remember."

"Yeah. But I should have respected what you told me at your door. I think you were right, we can't move forward until we discuss the past."

"What we did was fine, more than fine. It was amazing."

His facial expression softened. "Amazing, huh?"

The corners of my mouth lifted. "It was just my stupid reaction that ruined it."

"It didn't ruin it and it wasn't stupid. It was how you were feeling. I get it."

"No, I don't think you do."

Jeremy lay back on his pillow and I could see his naked chest. "Then help me understand. Tell me what's going on in your head."

I sighed. "I was broken after you."

He winced this time. "Phoebe, your ex-fiancé told me about it. He was only too happy to let me know that he was the one who put you back together."

I stared at him on the screen. "He was. But he shouldn't have told you that. Is that what the two of you were arguing about last Saturday night?"

He nodded. "He wanted to take you home and was pissed you wouldn't go with him. And believe it or not, I agreed with him."

"You did? Why?"

"I thought he was the right guy for you. I didn't see us being able to go anywhere."

"And what? Now you do?"

"Yeah, as a matter of fact I do. And after the way your ex acted, I actually think I'm the better guy for you."

My insides started to tremble. "And why is that?"

"Because I see something you don't."

I raised a brow. "Are you going to share?"

The corners of his mouth tipped up. "That you need someone like me in your life and I need someone like you in my life."

I tilted my head, contemplating what he'd said.

"If I were your ex, I would have picked you up and carried you out of there. I would have never let someone else take you home."

Yes, Jeremy and Dawson were very different.

"Phoebe." His voice was low. "Talk to me. We're face-to-face. Get it out. I can see there's more you're not telling me."

I pulled my thoughts together for a moment and then spoke. "When I closed my eyes and let myself go, I felt something I hadn't felt in so long. Since the last time I was with you actually. And I couldn't figure out if it was real or just what I wanted to feel. I don't know if that makes sense but it scares me."

"Don't be scared. It was real. Trust me, it was real. I felt it too. And when we're finally together, I know you'll have no doubts."

I gave him a slight smile. "You're awfully confident."

"There are some things you just know. And you, Phoebe St. Claire, are one of those things. Anything else?"

I shook my head. "I think that's enough for now."

He chuckled. "Okay, my turn then. Since I got a small smile out of you, I have a personal question to ask you."

Feeling slightly nervous, I piled the covers up over my head. "Go for it."

His laugh was free and easy and it relaxed me. "Are you on the pill?"

That got my attention. I lifted my head from my cocoon. "Yes."

I heard the bed shift and he went out of focus, then he came back on the screen. He waved a piece of paper in the air. "I went and got tested on Tuesday. I'm clean. I'm not trying to rush you, but when we are together, I don't want any barriers between us."

"How do you know if I'm clean?"

"Are you?"

"Yes."

"Then there you go."

Again, I laughed at how simple he made everything seem.

"Your turn. Anything else?"

I hesitated. "One more thing."

"Shoot."

"Where did you go after you disappeared that summer?"

His mouth thinned. "When I found out, well, when I found out you weren't who you said you were . . . Hang on, let me start again. I had gone to see you that day to not only try to smooth things over but to tell you that at the last minute I had gotten that scholarship to Stanford after all. It all happened so fast and I had to be there the next day to register for classes. After I left your house, I just packed up and headed to California. Kat was the only one who knew—I wanted it that way."

Kat.

Kit-Kat.

My blood boiled at her name.

I pushed the immaturity away.

But then my throat went tight over his entire admission and I tried to hold a new wave of tears back. When I couldn't, I covered my eyes.

"I can't change any of that. But I am sorry," he said.

"I still don't understand how you can forgive me now."

"I already explained it."

"Tell me again."

"I matured. Realized everything that happens in this world doesn't have to be blamed on someone else."

"What do you mean?"

He tensed. "I don't know how to explain it any more than that. If I wasn't so closed off, you wouldn't have had to lie."

I drew in a breath. I hated that I had.

"When I saw you in trouble, I had to help. And then when I looked into your eyes, it all went away—all the hurt I'd been feeling was gone. Phoebe, it was as simple as that."

"But how? I lied to you." *I feared it would always haunt me.*

"Because you knew me. You figured me out from our very first exchange. You knew I would have never even talked to you if I had known who you were. I can't change that. Just know I'm different than I was. I don't believe everything is black and white anymore."

I could see that. At the same time he was still the same and the dichotomy was confusing my heart.

Jeremy continued, "I realized that what you did wasn't important. That you were the same girl I had grown to . . ." He didn't finish but I knew he meant to say love.

I had loved him too.

"Jeremy." My voice was soft.

"Yeah." His was equally soft.

"After you left, I lost myself. I lost myself in you and then I lost myself even more after you. And now I'm scared. I can't do that again."

He stared at the screen. "What if I want you to . . . to lose yourself in me?"

I shook my head. "I can't be that girl ever again."

"Jeremy, I'm home." It was a woman's voice.

The screen turned and went black but we were still connected. "Fuck, how about knocking," Jeremy said.

"Sorry, I heard you talking and—"

Jeremy cut her off. "Just close the door."

His face was back on the screen. "Give me a minute."

"Who was that?" I asked, not about to give him a second.

"Kat."

Kat!

Kit-Kat.

"Kat! The girl you were kissing the last time I saw you that summer? Kat, the only person you told where you were going? The girl who never liked me."

"Phoebe, I wasn't kissing her. I had given her a peck on the forehead to try to comfort her. Her boyfriend had broken up with her and she was upset. We were friends. We are friends. You knew that then, and now you know it again.

She runs Jet Set Miami and lives at my place here in Miami. And she never disliked you."

The air rushed from my lungs. "You live together?"

He exhaled and looked away. "No, I live in New York now. She lives in my house in Miami. The business is run from here and it was just easier if she lived here."

I made an unintentional noise in my throat and his gaze met mine. Jealousy was rearing its head but I began to realize when it came to Jeremy, I might not always see things clearly. I was so easily driven to anger and jealousy. I had to control those emotions and part of controlling them was not getting lost in him.

His words were quiet. "There's nothing between us. She's like a sister to me," he insisted.

I swallowed, trying to be so much more mature than I felt at that moment. I wanted to scratch her eyes out. But instead I bit my lip and said, "I believe you." And I did. Or I wanted to make myself believe I did. And I was going to make myself do it. I had to for my own sanity. "Does she have a . . . boyfriend?" I asked hesitantly.

He was moving around. "To be honest, I can't keep up with her. New guy, new girl, every time I turn around it's someone different. It's just who she is and I accept her for it."

"She's lucky she has you."

He was dressed when he looked at me again.

"Jeremy?"

"Yeah." His voice rumbled through the line.

I wanted to tell him I was lucky to have him back in my life, but I lost my nerve. I shook my head. "Nothing."

"Well, since we are talking face-to-face and confessing, I have something I should tell you. I already told you but you probably don't remember."

I covered my head again.

He snorted with laughter.

I loved the sound of his laugh.

"Go ahead," I murmured from the under the sheet, but then pulled it back.

He shook his head at my antics, then grew serious. "I saw you a few times in New York before the night you came home with me."

I shivered. I'd felt like someone's eyes were on me at times, I just couldn't explain it. It made sense though. He'd been in New York for over a year and I had been out with Danny a number of times to Jet Set locations. "Why didn't you ever say anything?" I asked.

"I just didn't think we had anything to say to each other. But then I saw that douche bag harassing you and I had to put an end to it. After that, I didn't want to stay away from you."

Groaning, I sat up. "Hmmm . . . So now you're telling me I owe Lars Jefferson one."

He scowled. "You don't owe him shit."

If only he knew.

"Jeremy."

"Yeah." His voice was sleepy.

"Where does this leave us?"

"You tell me," he said in a serious tone.

I felt the resolve leak out of me. I was diving in whether I should or not. "If we're going to try this again, then we need to take things slow this time."

"We'll go as fast or slow as you need to go," he promised softly.

Feeling good about where that left us, I looked at him a little too dreamily, I'm sure. "I'm glad we ran into each other again, Jeremy McQueen."

He made like he was kissing me again. "Get some sleep. I'll pick you up Saturday at five."

"Jeremy."

"Yeah," he answered.

"Thank you for not making a big deal out of my freak-out after we, well you know."

His grin grew devilish. "Had amazing phone sex."

I nodded and gave him a smile.

"Good night, Phoebe," he said and ended the call.

The room was dark and I stared at the blank screen. While it was still alight, I thought about that conversation—I was glad we talked. I wasn't happy he was staying with Kat, but I still felt closer to him. Then, I almost laughed out loud when I thought—Jeremy McQueen was never going to want to have phone sex with me again.

CHAPTER 16

A Silly Grin

For hours, I walked around with a silly grin on my face.

I went to work with that grin on my face. I sat in meetings with that grin on my face. And I ate lunch with that same grin on my face. I even wore that stupid grin all afternoon.

A weight had been lifted off my shoulders—I was going to agree to his terms. I was going to say yes to giving us a second chance. I didn't want to define what that meant. I wanted to take things slow. I wanted to do things differently than we had done the first time. We had jumped in back then; this time I wanted to wade in. I had decided to tell him at the video launch party.

My office phone rang shortly after five.

I thought it might be Jeremy, so I reached to answer it. I hadn't talked to him all day, but I knew he was flying back. I hadn't asked him when and I hadn't really thought that much about it. I had, however, been thinking about his mouth. How I wanted it on me. The sounds that came from it. The words he spoke. The erotic tone his voice took on when he whispered his sexual desires into the phone.

I also couldn't stop thinking about how hard he made me come the night before. I wanted him to do that again—in the flesh.

My mind was not where it should have been while at work.

My phone rang again and I realized I hadn't picked it up. "Phoebe St. Claire," I answered.

"Are you sure?" His voice oozed sarcasm.

"Hi, Jamie."

"Don't *Hi, Jamie* me. Where the fuck have you been?"

"What do you mean?"

"I've called and texted you for two days and you haven't returned a single one. I was just about to call your mother."

The threat of Poppy St. Claire meant he was serious.

"Oh God, I'm doing it," I admitted. I hadn't even told Jeremy yes and I was losing myself in him.

"Doing what?"

"Losing myself in Jeremy."

"Okay, whoa, back up. You need to explain."

"We've been talking and—"

His buzzer rang before I could tell him anything.

"Hang on."

"Sure," I said. While I waited, I thumbed through the blueprints of the four apartments that would soon be converted into nightclubs. My stomach started flipping.

"Look, I have to go," Jamie huffed when he came back on the line.

"Okay, but you called me. Don't sound so annoyed."

"I didn't expect you to answer." He sighed, then said, "I'm sorry. I'm just not looking forward to tonight."

"Oh, what do you have going on?"

"I have the Annual Rockefeller Foundation Benefit. Cocktails were at five and I'm already late. That was my mother on the other line. She's waiting for me to go in. Anyway, tomorrow I have the annual Ashton Christmas card photo shoot and all the shit that goes along with it. How about a run in the park Sunday morning? I'll meet you at nine."

"Sounds perfect. Have fun promoting humanity throughout the world. You can warm your smile up there."

"Fuck that. It's the most boring event of the season. I'm only going because my father is a trustee and it would look bad if I didn't represent in his absence. I'll be home early, I'm sure."

Charles Ashton had taken off three months ago with a younger woman and no one had heard from him since. His absence from society had been covered up from the press quite easily as he was an eccentric man with a passion for painting and known to take off on sabbaticals and pilgrimages to find inspiration. That wasn't the truth. His paintings transpired after his binges as apologies to his wife. He was addicted to young models and often disappeared with them for months at a time. In the past he'd always returned alone. Having gotten his fix, he knew when to drop them but this was the longest he had been gone.

Jamie's mother was a Vandermore and her social status meant everything to her, maybe even more so than my mother's, and that was saying a lot. She allowed her husband his indiscretions as long as he kept them discreet. And so far, no one was the wiser.

"Well, I'm not so sure. I'd say try to have fun, but you always do," I said.

"Phoebs, you know it's all blue hairs at this one."

Somehow I was certain he'd find a hot twenty-something.

He always did.

Jamie had some of his father's tendencies and sometimes that worried me but he also loved to work, which gave him purpose and made him different from his father.

I laughed. "We'll catch up Sunday. Love you."

"Back at you," he said and hung up.

Once I settled the phone on the cradle, I clicked my keyboard and brought up the Excel spreadsheets Hunter had put together. But all I could do was stare at the financial models on my screen. Each one showed a glimmer of hope. All were doable. All depended on a successful launch of the clubs. It was a big risk. Could this be done in such a short time frame? Would it be successful?

My worry shifted to Jeremy and me. I knew the venture could be successful, but I had to put all my energy into focusing on rebuilding the business. Would Jeremy be a distraction? I couldn't afford any distractions.

I shook off the ill feeling that maybe I should say no to his proposal and got to work. I drafted my vision for the Saint's reemergence into the world of luxury hotels and the international expansion I wanted to relaunch someday. I wanted to attach this to the request for investment portfolios that would be sent in just one week.

A light knock on my open door startled me. I looked up to see Dawson standing there.

"Dawson." He never just showed up. "Is everything okay?"

Concern etched on his brow. "Can we talk?"

"Yes, sure of course." I nodded for him to sit down.

"Not here. Can I take you out for a drink?"

My eyes searched my desk, but I had nothing pressing left to accomplish. There was still so much to do to prepare for next Friday, but I'd done all I could until the construction bids came back on Monday. I glanced at my watch. It was almost seven. Where had the time gone? I smiled at him. "Sure, it's time I left anyway."

I slipped on my shoes that I had taken off after lunch and stood, flattening my dress as I did.

"You look really nice today," Dawson complimented me.

"Thank you," I said as I grabbed my red leather swing coat and purse. I had worn a short body-hugging sweater dress to work that I normally would have reserved for a casual evening out. My hose were a floral fishnet. My shoes were snakeskin pumps. I had even snuck out before lunch for a blowout.

I was secretly hoping to see Jeremy that evening.

As I circled the desk, Dawson came toward me and placed a kiss on my cheek. I kissed him back. Then he offered his arm and I took it. I wasn't sure if I should, but I didn't feel right not doing it. Friends acted this way all the time. Jamie and I did, so why not Dawson and I?

He glanced over at me. "I called you Wednesday and Thursday and asked you to call me back. Is everything okay? It's not like you to not return a call."

"I've been"—I thought about the best word to use: crazy, chaotic, wanton, out of sorts, preoccupied, but settled on—"focused. I'm sorry."

If guilt could have stamped itself on my forehead, I'd be wearing its equivalent to a scarlet letter. I hadn't even listened to either of his messages. That was the thing with getting lost in someone; they were like a poison, making everything else around you become secondary. I was going to fix that though. This time I was aware it was happening and I wasn't going to lose sight of everyone and everything else around me.

We walked down the quiet hallway. Last month I had let a quarter of the staff go. And everyone that was still employed had gone home already. Fridays were half days at TSC. That was the one and only benefit that remained constant through the years.

Dawson's Mercedes S Class AMG sedan was out front when we exited the hotel. He never drove, although he had his license; he always had a driver on call.

We slid into the luxurious car and Dawson leaned forward and said to his driver, "Morimoto's."

I looked at him. "You said a drink?"

He gave me a smile. "I'm certain you haven't eaten. So I thought we could get some sake and sushi. If you'd rather go someplace else that's fine."

He knew my weaknesses. I was hungry. And besides, it was a good opportunity to talk to him. To tell him it was finally time we both moved on. Odd, it wasn't even a week ago that the thought of seeing him with someone else unsettled me. Now the thought only eased my mind.

I glanced at him in his wool blazer and turtleneck. He was so distinguished-looking. He might never be classified as one of my great loves, but he would always be *my* Prince of Camelot. "No, Morimoto's sounds really good actually."

Once we pulled into traffic, Dawson looked over at me with concern.

"What is it?" I could see trepidation in his stare.

"Your father called me."

"Why?"

"He said you aren't returning his calls and was worried about TSC."

I twisted my butterfly ring. "He's right, I'm not returning his calls. He wants to run TSC from his jail cell and he can't do that. I already let him do that for too long. The company is in too much danger of going under to continue to allow it."

Dawson looked even more nervous.

"Dawson, what is it?"

With resignation in his eyes, he answered, "I've been telling you TSC's stock has been bought up in small blocks by a number of different companies over the past year."

"Yes, I'm aware. Hunter has also been keeping me informed."

"Like me, your father is worried."

"Dawson, I appreciate the concern but Hunter is watching the market."

"Well, it seems on Monday, even smaller blocks of stock started being sold back on the market, and it's happened every day since."

This was news to me. Why had Hunter not informed me? "Okay."

"You know how it works, don't you, Phoebe?"

Incredulously, I answered, "Yes, Dawson, I understand how the stock market works."

He shook his head. "I mean stock dilution. You can lose control before you know it if you don't keep a tight watch on what you're selling and who's buying it. I looked into what's been going on and luckily the blocks aren't being bought by any one entity, so I don't think it's an issue."

Blinking in confusion, I tried to process what he was talking about. "We haven't sold that much, just enough to keep operations running. And why would anyone sell TSC now? The price has declined, not increased."

He furrowed his brows. "That's the strange part. It's insanity to sell now. Like whoever is doing it needs to get rid of the stock quickly or maybe they are purposefully trying to dilute the stock price to put you in a vulnerable situation."

Aghast, I refused to believe the latter. Who would want to do that? "Maybe they just decided to unload. Take the loss for taxes?" I second-guessed.

His words were quiet. "Yes, I was thinking that as well but why so little and with such a small incremental change in value? It doesn't make smart business sense at all. It seems more personal."

I pushed my worry away. "They could just need the money."

"I suppose." He didn't look convinced.

Concerned, I had to ask. "Are you really that worried?"

He shook his head. "No, but do you want me to look into it further? See who it is?"

"No, I don't think so."

His jaw twitched and I could tell he wanted to. "Okay, but if you change your mind, let me know."

"Yes, I will. What else aren't you telling me? Did my father say something else?"

He drew in a breath. "As a matter fact he did. He heard you're looking for financial backing for a new project. He wanted to know what I thought. Since you hadn't mentioned it, I couldn't really render my opinion. That's what I wanted to talk to you about."

My father had named me CEO of TSC when I was engaged to Dawson. At the time, I thought his faith in me was tremendous, but after my breakup with Dawson, I learned it had more to do with his faith in Dawson and Dawson's ability to guide me toward the right decisions. That conversation was the last one I had with my father.

The traffic was stop and go. Horns were honking and people were every-where. Friday nights were always crazy. I sighed and turned sideways to face Dawson. "The idea is new. I want to move quickly and need to get financial backing just as quickly."

"I get that, but for what?"

I lifted my chin, hoping he could see my confidence. "Nightclubs; exclu-sive-access night clubs."

He rolled his eyes. "Tell me it's not him."

I threw him a look.

"Phoebe, the hotel business is a completely different animal from that entertainment sector."

"Dawson, I know that. It's not the nightclubs that are going to rejuvenate the Saint Hotels; it's their draw that will increase occupancy. Hunter ran the numbers. This can work."

I didn't need Dawson's approval but I wouldn't have minded his reassur-ance. Yet, even without it, I knew this plan would be successful.

It had to be.

He looked doubtful. "You really think these nightclubs will be a draw for more overnight stays?"

I slanted him a look of consternation. "Yes, I do. If marketed right, I do."

He paused a moment. "This doesn't have anything to do with your run-in with Jeremy McQueen last Saturday night?"

I drew in a breath. "He has agreed to consult with me on the project."

Dawson looked upset and took a moment.

"But it was my idea."

He took my hand. "Do you think that's wise? Working with him."

My phone rang. I tugged my hand away but didn't pull my phone from my purse. "Dawson, I can separate business from personal matters. And it's good business to gain the expertise of someone who has been successful in a very similar venture."

"What about you? Are you interested in him on more than a business level?"

I couldn't lie. "I am."

"You know he's seeing Avery Lake?"

Ice formed in my belly. His belief that, *once a cheater, always a cheater* was evident on his face. Dawson knew only what I'd told him and I hadn't told him what I recently learned—that Kat was only Jeremy's friend. There was nothing romantic between them. Still, his words stung and I sat up straighter. "I know he's worked with her."

Dawson didn't look convinced. "Is that what he told you? Because he's with her tonight at the Rockefeller Foundation Benefit."

I gaped at him. "How do you know that?"

Dawson furrowed his brows. "See for yourself. It popped up in the news feed on my ride to your office." He pulled his phone from his pocket and tapped a few buttons. Then he handed it to me.

Right there on Page Six was a picture of Jeremy walking into the event with Avery beside him. Tension filled every muscle in my body as I found myself wondering again if there really wasn't something more to the two of them. Contrary to what Jeremy had said, evidence seemed to prove otherwise. I thought about what he had said for a moment, and realized he hadn't denied they were seeing each other. I might not have had the right to care, but I did. I cared a lot. How dare he ask me to consider starting something with him when he was involved with someone else?

Dawson's eyes met mine. He had to see the sadness that lingered there. But if he did, he ignored it and kept talking. "I looked into what he's been doing. The new money he brings to New York comes from his business. Jet Set is very successful, I agree with you there. But I have to caution you, there's a big difference between what he's done and what you want to do. He purchased successful businesses and left them intact. He manages them from a bird's-eye level."

I gave him a questioning look.

Annoyance plagued him. "Phoebe, he checks on them, but doesn't get involved in the day-to-day operations. What you want to do is build something from the ground up and manage it under the hotel's structure. It's not the same."

My phone rang again and again I ignored it. "I know," I said, feeling exasperated. "That's why it's so very important to find the right people to run the clubs. They have to have experience."

"Have you found them yet?"

"No. Not yet."

Dawson shook his head.

The truth was—I didn't have those contacts. Jeremy did and he hadn't been around this week. I averted his stare and glanced out the window. We were in the Meatpacking District and had just passed the Rose Bar. My mind wandered. I wondered when Jeremy had gotten back. I wondered why he was out with Avery. I wondered about his business. Was Dawson right? Was he successful because he bought successful businesses? What did that mean for TSC?

As we pulled up to Morimoto, my confidence over my decision to move forward with this new venture, not only the one for TSC, but for myself as well, started to wane.

The car door opened and Dawson and I went inside. Once there, neither of us spoke of Jeremy again. I also didn't bring up my thoughts on moving on because I think Dawson saw it in my eyes when he brought up Jeremy's name.

We had a few drinks and ate dinner. Dawson kept the conversation light at first, telling me about his five-year-old niece, Elise, who had arrived in town earlier this week with his sister. He loved her and animatedly told me what they had been doing together. I adored her. Then he told me what brought his niece and sister back to the city. Blaine had always hoped to move back to New York one day but her husband loved living in London. It seemed they had come to a crossroads and were divorcing. I was shocked. We spent the rest of the evening talking about his family.

Before we left, I used the ladies' room and checked my phone. My mother had called and Jeremy had called three times. There was a text message from him as well. He had sent it two hours ago. It read:

Where are you?

I'd call my mother tomorrow. But Jeremy I would call when I got home. Jealousy burned through me. Why was he wondering where I was when he was out with someone else? I had to suppress it. I had to take the best course of action. I had a couple of them in mind. I could call him back and invite him over. I could ignore him. I could send him a link to his photo. In the end I sent him a quick text, deciding I'd call him later.

Me: I'm out for the night

Him: I want to see you.

Me: Two women in one night? I think that's a bit much.

It was snarky. I shouldn't have sent it. I knew I shouldn't have. He could go out with whomever he wanted. I hadn't told him yes. Yet, I felt like something was tugging at my heart at the very thought of him with someone else. As I looked at myself in the mirror, I knew what I was going to say to him. I was going to tell him the truth.

I glanced at my phone. He hadn't responded. There was a chance the truth wouldn't have mattered. My nagging jealousy may have stolen the deal off the table. I shoved my phone into my purse, and then went to tell Dawson I was ready to leave.

It was still early when his car pulled up to my apartment. I turned to say good night to him but he was getting out behind me. He walked me about halfway to the lobby door.

"Phoebe," he said, taking my hand.

I stopped and turned around.

"I'm going to say good night here. But I want you to know I'm always here for you. And I hope you know I'm only trying to help you. I'm worried about you, not just TSC."

I kissed him on the cheek and hugged him. "Thank you for everything."

He held me for a long time before he looked at me and kissed me one last time.

We both knew this was really good-bye.

Then he turned around and started for his car, but he stopped. "Don't forget to send me a proposal. If your plan is as solid as you believe it to be, I'd like a chance to invest."

"I will." I smiled, thankful the friendship we had built over the years might still be in place.

I watched him walk to his car feeling the same as I had a week ago—knowing I made the right choice, but still heartsick over it.

In a daze, I turned back around and walked toward the door. The door opened and when I looked up expecting to see Jack, Harry, or the new door-man, whose name I still didn't know, it was intense blue eyes I was staring into.

It was him.

"Jeremy," I said and my body started to tremble. "What are you doing here?"

He looked as he had the morning I awoke in his loft. Removed. Uncaring. Hard. "I came to explain what you had seen but it looks like I didn't have to."

His tone was harsh.

His stare harsher.

"Jeremy, it's not what you think."

But he wasn't listening. He was walking away.

"Jeremy," I called frantically.

"I'll call you Monday. I found three managers for the clubs," he said over his shoulder.

My heart sank. I wanted to run after him but my legs felt too weak. And then before I knew it, he was in a taxi and gone.

"Oh darling, come with me. I think we need to talk." It was Mrs. Bardot and she was standing just inside the door.

I walked into the lobby and across the marble floor. The air smelled of flowers and I glanced over to see a bouquet of peonies set on the table between the two leather chairs that were placed near the doorman's desk.

Mrs. Bardot picked them up along with a brown-handled grocery bag and handed them to me.

I gave her a questioning look.

"They're for you. From your James Dean."

Tears filled my eyes and my stomach dropped.

"Come along, dear," she said, and pressed the elevator button.

I followed her but an unbearable emptiness had opened up inside me. "I have to go after him," I managed to say.

She stepped into the elevator and held the door. "I think you could use some advice first."

She seemed to know what she was talking about and so I boarded the elevator with her. It was going down. The doors opened seconds later and we were facing the wine cellar. The room was small with chilled wine lockers, a leather sofa, two chairs, and a fireplace, which was surprisingly burning.

She took a set of keys from her purse and opened a locker, pulling out a Chateau Latour 1982. She collected the most sought-after vintages.

I plopped in a chair and watched as she skillfully uncorked the bottle and poured us each a glass.

She offered me one and then she sat in the chair beside me. "Glorious," she mused as she took the first sip.

I took a sip as well. Then I was surprised to enjoy the wave of fruit that hit my senses. I always drank white wine, but the taste was worthy of competing with my very favorites.

"Your James Dean was waiting at your door when I brought him to the lobby for a chat. I have to say, I was surprised that he opened up to me."

I blanched. "He talked to you about me?"

Not that I really minded. It was just so not like him.

She took another sip of her wine. "He did, but then again I do have a way with brooding men."

Even through my heartache, I couldn't help but smile at her.

"But actually, my mention of a part I had in a James Bond movie once helped."

I offered her an even bigger smile.

She grew serious. "I want to caution you about jealousy, Phoebe. It's toxic. It can tear relationships apart. Trust me, I know. In the height of my acting career, I met one of my two great loves. We were inseparable. Then he took a part where he had to film in Paris and I couldn't join him in my beloved city. He was starring opposite a beautiful unknown actress and my insecurities ate at me. Elizabeth Taylor, Sophia Loren, or even your Audrey Hepburn, I wouldn't have worried about them. I knew they weren't women he'd be interested in. But new blood, that was different. I couldn't be there with him so I called nonstop. Asked others on the set if he was spending time with her. Questioned him about her. Made him tell me how he felt after he filmed romantic scenes with her. My jealousy strained our relationship. I started to see things that weren't there. Even after he came back, I accused him of cheating on me with the next woman he starred opposite. Six months later, he broke up with me. He couldn't take it any longer."

I set my glass down and picked up the flowers. "That's not what Jeremy and I are about. It's more complicated than that."

"I'm sure it is. But tonight he told me he was coming here to make sure you understood you were the one in whom he was interested. You must have made him doubt that you believed that. Then he sees you with your ex-fiancé and his own jealousy overtakes him. That's the thing with jealousy—it festers and builds until there is nothing left."

I sighed, and inhaled the scent of the flowers. "What can I do about it? I can't help how I feel."

"My advice to you. Show him he's who you want and do your best to accept what he tells you about these other women in his life."

My head snapped toward her. "He told you about Kat?"

She shrugged. "He actually said very little. I didn't know either girl's name. All he said was that he didn't know how to make you believe him. Look in the bag. He told me he hoped that would do it."

I opened it up. Inside were two DVD sets—the complete library of James Bond and the complete library of Audrey Hepburn. There was also a box of microwave popcorn. I was sure it was his way of wanting to reconnect. It was twenty questions brought face-to-face.

I pulled out the movies.

She took another sip of wine.

"Both of our favorite movies."

She smiled. "Your James Dean has a temper. All men with tempers need a cooling-off period. So here's what you're going to do . . ."

CHAPTER 17

The Start of Something Great

Usually strapless black dresses made me think of prom.

The one I was wearing definitely did not. I looked in the mirror as I zipped it up. The expert draping and structured shape of Mrs. Bardot's vintage Chanel totally elevated the silhouette. The low U-neck added a little sauciness, making the piece both elegant and flirty at the same time. Mrs. Bardot also lent me the most spectacular little black lizard clutch. My own studded Manolo Blahnik ankle-strap heels added some additional edge to the otherwise all-black look.

Mrs. Bardot touched my bare skin with her finger. "You're practically sizzling, my dear."

I had to admit, the plunging strapless confection totally raised the bar on LBDs. "I love this dress." I looked around her closet. "I love all of your dresses."

"Come over to browse anytime. I have something for every occasion. And you keep that one."

I swung my hips and watched the way it swayed with my movement. "I couldn't possibly."

"You can and you will. In fact, I'll send some others over this week. This old body is never getting in some of these again. And you can't turn me down when empty closet space gives me a reason to go shopping."

I gave her a hug. "Thank you."

"Nonsense," she said. "I'm just glad I can share my things with you."

I picked up my leather jacket and bag. "Here goes nothing."

She walked me to the door. "Let's hope, here goes something. Now hurry along, I have my own young man waiting for my attention this evening."

She was one of a kind.

I laughed and pressed the DOWN button.

Logan was waiting for me in his car downstairs. I was nervous and felt more at ease riding with him to Pier 60. He was a huge video gamer in his day and I reached out to him this morning to see if he was attending the launch party. Of course he was. He'd already gone to the West Coast release and had a blast. When I asked him if he could snag me an invite, he insisted I go with him. I didn't argue.

Mrs. Bardot's plan included not only me still going to the launch but also going after what I wanted. "It's the grand gestures that really matter," she insisted.

I didn't know if Jeremy would think my attendance was a grand gesture, but I was willing to try. I had texted him last night that I was sorry and again in the morning but he didn't respond. My hope was that he would still show up.

I had to believe he would.

We arrived to a mass of photographers, press, and guests. Logan hated press as much as I did and we slipped easily in the back door.

The high ceiling and huge windows provided a beautiful view of the Hudson River. Large black partitions formed a maze of corridors in the large space and inside each cubicle were two swivel chairs, a TV, and of course, a console gaming system. Logan ducked in the first unoccupied one he found.

I opted to pass.

I had to find Jeremy.

I walked the perimeter of the room. I was overdressed but I didn't care. I wanted to look my best for Jeremy.

The daylight was slowly easing down over the horizon and dusk was approaching. The colors in the sky were magnificent shades of blues and purples. They caught my attention. The simple beauty of a sunset was something I hadn't admired in so long.

The outer corner of the maze led to a set of doors and I opened them, yearning to see the skyline with its unobstructed view. The terrace was crowded but as soon as I set foot on it, my eyes landed on him.

Him.

My pulse quickened at the sight.

He was standing near the outdoor bar, casually dressed in a pair of distressed jeans that rode low on his hips, a plain blue T-shirt, and a navy baseball hat worn backward. He was wearing sunglasses and he hadn't shaven. There was a glass of liquor in his hand that looked like it hadn't been drunk.

He looked sexy as hell.

I knew the minute he noticed me.

The current that traveled between us was electric.

He took his sunglasses off and his eyes devoured me. They were intense, raw, and oh so blue. He lifted his gaze and our stares collided. Just then, there was nothing between us. No barriers, no issues, nobody else but him and me.

My heart beat wildly and I mouthed, "Hi."

"Hi," he mouthed back and then he smiled a smile that was wide enough to highlight his dimples and told me so much.

I melted.

Mrs. Bardot was right; a cooling-off period was wise.

He was talking to Harvey Majors. An enigmatic man, Harvey was the most socially connected thirty-something in Manhattan. His ties ran from old money to new. He made a job out of networking.

Jeremy was going after the right man to help him grow his business—that was for sure. I wondered if I shouldn't have come. I didn't want to interrupt whatever deal he was working. I realized then Jeremy wasn't attending these functions to socialize—he was networking, growing his business, becoming more successful by the day.

Just looking at him, I could see the power he held. He was building his empire and if things worked out, I'd get to see him do it.

Harvey nodded when Jeremy next spoke, and then Jeremy held his hand out. They exchanged a few more words and he set his glass down. His eyes were hypnotic as he strode my way. The hungry expression on his face grew more ravenous with each step and my pulse raced with excitement.

I couldn't help but watch the way he moved. I loved how he walked. I loved the look on his face. I loved how I felt in his presence.

Whoa.

Except the closer he got, the more nervous I became. What if he didn't want to talk to me? Maybe I was misreading him. What if he was coming over to tell me to leave? I was twisting my butterfly ring by the time his body was in front of mine.

God, he smelled so good.

"I was going to call you later tonight," he said very matter-of-factly.

I couldn't judge what he meant. "I didn't want to wait."

His eyes looked me up and down again in the most blatant way and the heat in his gaze was almost too much to bear. "Let's talk," he said and took my hand.

I nodded. Heat flowed through my veins. I was on fire.

He, on the other hand, seemed cool as a cucumber as he led me to the railing and casually leaned against it, taking in the very last of the sunset.

"Jeremy," I started to say.

He pulled me close and looked right into my eyes. "I'm not sure what last night was about but I'm not seeing Avery."

The last thing I wanted to talk about right now was Avery. Red lips was getting on my nerves.

His fingers dug into my hips. "She arranged for me to meet with her brother before the event but my flight arrived late and I was in a rush to get there. I didn't want to call you when I was in a hurry. Her brother was interested in Jet Set membership for his entire men's club and it was a big deal. I had to go. She met me outside and we went in together. That was it. Then I talked to Theo and I called you as soon as I left."

I stepped into him, closing the distance between us.

We were close.

So close.

"I believe you," I whispered.

His grip at my hips tightened. "Good."

Delighted, I held my grin. "There's nothing going on with Dawson and me either. My father had called him and he wanted to talk to me about what he had to say. That's it."

My hands slid up his chest.

"I believe you." He grinned.

I eyed him carefully. "You do?"

"I do. Now where does that leave us?"

He always made things seem so simple.

He always had.

"Us?"

"Yes, us. You and me."

I loved the sound of that.

"Yes," I blurted out.

His eyes darkened. "Yes what, Phoebe?"

Ripples of desire moved through me. "Yes, I want to see where you and I go."

He pulled my body flush to his and stared into my eyes. A wave of arousal went right to my core when he smiled at me salaciously.

"You look fucking amazing."

His raspy voice carried such a sexual cadence to it that my cheeks started to burn. "I wore this dress for you."

He leaned even closer. "Good, because I want to fuck you in it."

I swallowed at the deliciousness of his naughty words.

Although the place was packed, Jeremy still searched our surroundings. "Right now."

"Here?" A thrill ran through me.

He nodded. "Yes, here."

"Where?"

Challenge danced in his eyes.

We always had a hard time waiting—time hadn't changed that.

I bit down on my bottom lip, unable to argue.

I wanted that too.

"Come with me," he growled.

It had been five long years and I didn't hesitate to obey his command.

He led me through the maze. The deeper we got, the darker it became. Open ropes indicated the cube was unoccupied. We wove our way deeper into the core but they were all taken. We were almost to the middle when two guys exited one of the makeshift gaming rooms.

Jeremy closed the rope and tugged me inside the curtain. The TV glow was our only light. It didn't matter that the room was small. I had burned for this man for so long, I didn't care about anything but him and me.

"I need you right now," he said in a husky voice.

"I need you too." My voice was weak, raspy, and full of desire.

He looked down at me with smoldering eyes, and then his lips were on mine. *Finally.*

As soon as our mouths came together, something unleashed and his calm exterior was gone. His hands were on me—everywhere. "Do you know how long I've wanted to feel you again?"

I knew. Oh, how I knew.

My lips parted as soon as I felt the brushes of his velvety smooth tongue against them. I too had waited for this moment for so long. "Jeremy," I breathed, unable to say anything else.

His mouth.

It was finally on mine and it felt so good. His lips were soft. And the passion that had been building between us exploded as we finally connected in the most carnal way.

With whispered breaths he groaned, "I want to feel every single inch of you."

"I'm yours," I moaned.

His hands were clasping my face. Mine were around his neck. We were kissing frantically. Our tongues clashed, our lips moved in sync, and our breathing was labored.

God, he tasted so good.

In an instant, he tugged my dress down with one pull and exposed my nipples. Another piece of Mrs. Bardot's advice had been stockings, no further undergarments. I didn't have the whole garter belt and thigh highs so I went for hose. Still, at that moment, I was glad for the advice.

"Fuck," he groaned as he connected with my bare skin, and then his soft mouth closed around my nipple. I was frozen to the spot as electricity shot through my body. My eyes closed and my head tipped back in dizzying arousal. As he sucked at me harder and harder, I could feel myself growing wetter and wetter.

He felt like I remembered, but even better.

The real thing was so much more than I had ever dared to recall.

I wanted to run my fingers through his hair but his hat was still on, so I took it off and fingered his soft silky locks.

When he moved to my other nipple, I wanted to do more. I wanted, no needed, to feel his cock in my hands.

My fingers skimmed down his firm chest and over his taut abs and then I pressed my palms against his denim-clad cock. He was hard and he groaned so loudly when I touched him, I was certain the cubicles on either side of us could hear.

It surprised me that I didn't care, but I was too lost in him.

My touch seemed to unleash the beast in him. His hands darted under my dress and frantically roamed for access to my core. The feel of his touch caused my heart to beat so wildly in my chest, I felt it skip a beat or two. He hissed as soon as his fingers grazed my core and the sound was music to my ears.

Then his lips were back on mine and as he pressed his fingers to me, he shuddered. I did too. He tried to push his hands under the elastic band of my hose, but when it seemed to be too much of a burden, he simply tore a giant hole. Without falter, his fingers sought out the treasure he had been searching for and he groaned loudly as soon as he discovered I was bare there as well.

We were frantic for each other—time hadn't done anything to quash what we felt physically for each other. In fact, it had only fanned the flames and the fire was bigger than ever.

With burning need, I unzipped his jeans and his beautiful cock sprang free. My fingers were trembling as I tentatively touched his tip and my pulse practically exploded.

But then two things happened that made me pause.

First, I was momentarily overtaken by the sudden awareness of how wet I was. Wetter than I'd ever been.

Second, small fissures of desire seemed to radiate from my core and made me gasp in pleasure.

Before I could regain any small semblance of composure, Jeremy dropped to his knees and started trailing openmouthed wet kisses down my bare stomach. My heart zipped around my rib cage and I inhaled sharply as soft, velvety smooth strokes lapped around my clit and an even more intense tingling radiated from my core.

Oh God, that mouth.

That tongue.

The feeling was so intense, my fists clenched and I moaned from the sheer pleasure that was exploding through every nerve in my body.

Jeremy's mouth was like magic. He licked, sucked, and lapped my pussy as he kept me on the edge.

I wanted to fall off it and stay there forever at the same time. The feeling was just that good.

But then he inserted a finger inside me and stroked it up in such a way that I could feel every inch of him inside me. Up and down he moved it. Again keeping me just on the cusp.

"Jeremy," I gasped. "Please."

At my words, he inserted another finger and in harmony his mouth and hand moved together. The first wave of an orgasm started to flood me at that very moment and it was so strong, I had to grip his shoulders for support. The feeling was so intense that everything around me went blank. All I saw was light shining everywhere. I bit my lip to contain my moans as my body clenched in pure pleasure.

Before I floated back down to earth, Jeremy stood. "Wrap your arms and legs around me," he panted into my ear.

As I shifted position, he braced a hand on the partition behind me and then he was inside of me, moving with such primal need I wanted to scream out.

I think I started to yell.

He stopped me with his mouth.

That mouth.

His cock was thrusting inside me.

And I was feeling something I hadn't felt in so long—utter bliss.

As the rapture started to take root, I felt lost to him. No, maybe not lost, maybe I was finding myself in him.

I didn't know.

I didn't care.

Because at that moment, we were both taking in the complete pleasure we were creating as one unit.

"Fuck, you feel so good," he growled over and over.

My body tingled and another orgasm hit me harder than before. He swallowed up my cries of pleasure but soon his own pleasure echoed in the space.

"Phoebe, oh fuck, Phoebe," he groaned as his cock pulsed inside me and he found his release.

My hold around him tightened as the world stopped for the both of us. He buried his face in my neck and I allowed myself to be absorbed by him. It felt so good. I was soaring. I was flying. I was free.

Sex was sex.

Sex was good.

But sex with someone you have an explosive reaction with takes you to a whole new level of good. My body was shaking, I was breathless, and I was really happy. But at the same time, the warmth that filled me made me apprehensive.

A few moments later Jeremy pulled back. "How is it that when I'm with you, you're all I see?"

I couldn't answer him, but I knew exactly what he meant. I felt the same.

"Whatever this is between us, I want to take it as far as we can. I want to take it all the way."

I ran one hand down his chest. "I want that too."

Wherever that meant.

My body cartwheeled with a surge of emotion that I knew better than to acknowledge this early into our reunion.

"Promise me, no matter what, you won't give up. You'll see us through."

Was he sensing my apprehension?

I bit my lip. "I promise."

His mouth captured mine in a frantic kiss, one that felt like he longed to seal the deal.

Breathless, I leaned back. "Is everything okay?"

He set me down. "It is now."

I looked at him with concern. "What is it?"

Jeremy shook his head. "Nothing."

It didn't seem like nothing.

He kissed my concern away. "Come on, let's get dressed before someone walks in."

I tugged my dress back up and fixed myself as best as I could. The hole in my hose was irreparable but it was dark and hopefully no one would notice.

Jeremy zipped up his pants. "Spend the night with me," he said.

Old memories surfaced. How I felt after he'd disappeared. And I hesitated for a moment, wondering if I should say no, or if we should go to my apartment instead. After all, five years ago he said the exact same thing to me and once I got to his apartment, I never left.

I couldn't let that happen. My life was different now. I had responsibilities.

He squeezed my waist. "What is it?"

That unwelcome warmth flooded my chest and I had to push the words out. "I can't get lost in you again."

He yanked me to him. "What if I want you to?" he growled.

I knew then—I already was.

CHAPTER 18

Every. Single. Morning.

Soft, luscious lips were licking at me. And I had a sudden awareness that I was wet.

Really wet.

I thrust my hips up and moaned in pleasure.

It felt so good.

The dark fringe of his lashes brushed against my skin just before his eyes lifted to mine as Jeremy rose from beneath the covers. They were bluer than blue. With a wicked grin he said, "Morning."

"Good morning." A smile slowly spread across my face as I took him in. I couldn't help licking my lips at the delicious sight of him. My fingers were itching to touch him and I ran them over his chest and down his flat stomach, both of which were soft and smooth but ripped with strength. His thigh muscles bunched as he knelt above me. He was beautifully erect. Ready for me. And I was more than ready for him. I couldn't get enough. I felt like I was never going to get enough.

"What do you want to do today," he said with a smug grin.

I slid my hands around to his ass and purred, "Everything. Nothing. I don't know." I was still in a lustful haze.

Last night we'd left the video launch immediately after our tryst in the gaming cubicle. I'd lost Logan long before and texted him in the car that I was leaving. Jeremy had driven there himself and once I conceded to go back to his place, he drove here as fast as he could. I didn't want to wait to have him again. To taste him. I couldn't. I was hungry for him. So hungry that I unzipped his jeans and sucked him until the screams of my name echoed in the small interior of the Porsche. I had never felt so powerful as I did then. I'd watched him stiffen under my touch, heard the increased sound of his breathing, and brought him to orgasm at my own speed.

So powerful.

When we arrived at his loft, he'd hoisted me over his shoulder and took me right up to his room. The rest of the night was filled with frenzied fucking. At around midnight we had ordered pizza and ate in his bed.

I'd loved the feeling of being with him, boneless and sated.

It was early now. I could tell because the sun was just rising. He leaned down and kissed me tenderly. His lips felt good against my swollen ones. It wasn't long though before he gently parted my lips with his tongue and met mine in a deep kiss. "That isn't very decisive," he said.

Desire coursed through me.

"Do you taste how sweet you are?" he breathed into my mouth.

I couldn't answer. I couldn't speak. I was caught in his web of seduction.

"Do you?" he asked again.

I nodded as his warm breath tantalized my neck and his lips glided down it.

"I didn't hear you," he said as he closed his mouth around my nipple.

"Yes," I called out both answering his question and succumbing to the moment.

He bit down on my breast and the slight pain brought a jolt of desire so deep, so wanton, all I could do was moan in ecstasy. "Do you like it when you taste yourself on me?"

I nodded.

"That's not an answer," he taunted. "Tell me you want me to do that again?"

"I do," I moaned.

"You do, what?"

I looked at him breathlessly.

"Tell me," he demanded.

Years ago, Jeremy had liked to talk dirty during sex and he really liked it when he got me to do the same. That was one thing that hadn't changed. In fact, everything felt the same between us, just deeper, stronger, and more intense. The twenty-one-year-olds had aged. For him, that meant an even greater confidence. He always knew what he was doing—now he was even more skilled. But for me, the change was greater. Time had made me aware of what I wanted and I wasn't shy about asking him for it.

"I want your face between my legs and your tongue on my clit and in my pussy."

I knew my words excited him when I felt his smile as his tongue dipped into my navel. "Good, because that's what you're going to get."

A thrill ran through me. I couldn't think of anything I wanted more, other than having him inside me.

But then he moved back up my body and collapsed beside me where he proceeded to draw me to his chest. He drew hearts on my back with his fingertips. "As soon as we make a plan for the day that is."

"You're evil, pure evil."

His grin told me he knew he was.

"So what do you want to do? Where should we go?"

For some reason the thought of doing something as normal as planning a fun day out terrified me. I was suddenly feeling more frightened than thrilled. This was real. This was his way of trying to make us about more than just sex. I pushed myself up to look at him. "I'm scared," I finally admitted.

He raised a brow. "Scared to make plans for the day?"

I shook my head no.

His arms drew me in closer. "Then what?"

I kissed him softly so as to lessen the blow. Then I motioned between us. "This is too much, too fast. We have to slow it down."

He propped his head on an elbow and stared at me. "Phoebe, talk to me. What's going on in that head of yours?"

There was so much—the fact that he knew me so well. That he spoke to me like he always had. It scared me even more. I sucked in a breath. "It's just—" I stopped, unable to say what I wanted to say,

Somehow he picked up on my feelings and sat up, taking me with him. Both on our knees, he took my face in his hands. "I know exactly what you're thinking and I want you to put it out of your head."

I stared at him.

He stared back and his eyes glittered with honesty as he said, "This time I won't leave."

Unable to bear his reaction to what I was about to say, I looked down. "But you did once."

He lifted my chin. "Never again."

My body started to tremble. How was it he knew exactly what scared me the most—that he would just up and leave me again.

"I promise. I'm not going anywhere. With you is the only place I want to be," he reassured me.

I rested my forehead against his and closed my eyes. "What if something happens that you don't like?"

He pulled back. "I'm not the same guy I was then. I was young and immature and didn't understand the world. I'm different now."

And he was. I could see it. But for some reason that wasn't entirely reassuring. I had an uneasiness in me I couldn't calm. I didn't know why or what it was. It was just there.

The ringing of my phone jolted my thoughts. "Oh no, Jamie," I remembered. "What time is it?"

Jeremy reached over to his nightstand. He looked at my screen. "It's eight fifteen and it's Jamie," he said, handing it to me.

"Hello," I answered.

"Don't kill me but I have to cancel." Jamie's voice was scratchy, uneven.

Jeremy pulled me down to the bed and I rested on his chest. "It's fine, but is everything okay? You don't sound well."

"Let's just say I did something completely unlike me and I'm trying to figure out what to do about it."

I circled the dark skin of Jeremy's nipple as I talked. "Okay, you have my mind working overtime. Care to elaborate?"

He drew in a sharp breath and it sounded like he was inhaling.

"Are you smoking?" I asked incredulously.

"Just a joint or two. I needed to take the edge off."

I bolted upright. "Okay Jamie, you're scaring me. What's going on?"

Jeremy sat up too.

I covered the phone. "Jamie's in some kind of trouble."

Jamie had been clean for five years. There was a time when he lived off blow and a long string of women. But then he almost overdosed that summer we all rented a house together and it was his wake-up call. He still drank, but he hadn't done drugs, of any kind, since.

I heard a door closing. "Phoebs, I don't want a lecture."

"I'm not going to give you one. I'm just worried about you."

Finally Jamie spoke. "It's just a joint."

"Tell me what's going on," I insisted.

He heaved a heavy sigh. "Friday night after the benefit, Avery and Theo were going to Provocateur, so I went along with them. Oh, by the way, she wants to get back together with that man of yours in the worst way."

Back together?

I narrowed my eyes at Jeremy but swallowed back my ire and focused on Jamie. "Go on."

"Yeah, so I met this Victoria's Secret model there, and you know how I have a thing for models."

"Yes, I'm aware," I said in a clipped tone.

"Well, sometime that night we all got on a chartered flight to Vegas and when I came back last night, I was married to Lindsay, the model."

"Married!" I almost screamed it. "Are you out of your mind?"

"Not so loud," he whimpered into the phone.

"You have to go back and get it annulled," I demanded.

"I know that, Phoebs. The problem is Lindsay doesn't want to."

"Is she insane? You just met."

"She wants to give it a try." I could hear the smile in his tone and it irked me.

"Did you tell her no? Go find her and tell her no. Do you know where she is?"

Silence.

"Jamie?" I drew out his name.

"Yeah, I know where she is. She's in my bed right now."

"Then go wake her up and get yourselves back to Vegas."

"That's the thing. I'm not sure I want to either. I'm getting sick of all the parties. All the women. Maybe settling down isn't a bad thing."

"Jamie, settling down is great. But with someone you love. Not someone you just met." I tried to sound logical.

"Have dinner with us this week. Meet her and you'll see. She's perfect for me."

I flopped myself on the bed and noticed Jeremy was intently watching me.

"Sure, I'll have dinner with you both. But you really need to think this through."

"Yeah, well, my mother rescheduled the family picture for today. Guess she'll be surprised at the new addition to the family."

I gasped. "Your mother is going to blow her lid, Jamie. You can't do that to her. You have to warn her."

"Nah, I can't deal with her right now and we have to be there at noon. Speaking of, I really need to get some sleep. I'll call you tomorrow. Love you, Phoebs," he said.

"Love you too," I said back and hung up.

Jeremy was sitting on the side of the bed. "What was that about?" he asked, sounding slightly agitated.

I reiterated the entire conversation except for the Avery part.

When I finished he said, "So why are you trying to talk him out of staying married?"

"Because he just met her."

He shrugged. "Sometimes you just know."

His back was still to me. Something had created distance between us. He must have sensed my animosity toward him but I wasn't sure he knew why. I couldn't hold my jealousy back any longer. "Did you and Avery sleep together?"

Jeremy turned to look at me. His eyes were no longer bright blue. They were dark and cold.

I pulled the sheet up farther as I shivered.

His answer was clipped. "Once."

I gaped at him as fury blasted through my entire body. "And you didn't think to tell me that any of the times her name came up?"

He narrowed his eyes at me. "Why would I tell you that?"

"Because you still see her. Because she still wants you and she's not shy about telling anyone either."

He shrugged. "She knew what it was. I made it clear I wasn't interested in anything further."

I didn't know what to say. He sounded so cold. "And it doesn't bother you that she still has hope for the two of you?"

"No. There was never anything between us."

"Well, you slept with her."

"Once," he reiterated. "Look, she just wants someone on her arm to be photographed with for Page Six. Our relationship started as a business one and as far as I'm concerned that's the way it will remain. She knows that. She's not under any illusions. Trust me."

I stood up, dragging the sheet with me as I picked up my clothes that were strewn across the floor.

He pulled on his boxers. "It isn't any different than you still seeing Dawson. And I didn't ask you if you fucked him."

"I was engaged to him! Of course we slept together."

He grabbed his jeans and headed toward his bedroom door. "Yeah, I'm well aware."

"Jeremy, let's talk about this."

He put a hand up. "Not right now. I'm still trying to get over you telling some other guy you love him while I'm in the fucking room."

He didn't give me a chance to explain. He walked out the door and slammed it behind him.

I couldn't help but stare at the closed door. Jealousy was going to tear us apart. I knew it in that moment. I just didn't know how either of us could stop feeling the way we did long enough to keep it from happening.

His T-shirt was at my feet and I picked it up and pulled it over my head. It smelled like him. My gut twisted. I wanted this to work.

I stood there trying to figure how it ever could when the door opened.

His long strides had him standing before me so quickly that I could barely blink. "Look, I don't want to argue with you. I didn't tell you about Avery and me because I knew once I did, you'd think there was something between us. Even before last Saturday night, she and I were nothing more than business associates. What happened between us took place during one of her and her brother's excursions. There were at least a dozen of us squeezed into one limo from here to the Hamptons and things got a little wild."

This time I put a hand up. I didn't want to hear the details. The thought of Jeremy with anyone else, doing the things he did to me last night was hard enough to bear. But the thought of him with her sickened me.

Avery Lake was one of those women you knew better than to ever trust. Years ago she went after Jamie with a vengeance. He wasn't interested in her though. She was also Dawson's girlfriend before I was and when Dawson and

I started dating, she didn't take it very well. She continued to have lunch with his mother, show up at his apartment whenever she wanted, and just as she was doing with Jeremy now, trying to be photographed with him at whatever event we were attending—stirring up rumors of a breakup.

I didn't want to go through that again.

Jeremy took my hands and laced his fingers with mine.

I looked up at him. The tenderness was back in his features.

He took a step closer and brought my hips to his. "The bottom line is she has connections that I have benefited from immensely. The only cost to me was that I had to show up at a few events and spend some time with her. I didn't care then. But now it's different. I'm with you. And I can see where what Avery wants from me might blur the lines of business so I'll make sure in the future that doesn't happen."

I lifted on my toes and gave him a light kiss. "I'm with you too, and I have to trust you just like you have to trust me. Jamie is my best friend. There's never been more than friendship between us."

He leaned down and kissed me. "I know that. It was a knee-jerk reaction. I shouldn't have said anything. And besides, we have a more pressing matter."

I smiled at him. "What might that be?"

He walked us toward the bed. "We need to get some breakfast and you have no clothes."

I looked down at myself. "Yes, that's a problem."

He picked me up and tossed me on the bed. "I guess that just means we know what we're doing today."

I raised a questioning brow.

"Staying in," he replied with a wicked grin.

I giggled. "Do you have any leftover pizza?"

He crawled up the mattress and stopped when he was hovering above me. "I might and I think I have eggs too."

"Mmmm . . ." I moaned. "Sounds delicious."

His tongue circled my ear. "Then the breakfast dilemma is solved."

"I still need to go home at some point."

He licked down my neck. "I'll take you there later to get some stuff."

Reluctantly, I lifted his chin so I could gaze at him. He looked magnificent above me and I wished I could have captured the fire in his eyes. They were burning. And so was I, but I knew my next words very well might douse the flame. "I can't stay here."

Jeremy pushed my hands over my head and held them there as he gazed down at me. "Sure you can," he said as he trailed featherlike kisses down my neck.

"I can't. I have to work," I managed to say.

His free hand lifted the hem of my T-shirt and his fingers trailed up my bare thigh. "You can go to work from here. I'll drive you. In fact, I'll split my time."

Perplexed, I asked, "What do you mean, split your time?"

His mouth and teeth were working right at the base of my throat. "I'll spend the mornings at TSC and the afternoons here working on Jet Set contracts, then I'll return to get you."

I remained silent as I thought about his offer. I had a funny thought about having my wicked way with my driver but honestly everything about what he was doing to me right now had me slipping into a lust-induced coma.

"Phoebe." He tugged a little on my wrists as if he sensed he was losing me. The stretch followed by a tinge of pain felt good.

I arched my body, giving in to the sensations and purred, "You have it all worked out."

Jeremy's gaze roamed my face. "It wasn't that difficult. And we do have a lot to iron out in a short period of time."

"A lot of what?" I moaned.

His trail of kisses led to my chest. "Work for Sinners."

Gooseflesh covered my skin as I considered my options and what they meant.

"Of course, I'll be there either way," he assured me.

A pleasurable pain rushed through my body as he sucked deeply on my nipple. "I can't think like this," I said and bolted upright.

Jeremy McQueen's grin was devilishly wicked.

I pushed the hair from my eyes and took a few calming breaths before I dared look back toward him. When I did, I pointed my finger at him. "From now on, we keep business separate from pleasure."

That devilish grin turned downright evil and then a roar of laughter filled the room.

I joined in. There I was, sitting up, naked, still lolling in my post-bliss state trying to sound authoritative.

Quite abruptly I found myself on my back again. "I promise, from now on, I will try my hardest to separate the two."

As my arousal became more than evident in the new position we were in, I arched my back and gave in to him. "Okay then."

The mattress seemed to melt beneath me when Jeremy rested his fingers on my clit. "Is that a yes?"

My breathing became labored as I stared up at him. His eyes were low-lidded with his own longing. His hair was a mussed mess that I found to be such a turn-on. Everything about him thrilled me. And not just his looks. The way he held me. The heat and hardness of his body so close to mine. The way he was looking at me. The way I was anticipating his touch. The way he wanted to help me save TSC, and I answered with the only word that made sense, "Yes."

His fingers started moving and I writhed beneath his touch. "Good. And you don't have to set an alarm. I'll wake you up."

"You will? How do you plan to do that?" I teased.

His grin was wicked. "My tongue in your pussy should do the job just fine."

"Every morning?"

He inserted a finger inside me and said, "Every. Single. Morning."

Oh. My. God.

CHAPTER 19

Bedroom to Boardroom

I was in serious trouble.

Jeremy was everywhere—even when he wasn't around.

All I had to do was close my eyes, and I could feel the way his touch made my skin tingle, I could imagine his body as he crushed his to mine, I could hear the sounds he made when he came.

It had been only a week but he was already living in my head.

I was lost in him.

I shook off the thought.

It scared me.

Yet, in his presence, I was anything but afraid. Enamored, awed, consumed, ravenous, passionate, the list could go on for miles because those were just a few of the emotions I felt when he was near me.

And near me he was. Each morning I awoke in the most delicious way and then after we showered and got ready, he drove both of us to my office. Jeremy stayed at TSC to work on the Sinners project plan with the team we had assembled. The cross-functional project team consisted of a TSC staff accountant, a regional sales manager from a liquor distribution company, an interior designer, a Jet Set club manager, Hunter, Jeremy, and myself.

And as cliché as it sounded, Jeremy and I were equally as compatible in the boardroom as we were in the bedroom. We worked well together. Working side by side with Jeremy made it easy to see how he'd been able to make Jet Set as successful as he had. He was not only brilliant but he worked day and night. It felt like we were a real team and, to my chagrin, we had remained completely professional whenever anyone was around. Behind closed doors, not always so much.

Smoldering attraction aside, we made real progress during the week. Jeremy's contacts were innumerable and preliminary designs had already been drawn up, estimates received, and a high-level implementation plan completed. In a record five days we'd put together what I needed to move to the next phase of the Sinners project, which was securing funding.

The days started dreadfully early: We'd arrived at the office by seven every day this week. Sometime in the late afternoon, Jeremy would leave TSC to tend to Jet Set matters. He had mentioned that Theo Lake was a huge lead, as was Harvey Majors. Jeremy said he signed over five thousand members this week alone with their connections.

Huge.

And even still, he returned each night to pick me up without complaint. Sometimes he drove, sometimes he used the Rose Bar's car service. It depended where we were headed after dinner. Jeremy made it a habit to pop in the Jet Set locations to check on business nightly. Tuesday night he wanted to go to Finale. We ended up staying and having a few drinks. He said he didn't dance, but I was still smiling to myself at the way I got him to. Dark, crowded places lent themselves to wandering hands very nicely.

I'd been in such a lustful haze since Jeremy reentered my life. I'd tried to shake off the endless desire that's flowing through my veins and focus on work when I was in the office but sometimes I just had to force myself. And it was one of those times. I looked down at the first task for the next phase—the request for investment packets that had been expertly bound. There were five of them, but I would be submitting only four.

Since TSC's line of credit was already at its limit, I had to seek funding from potential investors in the private sector and Dawson was one of those potential investors. Jeremy vehemently disagreed with soliciting aid from him. I concurred with him, but for entirely different reasons. I knew Dawson would say yes regardless of what he thought of the project and I didn't want to put him in that situation. Jeremy, on the other hand, didn't want me working closely with him. He said he didn't trust him. I'd decided to bite my tongue and let the whole alpha male, macho man thing roll off my back.

Anyway, the packets were going to be hand delivered tonight. Included with the portfolio analysis and projections were 3D models. Looking at the packets gave me a jolt of hope. Hunter and I had decided on the personal touch—no e-mailed attachments. The packages were complete with a vision-ary letter I'd written myself. The proposal was thorough, analytical, and de-tailed. I just hoped it was enough to get the investors to buy into the resurrection of the Saint Hotels.

Biting my nails, I started to worry about what would happen if I didn't get the funding. It would mean the end of TSC. Even if I did get the funding, if Sinners wasn't successful, it would also mean the end of TSC. With cash flow in the red, we were dangerously close to having too much stock on the open market. If I lost control of TSC, the decisions for its future would no longer be mine. It was clear at this point, any sane business person would see the com-pany was hanging on by a thread and selling it off in pieces would be the most profitable decision. I, however, refused to do that. This was my family legacy and I was going to fight for it with all I had.

My cell rang and I welcomed the distraction from my dire thoughts when I saw who it was.

"Lily, I miss you," I answered.

"I don't see how you've had time. Page Six has you involved in the biggest love triangle since Jennifer, Brad, and Angelina," she scoffed.

I rolled my eyes. "If you would call me back, you wouldn't have to read Page Six to find out what's going on in my life."

"Yeah." She dragged the word out. "Things have been a little crazy around here but I'm calling you back now. Poppy must be a wreck with all the nega-tive attention you're getting."

I tried not to be offended by her word choice. "Honestly, when I talked to her this week, she didn't even mention it, so neither did I."

Lily snorted. "Really?"

I slid my hand over the shiny clear cover of one of the packets. "Really."

I was just as perplexed as she was. I was almost certain the wrath of my mother would cause chaos this week when I really needed to focus but to my surprise she remained utterly silent about the situation.

"So . . . spill all the gory details," she demanded.

I gave a little huff. "Wait . . . you know it's not true. Don't you?"

Whereas I refused to peruse the gossip, entertainment, and pop culture source, Lily and Poppy were religious about reading the NYPost.com, specifi-cally Page Six.

"Sure, of course I do. But they're doing a good job of making the story believable. Jeremy's been photographed with Avery quite a bit, you know."

Lily didn't sound convinced that I wasn't involved in a love triangle. Was there something I was missing? *No, of course not.* He'd been with me every night.

Still, I sighed awkwardly. "I told you he was out with her for work."

Silence.

"Lily," I prompted.

She blew out a breath. "Okay, okay. It's just Brad denied it for a long time too."

An uncomfortable silence swelled between us and I frowned. The thought that Jeremy could be seeing Avery behind my back sickened me.

"Phoebe, look, I'm just being honest with you—the photos look like more than just work. But you're there and I'm here. So what do I know? I'm sure Jeremy is telling you the truth and besides, it's not like there's anything overtly sexual about their touches or the way he—"

Touches?

I blocked her out and abandoned my caressing of the packets to click my mouse. As the computer came to life, I knew I shouldn't be doing this. I didn't need to see those pictures. Jeremy and I had both agreed it was best to ignore the media storm in order to avoid our own shit storm. Hmmm . . . which of us had actually said that?

My fingers trembled as they hovered over the keyboard and I contemplated typing Jeremy's name in the search bar. But as my index finger tapped the J, I couldn't do it. Memories of the intimacies we'd shared assaulted me and eclipsed all my doubts. So as Page Six filled my screen, I immediately closed the window. Nope. Not going there. I directed my attention back to Lily, who was still talking, and cut her off. "Well, I'm not worried about Avery. She and Jeremy had a short-lived thing. It's over," I reassured my friend and to be honest, I was reassuring myself as well.

"Right, right. I got your texts. They slept together once and that was it."

"You still don't sound convinced."

"Nonsense. I'm happy for you. I still can't believe you're living with him though," Lily said.

I chewed on my bottom lip. "I am not living with him. I told him I'd stay the week."

"Yes, so you said. And if things continue like they did in the past, you'll be there next week and the week after, and the week after that. So you might as well just move in now."

I hesitated. "No, that's not going to happen."

"Oh, come on, who wouldn't want to wake up like that every morning."

"Yes, a girl could get used to that," I said dreamily.

"So tell me some more. How's the sex? Has he tied you up yet?"

"Lily! You know I'm not into that kinky stuff."

"Well, give me something. Tell me it's better than that summer you spent with him at least? Something in his eyes tells me he only gets better with time."

"Lily! He's not a wine. What's going on with you? Isn't your own wild sex life enough?"

Her sigh was filled with exasperation. "If you must know, Preston and I have decided to hold off on having sex this time around."

"What? Why?" I asked, flabbergasted.

"We need to work on our relationship and Preston says sex dulls the real issues."

"Preston says that, does he? I thought you wore the pants in the relationship."

"I always did before. But he's been insistent."

"So no sex? For how long?" I couldn't believe it.

She took a deep breath. "I'm not sure but it's killing me."

I twirled in my chair to look at the park. "Well, are your problems getting better at least?"

"No. That's just it. Nothing has changed. We will always be on competing sides in the fashion industry."

"You can work through it though, Lily. I know you can."

"I'm not so sure that's even the problem anymore. We've been fighting so much this time. We're coming back to the city next Friday and if we don't feel things have improved between us, we're going to spend some more time apart."

I turned back around. "Do you want to talk about it?"

"Nope. But I do want to talk about Jamie. I can't believe he got married. Page Six is declaring one of the city's most eligible bachelors has been taken off the market. What do you think? Is he serious about . . . What's her name?"

I laughed. "Her name is Lindsay."

"Right, the Victoria's Secret model with the red hair that was on the Christmas cover last year."

"That's the one."

"So what do you think?"

I opened each of the packets and slid the personal note in. All that was left for me to do was sign each of them before putting them in the courier envelopes. "I'm meeting her tonight, so I'll let you know."

There was a knock on the door. It opened and I glanced up to see the courier was standing there. I held up a finger. "Lily, I'm sorry to cut you short but I have to go."

"So soon?"

"Yes, someone is waiting for me. But I'm so excited you'll be home soon."

"I'm excited too. And when I get there, I want dirt, St. Claire."

"See you," I said with a lilting tone in my voice and hung up.

I looked up. "Just one minute please."

Taking a deep breath, I signed the first one. Then I let the breath out and signed the remaining three. Once I stuffed them in the envelopes, I picked them up. "Here you go." I smiled.

"Have a good evening, ma'am," the courier said as he took the lifeline to my business in his hand and closed the door behind him. The deadline for responses was next Friday.

It was going to be a long week.

I stared at the one remaining envelope for a few moments and then shoved it into my top drawer. When I did, I saw the apartment keys Hunter had given me. I needed to get over to the Times Square penthouse this weekend. I knew I should probably just leave it alone, but I had a curiosity that needed to be settled. I shoved the smaller envelope in the little black lizard clutch Mrs. Bardot had given me last week and then glanced at the time. Almost six. Jeremy should have arrived by now.

Just as I started to pack up, my office phone rang. We had dinner plans with Jamie and his new wife, at six thirty. Jeremy thought it would be more intimate for all of us to eat at his place rather than go out, since the point of the meal was for me to get to know Jamie's wife—*wife*, the word sounded foreign on my tongue.

Jeremy had arranged for the chef at one of the restaurants he was considering adding to the Jet Set portfolio to come and cook for us.

"Phoebe St. Claire," I answered.

His gruff voice breathed into the phone. "Hey, I wanted to see if you received the design schematics yet?"

My eyes darted to the blueprints on my desk. "I did."

"And," he drawled out.

I turned in my chair to look out the window. "And, I think Sinners will be the hottest club in town before we even open."

"Hey, not that I mind a little competition, but let's take it one step at a time."

Way to spoil the fun.

My sigh was soft. "I know. I know. I shouldn't get my hopes up but I'm just so excited."

"Good."

"Where are you?" I asked.

His voice dipped to a low rumble. "Outside your door."

I laughed. "Do I want to know why you're calling me from outside my door?"

"I think you might." There was hint of naughtiness in his tone.

I found it hard to find my voice with all the noise the butterflies were making in my belly with their fluttering. "I'm listening."

"I didn't want to mix business with pleasure."

My heart started to pound. "Pleasure?"

"Yes, Phoebe, pleasure."

I looked around my office like someone might be listening before speaking. "I think you need to explain."

"Oh, no explanation will be needed."

My voice grew breathy. "I'm intrigued."

"Do you have anything else to discuss about Sinners?"

Estimates, contracts, and vendor agreements were piled on my desk but everything was labeled and straightforward. "No. You've made it all so easy to navigate."

"Good"—that delicious-sounding word again—"because I'm in trouble and I need your help."

I knew he wasn't in any real distress. I could tell by his tone. "Well, tell me what it is and maybe I can help," I purred.

The line went dead and I heard the door open. I grinned like the Cheshire cat as I slowly twisted in my chair and saw his eyes blazing bluer than blue. "I need you wet for me," he said as his tongue slipped out of his mouth to lick his lips.

A shiver ran down my spine but I kept my cool. "You do, do you? May I ask why?"

The door locked. "I think you know the answer to that."

I couldn't help myself. "No, I don't. I might need a little explanation," I teased.

Jeremy gave me a dubious look and I raised a more than curious brow. With a smoldering grin, he leaned back against the door and crossed his arms. "If you must know, I made the mistake of thinking about how sweet you tasted this morning on my way over here and now I'm hard."

Oh my.

His voice had dipped lower still, making it gravelly and irresistible. The sound liquefied my insides and watching him as his entirely too hot, too sexy body prowled my way, made me melt all over again. My pulse zinged as the rakish specimen of man began striding toward me and I could practically feel the air sizzle with each step he took.

Still, I kept up the illusion of being calm, cool, and collected, and laced my fingers together on my desk. I sat up straight to try to lessen the effect of butterflies fluttering in my belly and calmly said, "That's sufficient. I understand your predicament. But you want me wet in my office why?"

His lids lowered as the lustful haze that had only seconds ago overtaken his features began to shroud with a slight glimpse of annoyance. "I think you know," he repeated in a stern tone.

I fought to keep my control. "I have a vague idea, but I'm not completely certain. I'd like you to spell it out for me." My breathy tone was more of a whisper. I so wished I had a pair of reading glasses I could have pushed up my nose for effect.

He placed his palms on the desk and leaned forward. "Because I'm going to fuck you. Hard and fast."

If I wasn't already wet, I would have been then, and any semblance of calm and cool I had been putting forward quickly diminished. My lips parted, my breathing hitched, and my nipples peaked. I was, without a doubt, one hundred percent turned on.

"Now stand up and take off your hose and then your panties."

His demand completely obliterated the character I had created and all that remained was me, and I was wary. "Jeremy, I can't do that here."

His gaze roamed my body. "Yes, you can," he growled.

"Jeremy." My protest came out weaker than I would have liked.

"Phoebe, I need to be inside you and I can't wait until later." His voice was no longer gruff, but instead it was smooth like honey. Gone was the rough tone that proclaimed want and what had replaced it was so much worse. It was his seductive side. The one that not only melted me but also put me back together and made me melt all over again. I couldn't help but want him even if I tried to resist. Goose bumps arose on my flesh and I knew it was hopeless to even pretend I wasn't going to do what he asked. Because God help me, I was.

With those eyes blazing and watching my every move, I stood and kicked my boots off. I was wearing a slinky black turtleneck and a form-fitting long skirt. The skirt had some stretch in it so I pulled it up easily. Then, as his eyes grew even more lustful, I slid my hose from my hips, and then removed my panties.

"Sit back down," he commanded.

"Okay," I whispered with a thrill.

Arousal made me hot and I wished I hadn't worn long sleeves.

"Good," he said. That word. That word I'd never think of the same again.

While I waited for him to pounce, my whole body felt like a furnace—that's how hot I was for him.

He slid his hand along the desk as he circled it and my pulse raced. But he stopped just shy of me and perched himself on the corner. Chewing on his lip, he stared down at my naked bottom half. "Now take your finger and circle it over your clit. Just a few times. Not too much."

I was more excited than I should have been with his eyes watching me. I should have been nervous about doing this at work. Sure, Hunter had said good-bye already and chances were good no one else was still around. Plus he had locked the door—but he wanted me to touch myself. In front of him. Here? Now?

I flashed him a heated smile. "I think I should tell you that I'm already wet."

"Do it anyway," he demanded.

My heart raced. I couldn't do this. Sure, we had been having sex like rabbits but this was different. I stood up and let my skirt fall.

His eyes flared as he brought himself to full height. "Phoebe."

I met his hungry gaze and turned the tables. "Sit down."

He narrowed his eyes at me.

My eyes fell down the length of him and I think I let out a small gasp when I saw the huge erection straining against the fabric of his slacks. I swallowed, and then nodded toward the chair. "If you want my help, then you'll sit down."

His lips quirked up in bemusement.

I kept my finger pointed at the chair. "I mean it." I wasn't quite sure how this was going to go down, so it surprised me when he actually lowered himself into the chair.

I wanted to give myself a high five.

Jeremy didn't like giving up control. It should have bothered me.

It didn't.

Instead, it thrilled me all the more. But this was my office and it was my turn, my opportunity to take control. I put my hands on my hips and felt powerful. "Unzip your pants."

He looked at me with a sly grin that looked more like a wolf in sheep's clothing. "I think you should do that."

I shook my head. "You have a problem and I have the solution. If you want it, you'll do as I suggest."

"Is that the way you want to play?" he grumbled.

I swallowed. Not sure if it was, but I decided why not. "Yes," I replied sternly. Adrenaline pumped through my veins. This was fun. A lot of fun.

He unzipped his jeans and his long, thick cock jutted out.

Holy hell, he wasn't wearing underwear.

I licked my lips at the sight. He knew how much that turned me on but I kept my cool. "Oh, I see your problem."

He looked down, his gaze darkening and began stroking himself.

Damn, he was better at this than me.

My internal muscles clenched as I watched, mesmerized by the picture before me. His head had tipped back as his stroking became more aggressive.

I made a noise that might have been a growl when he started thrusting his cock into his fist. My pulse quickened and my clit pulsed in perfect harmony.

Jeremy flicked his glance toward me. "This feels good . . . but you'd feel so much better."

Damn him.

I couldn't hold out any longer. I tugged my skirt back up and put my hands on his shoulders to straddle his legs. He brought his head up and gone was any amusement on his face. All that was left was pure lust. Without any additional foreplay and without another word, I positioned myself over the broad, blunt head of his cock and eased my way down.

He threw his head back and grabbed my hips.

Ripples of desire consumed me as I rose up and slammed myself down.

"Fuck," he groaned.

I gripped the arms of the chair and did it over and over again, feeling like I would never get enough of him.

"Fuckkk," he groaned again. This time drawing out the word. Soon his hands were moving me as fast as my hips were already moving.

I leaned in to kiss him and his mouth devoured mine. His tongue stroked mine and his lips crashed against mine with a hunger that would have made me weak at the knees if I was standing.

I was climbing higher and higher and his groans were becoming more intense, even fiercer, with every passing second. One of Jeremy's hands had drifted down and his thumb was directly over my clit. With pressure he circled me, and my hips jerked as my thigh muscles tightened in preparation of my impending climax.

"Oh God, I'm going to come," I cried out.

"I'm right there with you," he groaned through clenched teeth. He had been there before me and he was holding back, waiting for me, I could tell.

We both exploded as shattering climaxes ran rapid through our veins. Time stood still as the pleasure only he could deliver consumed me.

When I could breathe again, I looked at him. "I think I solved your problem."

He nipped at my lip. "You certainly did. But I have to be honest, I'm not sure I like you taking control."

I nipped back at his. "So punish me."

I was joking of course. Too much Ana and Christian on the big screen.

A strange light glimmered in his eye. "Do you mean that?"

I swallowed. "I'm not sure. It depends what you have in mind. . . ."

Slowly, he stood up with me in his arms and turned around, setting me on my desk. His limp cock was starting to stiffen again already.

"What are you doing?" I asked him.

"Giving you what you want. What you need. Do you trust me?"

"Yes, I trust you."

He pulled my legs apart. "Good. I want access to you all weekend."

I gave him a questioning look.

"No panties, no hose, no pants."

I laughed. "I can't do that."

He dropped his head and drove his tongue into my pussy, thrusting it in and out and in and out in the most delicious way.

That mouth.

"Oh God, yes," I screamed as his tongue drove me to a state of near insanity.

I couldn't believe how fast I could orgasm again if I let myself go. And I couldn't believe how much I wanted to. I loved when his cock was inside me but now desire built fast and the explosion came quick as pleasure overtook my entire body. Usually when his tongue was inside me, the build was slower. He took his time. The blissful state lasted longer. I was rising higher and higher but then he just stopped.

"What are you doing?" I panted.

"Do you like that?"

"Yes, you know I do."

He didn't respond. Instead he drove his tongue into my pussy again and brought me slowly back to the brink. And just as before, he stopped.

"Did you like that?"

"Yes," I said desperately.

He did it two more times.

By then I was whimpering and begging for him not to stop. "Please Jeremy, please," I whimpered.

He licked his shimmering lips. "You taste so good. I could do this all day."

My arousal intensified as my release tempted me. I couldn't take his teasing anymore, so I moved my hand to my clit. I didn't care. I was desperate for a release. And he had wanted to see me. So why not now? It wouldn't be as sweet from my own hand, but at that point, I didn't care.

"I wouldn't do that if I were you. Not right now anyway. I wouldn't mind watching you later but if you don't move your hand, your alarm clock might not go off tomorrow morning. And that would be a shame—for the both of us."

"Okay," I cried out. "I'll do as you ask but first tell me why."

His grin was wide. "To be up front, I've never done anything like it before and I want to try it with you. You seemed to want it."

It would be the first sex game I'd ever played and from what he said, Jeremy too.

He dropped back down. Right then I didn't care about anything else because his face was right where I wanted it and unlike before, he didn't stop. He licked and sucked me until I screamed out in pleasure.

Once my breathing settled, he stood up and zipped his pants, then held out his hand. "Come on, we should go. Our guests will already be there."

I picked up my hose and went to step into my panties when he took them both from me and shoved them in his pocket. "Bare, remember."

"During dinner with my friend?" I asked incredulously.

A devilish glimmer flickered in his eyes. "Absolutely."

I shook my head and slid my boots on, barefoot. "I don't see how this is going to be a punishment to me anyway."

Just the thought of his touch thrilled me, excited me, and turned me on. I was wet again just thinking about it.

He handed me my leather jacket; he had never even taken his off, and he led me out of the office and to the elevator. "Oh, you will."

Butterflies took flight again in my belly at the thought of what he had planned.

The driver was waiting for us. When we got in the car, I couldn't help but think about Jeremy sitting where I was, thinking of me, and getting hard just minutes earlier. I smiled at the thought.

Unexpectedly, his hand crept up my leg and my body shivered in anticipation. However, we were not in private and I subsequently squirmed. "What are you doing?" I hissed as my head bopped toward the driver.

In answer, he kept running the tips of his fingers higher up my thigh. He stopped, but not until he allowed his fingertips to lightly graze my sensitive flesh.

Holy hell.

Realizing it was his intent to drive me wild didn't help make matters any easier. Even after his hand was gone, the feel of his touch still lingered.

The feel of his hand back on my leg sent shivers up my spine.

He chuckled. "Come on, we have guests."

I glared at him without moving. I was so lost in thinking about this little game of his and the frustration it was going to cause me, I hadn't noticed when we arrived at his loft.

Jeremy shrugged, so calm and cool as he exited the car. I tried to keep my distance as we entered the elevator, but he didn't let me. He stepped closer and lust whirled around us but the doors opened before he even touched me. I think he did it on purpose and I could see then how this game was definitely a punishment.

With his key, he unlocked the door but paused before he opened it. Turning around to face me, he crashed his mouth to mine and kissed me—long and hard. The hungry movement of his mouth swallowed up my gasps of surprise and excitement. However, the whimpering noise I made when his fingertips caressed my clit through the fabric of my skirt echoed in the hall. That's when my body thrummed with excitement as it roared to life. But the flash was short lived, because just as fast as he had turned around, he turned back and pushed the door open, leaving me desperate and wanting as I followed him in inside.

Bastard!

CHAPTER 20

Dinner with Friends

Jeremy's place was amazing.

The fully renovated loft was formerly part of a caviar warehouse. It was three floors with a double-height ceiling in the living room. The main floor was an open-space combination living room and kitchen. Two sets of open stairs appeared from just inside the front door, both with glass guardrails. The first set took you from the main floor to the second floor where Jeremy's bedroom took up half the space and the other two bedrooms, both of which served as office space for Jet Set New York, took up the rest of the space.

The second set of stairs led to a totally redone roof deck. The deck was high enough up that you got a complete view of the surrounding area. Jeremy showed it to me the first time he brought me here.

I loved it up there.

Everything Jeremy had was functional. All the walls in the loft were painted white and there was very little in terms of decor. Yet, the place was still somehow warm and inviting.

The loft was completely Jeremy.

Voices echoed from the kitchen. Jamie and Lindsay were in there talking to Max, one of the chefs from Catch.

"Jacket," Jeremy whispered in my ear and his warm breath gave me goose bumps.

I narrowed my gaze at him. "I got it." I took it off myself because the less he touched me, the better. I had to calm down my desire for the rest of the evening, at least. I could see what his game was. He wanted to drive me wild. And I was going to prove to him that I had some semblance of self-control.

While he took both our jackets and hung them in the closet at the bottom of the stairs, I checked my clothing to make sure I was put together. I hoped the lace bottom of my skirt didn't give away that I was bare beneath it. At least the top portion, to midthigh anyway, was solid black.

Once I was certain I didn't look *just fucked*, I went ahead of Jeremy into the kitchen.

Max was making sushi rolls and Jamie and Lindsay were busy eating them.

"Jamie," I squealed, happy to see him.

"Phoebs." He smiled and hopped off the bar stool to meet me in the middle of the kitchen. He hugged me and whispered, "I think you're going to love her."

I pulled back to look at him. "I think you already do."

"Jeremy," Jamie said, letting go of his hold on me and grasping Jeremy's hand.

"Good to see you, James. How's the head?"

"Harder than ever," he joked.

We all laughed.

"Lindsay," Jamie called, outreaching his arm.

As she approached, I couldn't help but think she was even more stunning in person. Tall, in her heeled booties, she stood at equal height with both Jamie and Jeremy. She had hair that was more orange than red. It was long and hung in loose waves down past her shoulders. She was also waif thin and had legs a mile long. She wore a short, tight red dress with black fishnet stockings. I could see what Jamie saw in her. She was sexy and naturally beautiful rolled together.

"Baby, this is my best friend, Phoebe St. Claire and her—" He paused.

"Boyfriend," Jeremy quickly added. "Nice to meet you. I'm Jeremy Mc-Queen."

Boyfriend! My heart skipped a beat.

We had yet to define our relationship, but it seemed we just had.

"Hi, Lindsay," I said, giving her a quick hug.

"Max," Jeremy greeted the chef as he walked toward him and shook his hand. They spoke quietly for a few moments.

"Baby, Phoebs and I have known each other since ninth grade."

She clasped her hands together. "Oh, then she should have some really good dirt to share with me."

Jamie's hand went to her behind and he tapped it.

Lindsay jumped in surprise.

Jamie leaned in close to her and whispered, "You already know everything naughty about me that you need to know."

But his whisper wasn't soft enough.

I rolled my eyes.

"What?" he said, raising both brows.

I wrinkled my nose and gave him a slight shove. "There are some things I'd rather not know."

The three of us laughed at that but I couldn't help but stare at Jamie. He was just so different with this woman at his side. He was gazing at his new bride adoringly. I'd never, ever, seen him act like this, nor had I ever heard him call a woman *baby*.

"Congratulations are in order," I heard Jeremy say, but my state of shock wasn't interrupted until the pop of the champagne cork.

So lost in Jamie's actions, I had completely forgotten about their marriage. I hurried over to the table in the living room and grabbed the gift I had purchased for the new couple. I rejoined them just as Jeremy was filling the flutes with champagne. I hadn't seen those in the loft before. I was pretty sure that was because they were new.

Feeling a little close to gushing, I was touched that he had thought to get champagne and glasses. Jeremy had actually planned the entire evening. I was so caught up in preparing the investor packets for distribution, I had spent little time on anything else except Jeremy himself.

Excited, I handed the gift to Lindsay. "Just a little something for the two of you."

She beamed with enthusiasm. "James, it's our first wedding gift."

Jamie beamed as well and then kissed her on the cheek. "Go ahead, open it."

"Yes, open it," I assured her.

Lindsay carried it to the island where the plates of sushi had multiplied and looked to Jamie again.

With a slight huff of laughter, he nodded toward her in reassurance.

I was certain she was worried about breaking etiquette. Although she wasn't an Upper East Sider, she must have known that the older generation of

East Side women believed gifts were not meant to be opened in the presence of those who gave them. God forbid you hated it and had to pretend you liked it. I had to give Jamie props for not caring about what his mother might think about his choice in women.

Lindsay tore the package open with excitement and my heart opened to her immediately. She wasn't like anyone Jamie had ever dated. She was warm, kind, and genuine. I didn't have to know her well to know she was good for him.

"I like her," I whispered to Jamie.

His smile was brighter than I'd ever seen it. "I knew you would."

"Come on, let's join her," I said and tugged him that way.

When we reached the island, Jeremy had just set the glasses on it and I went to stand beside him. Butterflies were soaring in my belly and I felt a little giddy myself. Jeremy looked at me curiously and I rose on my toes and whispered in his ear, "Thank you."

Grinning in triumph, he whispered back, "You can thank me later," and he let his hand graze up my derriere. My back was to the front door. Thank God no one was behind us because he slid his hand inside my skirt and his fingers stroked right down the middle of my behind.

My pulse leaped.

"Oh my God," Lindsay cried as she held the pewter bowl in her hands and then clutched it to her chest.

I tried to focus on Lindsay and her excitement over the gift.

But it was difficult.

Poppy, for all her flaws, did have a terrific tradition. She always gave a newly married couple the perfect salad bowl. She searched high and low for one that fit the couple. She said it would be sitting on their table through many meals and hopefully the couple would remember it was given to them at a time in their lives when their love was the strongest.

I had adopted her tradition.

The only thing my mother valued in life more than money was family and it was the one thing I truly admired about her. I knew my bowl was waiting for me. It was old, and wooden, and had belonged to her mother. I remembered it sitting on our table for every family meal.

Jeremy's hand stayed where it was, caressing a place I wouldn't have thought would make my entire body tingle. I was starting to breathe heavy. I made a mental note to not wear anything jersey the next two days. Structure would inhibit easy access and hopefully a thicker fabric wouldn't elicit such a harlot response on my part. His hand moved lower and he slid a finger just barely inside me. The tingles I was already feeling turned into pulsing. If he kept it up, I was going to come right there.

And Jamie would be telling me there were some things he'd rather not know.

I fidgeted but when I did, he slid his finger deeper. It was a warning for me to stay still or he was going to drive me over the edge. I wasn't sure which would be worse—his constant teasing, or just coming right there in front of everyone.

I was incredibly turned on.

I shifted my focus, turning my attention back to Lindsay, who was still sobbing as she showed the inside script on the bowl to Jamie that read, "May your future be bright."

I didn't know Lindsay at all, but I knew Jamie. Fancy crystal or designer china wasn't his thing. So when I saw the antique pewter set at a small gift shop near my office, and read what was inscribed inside it, I thought it was perfect. I didn't include a note like my mother would have instructing the couple to use this bowl at each and every meal and remember the love they shared always, because I wasn't sure then if what they had was love. But I was now as I watched them.

"Hey," Jamie soothed her. "It's only a salad bowl."

He glanced at me and mouthed, "Thank you," and then pulled her in for a hug.

I in turn dared to raise my gaze to Jeremy.

"Are you okay?" he whispered. "You look a little flushed."

I pulled at my turtleneck. "It's just a little warm in here."

His grin was devilish.

I sucked in a breath and then slowly exhaled. "You're a bad, bad boy."

When Jamie pulled away and Lindsay still hadn't stopped crying, I knew something wasn't right.

She finally spoke. "Thank you so much for accepting me. It means so much."

"Is everything okay?" I asked her.

Jamie sighed. "It's been a rough week."

"His mother refuses to accept our marriage," Lindsay blurted out.

"She will," Jamie said softly. "Just give her time."

"And your friend too, she couldn't even look at me."

"Emmy," Jamie whispered and that said it all.

Obviously sensing the mood shift, Jeremy removed his hand.

I took the glasses he had set down and handed them out. "It's time for a toast."

Lindsay inhaled deeply and brushed away her tears and Jamie gave me a slight smile.

"To beginnings," I said. "They aren't always smooth but what matters is that the future remains bright."

"Cheers," Jeremy said, looking at me. The heat of his stare told me he knew I meant that for us as well.

"Cheers," Jamie also said.

"Cheers," Lindsay said as she clinked each of our glasses.

Max raised his own glass. "Cheers and it's time to eat."

We all laughed and moved toward the table, which was already set.

"So how's work?" Jamie asked me.

"Still walking the line, but I hope not for much longer."

He nodded. "The club renovation is still a go?"

"It is. In fact, Jeremy got me everything I needed to make initial projections and I sent out the requests for investment earlier tonight."

Jamie looked over at Jeremy and gave him a nod. "That's great."

I told him and Lindsay about the ultramodern fixtures and lighting, and the design of the bar. I went on and on and between the wine Jamie brought and the champagne Jeremy had bought, by the time we finished dinner, not only did they have a vivid picture of what Sinners would look like, we were all a bit buzzed. Max had left long ago, leaving dessert in the refrigerator.

Jamie cleared his throat and grabbed Lindsay's hand. "So, we were thinking," he said. "As long as everything continues to go as well as it has been and you open Sinners on New Year's Eve, I'd like to have our wedding celebration there that night."

My eyes widened. "Are you serious?"

"Fuck yeah, it would be a great way to bring in the New Year."

I clasped my hands together. "That couldn't be more perfect."

"Next Friday night, dinner and a preliminary discussion," Jamie suggested.

I glanced toward Jeremy. "Sounds like a plan," he said.

"Oh wait. I can't Friday. Wednesday?" Jamie asked.

Jeremy nodded and so did I.

"Does that mean we should wait to make a public appearance together until the New Year?" Lindsay asked, looking hopeful.

Jamie shook his head. "No, we have a season of events to attend. It's perfect. That way, you'll get to meet everyone before the celebration."

Lindsay didn't look happy.

Jamie squeezed her hand and then looked at Jeremy and me. "Are the two of you attending the White and Black Jack Ball tomorrow night? It's stressing Lindsay out for some reason."

The makeshift casino fund-raiser was Avery Lake's crowning achievement and she basked in the attention she received for her philanthropic ways. Much to her credit, she did raise millions every year for the families of the victims of 9/11. She had a very personal connection—she had lost her father in the collapse of the World Trade Center towers. Her stretch continued to be far reaching, providing college funds to those who needed it, senior care to those who didn't have the proper insurance any longer, and trusts had been set up for the children of firefighters and police officers who lost their lives that day. Her support was appreciated beyond measure and everyone joined forces to make the night an annual success.

It was the event of the year and yet the thought of attending put dread in my belly. Jeremy had left the choice up to me and with everything going on during the week, I had pushed the decision aside. I think I was secretly hoping it would just disappear. But Mrs. Bardot had sent over the most spectacular black-and-white gown during the week and of course I knew going would be good for Jeremy's business.

I looked at Jeremy, who remained neutral. "Yes, we'll be there," I said.

Lindsay looked extremely relieved.

I wondered if she had met Avery yet and if that was her reluctance. Long before Jeremy and even Dawson, Jamie had been Avery's target and she gave up hope of landing him only after many years and many unsuccessful attempts. I even think she and Emmy had joined forces for a bit in order to coerce him away from other women. I believe it was because of the threesome that Avery and Emmy no longer spoke to each other.

"Phoebe?"

Jeremy had stood and was talking to me, but my mind was wandering. The sound of his voice pulled me back. "Hmmm?"

"What do you say we make some coffee and see what Max left for dessert?"

I stood too. Thinking about Avery had rattled me and I had to shake my thoughts away. Tomorrow night would be fine.

"Here, I can help," Lindsay offered.

"No, no. You two go sit down over there." I motioned to the large living area. "We'll bring everything in there."

"Great, there's a b-ball game on; I can catch the score," Jamie said.

I shook my head at him. "Did you bet on it?"

He gave me a coy look. Of course he did. My guess was he hadn't told Lindsay about his penchant for gambling. All in due time, I thought.

I grabbed some plates and took them over to the sink. The dirty dishes from the dinner prep were piled next to it. Jeremy didn't have anyone to clean so it was him and me. I liked it that way. I turned the water on and while I waited for it to warm, I stole glances at him as he made the coffee.

"What?" he said when he caught me.

I couldn't help but smile. "Nothing."

The TV turned on and the sound of the Knicks playing and Jamie cursing at a play made me laugh. I turned back and started rinsing the stack of dishes. We could load the dishwasher later but it would make the job easier if I removed the leftover food before it dried onto the plates and bowls.

Arms circled around me just as I finished the first stack. "Did I catch you staring at me?"

"Maybe."

"Do you know what that does to me?" His low groan across my neck sent shivers down my spine. But it was his hand sliding inside the elastic of my skirt that made me tremble. Before I could lean against the counter to stop him his fingers found my clit and instant heat flooded me.

"Jeremy," I gasped.

"Keep doing what you're doing and no one will notice when I make you come."

Oh God, I was already halfway there.

I wanted to protest but it was too late. His thumb was already circling my clit with just the right amount of pressure. I bit my lip to keep from crying out as that familiar oblivion overtook me. I squeezed the metal bowl I was holding and dropped my chin, hoping my moans of pleasure would get sucked up into the flowing water.

"Hell yes," Jamie yelled from the other room. At least I knew he wasn't paying attention to us.

"That's it," Jeremy prompted me. "Let go."

And I did. I bit harder on my lip as he coaxed every lingering drop of pleasure from me.

"You are the one I want."

"I know," I said with small huffs of breath.

He put his hands on mine and grabbed the bowl, rinsing it with me under the warm water. "I just wanted to make sure."

I was not good at hiding my emotions and obviously he knew the talk of Avery's party had rattled me. In that moment, with the two of us standing together at the sink, I knew my feelings for him were stronger than they should have been after only one week together.

The problem was, I didn't know how to stop them from flourishing.

"I want to watch you make yourself come."

I shivered at his breath on my ear.

Jamie and Lindsay left shortly after we finished dessert. Jeremy and I had started to clean up but I sent him out for his nightly club check and finished it myself. I was too tired to go out anywhere. While putting things away, I knocked over his pile of mail on the counter and a letter drew my attention. The name on the return address, a J Truman in North Carolina, seemed familiar, but I couldn't place it. Once I finished in the kitchen I read for a bit. When I couldn't keep my eyes open, I changed into one of Jeremy's T-shirts and was brushing my teeth when he returned.

I spit out my toothpaste and looked up at him in the mirror. Then I turned to look at him. "What?" My throat was dry despite the fact that I was rinsing my mouth and I knew this was coming from earlier this evening.

His lips were on mine in a long kiss before he broke the suction of our mouths and buried his face in my neck. "I want to watch you make yourself come," he groaned into my throat.

I didn't know how to reply so instead I stared at his reflection in the mirror. His handsome face was so serious and I watched as he studied me without an ounce of amusement dancing in his eyes this time.

The intensity of the moment caused goose bumps to rise on my skin.

He was serious.

Dead serious.

He dropped his head to the curve of my shoulder and with his teeth bit me gently. He lifted his mouth and looked at me in the mirror. "I'll help you."

My blood felt like gasoline as it flowed through my veins. Hot. Explosive. Ready to catch fire. With his eyes still on me, I swallowed and gave a slight nod.

"Take your shirt off," Jeremy commanded.

I didn't hesitate.

Jeremy stepped back and started to pull his own clothes off and I couldn't help but watch him. His eyes were burning with desire and his body was utterly glorious. Once he was naked, he pressed his body to mine and I could feel him starting to get hard.

But then he took my hands, which were gripping the counter, and lifted them to my chest and a nervous flutter swept through me. I had twenty fingertips touching me as he slid our hands over the small swell of my breasts and my nerves dispersed into full-out desire as the eroticism of it all took over.

"Do you feel how hard your nipples get with the slightest touch?" he whispered in my ear.

I nodded while he slid our hands lower to my navel and flattened my palms against it beneath his. Four hands covered my lower body and desire pulsed in my core.

"Open your legs wider," he growled.

God, the commanding tone to his voice made my heart beat frantically.

Once I did as he instructed, he moved one of my hands between my legs and put the other back on my breast. He concentrated below as he manipulated my finger so that I was gently stroking myself in a circular motion.

Stroke.

Circle.

Stroke.

Heat spread through me.

I could hear his deep breaths.

I shuddered in ecstasy when I looked down and watched as his hand moved mine.

"Pinch your nipples." His voice was hoarse as he bent to kiss my neck. It was more like a lick from my ear to my shoulder.

I pinched.

My pulse was racing.

Jeremy released the hand holding my breast and left me to that task but his hand down below kept up the slow torturous movement.

Stroke.

Circle.

Stroke.

Each stroke across my bare flesh was better than the last.

God, I wanted him.

Suddenly, his free hand went to my behind and his fingers trailed down the middle of it. He stopped in the spot he had caressed earlier that night. Jeremy gently circled it, just applying the slightest bit of pressure, all while his other hand was still guiding mine.

Stroke.

Circle.

Stroke.

His mouth covered my ear. "Tell me if you want me to stop."

To be honest, I was having a difficult time processing all of the sensations I was feeling but in no way did I want any of them to go away.

Slowly, he stopped his circling and even slower, he slid his hand farther down, meeting where our joined fingers were already stroking my clit. His hand though, didn't move, it just hovered over my opening, teasing me with the thought of what he might do.

I had no hair down there, on my legs, or under my arms. Laser hair removal had been my mother's gift to me for my sixteenth birthday. The sensation I was experiencing wasn't something I'd felt before. Maybe it was because I was standing naked in front of a mirror with Jeremy's hard body and lengthening cock behind me, maybe it was the eroticism of the moment, that I was doing what he had asked me to do, or maybe it was simply the stimulation all over my body. Whatever it was, I didn't want it to stop.

Jeremy took a step back away from the counter and I instinctively followed. "I'm going to let go of your hand. Don't stop. Keep doing what you're doing and I want you to look in the mirror. See how beautiful you are. See what I see."

My lids flicked up. My body was visible until about midthigh.

Jeremy's free hand went to my other breast. He circled my nipple and then pinched it. Circled it again, and then pinched it. He kept the same rhythm up and I followed with the hand I had on my own breast.

"That's it. Don't stop. How does it feel?"

I let my head fall back. "Incredible."

Jeremy captured my mouth and hungrily kissed me for a few moments before releasing my mouth and resuming his stare in the mirror. "Fucking hell," he groaned as he watched me.

My whole body hummed in delight and I knew his had to feel the same. Just to make certain, I arched my back so I could feel his hard cock, how much he wanted me.

His free hand rested on my navel, the other slid back up my behind and circled that spot again. "Now I want you to rub even smaller, gentler circles around your clit. You're already so wet it shouldn't be difficult. But not a lot pressure. Not yet."

My entire body was tingling now, not just my core but rather from my head to my toes.

He slid his hand back down and put a finger inside me. "Oh fuck, you're so tight, so hot and so wet," he hissed. He added a second finger, and a third, and I was moaning when he pulled them out. But then he moved his hand back to my behind and resumed circling that tender spot, adding a little pressure, and the tingles turned into tremors.

"Jeremy," I screamed. "I want to come."

"Not yet," he breathed. His own voice was ragged. "Not yet, just hold on a little longer."

My eyes met his half-lidded ones in the mirror. "When I tell you, add some pressure to your clit. When you start coming, I want you to bend over and grip the counter. I'm going to fuck you while you're coming."

"Where," I asked. At that point anal sex wasn't something I was opposed to, in fact I think I wanted it but I just wanted to be prepared.

"Not here," he said as he added a little more pressure. "Not here yet. This is just for added stimulation."

"Oh God," I cried out. "It feels so good."

My words must have undone him because a barely audible, "Now," escaped his throat.

Jeremy let go of me and his eyes were on me in the mirror and I added that little bit of extra pressure and my orgasm consumed my entire body. I was riding the intense waves of delicious pleasure when I felt him enter me from behind. His body slammed against mine. He was thrusting fast and I absorbed each and every one. Reveled in it. My orgasm started to wane but then out of nowhere started to rise again. I was climbing higher than I ever had. His hands were gripping my hips, mine were squeezing the countertop so tight that my fingers hurt. He was slamming into me.

I didn't care.

He called my name as he came, whispering something I couldn't hear.

I closed my eyes. "Jeremy," I cried out again. Beneath my lids, I saw stars, the moon, and lightning. With my eyes closed, I felt the earth move and the sky shift. In my own darkness, I felt a million different things but I didn't feel lost in him. I knew then for certain, I wouldn't get lost in him.

There was no way I could.

Not when I had found myself in him.

CHAPTER 21

The Green-Eyed Monster

It had officially been one week.

Jeremy and I had been together for seven days but I felt like it had been so much longer. We seemed to have come so far in such a little time.

I won't lie. I was slightly scared.

Intense.

All-encompassing.

Consuming.

Passionate.

Did I say intense?

And those were just a few words I would use to describe our relationship.

It was Saturday morning and Jeremy woke me up with a kiss on the cheek. "I'll be back in a couple of hours."

I blinked up at him, those thoughts tumbling through my mind. "Where are you going?"

"My weekly manager's meeting."

"I thought you held those here?"

"Normally, I do."

I shaded my eyes. "And you're not because of me?"

He kissed me again, this time on the mouth. "No, not entirely. I've been thinking of rotating between Jet Set locations so each manager can familiarize himself with the other operations."

"Oh, that makes sense." I felt better that it wasn't because I was there.

He grinned. "It does. But not every week, I was thinking every other. I can stay in bed longer when they all come here."

The smirk on his face was a turn-on and my insides turned to liquid.

His mouth found my ear. "You stay in bed and wait for me. I'll wake you up when I get back."

His tone told me just what he had in mind. The very thought had my sex clenching but then I remembered that I had plans. "I can't. I have to go home and clean my apartment."

He raised a doubtful brow.

"I do. Every other Saturday, I have an eleven a.m. lunch date with my mother and she always picks me up."

He lowered himself on the mattress and lay beside me with one elbow propped up. "That's really nice."

My gaze traveled the length of his body. He wore a simple long-sleeve black T-shirt, distressed jeans, and his scuffed boots. He looked edible in his Saturday work attire. I was certain a baseball hat would be going on his head—backward. "I guess. We've been doing it since I got my own place. She says it's the only time she gets my full attention."

He looked a little sad.

"What about you? Do you see your mother when you go back to Miami?"

He shrugged. "Yeah, I try to."

"I thought you were close."

"We used to be but we haven't been for a long time."

"Do you want to talk about it?"

He shook his head no. "When will you be done with lunch?"

I laughed. "That depends on how much my mother has to talk about and how much shopping she wants to do."

He leaned closer. "Then come back after."

I pecked him on the cheek and slid my mouth to his in an effort to lessen the sting of what I was about to say. "How about you pick me up at my place at seven?"

He leaned back and looked at me puzzled. "Ummm . . . sure, but what's this about?"

I ran my fingers through his hair. "Nothing. I promised I'd stay a week and I did. I have to go home sometime. I can't stay forever."

He captured my wrist and rolled on top of me.

The sheet separated my naked body from his clothed one, but the heat was undeniable.

"Move in with me," he rasped.

My body tensed. "I can't do that."

"Why not? You told me you were moving out of your place next month anyway. So why not move in here?"

"I just can't," I repeated.

He took my face in his hands. "So you've said. Now tell me why."

My eyelids fluttered shut at his close proximity. "Don't you have to go to work?"

His thumbs stroked my cheeks. "Not until we talk about this."

I sighed and pulled back. "First of all, I can't walk to work from here. And don't say you'll drive me because you can't drive me every day. That's just not realistic."

His jaw twitched as if he was trying to hold back some of his amusement. "I could but you're right, it's not realistic. But there are other ways people commute in this big city of ours. We can arrange for a car service, you could take a cab, or"—and then he allowed himself the grin he'd obviously been holding back and said—"or you could take the subway."

I wanted to slap the silly grin off his pretentious face but knew I wasn't getting out of the conversation on transportation alone. "Well, getting to work aside, all of my stuff won't fit in here."

He looked around and then let his eyes scorch me. "Get rid of anything of mine you want. I'm not attached to any of it. And I have an entire empty closet right there." He pointed to the second closet in his bedroom that I knew for a fact was completely bare.

Everything he was saying made sense but the swarms of butterflies in my belly made the idea seem preposterous. "Well, Mrs. Bardot will miss me and she's old."

This time he narrowed his eyes at me. "She's gone most of the time and besides if you're moving anyway you'd still have to stop by to see her."

I pushed his hair from his face and admitted, "Okay. So, I'm afraid."

With that he let go of my face and rose on his forearms. "Of me?"

I snaked my arms around his neck. "No, not of you. Of us together."

"What do you mean?" His voice was soft.

"It's just everything is so intense between us and I'm feeling things I've never felt in my life, not even when we were together before. I think space is a good way to help temper some of those feelings."

He dipped his head and kissed me long and slow with a tenderness that told me he wasn't trying to be sexual. When he released my mouth he said, "Space and distance won't cool this down. Trust me. But the bigger question is why would you want it to? I don't understand—" His phone rang. "Fuck," he hissed as he sat up. "I have to take this. It's one of my managers. He's out of town and giving me his update before the meeting. Just let me tell him that I'll call him back."

I sat up too. "No, take your call. You have to go to work. We'll talk about this tonight."

His phone rang again. "Hey, Mike, hang on one minute," he said and put the call on MUTE. "If you're not here when I get back, I'll call you. I want to finish this discussion, and not in public."

"Okay," I replied with a nod.

He leaned in and captured my mouth in a chaste kiss before returning to his call. "Mike, sorry about that. How were sales this week?"

The sound of his voice trailed off. I heard his heavy footfalls on the stairs and then the front door opened and closed.

He was gone and all of a sudden I felt lonely. I tossed and turned but couldn't fall back asleep. It wasn't even seven when I hopped in the shower, and by eight I was exiting a taxi and taking the elevator up to my apartment.

I heard Coco barking and knew Mrs. Bardot must be waiting for the elevator.

"Phoebe, darling," she greeted me as the doors opened.

"Mrs. Bardot, what are you doing up so early?"

"Oh darling, I have much to do. I'm returning to Paris this evening."

"So soon after your last trip. We hardly had time to catch up."

"It's my sister's eightieth birthday and I thought I'd surprise her."

I gave Coco a small pat. "That's really nice. How are you this morning?"

Mrs. Bardot looked me up and down. "Well, but I'm afraid not as well as you. Are you just returning from that James Dean of yours?"

I gave her a smile.

"Come with me to walk Coco and then we'll get a cup of coffee and chat. I missed you this week."

I stepped back into the elevator. "Oh by the way, thank you for the clothing. Every piece is exquisite. In fact, I'm wearing the black-and-white geometric one tonight."

She smiled and seemed to slip into the past as she spoke. "I wore that one to the Academy Awards in 1969. Such a great year for movies. I was up for best supporting actress, you know. The only nomination I ever received in my lifetime as an actress. It was the forty-first annual awards show and the only one I ever went to without a host. What a mess."

The doors opened and as we walked through the lobby, she continued, "I didn't win, of course, but it was still such an honor. It's a night I'll never forget. It's the night I reacquainted myself with the man who would become my husband."

Jack opened the door. "Good morning, ladies."

We said, "Good morning," in unison.

"Oh Jack, I'm just going to take Coco Chanel out for a quick walk and then I'll deliver her to you, if you could see her upstairs."

"Not a problem, ma'am." Jack smiled at her.

"You're such a dear," she said. As soon as we stepped out into the cool air, she set Coco down and began to attach her leash.

I waited, breathing in the fall air. October would soon be gone and the idyllic weather conditions were already fading. The thought made me sad. My favorite time of year was almost over and soon all the leaves would have fallen from the trees. Once Mrs. Bardot was settled, she started walking. I turned toward her. "Tell me about your husband. You never talk about him."

She sighed and buttoned up her coat. "Our time together was turbulent. We met again shortly after things ended with Rock. I was cautious at first. I didn't want to love anyone like I had loved Rock but Gaspard worked his way into my heart. He was very unlike me though."

"In what way?"

"Oh, not like you might think. It wasn't because he grew up in a working-class family. It was more because he had a lot of pride. Too much." She smiled when she said that but I could see the distress in her eyes. "I don't know if I ever told you this but I came from a very bourgeois, pious Catholic family. I grew up in a seven-bedroom apartment not far from the Eiffel Tower and summered in St. Tropez. From age twelve to fifteen, I attended the Paris Conservatory where I studied ballet. Gaspard and I met when I did my first photo shoot. He's the reason I stopped dancing and started modeling."

Coco stopped and I looked at Mrs. Bardot's face, when I realized for the first time she wasn't actually Mrs. Bardot. She was Miss Bardot or Mrs. De Gaulle.

"You never changed your last name," I blurted.

"No, darling. The world knew me as Bette Bardot or BB and Gaspard wanted it to stay that way."

I gave her a questioning look.

"It ensured a good living."

Mrs. Bardot's husband was Gaspard De Gaulle. He was one of the most famous fashion photographers of the sixties and seventies.

She seemed sad but then pulled out of it. "Well anyway, when I appeared on the cover of *Elle* magazine in 1960, I was fifteen and shocked the world. I was all curves. My body was toned and strong but not frail. I naturally had an athlete's build, which had been sculpted by the years of intense ballet lessons. Gaspard was Jean-Pierre Laffite's assistant and in charge of wardrobe for the shoot. He insisted I wear an un-corseted cotton dress with no lining and a bright colored bikini beneath. He also directed hair and makeup. Insisting that my eyes be painted with a dark kohl liner and that bangs be cut into my long, straight hair. He had a vision. He created BB."

"What happened? Did you date him back then?"

She headed back to our apartment building. "Oh, no, darling. I was fifteen and he was twenty. He was working for the hottest fashion photographer and had models at his feet." She laughed. "He was a bit of a slut. And besides, I left to come to the States right after the cover released. We never saw each other again until the 1969 Academy Awards. He had just moved to the States after two divorces and three children. He was broke and looking for a fresh start and I guess I was it."

I wrapped my jacket tight around me as we fought the breeze walking in the opposite direction. I couldn't help but wonder what she meant. "But he loved you?"

Mrs. Bardot picked up Coco and tucked her under her arm when we were close to our building. Jack was already outside waiting and took Coco.

Once we were walking again she said, "He loved me in his own way. And at the time, I thought I had enough love for the two of us. But as the years wore on, I realized I didn't. We fought about everything—from where to live, to his children, over his affairs, and even his drinking. I moved to New York for him because he despised California. I insisted his children visit, even though he thought it best he not interrupt their studies. He drank—a lot. We never had children of our own because he didn't want any more. But I could have handled all of that. It was the other women. He said they meant nothing. It was part of his job, he'd tell me. But it ate away at me until I hated him and the smell of perfume he'd come home wearing."

I looped my arm through hers. "I'm so sorry. I had no idea."

"No one did, my dear. I kept it a secret and he was discreet. You see even when we married, I knew we lacked that spark, that sexual chemistry that connects two people in ways life can otherwise tear apart."

We reached the coffee shop. "Shall we?" I asked.

She nodded. Still lost to the past, we sat in an empty booth and she continued, "He died ten years after we married. The papers called it a robbery."

"Coffee?" the waitress asked as she handed us each a menu.

Mrs. Bardot nodded and so did I.

As the waitress filled our cups, Mrs. Bardot said, "I'll have two eggs over easy and dry toast."

"I'll have the same," I said.

The waitress wrote down our order and was gone quickly.

I added cream and sugar to my coffee. "It wasn't a robbery?" I asked.

She opened an Equal packet and poured it into her cup. "No, Gaspard had been sleeping with a model and her husband found out. He shot Gaspard right in the stairwell of his apartment building as Gaspard left the man's wife one afternoon."

I reached across the table and tried to take her hand. "I'm so sorry."

She waved me off. "It was a lifetime ago. Enough about me. I'm an old lady. Tell me about you and your James Dean."

Her nickname for Jeremy made me smile. She'd been the one to nickname Dawson as well, calling him my Prince of Camelot.

I took a sip of my coffee. "Well, actually, he asked me to move in with him."

"And," she asked before sipping her own coffee.

"I think I said no, but I'm not sure."

"Why would you say no? Not because of Dawson, I hope."

I shook my head. "So many reasons. He's just one."

Her mouth drew into a thin line. "Do you love Jeremy?"

It was the first time she'd called him by name—and for that matter, Dawson as well.

"That's just it, I feel like I do."

"And he loves you?"

"I'm not sure, but it's way too early to bring it up."

The waitress set our plates on the table with our check and scurried off. It wasn't that busy in the restaurant but she was the only waitress.

Mrs. Bardot picked up the pepper. "Time doesn't dictate love. And I've seen the chemistry between the two of you. The spark that's there was never evident with Dawson."

I broke my yolk with the fork. "I know."

"Then you have to embrace this time. Run with it. Tell him how you feel. Life is too short not to."

I stared at her for the longest time, reading into her words what she wasn't telling me: *Don't make the same mistake I did or you might end up like me— alone.*

My apartment was an absolute wreck.

I'd been in and out all week and hadn't cleaned it up in more than two weeks. Needless to say, I was never so happy to have my mother call to tell me her stylist at John Barrett was running behind. She asked if I would meet her at BG's.

Bergdorf Goodman's modern interpretation of the social salon was always my mother's favorite place to dine. Located on the seventh floor, the restaurant showed more evidence than any other floor that the stately building had once been the Vanderbilt mansion. For some reason, it still held on to its cosmopolitan glamour.

Poppy and I had been lunching there for as long as I could remember. And I had to admit, I did love it there too. The bright atmosphere and light menu, plus a view of the park, made dining there with my mother actually fun. And of course, every lunch was followed by a shopping spree. Although, to my surprise, today my mother skipped that part of our once-valued tradition.

In fact, she was so preoccupied during our lunch that I didn't even tell her about the nightclubs or Jeremy. She asked me a few questions about work and then as soon as we finished our salads, she left under the guise of a migraine. I wasn't sure what was going on, but I could only guess she was beginning to realize just how little money we had left.

Jeremy had called me as promised, but I was with Mrs. Bardot and promised to call him when I returned from lunch. As I entered my apartment building, I pulled my phone out of my pocket and called him.

"Hey, I'm sorry it took me so long to call you back. But I'm back from lunch with Poppy and can talk now."

"Good, because I'm right behind you."

Jack was just opening the door for me when I whipped around. Jeremy was getting out of a cab with a suit bag in one hand and a duffel bag in the other.

I shoved my phone in my purse and walked toward him.

He kissed me. "Hi, perfect timing."

I looked down at his stuff. "Hi. What are you doing?"

He put his duffel bag in the same hand as the suit bag and grasped my fingers. "I thought I'd come over early so we could talk and since I'd already be here, I figured I'd just get ready at your place."

Jack opened the door again. "Did you now?" I teased.

He stopped just inside the lobby. "But if you'd rather I get dressed down here, that's fine too."

I pulled his hand. "Come on. I was thinking of a movie and a nap."

We got on the elevator and his eyes swept me. Before I knew it, he dropped his belongings and pushed me up against the wall. My pulse started to race. His mouth was on my throat and his hands were skimming up and down my derriere.

I'd worn a wool dress and the fabric was thick. I knew he couldn't feel what he was searching for.

"I'm up for a movie and a nap after you show me what's underneath your clothes."

Arousal flooded between my thighs. "I thought you wanted to talk first."

He pressed himself against me. "I changed my mind."

The doors opened and I couldn't get inside my apartment fast enough. He dropped his things once more and I did the same. We didn't say anything. The only communication was the heat in our eyes.

I kicked my boots off and unzipped my dress. Letting it fall to the ground, I stood before him in only my bra and a pair of socks.

His eyes simmered in appreciation. I had done what he asked even though I didn't know if I'd see him before the evening. As soon as he saw me, his hands were on me and my body was humming. He cupped my sex and groaned when he felt how wet I already was. I reached for his jeans and without even undoing them I shoved my hands down his pants and started stroking.

"Oh fuck," he muttered as his fingers started to move.

In.

Out.

Pressure.

Pleasure.

"Oh God, Jeremy," I called as I came lightning fast standing in the foyer of my apartment.

He started to lower us both to the floor but I flattened my palm to his chest and dropped to my knees. I unzipped his pants and pulled them down slightly. When I did, his erection jutted out. I licked my lips as I looked up at him. His eyes caught me, and in response, he gave himself a few strokes with a practiced hand. I knew then that at some point, I wanted to watch him make himself come.

"Fuck," he said again through gritted teeth as I sheathed him with my mouth. His hands went in my hair and he pushed his hips forward to go even farther into my eager mouth. I let him guide me.

I chose to get on my knees in front of him and I was relishing how much pleasure he found in it. I licked him, sucked him, and took him deep. This wasn't about teasing, this was about pleasure, plain and simple. And just as he had delivered it to me, I was going to do the same for him. I fucked him with my mouth, using my lips, teeth, and tongue and it wasn't long before I heard his guttural grunt, felt his body tense, and then tasted the salty sweetness of his release.

He pulled me up. "Fuck, what a way to say hi," he told me as he buried his head in my neck.

"Well, actually, that was my way of saying yes."

He pulled back. "Yes, you'll move in with me."

I nodded. "Next month, when my lease is up. Until then maybe we could stay here more often?"

He kissed me. "I'll stay wherever you want to stay. Fuck, if you want me to move in here instead of us living at my place, we could do that too."

I looked around. I did love my apartment but it was so much smaller than his place, it just didn't make sense. And then there was the reason I was moving out to begin with—the steep rent.

"I can pay the rent, if that's what you're worried about."

"No, I'm not sure. Where would you work then? And your place is so much closer to your clubs."

He pulled me to my room. "Think about it. I'll live wherever you're living. Now get dressed and let's watch a movie. We can figure out the logistics later."

Once I'd thrown on some sweatpants and a T-shirt, we both climbed into my bed. Then Jeremy pulled me to his chest. "We're a good team, you know."

I lifted my head in question.

"We fit together well."

I threw him a saucy look.

He smiled a rueful grin. "Not like that."

My heartbeat went sky high but I contained the effect he had on me and raised a sensual brow.

"Well, yes like that, but I mean in business. We work well together."

I relaxed back down against his chest and murmured, "We do," before hitting PLAY on the remote. It meant a lot to me that Jeremy valued my opinion when it came to business decisions. He'd confided in me about his plans for Jet Set and we had even discussed the best ways to grow membership as well as which cities would be ideal targets when he was ready to expand. I pondered our business savvy as he drew shapes on my back but when the movie started, I dedicated my attention to *Breakfast at Tiffany's*.

Sometime during the movie, we must have fallen asleep because a pounding on my door woke me up. "Stay here, it's probably Mrs. Bardot wanting to see her dress on me. I'll just tell her I'll come by before we leave."

"Sounds good," he mumbled as he covered his head with the pillow. All the sex we'd been having was probably wearing him out. I knew it was me.

I opened my door to find Lily standing there.

"I kissed a girl," she announced.

I simply blinked at her.

"And he liked it."

I stepped aside for her to enter. "Preston?"

She traipsed over to the couch and flopped herself down. "Yes, Preston."

I pulled a blanket off the back of the sofa and sat in the chair. "I thought you weren't having sex?"

"We weren't. That's the point."

"Lily, I'm just waking up. Help me out a little."

She covered her face in her hands as she spoke. "After I got off the phone with you, I went to go find Preston. It was late and he wasn't in his room. When I called him, he told me he was in the hotel bar. I went down there to find him sitting with a French woman who didn't even speak English."

I was confused. "What was he doing with her?"

"I asked him the same thing. He told me it was nothing. That he was just sitting with her. I asked why and he told me he had overheard my conversation with you and felt bad that I was feeling sexually frustrated. Well hello, I told him, he could fix it."

I grimaced.

"At least I wasn't sitting in the hotel bar staring at a dude like I might fuck him."

"Is that what he had planned?"

"No! That's when he told me he'd never cheat on me. She was for me, for us, not him. And then he asked me to kiss her."

"And you did?"

"Yes, I did, to prove a point to him. I wanted him to know I was sick of this no sex thing and if he wanted me to show him just how sick of it I was, I would. So I brought her to our room and we sat on the couch and I kissed her. Then I stood up and looked at him and asked him if I'd proven to him how much I wanted him now."

I pulled my legs up under my chin. "And he said what exactly?"

"That he wanted me to kiss her again."

The situation wasn't at all funny, but I had a hard time not laughing. It was just so unbelievable. "So what did you do?"

"Packed my stuff and left him there to stare at her as I caught the next flight back to New York City."

"Did you ever think he might have a mechanical problem and was looking for a way to . . . you know." Jeremy was standing in my bedroom doorway looking yummy, all sleepy and crumpled.

Lily's eyes shot to his. "To get it up?"

Jeremy cleared his throat. "Yeah."

She looked at him, deep in thought. "Why would he have a problem like that? He never has before."

Jeremy shrugged. "Stress, medication, I'm really not sure. I've just heard it happens."

"We have been under a lot of stress," she admitted.

Jeremy walked toward me and put his hands on my shoulders, massaging them.

I sighed and leaned forward.

"St. Claire, focus on me."

I laughed. I had really missed her. "You need to talk to him. Ask him about it."

"What if he says yes? Then what? I have sex with a girl to see if he can get off?"

"Men do like girl on girl action."

I cranked my head around. "Jeremy!" I scolded.

"I'm just being honest."

I narrowed my eyes at him. He raised his palms. "Not me of course."

Lily jumped up. "I have to run. I have to talk to Preston and find out what's going on. I'll call you," she yelled as she slammed my door.

"What if that's not the problem?" I asked Jeremy.

He plopped on the couch. "At least it will get them talking."

"That's true." I moved over to lie on top of him and then we both closed our eyes.

We woke with little time to spare before the event.

I showered while Jeremy shaved and put on my makeup while he showered. We moved around my bathroom with the synchronization of an older married couple.

I started to dry my hair while he got dressed and when I flipped my hair over, my eyes landed on him.

There he stood in a black tux with a white lapel, black shirt, and bow tie. He looked utterly dashing. My heart swelled. He was mine. He didn't have to tell me he loved me for me to feel it in my soul.

The fabric of my strapless gown was thick enough that I didn't have to wear anything beneath it. I made a show out of slipping out of my robe and pulling it up, completely naked underneath it.

Jeremy came behind me and zipped me up. "I could get used to this," he said. "But there's this little issue." He rubbed his semierect cock against me and I felt my body tingle.

I turned around to face him. "We have to go."

He pressed into me. "I know."

"Do you think too much sexual chemistry could be harmful?"

He laughed. "Are you kidding?"

"No. We're exhausted. Horny as hell. And can't go twelve hours without having to rip our clothes off."

"What's wrong with that?"

I shrugged.

"Is this what you were talking about this morning?"

"Yes, partly."

"I don't see it as a problem at all but if it will make you feel better, I'm sure I can keep my hands to myself."

I had to think about that for a minute. It was not exactly what I wanted but truthfully, I didn't know what I was after.

He smirked at me in a knowing way.

I put my hands on my hips. "Okay, prove it. Make it through the night without having to take me before we get home."

He held out his hand. "What do I get if I do?"

I shook it. "Me."

He tugged me toward me. "I think I get you either way."

"True." I smiled.

He raised a brow.

I shrugged. "Isn't that enough?"

"Always," he whispered in my ear.

Butterflies took flight in my belly. I wanted to tell him I loved him but instead said, "Now come on, we have to go. Jamie and Lindsay are waiting in the limo downstairs."

CHAPTER 22

A Sex Tape

Gotham Hall always reminded me of a Batman movie.

And as the four of us passed through the filigree brass doors and stepped onto the inlaid marble floor, it didn't disappoint. I also couldn't help but think the place looked like a casino that had been plucked right out of one of the finest hotels in Las Vegas and dropped into Gotham Hall with a little bit of intrigue that could have come from the bat cave with its dark spotlights.

Unfortunately, Cat Woman with the ruby lips wasn't far away.

"Jeremy," Avery greeted as she threw her arms around him and kissed him right on the mouth. "I just got back from Miami. The deal is done. I'm the official owner of the Ballroom." She winked. "And Nate Hanson was a dream to work with."

My stomach dropped; we had just barely crossed the threshold and she was already throwing herself at him.

It was going to be a long night.

"Phoebe," she said in turn, as she looked me up and down. "Gorgeous dress. I haven't seen that at any of the runway shows this season."

I ignored her attempted dig. I knew the dress was spectacular. "It's vintage," I said and glanced around. "And you've outdone yourself."

"I know. This is the best year yet. Wait until you see some of the things I have planned to make the evening even more exciting."

"I can hardly wait," I lied.

Jeremy tugged on my hand and moved us forward toward her brother.

I itched to wipe her lipstick from his mouth but I kept my hands at my sides.

Then I heard Avery say, "James, I haven't seen you in so long. What happened to your hair?"

I could tell she didn't care for it. It was too bad he didn't shave his head when she was pursuing him.

"It was time for a change," was his clipped response.

I wished I could have seen her face.

"Mitzi," she exclaimed. "You look lovely. Is that VS?"

"It's Lindsay," Jamie corrected.

And really, Avery knew her name as well as she knew she wasn't wearing something from the Victoria's Secret catalog.

"It's Cavalli," Lindsay's meek voice responded.

"Of course, I saw it on the rack at Bergdorf's. I completely forgot."

I rolled my eyes. I would have to tell Lindsay to ignore Avery's jabs because they never stopped. And besides, Lindsay's dress was spectacular and couldn't be worn by anyone that wasn't at least five ten. It was a long, black halter dress with a plunging neckline and a foil print of a peacock spread across the entire skirt. She looked amazing.

Jeremy was talking to Theo when Jamie whispered in my ear. "Meet us in the bar. I've had enough of the greetings."

I was certain it was because Emmy was standing beside Theo and Jamie just didn't want to upset Lindsay any further.

"Be there shortly," I said and squeezed Lindsay's hand before I turned back to Theo, who was as charming as ever as he talked about his latest mission trip.

"Hi, Phoebe," Emmy said, coming to stand next to me. Maybe now that she had let Jamie go, any resentment she had been feeling toward me was gone too. "I have something to confess."

"If it's about Jeremy and that summer, I already know."

Tears welled in her eyes. "I'm so sorry."

I shook my head. "It wasn't your fault."

She took a deep breath before continuing, "I'm glad you understand. I'd never do anything to hurt you."

"I know."

"I'm leaving for California right after Christmas. I got a part on a CBS pilot."

I hugged her. "That's awesome. Congratulations!"

"Emmy." Avery's cool voice interrupted us. "This is my best friend Beatrice. I think the two of you know each other."

I mouthed "call me" and turned my attention back to Jeremy who was just saying his good-byes to Theo.

Once Jeremy and I were alone, the first thing I did was rub my fingers over his lips and erase any traces of Avery from his mouth, then I kissed him, hard.

He pulled back with a raised brow.

I simply shrugged and asked, "What was Avery talking about earlier?"

He looked at me cautiously.

"In Miami?"

"I brokered a deal for her to buy a club that I used to own."

I pursed my lips. "Why? You still own Jet Set Miami. Why would you sell one of your clubs to her?"

I could hear that I sounded bitter and didn't like it.

He kissed my forehead. "It wasn't mine. I sold it over a year ago and the guy I sold it to was looking to get rid of it."

That just didn't make sense. "Why?"

He ran a hand through his hair. "Do you really want to know?"

"Yes," I said sternly.

"The Ballroom is a front for a sex club known as the Estate."

My mouth dropped. "Sex club?"

He nodded. "I really don't want to get into it here but when I first started my business in Miami, I ran a bunch of underground clubs and then invested in sex clubs. It was a way to make a fuck load of money—fast."

I didn't know what to say.

"Once I had enough cash, I wanted to go legit, so I sold everything that wasn't legal."

"How did Avery even know about it?"

He looked around. "Theo told her. Theo and Danny used to meet up there."

Well, I knew Theo had a thing for Danny. I didn't know it was reciprocated. But I did know Theo wasn't out and was never going to be while his mother was alive. Hence, the Emmy front.

"Why did she want to own a place like that?"

"I never asked."

Before I could ask any more questions, Jamie tapped Jeremy on the shoulder. "High-stakes tables are downstairs. What do you say?"

"Let's do it."

We took the elevator down to the ground level. The venue had once been a bank and the vault was the perfect backdrop for the high-stakes games.

It was a small room but there was a table with two empty seats. Jamie took one and Jeremy looked over at me. "Do you want to play?"

I looked at the giant stack of hundred-dollar bills Jamie was cashing in for chips. "No, go ahead."

"If you change your mind, let me know."

"Drinks?" a cocktail waitress asked.

"A scotch, neat," Jamie said as he lined his chips up in front of him.

She looked toward Jeremy, who was cashing in an equally large stack of hundred-dollar bills. "I'll have the same. And a pinot grigio for the lady." He nodded toward me. "And Lindsay, what would you like?"

Jamie turned. "Sorry baby, I was preoccupied." He looked at the waitress. "She'll have a merlot."

Lindsay and I exchanged glances and started giggling. The men had already turned back around.

"Damsels in distress are incapable of ordering for themselves," I whispered to her.

"I guess we should be flattered that chivalry isn't dead," she laughed.

Jamie rubbed his hands together. "Let's do this."

Frank Sinatra played from the speakers above us as initial bets were placed on the table and the poker game began.

The dealer's hands were flying around the table as she pushed chips and flipped cards. By the time our second round of drinks arrived, I was lost. Everything was moving too fast and I didn't really understand poker.

The player next to Jeremy stood up. "I'm out."

He'd lost all his money and Jeremy's stack was dwindling. Jamie's looked about the same.

There had to be over a hundred thousand dollars at stake and suddenly I had to get away from the table. I bumped into Lindsay, who was intently watching Jamie's every move, as I stood. "Shall we go back upstairs and walk around? They have blackjack up there."

"Do you mind?" she asked Jamie.

He turned his head slightly. "Mind what, baby?"

"If I go upstairs with Phoebe."

He handed her some chips. "Sure, go have fun."

"I'm going upstairs," I told Jeremy.

The hand had just ended and he turned around. "You okay?"

I nodded. Sure I was a little irked about the Miami thing, but I was getting over it and losing tens of thousands of dollars in less than an hour made me nervous. But it wasn't my money and I knew I shouldn't be concerned about it.

"You in?" Jamie barked.

"I'll sit this one out," Jeremy said, then pulled me to his mouth, kissing me. He turned and handed me half the chips he had left. "Maybe you'll have better luck than me."

"You don't have to give me money."

"No, I don't have to, but I want to."

I kissed him to thank him for his chivalry.

"Come on man, get your head back in the game," Jamie barked.

"We won't be long." I kissed him one last time.

"Is everyone having fun?" Avery took a seat next to Jeremy before I had taken even one step away.

I froze.

"Do you want to stay?" Lindsay asked me.

I didn't turn back. I had to trust him. "No, come on. Let's go have some of our own fun."

As we exited the elevator, Hunter was talking to Logan. "Hunter, Logan," I said, happy to see them both. "This is Lindsay, Jamie's wife."

It still sounded weird to say.

Hunter was Logan's father's brother, but Logan's wealth came from his mother's side, not his father. He'd moved to the city shortly after Logan had. Sean, Hunter's brother and Logan's father, had stayed in Boston.

"Phoebe," Hunter said. "Mind if I have a word with you for a moment."

"Sure, I'll be right back," I told Lindsay.

We stepped aside. "What is it?"

"I went to the office this morning and with the downtime between funding and construction, I looked into the condo in Florida. TSC has paid the mortgage for more than twenty-five years for a woman named Hanna Truman."

Truman? I couldn't place the name. "Do you know who she is?"

"I really think you should discuss this with your father. If we do have to declare bankruptcy, we need to know what to do with the holding."

"Hunter, if you know something. . . . Tell me."

He shook his head. "It's not my business as this has nothing to do with TSC. Talk to your father. And there's something else. About five years ago there was a donation made to Stanford University for fifty thousand dollars but no evidence that it was actually a donation."

Stanford. That's where Jeremy went. Why would my father have donated to the place Jeremy wanted to attend graduate school?

All kinds of alarms were going off in my head. I felt like I might be sick. "Excuse me please, I need to use the ladies' room."

I fled to the restroom near the mezzanine in hopes it would be quiet in there. Once I reached it, I locked myself in the very last stall and sat on the red velvet chaise. As I tried to calm my shaking body, I reminded myself that my father had never known anything about Jeremy and me. It must have been a coincidence that a donation was made the same summer I met him.

And it had to be a coincidence that Jeremy's fallen scholarship had been reinstated.

It had to be.

The alternative explanation was just too cruel.

"Oh Beatrice, he won't stay with her long." It was Avery's voice.

Who were they talking about?

"I'm not so sure. They seemed genuinely interested in each other."

"Is anyone in here?" Avery called.

I held my breath and pulled my feet up closer to me. Then I heard a click, like she was locking the main door.

"Let me show you something. But you can't breathe a word of it to anyone. He doesn't know I taped us."

"Of course."

There was silence.

"Get yourself wet for me." The voice was deep and husky.

It was *him.*

Using familiar, intimate words.

Oh God, I felt cold.

Hot.

Sickened.

Did he ask all his fucks to do that?

There was a knife twisting in my gut.

Jeremy's voice came from what I could only assume was a video—I knew then Avery had been talking about Jeremy and me.

"I can do more than that." It was Avery.

"It's so dark. Are you in your limo?" Beatrice asked over the sound of muffled voices that must have been coming from the playing video.

"Yes, he couldn't wait to have me. We were in the Hamptons at 1 Oak and we went out to the limo while everyone else stayed and partied. Just watch. You'll see why I think she's just a minor distraction."

"Oh. My. God. Are you touching yourself while he watches across the seat?" Beatrice asked.

"Yes, isn't that the hottest thing," Avery responded.

The knife moved to my heart and poked small holes in it.

There was the sound of heavy breathing and what might have been a zipper. "Come here." It was Jeremy's voice and it was extremely slurred.

I seriously thought I might have to jump up and puke but my need to hear what else was on the video overtook everything.

"Oh Avery, he's seriously hot but he didn't even take his clothes off."

"I know. That's how much he wanted me."

She had a warped sense of lust.

There was silence again and sounds that I knew weren't from Jeremy. "Oh, ohh, ohhh. Oh God. Oh, ohh, ohh, oh God. That's it. That's it. I'm coming. I'm coming."

She was so faking it. I think it was the same monologue from *When Harry Met Sally.* I didn't have to see her phone screen to know. I wondered if she'd ever had a real orgasm in her life. Jeremy must have known she was faking it. But I guessed he didn't care. That made me feel better—but not much.

"What are you whispering in his ear?" Beatrice asked. "I can't hear."

"I told him I wanted to suck him off. He was so into me, that even after I came, he was still hard."

Right, I thought.

"Do it," the slurred voice commanded.

"Holy shit, look at his face," Beatrice said.

"He's into me, right?"

"God yes. If a man looks like that when you have your mouth on him, I might have to do that to Tim tonight."

"You've never sucked your husband off?"

"God no. Not sober anyway. Now shhh."

"Fuck, that's it. Don't stop. Don't stop. Fuckkkkk yes." It was Jeremy and he was coming.

I closed my eyes as bile rose up my throat.

"Avery, he's seriously into you and seriously hot. Oh my God, is he pushing your head down?"

"Yes, he was guiding me. I loved it."

"That's it?" she asked.

"Yes, we were done and had to get back in." She sounded indignant.

"But he just zipped up his fly and got out—you didn't even kiss."

"That's what makes it so hot," Avery insisted.

"Yes, I guess." Beatrice didn't sound convinced.

"I'll share another secret with you."

"What? Tell me," Beatrice squealed.

"I just bought—"

There was a light tapping on the main door. "Phoebe, are you in there?" It was Lindsay.

Oh God. I was so busted.

I heard the click of the lock. "No, it's just us girls," said Avery. "But feel free to use the facilities. We have the scavenger hunt to announce."

"Toodles," Beatrice said.

I heard the door close and fell back. Had Lily been right about them?

"Phoebe. Are you in here?"

I peeked under the stall to make sure they were gone before I opened my door and stumbled out. My shock must have registered on my face.

"You look terrible. What happened?"

I couldn't speak.

"Why were you locked in here with Avery and that other girl?"

I ran back into the plush stall and kneeled near the toilet, where I promptly dropped my head, throwing up everything I had eaten and drunk and then dry heaving just for good measure.

"Are you okay?" Lindsay asked, handing me one of the rolled-up washcloths from next to the sink.

I sat back down on the chaise. My knees were wobbling. "I was in here when they came in. I didn't announce myself and because of my stupidity, I had to listen to something I wish I could unhear."

She wet a cloth and handed it to me. "What? What did they say?"

I shook my head, unable to even think about it.

"Oh Phoebe. She's evil. Pure evil. You can't believe anything she says."

"It wasn't what she said," I replied, snapping out of my daze.

"What was it? Tell me."

I wanted to tell her but wasn't sure even in my own head what I thought about everything. I looked at her. "I'm sorry. I can't right now. I have to go."

She walked toward the door. "Okay. Stay here and I'll get Jeremy for you."

I stood up and rinsed my mouth. "No, I need some time alone."

Her eyes filled bright with concern. "Are you sure?"

I stared at her. I had a sinking sensation that I was in trouble and I couldn't shake it. "I can't talk about it. I just have to go."

Hanna Truman.

Fifty thousand dollars.

Stanford. Stanford, the same college Jeremy had lost his scholarship to but then suddenly was able to get it back.

Was it extortion?

But for what?

And by whom?

As my hand gripped the door, an image of the name Truman presented itself on the unopened letter in Jeremy's kitchen. Not Hanna though, the initial on the envelope was J, not H. Were they related?

"What should I tell Jeremy?"

I opened the main door. "Tell him I have some things to work out and that I'll call him in the morning."

She scrunched her face.

I didn't know how he would react but I knew I had to figure things out before I could talk to Jeremy.

Too much had come to light.

I hurried through the drunken crowd and when the sign at coat check read BE BACK IN FIVE MINUTES, I went in and grabbed my own coat.

It was chilly outside as I wrapped the leather around me and walked up Broadway with no destination in mind. Just as I crossed West Thirty-eighth Street, my cell started ringing in my purse. I opened the flap and pulled it out to turn it off without even looking at who it was, and that's when I saw my father's apartment keys that I'd tucked inside last night before I left work.

With a destination in mind, I walked faster, ignoring my feet that were beginning to ache from my four-inch Jimmy Choos.

The closer I got to Times Square, the more crowded the sidewalks became. People were pushing and shoving but I was in a daze. Moving through them with purpose, I got to Seventh Avenue and was crossing the street before I realized I couldn't feel my feet. Not only were they aching, but they were also cold. And that wasn't all that was cold. I'd gone without undergarments or hose and the cool wind was flapping up my dress.

The sculpted waves on the far wall alerted me I'd hit the lobby. I kept my head down and hurried toward the elevators, not wanting to be recognized. Luckily, it was late enough that a crowd had emerged in the lounge area. I hit the UP button and as soon as I stepped in the elevator, I hit the CLOSE DOOR button and held it while I pushed the key card into the slot that would allow me to ride to the penthouse without stopping.

When the doors opened, I was surprised at what I saw. I had been envisioning black leather and steel—a modern fuckpad. But what was before me was warm and inviting. There was a step down into a large seating area where two large brown leather sofas were positioned in the middle of the room. There was a fireplace, and a desk near it. When I turned my head, I caught sight of a gourmet kitchen. I walked down the first hallway, which led me to a huge two-story library. A large flat screen on one wall and floor-to-ceiling bookcases on the other. A large cushioned chair faced the TV. This must have been where my father spent a lot of his time. I wondered just how much.

When I was growing up, he was rarely home before I went to bed and always gone before I got up—now I wondered if he'd ever come home.

I went back out to the main room and down the hallway beside the kitchen. There were three completely empty bedrooms and a hall bathroom. The bathroom was stocked with hotel toiletries and towels.

All that was left to explore was the large staircase. I climbed it slowly. Visions of a version of the Red Room of Pain horrified me. When I reached the top, the first room was a modestly furnished gym. The room at the end of the hall was the master bedroom. Just like the living space, it was warm and inviting. No sign of women or anything but a comfortable place to sleep.

This must have been his escape.

I wasn't naive though. I knew he'd had many other women in his life. I'd learned that for the first time the night my mother was arrested and we couldn't find my father. But then again, they'd both stepped outside their marriage.

My mother had yet to visit my father in prison, but I knew she wouldn't divorce him. Through everything, they had maintained a bond. It wasn't deep, can't keep their hands off each other love, but it was their own kind of love—and it worked for them.

I went into the bathroom and found a hotel robe. Then I stripped out of my dress and wrapped the robe around me before heading back downstairs and into the kitchen. I opened up the cupboards until I found the tea packets I knew would be there when I saw the teakettle that sat on the stovetop. I filled it up with water and turned it on. My father was a tea drinker. Never drank coffee. Hated it. Tea and bourbon—his drinks of choice.

I had a sudden longing to talk to my father that I hadn't felt since his arrest. I hadn't realized how much I missed him but he would be gone for another year and I had to stand strong.

With a deep breath, I walked over to the fireplace and hit the switch to turn it on. I stood there, warming myself, until the teapot whistled.

Once I fixed my tea with two sugars, I went over to the computer on the desk and turned it on. Going to Google, I typed in Hanna Truman Miami. What came up was nothing that would give me any clues. I got a Facebook page, but that Hanna Truman was twenty. I got a link to a YouTube video for a college experiment at Miami University. And a 1940 Census link to a woman who was eighty the year the census was recorded.

I searched again, that time without Miami, and got a slew of articles on a British sailor who had won a silver medal in the 2012 Olympics. I highly doubted she was the Hanna Truman for whom my father had bought a condo in Miami.

Trying something different, I switched to J Truman. J Truman was a manufacturer of brown bags and there were many articles on the company's meticulous attention to detail over the years. J Truman was also a jazz musician in the age of prohibition. There were about a dozen other J Trumans—none of whom were still alive.

With a sigh, I sipped my tea and went to sit on the couch. It was almost eleven and I knew everyone had to be worried about me.

I took out my phone and turned it on. Jeremy had called over twenty times. Jamie had called almost equally as many times.

I sent them both the same text.

Me: I'm fine. I'm sorry I took off. I just need some time alone. I'll be in touch tomorrow.

I turned my phone off immediately after sending the messages and went back over to the desk. My hand hovered over the phone. Then without any more thought, I picked it up and dialed nine plus the number.

"Hello." Dawson sounded like he might have been asleep.

"Oh God, did I wake you?"

"Phoebe?"

"Yes, it's me. I can call you back tomorrow though."

"No, it's fine. I was just reading. What's wrong?"

"I need your help finding out some information about two individuals named Hanna Truman and J Truman."

Dawson had all kinds of connections to people I didn't. And I knew if anyone could help me, he could.

"Yeah, sure, of course. What else do you have?"

"Not much. Just that a Hanna Truman owns a condo in Miami that TSC has paid the mortgage on for years."

"I'll get someone on it. Where are you?"

"I'm at my father's apartment at the Saint in Times Square."

He stayed silent.

I knew he was wondering just as I had—why did my father have an apartment and was it his fuckpad?

"Where in the hotel?"

"It's the penthouse level."

"I'll be right there."

"No, Dawson, I don't think that's a good idea."

"It's either me or I'm calling your mother. I don't want you alone."

I sighed. "Fine."

"Do you need anything?"

I paused, questioning the decision to let him come over but I decided we'd been friends before lovers and I needed a friend right now. "Do you think you could borrow something comfortable from your sister for me to wear?"

He laughed. "That, I can do."

"Okay, I'll call down to the front desk and tell them to give you a key."

"See you shortly," he said.

I knew I was playing with fire, but he was my only hope for answers. And I couldn't help but feel that I might have already been burned.

CHAPTER 23

Red Lips

I kept replaying what I heard in the bathroom over and over in my mind, adding my own images to the sound to the point where I was starting to feel a little perverted.

That's what I did though.

Play.

Rewind.

Pause.

Forward.

Pause.

Play.

In my mind the camera was zooming in on Avery's glossy red lips as she said, "I want to suck you off."

I wanted to purge the entire audio from my mind—no one should be subjected to a sex tape of his or her lover when they aren't the costar. But I kept hitting rewind in my mind, trying to catch a glimpse of Jeremy's face. I couldn't picture him at all, only her. And the image was entirely too vivid.

"Hey, are you okay?" It was Dawson standing at the edge of the foyer, staring down at me.

I stood up from the couch and set my cold tea down. "Yes, you know me, I'm strong."

I was kidding of course.

"You are."

I laughed at that.

He set down the bags he had in his hands and strode toward me. "You are strong. With everything you've been through with your dad, most women would have crumbled, but not you."

I gave him a slight smile. "You always see the good."

"In you I do."

I averted my face from his stare.

"I brought food. Sushi. I figured you probably hadn't eaten."

I eyed the bag and knew it was from Ayama. "Fried apple sticks?"

"Do you think I could order from the best sushi takeout around and not get your favorite?"

I went into the kitchen and found some plates and brought them out.

Dawson was already opening the bag.

I kneeled and helped him set everything out on the coffee table that sat between the two large sofas. My mouth watered when I saw the buffalo tuna sashimi and I realized just how hungry I was.

Dawson was watching me intently.

When I removed the large tin container that I knew was his, I lifted it up and down. "Wasabi beef?"

"Close." He grinned. "Red curry duck."

I shoved his arm. "That wasn't close at all."

He shrugged.

I liked to eat an array of food, so I always ordered appetizers or individual rolls. Dawson, on the other hand, always ordered a meal. Jeremy and I had never eaten sushi together, not even that summer we spent together. I knew what he looked like when he came but I didn't know if he liked sushi. I didn't know his favorite food. I didn't know very much about him, I realized.

The sexual connection was just too intense. I should have known it was too good to be true.

"Phoebe?"

I looked up, realizing I was still lifting the duck up and down. "Sorry. I'm not the best company right now."

"Does this have something to do with Jeremy?" He took the container from my hands.

"I'm not sure."

"He's bad news, you know. I don't think you should trust him."

"Can we please stop talking about him?" Even as the words left my mouth I wondered if he wasn't right.

"Sure. What's going on with the nightclubs?"

I rubbed my wooden chopsticks together. "I don't know yet. The perspectives went out last night. I hope to hear back by Friday, Monday at the latest."

The smell of curry filled the room. "Really? I didn't receive mine."

I bit into an apple. "I didn't send yours. You've done too much for me already and besides, we both know you'll only feel obligated."

He furrowed his brows. "What are you talking about? I haven't done anything."

"The donation for the ballet. It was way too generous."

The look on his face was blank. "I'm not sure what you're talking about."

"You made a donation in my name to the New York City Ballet."

He shook his head. "I'm sorry, but I didn't."

"But I texted you, and said thank you."

Dawson pulled his phone from his pocket and scrolled down the screen. Then he turned it to show it to me.

Me: I didn't tell you yesterday, but thank you so much.

Dawson: It was nothing. I'd do anything for you. Let me know when you have time for dinner this week.

Me: I will, promise

I stared at it. I guess I wasn't clear.

Dawson looked embarrassed. "I thought you meant something else."

Now I was the embarrassed one.

"Well, anyway, I wouldn't feel obligated, so I'd still like a copy of your proposal. I'm really interested. . . ."

I nodded as he talked, realizing it must have been Jeremy who had donated the money. Why would he do that if his intentions weren't real?

God, I was just so confused.

With a mouth full of food, I tried to figure Jeremy out.

I set my chopsticks down as tears sprang into my eyes. Those actions weren't from someone who had somehow managed to blackmail my father into a large Stanford donation so he could attend school there.

"Hey, don't cry. We'll figure out who J and Hanna Truman are. I'm here for you, just like I always have been."

I hadn't even realized Dawson had moved closer.

"You need to stay away from Jeremy. He's not good for you. He's like an addiction that you can't seem to break."

I narrowed my eyes at him. "He's not."

"Come on, Phoebe. He is. Have you forgotten the state you were in when we met?"

I shook my head. Like I ever could. It was the same day I let Jeremy go.

Snow fell all around me.

I watched it fall, mesmerized.

My friends and I had come here many times; it was our gathering place as kids. But tonight, the roofless old fort on the northwestern edge of Central Park looked magical. I took my shoes off and climbed the frozen concrete stairs. The flimsy railing lent such a sexy air of danger to the place, it caused my pulse to race. My toes were cold, but I'd drunk enough that my body was numb to any feelings. When I reached the top, I looked down at the steep drop and saw nothing but darkness.

It looked like I felt.

Empty.

Alone.

Lost.

Barefoot, I walked to the edge and stood with my arms out to my sides, letting the wind and snow cascade around me. My dress ruffled in the breeze and suddenly I felt free. Free to face the world from where I stood. Free to move forward. Free to leave the past behind. Free to let him go.

If only it was that easy.

"Hey, what are you doing up there?" I looked down to see a handsome man's concerned face gazing up at me. It was the first time since him that I had noticed any guy's looks.

I stared at the handsome stranger for the longest time before I stepped back, uncertain as to what I was doing up there. The alcohol I drank at the party had gotten to me and I wasn't thinking clearly. For that one brief moment before he spoke, I really thought I had wings and could fly free like a butterfly.

I was always seeking freedom. But freedom from what? I'd lost sight of what I was trying to escape.

The guy held his hand out. "I'm Dawson. Let me help you down."

He didn't have to remind me. I'd fought worries every day since Jeremy came back into my life of those same demons returning. But I was younger then, and much more naive. I wasn't the same person anymore. Dawson knew that. He'd even admitted it. I'd been through a lot and come out stronger. I didn't know who I was back then. I was a lost girl searching for a different life instead of taking charge of my own.

"Let me help you. Let me make sure of it," he whispered.

Worry plagued me. Was I headed down that same road?

Dawson's mouth was at my ear and his arms were around me before I realized it. "Don't cry." In the blink of an eye, cool, tender lips touched mine as he kissed me. I didn't kiss him back, but I didn't move away either.

"Lean on me. Let me help you," he whispered.

I did find a familiar comfort as he held me, and for a moment I let him in. But when he tried to lay me down on the carpet, something clicked. This was wrong. I didn't want to be with him. I turned my head. "Dawson, no!"

His lips found mine again and moved faster. I bit down on his lower one until I tasted blood but all he did was push himself on top of me and reach inside my robe.

I shoved him harder and when he didn't move, I did the only thing I could think of and scratched my nails down his face. "Dawson, stop it," I yelled.

Finally, he pulled himself back and jumped to his feet. "Oh God, I'm so sorry, Phoebe. I don't know what got into me. I'm so sorry."

I knew he would never hurt me but still, I was shaken. My body was trembling.

Blood was dripping from his lip and one of his cheeks. I ran to the kitchen and wet a paper towel. When I returned, he was sitting on the couch and rubbing his palms on his slacks.

"Dawson," I said softly as I handed him the paper towel.

His eyes were filled with regret when he looked up at me. "I'm so sorry. I have no idea what I was doing. I just miss you so much."

I pulled the tie tighter on my robe. "You should go."

"No, I'm not leaving you alone. You know that wasn't me. I won't touch you again. I promise. But let me stay with you. You shouldn't be alone."

I knew he was worried I'd fall into my old ways—drinking, partying, reckless behavior. The same way I had been when he first met me six months after Jeremy abandoned me.

I was worried too.

"Okay," I said and grabbed the other bag he had brought. "I'll just change and be back down."

I didn't wait for a response as I ran up the stairs with my heart pounding.

I knew he was someone I could trust and I didn't want things to be weird between us. That's why I let him stay, even though I knew he shouldn't.

Once I'd changed and calmed myself down, I went back down. Dawson was sitting on the couch, staring out the window. The bleeding had stopped but he had a scratch mark on each cheek and a puffy lip. I didn't feel bad, but I felt a little to blame. I had to watch my own body language around him. Make sure I wasn't giving false hope.

Things were over.

They had been over.

I had ended our relationship some time ago. But he was still hoping for a reconciliation I knew would never come, and honestly, I thought so did he. I knew he should probably leave, but I didn't have the heart to make him. So instead I grabbed the remote. "How about some TV?"

He nodded.

I sat on the sofa across from him and pulled the blanket off the back of it before I picked up my plate of tuna and picked at it. We didn't say anything else as we watched *Saturday Night Live*.

I was utterly exhausted.

CHAPTER 24

Revelations

The sound of the elevator dinging startled me.

As soon as I opened my eyes I saw the light that poured into the room. I must have fallen asleep watching TV.

"Phoebe." My mother's voice made me panic.

I quickly scanned the room searching for Dawson. He wasn't on the opposite couch. *Perhaps he'd left?* In true Dawson fashion, most of the dishes were cleaned up, as were the takeout containers.

I sat up. "Mom, what—"

I froze.

All of the air whooshed from my lungs when I saw she wasn't alone. Jeremy was standing beside her and he looked like he hadn't slept. His hair was more rumpled than usual, he hadn't shaved, and he was still wearing his tux pants and shirt from last night. Even in his haphazard state he was a delicious sight. Yet, the longer I stared, I could see he wore a blank look on his face and that concerned me. My concern began to mount with each stride he took. As he crossed the room his face seemed to morph with a mixture of warmth and anguish. I didn't understand what was going on. My heart was beating wildly by the time he knelt beside me.

Jeremy took my hand. "I'm so sorry. I should have told you. I wanted to tell you so many times but I could never seem to get the words out."

I jerked my hand away as I felt the floor shift beneath me. Everything about those words scared me. Was he referring to Avery or something else— something much worse? "What are you talking about?" I somehow managed to ask.

"Phoebe honey, hear Jeremy out." It was Mother. I'd forgotten about her.

I flicked my gaze toward where she sat on the opposite couch in her perfectly tailored slacks and finely knit sweater. "What are you doing here?"

Looking distraught she answered, "Hunter called me and told me everything he shared with you last night."

I bristled, not realizing they were in contact. "Still, how did you know I was here?"

She blanched and I knew this couldn't be easy for her. "When I met with Hunter this week, I asked him about the status of your father's apartments. He was surprised I knew and told me you were making plans to utilize them for a new project."

"You met with Hunter?" The breath rushed out of me.

She nodded. "I do every quarter to review our finances."

Surprised, I sat there feeling lost. "I had no idea."

Her voice strong, she responded, "I've been meeting with the CFO for years."

I nodded. It made sense.

"Phoebe, Jamie and Jeremy showed up early this morning telling me they'd looked everywhere for you—Lily's, Mrs. Bardot's, Emmy's, your office, and couldn't find you. Worried, I called the hotel to see if anyone was up here and the front desk told me you were."

"You knew about this place?" I asked, shocked.

She nodded and tears leaked from her eyes. "Yes, honey. I've known about your father's apartments for a long time."

I was confused. My eyes shifted between Jeremy and my mother but ultimately, my attention landed on Jeremy. "What's going on? Why are you here with my mother?"

He took my hand again and this time I didn't pull it away. I couldn't. Warmth flooded my veins and I knew then whatever web of malice I had conjured up in my head about this thing between us, was just that, something I had contrived in trying to make sense of the circumstances. But as I looked into his intense blue eyes, I knew it wasn't the truth.

What we had was real.

He caressed my hand with his fingertips. "Promise me you'll listen to what I have to say before you react."

My eyes dropped to our joined hands as my confusion over what Jeremy and my mother were doing here together turned into dread.

"There's no easy way to say this, so I'm just going to say it. Hanna Truman is my mother."

My gaze found his troubled one. Tension coiled tighter and tighter in my belly, as my world seemed to be falling apart around me.

Oh God.

My vision started to blur. Had my father been hiding his mistress for all these years? Was Jeremy my brother? I slapped my hand over my mouth. "Oh God," I said out loud this time.

Oblivious to my turmoil, Jeremy continued, "And Justin Truman is my father."

Justin Truman.

J Truman.

Relief.

More relief.

I could breathe at least.

Then realization dawned.

I knew that name.

My eyes darted to my mother, then back to Jeremy.

Bars of early morning sunlight stripped across his face. "My father is the man who orchestrated the first insider trading scandal your father was involved with. Since I was so young when it happened, my mother thought it would be better for me if she divorced my father and changed our last names to her maiden name. There was so much backlash from the trial, she didn't want me to suffer for my father's mistakes."

I swallowed bitterly at the reasoning behind his hatred all those years ago for anyone who had money as I just stared at him, trying to process what he had said. "Why didn't you ever tell me?"

He squeezed my hand, his eyes full of despair. "I don't know. It wasn't something I was proud of. I never thought about him. I hated him and didn't want anything to do with him. He wasn't in my life and I left it like that."

My mother spoke up. "Phoebe honey, your father is the one who turned evidence against Justin Truman to save himself."

I yanked my hand away from his. "That's why you hated my father so much?"

He flinched but nodded in concurrence.

Looking into his grief-stricken face I asked, "So what changed?"

He hesitated. "I'm not really sure. I guess I matured and accepted my father's sins were his own."

Confusion clouded things and I fought off the anger. I could accept the fact that he hadn't told me that summer; after all, I had lied about who I was. "Why, after you knew who I was, wouldn't you have told me everything when we first got back together?"

"It hasn't been that long," he countered.

"Long enough to tell me we were connected in some deep-seated way," I replied tightly.

"I was going to tell you, when I thought the time was right and you could handle it."

Aghast, I couldn't believe he thought I was that weak. "So while you waited, you lied."

His sigh turned harsh. "No, I didn't."

"Yes. You. Did." My words were sharp like glass. While he was trying to stay calm, I could see he was struggling. His brooding side was peeking through and making an appearance. I, on the other hand, didn't try to suppress mine.

The muscles in his jaw twitched. "I just hadn't told you yet; that's not lying."

His words stung. I had lied. Told him my last name was Saint. I shoved that thought away. "Was this"—I pointed between us—"some sick game of revenge? Is that why you didn't tell me?"

He stared at me in disbelief.

"Phoebe, honey. Let us finish," my mother spoke up.

Suddenly all I could see was a haze of red. I stood and picked up one of the plates on the table and slammed it down. "Was it? Say something, Jeremy!" I shouted.

Scowling, Jeremy stood and replied tersely, "I can't believe you'd even think that."

Tears fell down my cheeks and regret shrouded me. We were both so insecure about our relationship. I had done the same to him once—lied about who I was because I was afraid he wouldn't accept me. Was that what he was doing? I could almost understand it if it was. Or was there more to it? I stared at him looking for the truth. Looking out for a lie. "I don't know what to believe anymore."

He stepped so close I could feel his breath on my neck. "Yes, you do. I know you do."

Dazed, I finally nodded. "I still don't understand. There's more to this. Why would my father have bought your mother a condo? And why did he donate fifty thousand dollars to Stanford the summer you went there?"

I wanted to believe him.

I did.

But it still didn't make sense.

Jeremy's face went utterly blank and I knew he had no idea what I was talking about.

My mother cleared her throat. "That's why I'm here, honey—to help explain some things."

My stomach jumped nervously as I slowly turned to look at her. What else was there hidden away?

She fidgeted with her necklace. "Hanna and Justin traveled in the same circles as your father and I, and over the years, Hanna and I had developed a close friendship. You could say we were best friends."

My mother had a best friend I never knew about?

"Even after she moved away, we kept in touch. Phoebe." She put her hand on my knee. "It wasn't your father who did those things. It was me."

"You?" I was in shock.

She reached into her purse and pulled out a hankie, dabbing her tears with it. "Hanna was my best friend and when her husband went to jail, her life was torn out from under her. I had to help her. Her mother was ill and losing her house, so I helped her in the only way I could."

"By throwing money at her," I spat.

"She needed help, Phoebe. Sometimes money is the only thing that can do that."

My gaze darted to Jeremy's. "Did you know about this?" Except I already knew he didn't. I could see it in his face.

"No." He seemed to have gone somewhere in his mind.

More tears clouded my vision. "What about Stanford?" I asked both of them.

Jeremy blinked a few times and appeared to become more alert and his body filled with tension as he narrowed his stare on Poppy.

Poppy closed her eyes. "Hanna called me that summer the two of you met and told me Jeremy had been talking to her about a girl he was spending time with—a Phoebe Saint. She guessed who you were and I confirmed her assumption—I'd seen the two of you together. Hanna had spent so much of her life shielding her son from the truth and she feared if the two of you stayed together, it would be made public. She didn't want that for him. So she asked me to help her one last time. She wanted Jeremy to go to California. She offered to sell her condo and pay me back. But I owed her. I owed her more than that. You know your father was not an innocent. Justin may have very well gone to prison without his testimony, but he still aided in putting him there to save himself."

The intensity of Jeremy's gaze settled on Poppy. "So you paid for me to go to grad school? I didn't receive a scholarship?" His voice was gruff and my heart bled for him.

Poppy pulled in a shaky breath. "I did, but please don't be upset."

"How could my mother have asked that of you?" he asked tightly.

"Don't be upset," she repeated. "Hanna did it for you. She only wanted what was best for you."

"Did she?" he asked bitterly. "Or what was best for her," he retorted in anger.

"No, you know that's not true," my mother soothed.

It all came together then. My mother's drunk-driving arrest had taken place at the very same time. She must have been upset about all of this.

"Hey, Phoebe, I'm going to order room service. Do you want anything?" Dawson was walking into the room with his head down.

Oh no.

Watching in horror, I saw Jeremy's features twist as he assumed the wrong thing. He jumped back, tension rolling off him in waves as he glared at me. "You've got to be fucking kidding me."

"Dawson," my mother said in surprise.

My gaze darted to Dawson, who looked way too smug for the situation we were in. Worry overtook me and when my knees started to tremble, I had to grab the arm of the sofa for support.

Silence swelled in the room as we all stared at one another.

"What happened to your face?" Poppy asked Dawson, cracking it.

Dawson cleared his throat and started striding toward me.

My throat went dry and I finally dared to steal a glance at Jeremy.

His eyes burned with fire. He had already been teetering in the face of overwhelming anger and this situation only seemed to push him over the edge. "You didn't waste any time, did you?" He glowered.

Hesitantly, I took a tentative step toward him. "It's not what you think."

"Looks like we're both using those words today." His mouth twisted with bitterness.

I ran my hands up his chest. "Jeremy, it's not. Let me explain."

He shrugged me off, and then strode past me as he headed toward the elevator.

"Jeremy," I yelled.

Dawson jerked forward. "Let him go."

"No," I barked.

He made a move as if to grab me but I held my hand out for him to stay where he was. "Be smart, Phoebe. See this for what it is," he pleaded.

I ignored him and ran after Jeremy. I caught up with him just as the door opened. "Jeremy. Please. Listen to me," I pleaded.

Jeremy glared at me with that same flat stare he had done the morning I woke up in his bed. "I'm done listening to you and done trying to explain."

The doors started to close and something inside me told me this time, I had to fight for him. I stopped the doors with my hand and stepped in. He just stared at me with those intense, cold eyes. I knew the demeanor well. I had experienced it from him before.

I stepped closer. "I'm not letting you walk away from us."

"Good thing it's not your choice." His voice was cold as ice.

At that moment, I had to wonder if his heart was too.

I frowned at the chilliness pouring out of him. "Jeremy, just listen to me. Dawson only came over to help me."

His hand hovered over the buttons. "Get out now or take a ride down. It's up to you. I really don't fucking care."

I moved to the back of the car. Resolute.

I wasn't going anywhere.

"Suit yourself." He pressed the L button and leaned against the wall. Everything about him was hard.

It would have scared me if I hadn't seen it before. It was his coping mechanism. My response had always been to flee, but no more. I was going to stand and face his wrath and make him talk to me. I didn't care. I spoke to his back. "Jeremy." My voice was soft and when he didn't acknowledge that I'd spoken I continued on anyway. "We have to find a way to learn to trust each other."

He was clearly pissed off.

But I was determined. "We have to stop this poisonous reaction to things that aren't what they appear."

Jeremy dropped his head, still ignoring me as the elevator descended.

Uncertainty roared in my head. I was worried I wouldn't be able to get through to him in time. "I know you're mad but so am I."

"You're mad because I didn't tell you my father was a criminal who ruined people's lives?"

"No, that is not what I'm upset about."

He stood silent, acting like he didn't care.

It hurt me to even give voice to my thoughts, much less think about it anymore but I knew I had to do this. "So much happened last night—the information about the condo, learning that it was owned by a Hanna Truman when I saw a return address with the same last name in your mail, and then finding out about the money to Stanford—and I needed some time to think."

Unhappiness radiated from him. "Yeah, believe it or not I figured that much out for myself," he practically growled.

I held my breath, I was worried he just didn't care and I had to find out. A moment or two of silence passed until I let out a much needed exhale. "But that's not the only reason I left. After I talked to Hunter, I took refuge in the bathroom. I wanted to clear my head before I saw you and somehow I ended up getting locked in a stall listening to a tape of you and Avery Lake having sex."

He visibly cringed and I knew if he hadn't been listening before, he was now.

The trembling spread throughout my entire body. "I had to sit there and listen to the sounds you made when you came with another woman. Do you have any idea how that made me feel?"

He turned, his anger seemingly depleted. "I'm sorry about that, Phoebe."

I chewed my lip in contemplation, not certain I should go on.

Jeremy took a tentative step toward me but perhaps feeling the same uncertainty, he stopped and pressed his back against the side of the elevator car, not daring to get too close. "I didn't know she taped us."

Anger flared within me as I relived the poignant picture I had created in my head. "I hated everything about it, from the fact that you couldn't wait to have her, to the fact that you were in a car in the Hamptons, our place. *Ours*. But do you want to know what hurt the most?"

His eyes filled with tenderness and I could see the anguish on his face.

I didn't wait for him to respond. "It was the way you told her to do the same things you told me to do just last night."

He cut me off. "It's not like that. I was so drunk, I don't remember much about that night but—"

I put a hand up. "Let me finish."

He nodded, shoving his hands in his pockets.

At least we were communicating.

That was good.

"But listening to it helped me realize she couldn't have meant that much to you."

He propped a foot against the wall. "She didn't. She doesn't. I keep telling you that."

I looked into his eyes. "I didn't tell you that for reassurance. You had sex with someone before we got back together. I get that. And I had sex with other men before we got back together. Let's just leave it at that. But you have to know, there's nothing going on between Dawson and me. I know you know that. I called him last night to help me find out who the Trumans were. I wanted to trust you, but I saw that envelope on your counter from J Truman and then when I heard the information about the condo, and the Stanford money, I just didn't know what was real anymore. I had to sort it out in my own mind before I could talk to you. I don't know if you can understand that. But everything I learned made me question your true interest in me."

He took two steps and resumed leaning again, this time against the back wall with his hip pressed to it. "Don't ever doubt that. Ever. And don't ever doubt that what we have is real."

"I can't help it. Talk to me, help me understand instead of walking away."

Jeremy's expression softened and he lifted my chin with his thumb. "I don't want to walk away from you."

I leaned into his touch. "Then don't. Tell me what you're thinking."

He pressed STOP and the car came to a halt at the same time his gaze flashed dark. "We need to get one thing straight first, Phoebe."

I held my breath and waited.

My back was to the wall before I knew it. "You're mine. And I don't share," he whispered in a guttural tone.

I realized then that we both had jealously issues. "I only want you."

His hard body pressed into mine as he pointed over his shoulder toward the elevator doors. "Whatever that was in there makes me doubt that you understand that."

"Dawson's just a friend."

Jeremy practically growled at me in response. "He's your ex-fiancé."

I caressed his cheek. "Yes, ex," I reassured him.

He threw me a doubtful look and stepped out of my reach.

"Don't, Jeremy. Don't pull away from me over something that means nothing," I pleaded.

He just stared at me with those intense blue eyes.

"Please. I called him and he came to help. That's it. There's nothing left between us."

He nodded and hit L again. As the car descended we looked at each other. Floor after floor we kept the visual connection until he cleared his throat and spoke. "My parental situation is so fucked up. I don't like to talk about it. I've barely spoken to my mother in years and I don't remember my father."

"Why don't you talk to your mother?"

Tension filled his body. "She had some odd sense of righteousness that came out of nowhere and felt the need to tell me about my father, but then refused to let me talk to him and at I first I let it go. But then, two years ago, out of the blue, she decided it was time for me to meet him."

Confused, I inched my way toward him. "Why would she want that?"

He shrugged. "Because she's fucked up in the head. Because she regrets her decision." He threw his hands up in the air. "Who the fuck knows. All I know is she went to see him and came back informing me he wanted to be a part of my life. That letter you saw from my father, he sends me one once a month. I never read them. I just throw them away."

"Why not?" I was shocked he would do that.

He looked at me like I had three eyes. "I don't want anything to do with him. He purposely stole from people and hurt them."

My heart broke for Jeremy and the tough exterior that did nothing to cover up the pain in his voice. I knew what he felt. I had been feeling it too. "He's still your father. Maybe you should . . . open them."

He shook his head. "Do you have any idea what it's like growing up thinking you were a bastard and then learning you weren't? Only to be left wondering which was actually worse? Being a bastard or knowing your mother lied to you because she was ashamed of your father?"

I moved closer and gently wrapped my arms around him. "None of that changes who you are."

The doors opened. "Doesn't it?" he said softly.

I pulled him tighter. "No, it doesn't. You're an amazing man. You're strong and kind and generous."

"I'm not." He shook his head.

"Yes, you are. I mean it. I know you donated money in my name to New York City Ballet. Who does that when the girl lied to him about who she was five years earlier if they don't have compassion?"

All he did was shrug. "We said we'd leave the past where it was."

"I know. I just wanted you to know how much I appreciate what you did."

He didn't seem to care but then he said, "I do."

"Are you going up?" an older man with a suitcase asked.

I hadn't even realized we'd reached the lobby. I nodded, not caring where the elevator went, and the man stepped in, pressing the button for the eighteenth floor. The man had his back to us and when the car started to ascend, Jeremy finally returned my embrace.

I let myself fall into him.

I breathed him in.

Relished the feel of his arms around me.

I didn't care if I lost myself or found myself in him anymore. It didn't matter. "I love you," I told him for the very first time.

He pulled back and looked at me, studying me intently before speaking. "I love you too," he whispered.

My stomach swirled with butterflies. "Do you like sushi?" I asked.

He laughed. "Once in a while, but it's not my favorite."

"What is?"

He raised a brow.

"Food," I clarified with a smirk.

"Hands down, pizza."

That hadn't changed.

The older man spoke up. "Joe's, I hope."

Jeremy grinned. "You know it."

The doors opened and the man got off the elevator. "Have a nice day," he said with a huge smile on his face.

I waved good-bye. I could tell by the way he looked at us, he must have heard our declarations.

Who cared?

Not me.

With my own huge smile, I pressed the button for the lobby. "What's your favorite color?"

Jeremy aligned his body with mine. "What's with the twenty questions?"

My pulse was racing as our bodies connected in the most perfect way. "I felt like I didn't know who you really were and it scared me. I want to know what has changed about you and what hasn't."

"Blue," he said with that smirk that melted me. "I prefer still water to sparkling, I'd rather drink beer than wine, basketball is my favorite sport to watch on TV, but I love to go to baseball games. The White Stripes is one of my favorite bands. I'm all over the map when in comes to music. I like old-school hip-hop, Sublime, Nirvana, and old rock, but despise pop. I used to love watching *The Real World*. I'm a huge James Bond fan and watch every DiCaprio movie. There was a time I was addicted to Break.com. I hate doing laundry. Oh, and my favorite place to be is anywhere near a beach."

I listened intently. Some things had changed. Some things were new. But through his words the familiarity of his voice rang true.

I knew him.

I had been focusing on his lips, those lips, from a distance long enough. Without hesitation, I got up on my toes and kissed him, sucking on his bottom lip before I stopped. "That last one I already knew, and the laundry too, that's evident. And of course the music. And the pizza. Well, actually, I knew a lot of that already."

He chuckled as he slid his lips down my neck. "See, I haven't changed that much. So does any of that change the way you feel about me?"

I threw my head back as he kissed his way down my neck. "No."

His hand went to the small of my back and drifted down.

The heat.

The need.

The want . . .

It was consuming me.

We had to work on the give and take between the two of us.

Trust.

But I knew we could.

Our gazes collided, all words gone as we looked into each other's eyes. I was ready to throw him down right there by the time the elevator doors opened again. It was early and no one was moving around the hotel yet.

No, I chastised myself.

His hands lazily moved down my body. "We'll get to know everything about one an other all over again, it just takes time. But I'm happy to do it now if you'd like."

"Later is fine." I let out a small moan at his touch.

Jeremy's hands had moved to my hips and he pulled me into him. *Oh God, his erection was a hard, thick demand.*

We were in trouble. "Jeremy?"

"Yeah," he growled.

"We have to stop." I was breathy and very unconvincing.

As if he knew what I needed, he pressed himself further into me so I could feel every square inch of him.

"We can't, not here." I pointed up. "Cameras."

"Phoebe." He looked up, then down at my bare feet. "We can't get back up there, can we?" His tone was sensual, erotic.

I knew what was on his mind.

I shook my head. "Not without the key."

"And we can't leave because you aren't wearing any shoes."

I shook my head again.

Sweetly, he held me tighter and kissed me long and slow. His warm lips on mine felt so soft as he kissed me and kissed me and kissed me, until the doors opened again.

I wasn't ready for the ride to end.

"Do you want to go for another ride?" I murmured.

He turned us and pressed me against the wall. "Absolutely," he growled and blindly pushed a button that I wished was to heaven.

I could have kissed Jeremy all day in that elevator, but it was where I worked, and my mother was waiting upstairs—with Dawson, and things were starting to get a little too hot and heavy.

We never could just kiss.

When we landed on the lobby floor again, I pulled away. "I changed my mind. I do want to spend the day learning things about each other."

Jeremy raised a highly arched brow. "Are you telling me no sex?"

I gave a little shrug. "Not a Lily and Preston thing if that's what you're thinking. But just for the day. Let's explore the city together and tell each other stupid things about what we've done or want to do or what we like."

His tongue licked up my throat. "I like the taste of you."

I shivered and I might have moaned. I was about to tell him never mind when he stopped and took my hand. "But I'll behave," he said with a wink and led me out of the elevator—that glimpse of bad boy shining through that made me weak in the knees.

As we walked to the front desk, I knew that I had to tell Jeremy about the kiss with Dawson, but thought it was best to wait. He was going to be extremely upset either way, and I felt I owed it to Dawson to wait until after he had left the apartment.

With a new key card in hand, we rode the elevator up one more time. Jeremy pulled his phone out of his pocket and handed it to me. "You should text Jamie that you're okay. He spent the night looking for you with me."

"You looked for me all night?" I took his phone.

"Yeah, I was worried about you."

Guilt festered inside me as I typed a short note to Jamie telling him I was okay and I'd call him tonight. When the elevator doors opened, Jeremy took my hand and led me back inside my father's penthouse apartment.

My mother was still sitting on the couch and still visibly shaken. Dawson was sitting nervously beside her, not saying much. He stood immediately when he saw us and focused his gaze on me. "Listen, I'm going to leave the three of you to talk. But if you need me, you know how to reach me."

Jeremy's grip on me tightened.

"I know, Dawson, and again thank you for everything."

As he stepped into the elevator, Jeremy asked, "What happened to his face?"

Poppy's sobs shifted the focus though and the question was left dangling in the air. I wanted to tell him then, but I couldn't. I just couldn't. I didn't want to ruin all the progress we'd made.

"Mom." I sat beside her and hugged her.

She hugged me back. "All I ever wanted was for you to be happy."

"I know that," I told her.

"And when I saw Jeremy was back in your life, I was afraid and happy for you."

"Is that why you pretended not to know?"

"I figured you would tell me when you were ready."

I pulled Jeremy down to sit next to me. "Mom, I know you've already met, but I want to be the one to introduce you. Jeremy, this is my very special mother—Poppy St. Claire. Mom, this is the man I love—Jeremy McQueen."

She shed more tears as she hugged me tighter and then hugged Jeremy. When she sat back down, she looked around. "Can we please get out of here? I would offer to take you out for breakfast but"—she looked me up and down—"I don't think you should be out in public."

I shook my head. Poppy was Poppy after all. Not that I disagreed with her. I had on sweats and a tee, no bra or underwear, and my Jimmy Choos my only available foot attire.

I was a mess.

"Hugh is downstairs. What do you say to letting me make the two of you breakfast?" my mother said.

I looked toward Jeremy, not for permission, but more for reassurance, I think. Technically, we were still sticking to the plan. I'd be showing him the house I grew up in.

He answered before me. "We'd love to, Mrs. St. Claire."

"Oh, call me Poppy," she said, her tears finally slowing.

He nodded at her. "We'd love to, Poppy."

I squeezed his hand, silently thanking him. I popped up. "Sounds like a plan," I said and then looked toward my mother, who was still eyeing my clothing. "But Poppy, when was the last time you used your stove?"

She laughed. "Oh darling, to you I'm Mother, not Poppy. And coffee and toast don't require use of the stove."

"That's very true, Mother. Let me go up and grab my things."

I realized I'd called my mother Poppy on and off since her little indiscretion. I think it was my way of punishing her. But until just then, she'd never said anything about it.

I wondered what had changed.

Having no idea, but wondering if easing her guilt was the reason, I hurried up the stairs to brush my teeth with the hotel spare in the medicine cabinet and wash my face with soap and water. I couldn't help but think how Poppy would cringe at what I was doing to my skin. I dried my face and ran my fingers through my hair before I picked up my dress and shoes.

When I came back down, my mother was huddled with Jeremy, who was sitting on the coffee table, holding her hand. I couldn't remember the last time I'd seen her interested in getting to know someone new. She'd closed herself off from the world after my father's arrest. Partly because she was shunned, partly because she was embarrassed, and maybe mostly because she missed my father.

I really should spend more time with her.

They looked up at me and my mother whispered to him, "Call her. She's your mother and she loves you."

I didn't ask any questions. She'd been talking to him about Hanna and it was obvious they both cared for her. Whatever advice he had sought or my mother had delivered on her own, was between them.

I shoved my feet into my four-inch heels and tried to suppress a groan. My mother hid her smirk, but I could see it. I laughed and grabbed each of their hands. "Come on. Change of plan. I think we should stop and get coffee and bagels and let Hugh drive us through the park a few times. All the leaves will be gone soon and I'd hate to miss the last of them."

"You always did love the fall," my mother said.

"See, I already knew that," Jeremy whispered in my ear.

Jeremy pulled me close and so did my mother.

Sandwiched between the two of them, I couldn't remember the last time I had felt more loved. With my mother on one side and my boyfriend on the other, I was on top of the world.

CHAPTER 25

The Art of Kissing

We had perfected the art of just kissing.

It was something we were never good at stopping at, but as the day progressed, we were starting to perfect the technique.

Jeremy and I had spent the morning out with my mother and the afternoon together—just the two of us and the city beneath our feet.

When Jeremy suggested Hugh drop each of us off at our own places, I couldn't contain my shock. I wasn't sure how I felt about that. But we showered and changed and met in the middle where we embarked on something called subway roulette. Get on at one stop, pick a number, and get off at that corresponding stop. The rule was we had to find something to do at each stop that neither of us had ever done.

We had a blast. We went to the hidden subway station beneath City Hall, we explored the whispering gallery in Grand Central, and we walked through the cemetery behind the Bowery Hotel. Around four, Jeremy asked if he could take me to Brooklyn so he could show me the neighborhood he had grown up in.

Of course I was thrilled.

We toured the area he knew so well and ate at one of his favorite restaurants. At dinner we sat and talked. "Tell me, what are your ambitions when it comes to Jet Set?" I asked him.

He dropped his gaze, as if he was shy about it.

"What?" I asked.

Light twinkled in his eyes. "To grow it, city by city, a little at a time, until there's no big city left untouched."

I smirked at him. "That's no small ambition."

"Nope. What about you? What do you want to do with TSC?"

Blowing air out between my lips, I tried not to sound as heartless as my words would come across. "I want a career, I want to be a part of something great, but I'm afraid TSC might not be it."

He looked a little surprised. "I thought you wanted to save it?"

"I do. I don't want my family's legacy to die or to be stolen out from under us. But I'll be glad when my father's back and takes the helm."

There was hint of sadness in his eyes.

"I'm okay with it though. You see, I'm temporary for this position and I know that. And when my father returns, I hope to be able to hand TSC back over to him intact. Then, who knows, maybe I can be a part of something I can help build."

He reached across the table for my hand. "You will be. I know it."

I looked at him and loved the support I saw in his eyes. He wanted for me what I wanted. It meant so much to me.

Later that evening, once the heavy conversation had faded away, I took him to see the film adaptation of my favorite book at the theater around the corner from my apartment because come on, Christian Grey was still on the big screen and he'd never read *Fifty Shades* nor had he seen the movie.

The theater was empty. We were the only people in the cinema and we were behaving—up until the part where Christian threw Anastasia over his shoulder and took her into the boathouse. The more intense the scenes got, the more petting and stroking that was taking place in our seats.

We'd started out innocently enough, holding hands, a few kisses, then Jeremy's arm went around my shoulder, and my hand floated to his thigh. We'd been good all day, but by then, I wanted him beyond a simple need.

It was an ache that went down to my core.

As the scenes got hotter on the big screen, I could feel the muscles in Jeremy's body tense.

I guess you could say, I took my boyfriend to see girl porn and he liked it.

As my fingers glided up his jeans, his hips thrust forward in a jerking motion and I knew he felt the same way I did.

Enough was enough.

But then he stopped me by grabbing on to my wrist. He leaned over, whispering into my ear. "I want you to touch me so much right now, I can't stand it. I want you on my lap, straddling me so I can bury myself deep inside you."

A shiver ran down my spine. I wanted that too. I was so done with the no sex thing.

"But not here. Not now."

I pulled my hand back. Was he rejecting me?

I had these crazy visions of us not being able to wait, of me going down on him in the dark theater, of our lust for each other too much to bear as it exploded in a passionate union.

And he was saying no.

Something had changed between us.

Saddened, I worried he didn't want me like he had.

As if reading my mind, Jeremy's lips twitched. He stood up and took my hand. "Let's go."

Okay, so maybe I was wrong.

I glanced up quickly. "But the movie isn't over."

He bent his long, lean body down. "I want you—now. And I'm not waiting for the movie to end."

Excitement pinwheeled through me as I stood up and followed him out of the theater. My stomach fluttered as I realized he had been listening to my concerns about our relationship. All the frantic fucking wasn't healthy, is what I had thought, but maybe that wasn't the case. It was the way we showed each other how much we wanted to be together. The rest, he was right, would come.

And it was.

It had been.

I just hadn't seen it.

I was too worried about the bad to see the good.

He walked fast and I walked faster to keep up, cursing the heels of my boots with each hurried step. We made it to my apartment building quickly and we were inside my apartment door even quicker.

Jeremy didn't shove me against the wall or push me down onto the couch though; instead he helped me out of my jacket and then took his off. After he hung them both, he surprised me by picking me up in a cradling position and carrying me to my bed.

I stared into his hungry eyes as he set me down.

We didn't talk.

He opened my drawer and found the lighter I kept there and proceeded to light the candles I had scattered around my room. He took his boots off and I did the same. The room stayed silent as he moved about, reaching into his pocket and retrieving his phone. He tapped the screen a few times and plugged his iPhone into one of the two glass speakers on my dresser. Soft music started to play. He turned the lights out and his beautiful silhouette was all I could see in the glow from the candlelight as he moved toward me.

My heart was pounding with anticipation and I inched my way farther up the bed. The mattress shifted just as my elbows settled on one of the pillows. My heart pounded even harder as he crawled up to me.

When he reached the pillows, he loomed over me and his gaze overtook me. His mouth was parted and those intense blue eyes were shining down on me. He leaned forward and I eased back until my head was on the pillow.

"I love you," he whispered as his hands slid to the hem of my sweater.

Goose bumps rose all over my skin.

"I love you too," I whispered back.

He slowly pulled my sweater over my head. I had opted for underwear and was wearing a sheer black bra—our game of Friday and challenge of Saturday seemed so long ago and had been abandoned after the events of last night.

I, in turn, lifted his shirt and pulled it over his head.

He hadn't kissed me yet; instead his gaze continued to burn down on me. I felt warm under his stare even though the room was a bit chilly.

Jeremy traced a shape on my bare stomach.

It was a heart.

"I'm going to marry you one day," he said softly.

My breath caught. He wasn't asking me then though, he was just letting me know his intentions. I smiled up at him. I'd never thought about us marrying but then, thinking about it, I couldn't help but melt when I thought about him calling me his wife.

I couldn't believe how much I wanted to be his wife.

That, to me, didn't sound strange at all.

His fingers trailed down and he unbuttoned my jeans. I lifted myself as he slowly slid them down to reveal the matching sheer lace thong I was wearing.

His pupils had gone dark, swallowing the blue of his eyes. And his lips were glistening from where his tongue had snuck out and licked them.

I swallowed as I felt my pulse leap.

With shaky hands, I hooked my fingers in the denim at his hips and tugged them down. He moved a little, helping me, and then took over removing them and letting them drop to the floor in a neat little pile along with our other clothes.

Our gazes never left each other's as we both breathed hard.

He rolled to his side and propped himself up on one elbow. With an easy hand, he traced the lacy edge of my bra from one side to the other.

My nipples tightened until they were hard and aching. When Jeremy's thumb caressed one over the material, I sucked in a breath.

His eyes were dark and intense as he watched me and I closed my eyes when he pushed one cup aside to expose my nipple. When I felt his lips on my exposed skin, I bit my lip to stop from moaning but my body shuddered beneath his soft touch anyway.

With precision, he reached around me and unhooked my bra, pulling my arms from it as Phil Collins played in the background.

I opened my eyes to watch when he moved back over me and slid my fingers in the waistband of his boxers.

He too had decided on underwear today.

I eased them down and he kicked them off. Those didn't land in the neat pile on the floor, but rather wherever my foot had flung them. I was driven by the need to touch him, one that didn't allow for this slow pace. He made a noise when my hand wrapped around the length of his long, thick cock. He was warm, and his skin felt like silk as I slowly stroked him.

He didn't stop me, but he did press his body closer to mine as he trailed his lips down my belly and his fingers followed, forcing me to let go of him.

Sensation overtook me as he slowly licked down the center of my panties and with a light touch, slid them down my hips.

We were both finally naked.

His mouth was on my core and I started to tremble when light flicks of his tongue entered me once, twice, three times but that was it.

He trailed his tongue up my body and that hint of stubble tickled. When he reached my mouth, he finally kissed me.

That mouth.

Those lips.

I loved them.

I loved him.

Decadently happy, I wrapped my arms around him and when I did, I could feel his muscles bunching.

Staring intently at each other, we looked into each other's eyes as he ever so slowly slid into me.

Oh God.

My head fell back and an echo of soft moans escaped my throat, he felt so amazing.

And the way his eyes blazed down at me, I knew he was feeling it all too.

When he moved, he moved slowly, with steady strokes.

In.

Out.

Up.

Down.

In.

Out.

Up.

Down.

We were in rhythm, in sync, and my clit rubbed against him with every thrust. The pressure felt good, but not enough to push me over the edge. Which was good, because I liked the tantalizing way he was making me feel.

He didn't increase his pace as we both absorbed the pleasure of making each other feel good.

He was making love to me.

For the first time in our sexual history, our union wasn't about frantic fucking with a driving need for release.

It was about him, and me, and the love we shared for each other.

There wasn't any doubt we'd always have the frantic fucking, but now I also knew we'd have this too. And if I had been feeling any ounce of reservation about our relationship, it was completely gone.

We were going to be a couple. And we were going to be happy.

My mind focused on the splendor of it all, I didn't realize what the tingling meant, until my orgasm crashed over me so fast, it overtook my entire body.

I arched my back and watched Jeremy's face contort. He'd lifted himself a little higher and his thrusts had sped up just a bit.

Warmth rippled through me.

"Jeremy," I whispered.

"Phoebe," he managed.

"Oh, Jeremy," I whispered again.

His eyes closed and his body stilled, as he let out one long exhale before his body collapsed on top of mine and he buried his head in my neck. After some time, he rolled onto his side and propped himself on his elbow again.

We stared at each other with knowing eyes. We weren't done. We weren't done by any means.

Minutes passed before Jeremy hovered over me and covered me with his body and kisses. He kissed every inch of me—from my head to my toes.

Later that night when we were finished—for the moment anyway—he pulled me to him so that my back was to his chest.

When he did, I twisted so that I could see him. "I love you."

He sounded sleepy when he replied, "I love you too. No matter what happens."

I didn't know exactly what he meant, but after everything we'd been through, I was certain he meant: If we could make it through what we had, we could make it through anything.

CHAPTER 26

No Ring

I wasn't sure what to do about Dawson, so I didn't do anything.

Days flew by and I hadn't sent the prospectus to him, nor had I called him—and I also had not told Jeremy about what had happened between us.

It was Wednesday night and Jeremy and I were meeting Jamie and Lindsay for dinner. We would be discussing their wedding celebration, which was planned to take place at Sinners at the New Year's Eve opening of the club. The problem was, the week had gone by and I hadn't heard from any of the potential investors yet, so there was a chance there would be no club.

A knock at the door pulled me from my dire thoughts.

Hunter was standing just inside my door. "I'm headed home. I just wanted to remind you I'll be out until Tuesday. I'm sorry I won't be here, but call me the minute you hear from the investors."

"I will. Take care of your father."

He nodded. "Going into the home has been a long time coming."

"Logan's still going with you, isn't he?"

"Yes, he and my father are very close. This is killing him."

I pressed my lips together as sadness swept through me for Hunter and for my friend. "Tell him I'm thinking about him."

"I will. Oh and I had the Vegas and LA apartments emptied. The hotel managers told me there were no personal items in either of them."

"And the Times Square one?"

"Just as you instructed. I haven't touched it."

I gave him a solemn nod. "I'd like to talk to my mother about it but I think it's best if we just have everything of a personal nature stored here."

"I'll take care of it on Tuesday. And one last thing I thought you should know. Hanna Truman called this afternoon and wants to buy the condo."

I stared at him. "Buy it?"

"That's what she said. The problem is, on paper she already owns it. What do you want me to do?"

I had no idea but I knew my mother's good intentions happened for a reason and I didn't want to undo them. But I also knew TSC couldn't keep paying for her mortgage, regardless of how small the monthly amount was. "Let's just have her take over the payments."

"It's almost paid for anyway."

"I know."

He nodded and closed the door.

I leaned back in my chair. It was five and Jeremy and I would be meeting Jamie and Lindsay in an hour. I should probably tell Jeremy his mother called about the condo.

No time like the present.

I picked up my phone.

"Hey." His tone was dark and brooding.

"Hi there." Mine matched his.

"Did you miss me?"

I smiled. "Always, but there's a reason for my call."

"Okay shoot."

I heard bells ringing. "Where are you?"

"Walking down Fifth."

"Is that St. Patrick's?"

"Yeah, I think so."

"What are you doing walking around uptown?"

"I had some things to take care of after my meeting with Theo at his house. The place is like a castle, by the way."

"Theo, really?"

"Phoebeee." He drew out my name.

"I used to play there when I was little; it has seven floors and is over fifteen thousand square feet."

"Yeah, and it has twenty-two rooms," Jeremy teased. "I got the tour. And before you ask, Avery was not home."

"I wasn't going to ask." I took a deep breath. We were past all of that. "I wasn't," I reassured him.

"Okay good. Well, anyway, he wanted to meet with me to discuss membership for his men's club."

"I thought both he and his club already joined Jet Set?"

"He did and so did his friends at the Harvard Club, but now he's interested in membership for at least five hundred of his friends from the University Club. He also wants me to meet him next week at the Soho House, which presents opportunities for Miami as well."

"Wow, Jeremy, that's great news."

"Yeah, it is, but that's not why you called. What's up?"

"Well." I was tongue-tied. I suddenly felt like I didn't know what to say. Telling him his mother called here had awkward written all over it.

"You can say it." His voice was seductive.

My stomach did a little flip. "Say what?"

"Tell me you want my tongue in your pussy before dinner."

The dirty talker was back. He'd taken a leave all week, making love to me every morning and every night with an intensity that told me just how much he cared about me. But I liked this side too and I didn't want to ruin it by bringing up his mother. Besides, I knew he must have given her the money, so what was there to talk about. I'd call her back Monday and make the arrangements and then talk to Jeremy.

"Jeremy," I gasped.

"Tell me," he groaned.

"We have early dinner plans," I informed him in case he had forgotten.

"We have thirty minutes. Now tell me," he demanded.

I loved this side of him as much as I loved the tender side.

"Say 'I want your tongue in my clit.'"

Desire raced through me. "I want your tongue inside me," I shyly admitted.

The door opened and there he stood, looking very smug and extremely hot in his herringbone jacket with contrast peaked lapels. His hair was more disheveled than normal, sticking up in the front as well as the back. His eyes gleamed with mischief as he removed his jacket. The display of the way his slacks rode low on his hips was a sight I wouldn't have wanted to miss.

I drew my brows together as my pulse raced. "Jeremy." I was shocked to see him there. Although I had to admit, I could get used to him being behind my door when desire ran hot.

He shrugged. "I just turned town Fifty-seventh when you called, so I was close."

I looked down at what I was wearing and cursed the coming of winter for all the clothes it made me wear to keep warm. I had on a tight embroidered gabardine skirt with an equally tight turtleneck, and hose and ankle boots.

He strode toward me and my heart skipped a beat. His eyes were an intense blue as they stared at me. As soon as he reached me, his hands went to the zipper that ran the entire length of the back of my skirt.

With skilled hands, he had it off me, and my hose and panties were pulled down in mere seconds. He didn't bother to take them off, he just let them pool on top of my boots.

Without a word, he eased me back only slightly so that my behind was barely resting against my desk.

My desk—the things it had seen since Jeremy came back into my life.

Then he dropped to his knees before me. Spreading my legs as far as he could with the resistance of the hose, he wrapped his hands around me and drew me to him.

I went more than willingly.

He held me in place while his tongue flicked my clit.

Lightly at first.

One.

Two.

Three times.

I bit my lip to stop from moaning. The door was closed but it wasn't a Friday, and I didn't know who was still in the office.

With his hands cupping my behind, he pulled me even closer and when the flicks turned into licks, my core felt like it was on fire.

Oh God, I bit down on my lip even harder.

His finger trailed to that spot he'd darkly promised someday to enter and he caressed it, actually penetrating slightly for the first time.

I cried out, I couldn't help it. "Oh, God. It feels so good."

Spurring him on, his licks turned into sucks and then all at once his tongue was stroking, his lips caressing, and his breath tantalizing. My hand tightened around his neck and I pulled him even closer to me. His hot mouth kept up the slow, torturous assault on my pussy.

"Please, Jeremy, please," I whimpered.

He must have decided to take pity on me because he inserted a finger with just the right amount of pressure and in a matter of seconds, my thigh muscles clenched and I came in one hard rush.

Everything inside me turned languid as I felt like I might lose my ability to stand. Jeremy didn't stop until my thighs started to shake. When he stood up and I saw the tent in his pants, I wanted him all the more.

I was greedy. I'd come with his tongue in me and I also wanted to come with his cock inside me. Once I started to recover, I looked at him and told him, "I want your cock inside me."

He shook his head. "Later. We have to go."

I pointed to his pants. "You can't go like that."

His voice was hoarse. "I'll be fine."

"Jeremy," I said.

"I came here to take care of you. I don't want you to think that means we have to fuck."

It dawned on me then. It should have dawned on me earlier. Jeremy was trying so hard to be good. To show me we were more than just about the fucking. And I knew we were. But right now, I wanted us to be about the fucking. I turned around and bent myself over the desk. "I like the bad boy side of you just as much as the good man side. Now I want that bad boy side to fuck me—hard."

I didn't turn around because my cheeks were flaming. I couldn't believe I'd just said that. I really had read way too many romance novels.

But it worked.

He didn't hesitate.

I heard the telltale sound of his zipper and then his hand clutched my hip while the other guided his cock where I was dying for it to be, I was certain.

But I was wrong.

He teased his cock around that sensitive area he had been caressing during many of our sex sessions.

I gasped as the sensation flooded me but then he stopped and lowered his hand. He placed the crown of his cock against my entrance and then he pounded into me.

Hard.

Just like I asked.

I gripped the edge of the desk for support as he did it again.

And again.

Both of his hands were on my hips anchoring me by then, but I didn't need the support, with his fingertips pressing all the way into my hipbones and holding me in place.

I couldn't believe it but in a matter of a couple of more thrusts, I was soaring to orgasm.

I cried out to God, said his name like a prayer, and I think I might have even cursed.

"Fuckkk," he groaned and then I heard him shout and call out my name as he came buried deep inside me. Soon after, he collapsed his clothed body on top of mine and I fell to the desk, breathless and sated.

"I'm sorry," he whispered. "Did I hurt you?"

I pushed myself up and turned to face him. "No. No. I loved it."

He put his hands on my face and caressed my cheeks with this thumbs. "Are you sure?"

"Yes. I love it when you make love to me, but I also love when you show me just how much you want me."

"But you said—"

I put my finger on his lips. "Never mind what I said. What we have now is a healthy mix of lust and love and I want it to stay like this forever."

He stared at me for the longest time, as if he was in a trance.

"Jeremy," I said softly.

He shook himself out of wherever he'd gone and looked around. Then he walked into my bathroom and came out with a towel and cleaned me up first and then himself.

Once we'd righted our disheveled clothes and he'd put his jacket back on, he dropped to his knee.

"Jeremy, we have to go," I said, torn between the fact that he wanted to give me another orgasm and the dinner plans we had made.

But he had a completely different plan. He reached into the inside jacket pocket and took out a Tiffany's box. "Phoebe St. Claire, I love you like I've never loved anyone in my life and I don't want to wait any longer for you to be my wife."

My knees buckled beneath my feet as the earth shifted. I wasn't expecting his proposal—at all. But the electricity that traveled between us was undeniable.

Images of our life together flashed before me. Marriage, kids, a white picket fence, two rockers on the front porch where an older couple sat. It was our future and I could see it plain as day.

We were meant to be.

"Yes, yes, yes! I want to be your wife more than anything in this world."

He opened the box.

It was empty.

He stood up and took what I guessed was an imaginary ring from inside it and placed it on my finger. "Tomorrow at eight a.m., Tiffany's is all yours."

Tears filled my eyes. "Breakfast at Tiffany's."

He nodded. "I want you to pick any ring you want while you eat a croissant and drink coffee." His voice was hoarse.

"How did you arrange something like that?"

He shrugged. "I had some help."

"Jamie?"

He nodded.

Jamie and his connections. Years ago Jamie's mother's family owned the property Charles Tiffany bought to build his flagship store and somehow Jamie's family has been able to maintain that relationship through the years.

I threw my arms around the man who would soon officially become my fiancé. "I love you."

He squeezed me so tight. "I hope forever."

I pulled away. "Yes, forever." I kissed him exuberantly.

Again he held on to me like I was going somewhere.

"I have to call my mother."

He walked around my desk and took my coat from the hook. "I have something to tell you about that first."

I gave him a questioning stare.

He held out my coat. "I'll tell you on the way down."

"Okay," I said.

We walked down the hallway and hit the elevator and he didn't say a word. I was starting to worry.

When we walked outside, he hailed a taxi. "Perry Street restaurant," he told the driver.

As the cab jerked into traffic, Jeremy turned toward me.

Finally.

"On Monday, your mother and I went to see your father."

My voice caught in my throat.

"I went to ask your mother for her approval to marry you, but while I was talking to her, I felt I should meet your father and ask him."

"You went to visit him in jail? With my mother?"

He nodded.

"She'd never been, you know."

He nodded again.

I started to cry.

"Please don't be upset," he said.

"I'm not. I'm touched. I can't believe you did that for me."

He pulled me into his arms. "I'd do anything for you."

I looked up. "Your mother called today."

He didn't look surprised. "I figured she would. I called her."

"She wants to buy her condo."

He nodded. Again he already knew.

"I can't let her do that. My mother did what she did for a reason. But we're going to ask her to take over the payments."

"Phoebe, you have to do what's best for the company."

"That is what's best."

He kissed the top of my forehead. "If you change your mind, or things change, I'll make sure she has the money."

I knew he would. I snuggled closer to him and stayed tucked in his strong arms until we reached the Meatpacking District and our destination.

Life had never felt sweeter.

From outside the building was very nondescript. I'd never been and neither had Jeremy, so when we walked in, we were both pleasantly surprised by the relaxed elegance and tranquil setting. The walls and columns were a charcoal color and the booths and chairs were a light shade of beige. Single large lightbulbs hung over each table and sheer white panels covered the windows.

Jeremy approached the hostess and she immediately led us to a round booth in a quiet corner where Jamie and Lindsay were already seated. They both stood as we approached with smiles on their faces.

I knew they knew.

Lindsay looked like a knockout in a sequin-embellished metallic mini dress. She paired the elegant ensemble with gold ballet shoes to tone it down and the result was killer.

"Hi," she squealed as she hugged me. "How are you?"

"Much better than the last time you saw me." I smiled at her.

Jamie tugged me out of her hold and hugged me. We'd talked during the week but hadn't seen each other since Saturday night. "I hear congratulations are in order."

My grin was so wide, I thought it might split my face open. I already knew Jamie was aware, since Jeremy had arranged the Tiffany's visit and he must have told Lindsay as well.

"No decent champagne here. Can you believe it?"

I looked at the table. "How about we save that for another night anyway but I'll have whatever Lindsay is drinking with the apple in it."

"It's a siso apple and congratulations." She hugged me again.

"Shiso, baby," Jamie corrected.

"Thank you," I said to Lindsay, ignoring Jamie.

Lindsay rolled her eyes. "Sh—i—so," she exaggerated with a small laugh.

Jeremy kissed Lindsay and shook Jamie's hand. Then both men waited for Lindsay and me to slide in the booth. We looked at each other.

"Cavemen," Lindsay mouthed to me.

We both started to laugh.

Jamie furrowed his brows.

"Inside joke," I said.

"Can I take your drink order?" the waitress asked.

"She'll have a shiso apple martini and I'll have whatever he's drinking."

Jamie raised his glass. "Macallan eighteen years."

"Perfect." Jeremy grinned.

"And a carafe of the Koshino Omachi Sake," Jamie added.

"Yum," I said, not meaning to have said that out loud.

Jeremy raised a brow and settled a hand on my leg.

Tingles spread up my thigh and down to my toes as he traced heart shapes over my thigh.

Jamie and Lindsay asked twenty questions about the wedding, of which we knew nothing yet, and we drank our drinks and two more carafes of sake before we were ready to order.

"So Lindsay got the cover," Jamie said.

"For what?" I asked.

"She was in St. Bart's Monday and Tuesday shooting the 2016 VS swim issue."

"Are you kidding? And you're on the cover?"

She nodded. "I just found out."

"The pics are all over and I'm still not sure how I feel about my wife's ass being on Instagram."

"James," she soothed. "We've talked about this. When I'm wearing a thong, you can't see my entire behind, so technically, everyone isn't seeing my ass."

I almost spit my drink out.

"I don't know. Jeremy, what do you think?" Jamie took his phone out and passed it to him.

Jeremy pushed it back toward him. "I think I'm in a whole heap of shit if I even look at that picture."

"Pussy," Jamie mumbled.

"Whatever, dude, but looking at a naked picture of your wife is the kind of trouble I know better than to even get close to."

My hand went to his thigh—the word trouble elicited a flood of desire.

"I'm not naked," Lindsay insisted and handed Jamie's phone to me. I needed to take my mind off the trouble sitting next to me so I looked at the picture.

It wasn't that bad.

The problem wasn't the photo. It was the sheer amount of people who had seen it. I clicked over to his Twitter account and laughed. I already knew what I'd find there.

"Jamie, she isn't naked. But you might want to tell Danny to stop tweeting the pic."

He grabbed my phone. "That son of a bitch."

"Are you ready to order?" The waitress came just at the right time. A change of topic was in order.

"How about I order for the table?" Jamie suggested.

Lindsay and I couldn't help but laugh out loud.

Jeremy shrugged. "I'm easy."

That response made it too difficult to resist a little tease. I leaned over and cupped my hand around his ear and purred, "You are."

He snatched my wrist as I brought it back to my side. "Watch it," he growled.

Shivers ran up my spine.

Jamie cleared his throat. "Anything you don't like, man?" he directed toward Jeremy.

Jeremy glanced at the menu. "Not crazy about duck, but everything else is fair game."

"Cool," he said and rattled off enough food to feed eight.

When the truffles arrived, I knew it was time. "So Jamie and Lindsay, I have some bad news."

Jamie stabbed a ravioli with his fork and put it on Lindsay's plate and then passed the dish to me. "I don't like the way that sounds."

I could feel Jeremy's eyes on me. I hadn't told him yet either. "Hunter and I went back over the time line for the club openings and he feels it's way too tight to aim for New Year's Eve, so we've targeted Valentine's Day."

Jamie and Lindsay exchanged glances.

"Are you sure?" Jeremy asked me.

I nodded. "With no money secured yet and the holidays coming, it's just too tight."

"Well, hearts and flowers day it is," Jamie announced.

Surprised, I had to ask, "Are you sure you want to wait that long?"

"Yes, we want to have it at your club," Lindsay answered.

Jamie nodded. "But we don't have to discuss the details tonight. In fact I think you and Lindsay can handle that part of it."

"Sure," I said. "Let's wait until the time line is a little more solid first though."

"So, if that's set," Jamie concluded, "we have an announcement."

I stared at him. What else could he possibly announce? A baby came to mind but they hadn't known each other long enough for Lindsay to even know she was pregnant. "What?" I asked, feeling anxious.

"We've decided to have Christmas in the Hamptons and I'd love for the two of you, and Poppy of course, to join us."

I looked toward Jeremy. We hadn't discussed the holidays at all.

"No traffic, no restaurant lines, no party circuits, a hot tub, plenty of food, drinks, snowmobiles, and—"

Jeremy put a hand up. "Hey, man, you don't have to ask me twice." He looked toward me. "What do you think?"

I was actually excited. I hadn't been back to the Hamptons since the summer with Jeremy and loved the idea of going back with my fiancé. I looked toward Jamie. "We'd love to."

Jamie slammed his palm on the table. "Fuck yes. Christmas through New Year's in the Hamptons. It's going to be epic."

Shocked, I almost choked on my drink. "I can't go for a whole week."

"What are you talking about? Of course you can."

"Jamie, you know I have a lot going on."

"Phoebs, if anyone needs time off, it's you."

Jeremy squeezed my hand. "It's up to you, but I'll help you with what I can and we can come back and forth if you need to."

I squeezed his hand back and nodded. I had a lump in my throat. I appreciated his support—more than he knew.

Dinner arrived with more food than the four of us could possibly eat and by the time dessert was placed on the table, I seriously doubted if I would be able to eat for the next week.

"Carrot cake soufflé and chocolate pudding," the waitress said as she placed one of each in front of the four of us.

"Are those crystallized violets?" Lindsay asked with wide eyes.

Jamie had already prepared a perfectly portioned spoonful of pudding, cream, and the sugared violets and held it in front of Lindsay's mouth.

Her lips parted slowly, a little too slowly and I felt like I should turn away. Instead, I squeezed my eyes shut to avoid seeing anything I didn't want burned in my mind.

Jamie was like my brother, after all.

And I wasn't used to this type of behavior from him.

"Oh my God, so good," Lindsay mumbled.

I opened my eyes to see Jeremy watching me.

He licked his lips. "Which are you going to try first?"

Completely turned on, I leaned into him. "I'm too full."

He put a fork into the carrot cake soufflé and I watched him. His eyes locked on mine and he lifted the cakelike substance to my mouth. "Practice for the wedding," he whispered.

Finding that oddly perfect, I opened my mouth and let him slide the soufflé into it. Electricity crackled between us. Our chemistry was off the charts. Even more so than normal. I was glad the evening was almost over—I really wanted to be alone with him.

"So when's the big day going to be?" Lindsay asked.

"Oh, we haven't thought that far ahead," I said.

At the same time Jeremy said, "Soon."

I blinked at him.

"I told you I didn't want to wait."

"I know, but—"

"No buts, I want you to be my wife and I was thinking next weekend."

"Next weekend? Are you serious?"

"In the park, something small before it's too cold and all the leaves are gone."

"That's a great idea," Jamie said. "But I might need two weeks to get the permit."

"Try for next Saturday," Jeremy strongly encouraged.

Jamie raised a brow, but then smirked. "Yes, sir."

I was in shock and didn't even laugh, although it was funny.

"The terrace or the mall itself?" Jeremy asked me as his eyes practically twinkled.

How did you know my favorite places?

And, honestly, either sounded magical but things were moving too fast. "Jeremy, we can't," I said, still a little shocked.

The twinkle in his eyes was gone. "We can talk about it later."

"Well, let me know," Jamie interceded.

Everyone was quiet when Lindsay turned to look at Jeremy. "Not to change the topic, but my friends and I just recently joined Jet Set. Personally, I can't wait to see the fleet of white cars. Ever since I did a photo shoot on top of one, I've been dying to ride in a Lamborghini."

"Baby, you've been in my car. It's just as nice," Jamie said to Lindsay.

She kissed him and said, "I love your car, but there's something about a Lamborghini."

"I bet Jeremy could hook you up," I said.

He smiled. "Anytime."

Lindsay shot up from the table. "How about now?"

I looked at Jeremy in silent apology.

He shrugged. "Sure, we could head over to the garage. I'm not sure what cars are out though, I'm just warning you."

"Are you okay to drive?" I asked him, a little concerned and trying to give him an out.

He nodded. "I haven't had that much and after all this food, I'm fine. I can take her for a spin around the block."

"Can I, James, can I?" she pleaded with Jamie.

Jamie looked toward Jeremy. "You cool with it?"

Jeremy nodded.

Jamie looked back at Lindsay. "Yeah, sure, why not?"

She was up and on his lap with her hands around his neck before I could blink.

I couldn't help but notice how Lindsay asked Jamie's permission for almost everything she did and although I knew he had a controlling personality, it was interesting to see the dynamics of his new relationship at work. Lindsay knew Jamie had a need for control and she chose to submit to it.

I wondered if I should give that a try but quickly thought better of it.

I liked things the way they were.

After the bill was paid, we walked to the garage. It wasn't far, but it was cold.

Jeremy wrapped his arm around me as we walked. "What are your reservations about getting married?"

I looked up at him. "I don't have any. I just didn't realize you meant so soon."

"We can wait if you want; I just didn't see the need for a long engagement."

It struck me then that he was trying to make sure everything with us was different from what I'd had with Dawson.

But he didn't have to worry about that.

It already was different.

"I love you and I want more than anything to be your wife," I reassured him. "It's just we haven't even figured out where we want to live yet; getting married seems like we're skipping a few steps."

We crossed the street. "Let me take care of where we'll live. I'll take care of the wedding too. All you have to do is say yes."

I stepped up onto the sidewalk—my thought from a moment ago coming back to mind. Some things I could give up control of. And I trusted him to work those details out. Without further hesitation, I pulled him by his jacket so he'd stop, and then I kissed him. "Yes."

"Yes, to Saturday in the park?"

I looked at him. Into the blue eyes of the man I knew would make me happy for the rest of my life. "Yes."

"Yes?" he parroted back.

"Yes!"

He picked me up and twirled me around.

"Saturday's on, I take it," Jamie asked and I knew the real estate mogul extraordinaire would walk through fire to help us out.

Jeremy and I both nodded as our lips locked.

When Jeremy finally set me down, I felt giddy. He grabbed my hand as he started walking and turned backward to talk to me. "Come on, the faster I do this, the faster I can get you home."

Fairy tales might not be real, but as I watched the way he moved, I knew then that my James Dean was my very own Prince Charming.

And we were going to live happily ever after.

CHAPTER 27

Sins of the Past

"James Dean? I don't see it," Jamie said.

"Really? I do," Lindsay rebutted.

I was telling them about Mrs. Bardot's habit of giving everyone she met a nickname.

Jeremy laughed. "A rebel without a cause. I wonder if she knew me before my juvie record was sealed?"

My gaze pinned him. "You have a record?"

"Juvie," Jeremy clarified. "Too many truancies and the truancy officer wanted to prove a point. And he did. Scared the living shit out of me when I had to spend the night at Crossroads. I never skipped school again."

"What does she call me?" Jamie asked, nonplussed by the conversation that was taking place.

"Nothing," I answered hesitantly.

"Liar. Don't you forget, I can tell when you're lying. Come on, tell me."

I walked faster. "Are we almost there?" I asked Jeremy. "It's cold."

He wrapped his arm around me. "It's right around the corner. Do you want my jacket?"

"No. I'm okay." I curled into him.

"What does she call me?" Jamie asked again.

I turned to face him. "Are you sure you want to know?"

"Yeah, James Dean over there has my name, so I must have a pretty cool one."

"Are you jealous of a nickname?" I teased.

"Fuck no, just tell me mine."

"Okay, she calls you Richard Gere."

"Oh my God." Lindsay shoved him a little.

"What? I don't get it."

"You're the American Gigolo," Lindsay giggled.

Jeremy and I started laughing hysterically.

Jamie straightened his shoulders. "Richard Gere, that works," he said as Jeremy stopped in front of a garage. While he and Lindsay debated the merits of being a gigolo, I glanced up.

When I did, I remembered being here, at the garage where the Rose Bar's fleet of white cars was stored, that first night with Jeremy. Just snippets, but I remembered.

Jeremy zeroed in on me. "What's going on in that head of yours?"

"I remember being here."

"You do?"

"Just the sign above and what I remembered before."

"I don't want that to ever happen to you again."

"Trust me, I won't be drinking like that anytime soon."

He kissed me. "No, you won't."

I grinned at him. I liked when he wanted to take care of me.

"You didn't tell him," Jamie exclaimed.

"Tell me what?"

"Jamie," I chided.

Jeremy's eyes narrowed on me.

"Lily has this unfounded suspicion that someone slipped a Roofie in my drink that night."

Jeremy's entire body went hard. "And who does she think did it?"

I ran my palms up his chest. "I'm not sure it really happened."

"Who," he said so loud he made me jump.

"Fucking Lars," Jamie admitted.

Jeremy pulled me to him and ran his hands through my hair. "Why didn't you tell me?"

I shrugged and tried to change the topic. "Like I said. I'm not certain."

Jeremy shot a glare at Jamie and they seemed to exchange a few silent words, then Jeremy wrapped his arms around me and held me tightly to him.

My chest squeezed under his protective arms and I allowed myself to seep further into him.

"Is the lovefest over yet?" Jamie crooned.

Jeremy lifted my chin. His eyes locked on mine, but he spoke to all of us. "Stay here," he told us and then gave me a sweet kiss before he walked away. I watched him every step of the way. The way he competently strode up to the window and waved to the man behind the bulletproof glass. The way he moved his lips when he spoke.

God, I could watch him all day.

The three of us stayed on the sidewalk and soon, a metal gate unlocked. Jeremy breezed through it, and then a side door opened. Once it did, he spoke to the man for another few minutes and when he turned around, he was dangling a set of keys. "Come on, it's here," he said with a wicked grin.

My heart went thump-thump at the pure joy that was spread across his face.

The metal gate clicked open again and the three of us all entered the cover of the garage where Jeremy stood waiting for us.

He was so incredibly sexy.

My fiancé extended his hand and I took it. The heat of his skin burned against mine and I clutched his hand tighter. He peered down and a rueful grin slid across his face.

I shivered.

As we started to ascend the ramp, I pulled out my phone. "Hold on," I said. "I want a picture before we go in."

We all huddled together and Jeremy pulled me close as I snapped a selfie of the four of us. It was the first picture I had taken of Jeremy since the summer we met. As everyone separated, I tugged Jeremy back toward me. "One more of just us."

"Sure." He grinned and pulled me even closer than before. So close that shivers of desire went down my spine.

I snapped the photo and as soon as I did, he took my phone from me.

"Hey, what are you doing?"

"Sending myself a copy," he said and gave me a quick kiss.

I sucked in a breath. He wanted a copy of a picture of us. My heart swelled even more.

When he pulled away, he said, "Follow us," to Jamie and Lindsay as he threw his arm around me and walked into the garage.

I gazed up at him. I loved being out with him, knowing he was mine. I especially loved it when his arm was around me like it was. Like that—there was no mistaking I belonged to him. After all, he was going to be my husband.

Husband—that sounded strange, in a good way.

"There it is," Lindsay screamed as she leapt from Jamie's hold and ran toward the white Lamborghini.

"I won't be long." Jeremy nuzzled against my ear as we approached the car and he dropped his hold on me.

"I'll be here," I told him. I practically had to fan myself as I watched his narrow hips saunter away from me.

"Have fun." I waved to Lindsay after she got in the car and the roar of the engine came to life.

Jamie leaned against me. "Looks like it's just you and me."

I leaned my head back against him. "Baby? I still can't believe you call her baby."

He shrugged. "It just comes out."

"I'm happy for you."

He hugged me. "Thanks, Phoebs."

"What's the matter?"

"My mother is being extremely difficult."

"Give her some time, she'll come around."

He pulled away. "I'm not so sure about that. She won't return any of my calls."

"So go over there."

He cringed. "I tried. She refused to come down and when I went up to her room, she told me once I annulled my marriage, she'd be happy to talk to me."

Like his father, Jamie had a penchant for models and since her husband had yet to return from his latest romp with one, I was pretty sure that didn't help the situation. Sure Jamie's mother had a temper and a nasty streak but she always forgave his father and I was certain she'd accept Lindsay—eventually.

"Is that what Christmas is about?" I asked.

He shrugged. "Maybe. At least I know I can use the Hamptons house because she never goes there in the winter."

I shook my head at him.

"Hey, I know we didn't talk much about it, but I'm really happy for you."

The way he spoke touched me. "Thank you."

"I can see just how right Jeremy is for you."

I leaned against one of the cars. "He is. He makes me really happy."

Discussing emotions was never Jamie's thing, and as I talked, he scanned the area. "So, just how many cars does this future husband of yours have anyway?"

"There are twelve but they're assets that belong to the Rose Bar, not him."

He eyed each of the six that remained parked in the garage. "Still, pretty freaking cool. A fleet of cars at your command. I could get used to that."

I laughed at him. "I think you could get used to anything at your command."

"Hey now," he teased.

I shrugged. "The truth hurts."

Suddenly, his eyes narrowed on something behind me in the far corner. I turned to look.

"What's that one?"

Way over in the dark corner of the garage sat a car covered securely. "I don't know."

Jamie walked toward it. "Let's check it out."

I was hesitant. "Maybe we shouldn't."

"Come on, it might be brand-new." He was already at the car looking at the papers that were taped to the black cover.

"What is it?" I asked. Cars weren't really my thing, and honestly, I couldn't have cared less, but Jamie loved cars, so I indulged him.

"Interesting, he isn't buying it, he's selling it."

"How do you know?" I asked.

"These are pick-up orders."

"I think the fleet manager takes care of all the cars; I guess he decided to trade one in."

Jamie lifted the cover. "I don't think it belongs to the club, it's red."

"Jamie, don't do that. It's probably someone's personal car," I warned.

But it was too late. He'd already lifted the cover off the hood. "Fuck me, it's a vintage Ferrari." He studied it for a few minutes. "Not just any old Ferrari. It's a 250 GT Cabriolet Series II, 1961, I think, like the one your dad used to own."

My stomach knotted with dread with each step I took closer to it. As I stared at it, the blood drained from my face. It was identical to the rare car my father loved so dearly. The one Sotheby's had put up on the auction block a year ago and sold for one million dollars. I walked to the passenger side, and when I lifted the cover, there it was, the butterfly sticker I had stuck in the corner of the window so many years ago.

I felt overheated, sick to my stomach, and very confused. Why would Jeremy have bought my father's car?

Jamie was staring at it. He too must have realized it was indeed my father's car. "It might not be Jeremy's," he said with little conviction.

"It has to be. What are the chances it's not?"

Jamie was a betting man by nature and his refusal to wager any bet told me exactly what he thought. "Just talk to him. Hear him out."

The explanations I'd been given echoed in my head. The answers, the logic, were there, but the words—J Truman, Hanna Truman, and the condo, Stanford—still haunted me as I stared at my father's beloved car. They were spinning around me, weaving themselves into a knot inside my head. I couldn't think straight.

In horror, I looked at Jamie. "Do you think this really has all been about getting back at me? At my family? And marrying me is a ploy to get . . ."

I couldn't even finish that thought.

Had I been right weeks ago?

"No," he shot back. "There has to be a reasonable explanation," Jamie insisted.

"What possible reason could there be for Jeremy having the car he once took for a joyride when he was younger, in the garage where a fleet of cars are stored that belong to his company?"

Jamie braced his hands on my shoulders. "I know it looks bad, but just let him explain before you jump to crazy conclusions."

Just then the loud roar of an engine echoed from the street below and a few seconds later the sleek, white body of the Lamborghini came speeding up the ramp and my stomach roiled with emotion. The headlights illuminated the red paint of the one single car that didn't belong.

"Stay calm," Jamie warned.

My pulse thudded in my ears. My mind raced with the only reason he would have my father's car and I tried so very hard to expel it.

Suddenly, the tires squealed as the car came to an abrupt stop and the driver's side door opened.

"Do you want me to stay?" Jamie asked.

"No," I said as my body started to tremble.

"I'm going to take Lindsay home. Call me if you need me."

I nodded.

Jeremy was practically running as he rushed toward me. Concern was etched all over his face but I couldn't shake the memories of the way he looked at me that first morning I woke up in his bed.

Had he been playing me?

The look on my face must have said it all.

"Phoebe, I can explain," he said as his hands braced my upper arms.

I shrugged out of his grip. "I'm listening."

He opened his mouth. Closed it. Opened it again.

I felt my features harden. "Well?" I prompted.

For the first time, Jeremy was at a loss for words. Again his mouth opened but then shut, opened again but he said nothing. The words that he had spoken to me when we first reconnected came to mind: *We've both done things we're not proud of.*

My heart was pounding in my chest. Fear that he'd somehow duped me was all I felt. Each second that passed without a word forced me to believe that was the case. Finally, I couldn't stand it. "Nothing to say?" I hissed.

His eyes were bright with panic. "Fuck," he swore hoarsely. "I don't know how to explain this without it sounding . . ."

Again he was at a loss for words.

"Let me help you." Anger sparked within me and I couldn't control my ire. "You bought this car." I pointed to his bright shiny toy with a fury that was unleashing itself at an even greater speed with each passing second. "As one, big, giant fuck you to the almighty St. Claire." I inhaled a deep breath before I could finish. "So as to really ruffle his feathers."

Jeremy stood there shaking his head. "Phoebe. Calm down."

"Calm down," I screamed.

He stepped into me and tried to pull me to him.

I shoved him away. "Don't touch me."

At that moment I hated him. I loved him. No, I loved him and hated him in perfectly equal measure. The question was—how did he really feel about me?

Jeremy sucked in a breath. "What else? Get it out. Say it all."

I looked at him incredulously. "No, you say it."

His expression went stony. "I'm not going to do this. I'm not going to go round and round with you and be accused over and over of something you know isn't the truth."

I wanted to believe it wasn't.

I really did.

I held back my tears. "Say it then."

Jeremy huffed. "Say what? That you're right? Or that I want you to trust me. To believe in me. To not think the worst every time something presents itself in a compromising way."

I shook my head. "That's not what this is. How dare you turn it around?"

He raked a hand through his hair as if exasperated. "Yes, before we got back together, I bought that car as a giant fuck you to your father. Is that what you wanted to hear so badly? Does it make you feel better now to know that?"

I stared at him in disbelief. "How could you?"

He took a step back as if I'd stung him. "Be honest, Phoebe, that's not what this is about. That's not all you're thinking, is it?"

His words sliced through me like a knife and I was momentarily torn.

Was I overreacting?

I wasn't sure. I needed some space. Somewhere to breathe where he wasn't all I saw, heard, felt, wanted to touch. Yes, touch. I couldn't stand this. I wanted to say okay and throw my arms around him but right now I didn't know left from right or up from down.

My breath caught on a small squeak. "I need some time to think."

He stared at me in disbelief. As if I'd wounded him. I stood here helpless to think anything else. Feeling fractured, like a part of me was missing, I watched his throat work, as he swallowed hard, and his mouth slipped open, wordless once again.

A complete, emotional wreck, I did what I had to do and put distance between us. Somehow I managed to turn and walk away. I had no idea how. I was trembling from the cool air and nerves twitching in my belly. I couldn't believe I was doing this but I was a mess and I couldn't make a rational decision. I felt the burn of his stare on me the entire walk out of the garage and again as I hit the cool of the night, and although I knew it was best if I didn't, I turned around as I got into a cab and saw him there.

My throat was sore from holding back the tears and as I told the cab driver my address, I never took my eyes off him.

He stood there sullen, with his hands in his pockets and his head slightly down. It was as if I'd put a huge gaping hole in his heart, and not the other way around.

Staring at him, I couldn't shake the feeling he was waiting for me to change my mind.

And I wanted to.

I just couldn't.

He loves me.

He loves me not.

He loves me.

He loves me not.

I kept the chant up as I willed myself back to sleep. I tossed and turned and no matter how hard I tried, I couldn't find peace.

Finally, at six in the morning, I dragged my tired self out of bed and stared at my phone. He hadn't tried to contact me. I swayed back and forth about what had happened. Part of me understood what he had done, that he had done that before we got back together and it had absolutely nothing to do with me. But the other part warned me to be wary. He told me he had matured past that and made me believe that maturity had come way before he moved back to New York City. Obviously, that wasn't true.

Which part I should believe was where the divide lay, and I wasn't certain which line to cross.

I ached to call him. To see him. To be with him. But I had to get past all of this stuff messing with my head first. He was right. There was so much more to my accusations than just asking why he had bought the car. He wasn't wrong in knowing an admission would only lead to persecution.

So I busied myself getting ready for a slow day at work. I glanced at my phone and resisted the urge to call Jeremy the entire time.

I left early and took my time walking to work. I avoided any thoughts of where I should be right now. Tiffany's wasn't a name I wanted to think about, or walk past.

The office was unusually quiet. Tomorrow, I was scheduled to hear back from the investors but today Hunter was gone and my plate was surprisingly empty. I had all kinds of time to think.

Great.

I spent the day pondering the situation with Jeremy and trying to figure out his motives. Going over and over our conversation in my head my thoughts always paused on his wrecked expression as I rode away in the cab.

The text I received from Lily didn't help matters any.

She'd been MIA all week. She had left to go back to France last Sunday and the text I received from her yesterday said she and Preston were seeking alternative help in Paris. I'd texted her back asking for details and asking about her job. Her reply was short, telling me she had to give them one last chance and if it didn't work, she was ending it for the final time.

Von Furstenberg Fashions was headquartered in France, whereas the House of Monroe was headquartered in New York. The fact that she was staying in Paris as long as she was made me wonder what she was doing about her job.

Lily's text today asked me if I had plans to go to the Hope Gala at Capitale tonight. No, I didn't and as far as I knew, neither did Jeremy, but I was certain I knew who did and her name wasn't one I wanted to speak of ever again. I couldn't talk about what had happened yet between Jeremy and me, so I ignored Jamie's calls and kept my texts with Lily brief. I'd tell her the whole story but not today.

By the time five o'clock came, I was ready to run out of the office. When I got home to my quiet apartment, I wanted to scream. Instead I paced back and forth, wishing Mrs. Bardot was home or Lily was around. I settled on Jamie, but got his voice mail.

By nine that night, I didn't know what I was going to say but I knew I couldn't leave things the way I had with Jeremy. My mind had settled and the shock had faded. With the fog clear, the truth was, I didn't really believe he was using me.

His feelings were real.

I knew they were.

I mean, come on, I had felt them to my core.

No one could fake emotions like that.

Yes, he had done something that would hurt my father, but in no way was he trying to hurt me. Now that I had worked through how I felt, I was ready to sit down with him and discuss what had happened calmly.

I sucked in a deep breath of the cool night air and hailed a cab. I thought about texting Jeremy that I was on my way but I was certain his naturally brooding nature would engage and I'd have to break that wall down to even get in the door.

My prince had a brooding side.

Not that I blamed him.

I should have trusted him enough to have calmly listened to his explanation before I jumped to such despicable conclusions.

If I was honest with myself, I felt a little sick about my own behavior and wished I could take it back. After all, I loved Jeremy and yet I had assumed the worst.

What kind of woman does that?

With a trembling hand, I knocked on his door. No answer. I thought I'd come early enough that he wouldn't have left for his nightly club check. Perhaps, he like me couldn't stand sitting around. Or maybe he had a function after all. I thought about pulling out my phone and checking Page Six but thought better of it.

I didn't want to go in uninvited after how I'd left things yesterday, so I went back down and sat on the stoop. The night air was cold and I was thankful I had pulled out my warmer coat before I left.

People passed, walking their dogs, jogging, and even carrying groceries home in the later hours of the night. But it wasn't them I was watching. I spent my time going over and over my cruel accusations and I felt more and more sorry for the way I had reacted. For the way I had treated Jeremy.

I wasn't sure how much time had passed when something caused me to look at the stopped cab in front of me. Jeremy stepped out, wearing a tuxedo, and through the open door I spotted Jamie inside.

What the hell?

I stood up and I knew the moment he caught sight of me.

His eyes narrowed a fraction and his mouth tightened slightly, yet I still noticed his hesitation, and I had to close my eyes to will back the burn of tears prickling there.

I knew he was standing in front of me before I felt the warm breath of my name from his lips. "Phoebe," he sighed, and I heard the harshness in his tone.

But when I opened my eyes, there was nothing hard about him. All I saw was his sweet face. And everything about him seduced me—from his closeness, to the smell of his skin, even the familiarity of his soft breathing. It had been only a day and I longed for those things to be back in my life.

I didn't want another to pass without him.

He was dressed warmly. As if he'd been outside for a while. Up close, I could see his hair sticking wildly out of his knit hat. His wool coat was open, as was his tux jacket, and as my eyes slid down, I noticed small red splotches on his white shirt. My eyes darted to his face. I wanted to say I saw lipstick on his lips but I couldn't be certain. I did however know without a doubt that there was a slight bruising below his eye near his cheekbone, and I rubbed my fingers across it. "Where have you been?" I asked softly.

He gently took my hand and lowered it. "Nowhere worth mentioning."

I could smell the alcohol on his breath and knew he'd been drinking. I was standing on a step. He was on the ground. We were face-to-face. Eye to eye. That's when I noticed it. The blank canvas he wore and it wasn't from the alcohol. My heart thudded in my chest as I tried to ignore it. I'd seen it before. "Why was Jamie with you?" I pushed on.

He heaved a heavy sigh. "I had to take care of something and he came along with me."

"Lars?" I questioned. Somehow as soon as I saw Jamie, I knew that's where they'd gone.

He nodded but said nothing.

I, in turn, had nothing to say to that either. Concern started to mount. He wasn't being his normal self. Okay, we'd had a fight but he was completely disconnected from me right now. I couldn't stand it. "I'm sorry," I apologized. "Can we talk?"

His eyes seemed so dark as he took me in. I bit nervously on my lip, not certain if he was ready to talk to me. When he offered his hand, I exhaled softly and took it. His warm skin practically sizzled as it wrapped around my hand but he didn't hold it with the possessiveness he always had. My pulse was zooming as he led me up the stairs to his loft with such uncertainty. His mood was completely unreadable.

Guilt hailed down on me. I shouldn't have left him there last night. I should have stayed and talked this out. I had done what I asked him to never do to me—walked away.

From the moment he opened the door his movements seemed so mechanical. He pulled his hat off and let it fall to the ground. And then he took his coat and tux jacket off and threw them on the stairs before his white shirt followed. I had already taken my coat off by the time he turned to help me and I handed him my coat instead. He promptly tossed it on top of his.

My chest rose and fell with the anxiety I was feeling. Silence swelled between us as he walked into the living room and I hesitantly followed.

Was this it?

Had I ruined everything by overreacting?

Once there, he motioned for me to sit on the couch and stood a good distance away from me in his slacks and plain white tee.

I drew my arms around myself as I sat, ignoring the pit in my stomach and telling myself this was going to be okay. That the distance between us would dissipate as soon as we talked.

"Are you cold?" Jeremy asked. "I can turn the heat up or make you a cup of tea." His tone was despondent and he wouldn't look at me. I feared that he'd already shut me out.

I shook my head and tried really hard to keep it together but my exterior shell was crumbling with the detachment he was exhibiting. "I'm sorry I left like I did yesterday. I shouldn't have done that. I should have stayed, so we could talk things out."

He didn't raise his head to look at me but I heard him sigh heavily.

My heart lurched and my breathing stuttered. "Talk to me, Jeremy. Don't do this. Don't shut down," I begged. I was desperate to snap him out of wherever he'd gone. I'd take the brooding, sardonic man any day over the empty shell that was standing before me.

At my pleading words, he lifted his eyes to mine. I saw a glimpse of the fire in them I knew so well, the intensity I'd come to need, but there was also a dulled edge to him that scared the living shit out of me. "I'm not sure there's anything left to say."

I drew in a breath. "Please Jeremy, just tell me why you bought my father's car. Explain to me why you would have done something like that when you told me you had let that animosity go?"

He sat down on the chair and rubbed his hands on his pants. He stared at me, his eyes pleading in a way they never had.

I was shaking and frankly, I was terrified. It was what they were pleading for that made me panicky.

His voice was hard. "I told you why last night."

I wanted to shake him. Was this it? Was it my choice to accept what he'd done and if I couldn't then what? Then we were through? Well, I didn't accept that. He needed to fight for me more than that. With a shaky voice I said, "I love you, Jeremy. I want to be able to move past this. But you have to explain to me what was going on in your head."

He scrubbed at his jaw, which was covered in stubble.

I was losing him.

"Look at me," I demanded. "Are we over?"

His voice hardened even more. "Isn't that why you're here?"

"No, goddamn it, it's not. I'm here because I want you to fight for me. Tell me what was going through your head when you bought that goddamned car. Make me understand you," I yelled.

Something must have snapped inside him because he seemed to inflate right in front of me. He squared his shoulders and looked straight at me when he said, "I need to start from the beginning."

A glimmer of hope bloomed inside me. "That's okay."

He gave me an impassive look. "Some of this you know, some I never fully explained. I was eighteen when my mother first told me who my father was, and what he'd done. Why the fuck she bothered, I still don't know. I'd grown up thinking I'd had no father, so why tell me when it no longer mattered?"

He stopped as if waiting for me to answer but the question wasn't meant for me. I knew that.

"It hit me hard. I was at an age when I wasn't really an adult but I felt like I was. I demanded she tell me everything, but she wouldn't and it fucking pissed me off."

I gave him a reassuring nod.

He practically spat the words. "She said she couldn't bear to. Yet, she told me just enough to make me dangerous. She told me the names of the four men who were involved with his get-rich scheme and that he'd done it to make our lives better. Well, fuck that. He didn't even come close. So yeah, I knew the guys' names that had been a part of his plan and then I had to see them every summer while they tooled around in their wealth. Your father was one of those guys and every time I saw him, he made my skin crawl."

I bristled at the confession.

"Still, I wasn't lying. As the years passed, my hatred faded but what I didn't realize was that the resentment was still there."

My heart hurt for him and when I saw hurt on his face I wanted to tell him to stop but I felt this was as much for him as it was for me, so I clasped my fingers together when what I really wanted was to soothe him, and let him continue.

Jeremy ran a hand through his hair, making it even wilder. "Until two years ago when my mother asked me to go with her to see my father. Was she out of her mind? I knew then I had to get away from her and that's when I came back to the city. I know I said it was because this was always home, and although that was partially true, the other part was I had money and I wanted to take back the life I felt was stolen from me."

As honesty bled through his words, I tried to see things from his perspective. What it must have been like to grow up without a dad and then find out you had one, only to learn he'd chosen greed over family. Funny thing was, I could understand it—it had happened to me. But luckily I wasn't too young to remember my father.

Jeremy looked extremely pale. "I hadn't even been here a week when I went to Sotheby's with the fleet manager for the Rose Bar. And that's when I saw it, your father's car up for auction . . . and I thought why the fuck not? I never knew, all those years ago, if your father knew who I was. I wanted to hope he didn't. But just in case he did, I thought I owed it to him to stick it to him. He was in prison. I was out here, with enough money that I didn't have to take it for a joyride. I could own it. So on a stupid whim I bought it. Yes, it was my giant fuck you to him. But here's the funny thing—I never drove it. It never felt right. It has just sat where you found it for over a year."

My mouth opened to say something but I thought better of it.

Jeremy stood and crossed the room to sit beside me. My heart stilled. He didn't touch me but he did lean close. "You have to know, I never expected when I bought it that I'd be sitting next to you right now. That we'd be getting back together. And then, when we did, I knew what I had done was wrong and just wanted to erase it. I wasn't like him. I wanted to get rid of it and never think of the car again. I hated everything it represented and I didn't want you to see that side of me. But who would have thought it would be so fucking hard to find a private buyer?"

My breath hitched at his words. "Jeremy, I want to see all sides of you. You have to know that."

He shook his head. I could see how hard this was on him.

I took his hand and squeezed it. "You should have told me, and not just about the car. About your feelings too."

He brought my hand to his chest. "We've discussed this. Once I talked to you that first time, all my resentment was gone."

"Are you sure?"

He nodded. "Everything I had felt for you before came rushing back and I no longer cared what your father did to mine, or what mine did to yours. All I cared about was you—the girl I met on the beach that wasn't any part of their fucked-up world. And you're right, I should have told you about the car, but I didn't want to hurt you. And I knew what I'd done would."

All my composure dissipated as tears leaked from my eyes. I'd never seen him like this. He looked wrecked, ruined, and as seemed to be the case with Jeremy, while my mind told me I should proceed with caution, my heart told me he lived inside me and I didn't have to.

He let go of my hand and it worried me. "Talk to me. Tell me what you're thinking." His voice was hoarse, broken.

I looked at him. "That I'm not going to let this end us."

My heart hurt for him but this wasn't about that. It was about him and me. And all I knew was that I loved him with every bit of my being. I wanted to be his and I wanted him to be mine. I couldn't continue to be upset over a car. Over what he had been feeling before we reconnected.

I just couldn't.

He cradled his head in his hands. "Don't let the sins of our fathers ruin this. Ruin us."

Without any further hesitation, I dropped to my knees in front of him and took his hands in mine. "Look at me," I commanded.

He did immediately.

I searched those intense eyes for lies, but I didn't see any. All I saw was deep regret. "I love you so much."

He sighed and pulled me onto his lap. "You have to know that I wouldn't do anything to purposely hurt you. I want to spend my life taking care of you."

Butterflies swarmed in my belly. "I do know that, I do."

He touched his forehead to mine and then swiped his thumbs across my cheeks.

We stayed like that for the longest time.

Still, something was wrong.

Could we come back from this?

"Can I stay with you tonight?" I asked.

He nodded but didn't seem to care either way.

My sobs had waned, but my throat was still tight from holding back my tears. I stood up and offered my hand and for the first time, I led him upstairs. Once we got there, I went into the bathroom and when I came out, he had taken his shoes off and collapsed on the unmade bed, exhaustion clear on his face.

He held his hand out for me to join him and I removed my boots and went to lie beside him. Jeremy covered us with the blanket and pulled me to his chest.

I felt safe there.

Although things weren't anywhere near right.

I knew that.

However, as I closed my eyes to listen to the beat of the heart I didn't want to ever have to fall asleep without again—I pretended they were.

CHAPTER 28

Rumors

Ruby red lips.

Here, there, and everywhere.

The marks covered his face, his neck, and his shirt collar.

I awoke with a jolt.

It was just a dream. It wasn't real. It was just a dream.

As I clung to consciousness, I felt completely alone. Yet I wasn't. Jeremy's soft breathing filled the room. He was with me, not with somebody else.

Not her.

Me.

My back was to his front but his arms weren't curled tightly around me, as they had been every night for weeks, except the night before last. It was Friday, the deadline for the investors to respond to my request for funds, and so I was on edge.

With a stretch, I turned to face Jeremy. I studied him for signs I may have missed last night. We hadn't had sex, we hadn't kissed, he hadn't even really embraced me but that didn't mean anything. I was allowing my nightmarish dream to bleed into reality, and I knew better.

Even though faint glimpses of sunshine filtered through the skylight above us, the sound of water splashing told me it was going to be another rainy day.

Jeremy blinked a few times and then opened his eyes.

"I'm sorry we missed our official engagement yesterday," I whispered.

He sat up and scrubbed at his face. "We can do it whenever we're ready."

My stomach soured at the distance that was still between us. I reached up to brush his cheek, which was now much more purple than last night. "What do you mean?"

Jeremy turned to get out of bed. "Jamie gave me the number of who to call."

"Can you call now?" I asked.

Without looking at me he said, "Yeah, sure I can."

Warning bells lit up inside me. He was still so indifferent, so unlike himself. I sat up and wrapped my arms around his clothed body and then kissed behind his ear. He stiffened under my touch and I knew we still had more to talk about. I wasn't a fan of using sex as a means for making up but I could see where sometimes it might be useful.

And this was one of those times.

I just needed to break down the wall Jeremy had put up so things could go back to the way they were.

Slowly, I brushed my fingers down his T-shirt. I could feel the smooth strength of his stomach muscles as I pressed there. My lips lightly trailed down his jaw to the base of his neck, where I could feel his pulse throbbing in his throat.

I pressed my chest into his back and I could hear his increased breaths but it wasn't until I ran my fingers over the jut of his hip bones that he allowed his body to ease into mine.

Feeling triumphant and underhanded at the same time, I longed to see that lustful look on his face and desire in his eyes. With that, I scooted off the bed. I expected him to ask me where I was going or better yet, grab me by the wrist and yank me to him. But his only reaction came when I nudged his thighs farther apart so I could stand between them, and he closed his eyes.

Worry wove itself around my heart but I still had hope.

I pressed my palms to his chest and when I did, I could feel the increased thump of his heart.

He was going to come around.

I lowered my head to kiss and lick and bite every square inch of him. I didn't want to hurt him but I wanted to elicit a response that was Jeremy-like. As my teeth sank into the flesh of his throat, his hands gripped my hips and my heart got that little pick-me-up it needed.

It occurred to me then that what I wanted, no needed, to do was mark him. *He was mine after all.*

Just as my lips began to work a little harder, one of our cells started to ring. We both had the same ringtone and I leaned over to grab at the disruption. If it was mine, I had to answer; it could be one of the investors.

Except it wasn't mine.

"It's Kat," I said, handing him his phone.

"At six thirty in the morning?" he groaned.

"You should probably answer it."

He hit ACCEPT. "Yeah, Kat, what's going on? What? You've got to be fucking kidding me." He shot up. "I'm going to check it out now. I'll call you back." He hung up and hurried out of the bedroom.

I followed him. "What's going on?"

He was in his office across the hall, tapping some keys on his keyboard.

"Fucking hell." He slapped the top of his laptop down.

"What's the matter, Jeremy?"

He shook his head. "I'm so sorry."

I was already crossing the room, but when he spoke, I hurried. Once I reached him, I stared at him. "What?"

"Fuck, fuck, fuck," he spat.

I lifted the screen of his laptop to a Page Six article whose title read, "Sex Clubs, That's How Jet Set Owner Jeremy McQueen Got His Start."

I stopped breathing and sank into his chair. I didn't need to read the article to know two things. First, it wasn't going to affect Jet Set—in fact, it would probably increase membership. Second, it was going to ruin any chance I had of receiving private funding from the super-conservative channels I'd solicited because the prospectus had Jeremy's name on the byline as a consultant.

His gaze cut to mine. "I'll fix this."

I just shook my head. "There's no fixing this, Jeremy."

"I'll find a way."

My cell started ringing from the other room. "I better get that."

I felt like I was someone else as I crossed the hall and answered Logan's call. "Hello."

"Hey, are you up?"

I sat on the bed. "Yes, and I saw it. Did you tell your uncle?"

"Not yet. I wanted to know what you were thinking about doing first."

I gave a small laugh. "You know there's nothing I can do."

"Did you send a prospectus to Dawson? He won't care about the rumors. He'll invest, I'm certain."

"No, I left Dawson's prospectus in my desk drawer. I wasn't sure I should ask him. And after some things that happened last week, I know I made the right choice."

"Fuck. Look, when I get back let me see what other avenues you have."

Logan and I both knew I had none but I appreciated the effort. "Tell Hunter I'll call him later."

"I will. And Phoebe, don't give up yet."

I looked up. Jeremy was standing there. When our eyes met, he started stripping off his clothes as he walked toward the bathroom. A few moments later, I heard the shower turn on. "Logan, thanks for calling. I'll be in touch." I hit END and went over to the bathroom door. "What's going on?"

He was rinsing his hair. "I'm going to find out who leaked the info."

"Jeremy, it doesn't matter. It's done. It's not a lie, so there's nothing we can do."

He turned the water off and grabbed a towel. "This is something I have to do. I'll meet you at your office later."

Neither of us said anything about breakfast at Tiffany's. We both knew it wasn't the right time.

Jeremy brushed his teeth, dressed, and was out the door in less than five minutes.

It was only after he left that I realized: *He never kissed me good-bye.*

Next I went back into his office and stared at the article.

Why today of all days?

I didn't cry though. I must have been in some kind of state of shock.

Finally, I made myself get up and shower.

The winter solstice was still one month away, but somehow fall had passed. It was raining or maybe it was sleet, I wasn't sure. I wouldn't normally wear jeans to the office, but between my mood and the weather, I went for comfort and grabbed the only pair I'd left over at Jeremy's and a heavy sweater too.

Lily texted me asking if I was okay, and I texted her back in the cab that I was and I was certain everything was going to be fine, even with the scandal.

I didn't really believe that.

My phone pinged with another text from Lily.

Lily: Preston and I are close to reaching an understanding.

Me: I hope it all works out. Keep me posted.

The rain pelted against the window as I looked out. The day was dreary, a perfect reflection of how I felt. As I compared Lily's life to mine, the parallel between job and boyfriend was there, but that was as close as they came. Lily's priorities were different from mine, but then so were her situations. She was risking her career for the man she loved and I'd blown off what should have been something very special because of my job.

Maybe I should have been more like her?

I looked at my watch. It was eight forty-five. When I glanced at my phone I noticed I had missed a call from Jeremy. Had he gone to Tiffany's after all? Was he waiting for me? I should have asked him before he left. I called him back and when he didn't answer, I sent him a text.

Me: Where are you?

The cab arrived at the Saint and he still hadn't answered me. I surveyed the traffic, and knew I could walk faster. After I quickly paid the driver, I ran as fast I could in the rain to get to the corner. I made it in less than a minute. I pulled on the doors of Tiffany's, but they were locked. I peered inside and the place was dark. There was no Jeremy and no one else.

My heart sank.

I hurried back to the Saint and up to my office. I was wet and I pushed the water from my face. The door to my office was open, which I thought was strange. I usually always closed and locked it, but I was a little distracted when I left yesterday and must have left it open.

I shrugged out of my wet coat and threw it over one of the chairs across from my desk before I plopped down and began to shake my head dry. I finally gave up; it wasn't going to dry that easily.

I tried Jeremy again.

Still, no answer.

I turned in my chair and stared at the park.

Turned back and tried him again.

Still, no answer.

Finally, I set my cell on my desk. I couldn't obsess over yesterday right now; I had to concentrate on work. With my silent admonishment, I turned to face my computer and hesitantly pressed the button to ON and opened my e-mail.

I knew what I was going to find, but seeing the four e-mails stacked on top of one another brought tears to my eyes.

I opened each of them, but they all read the same, just a variation on the words, "I'm sorry I am unable to invest in your company at this time. . . ."

This was it.

The end of TSC.

There was nothing left to do.

Nothing I could do.

I spun myself around in my chair and had to grab the drawer handle to stop from going around again. In the process, I pulled open the drawer that held Dawson's prospectus, but it was empty. I stared at the space, wondering where it had gone.

"Are you looking for this?"

I snapped my head up to see Dawson holding the white envelope in his hand. "How did you get that?" I asked in surprise. *What was he doing here?*

His face had mostly healed; there was just one faint red streak that remained. Acting like he belonged, he picked up my coat and hung it up behind the door. "You know there's a serious change in weather when you switch from leather to wool."

I ignored his comment and went for blunt. "Dawson. What are you doing here?"

His eyes slid over me as he took an unwelcome seat. "Jeremy called me this morning and asked me to meet him here."

My eyes widened. "Why would he do that?"

He leaned forward and set the prospectus on my desk. "He wanted to talk about you."

The hairs on my neck stood up.

Dawson shot me a rueful glance. "Relax, Phoebe. Is everything okay between the two of you?"

An ache raked across my chest. "Everything is fine." I pasted on a fake smile.

He leaned back in the chair. "Good. I'm glad to hear that. It's just"—he waved his hand like he was drawing a circle around me—"you seem a little off today?"

I looked down at myself and knew he was talking about my disheveled appearance. Dawson did not like anything to be less than perfect. And today I was far from perfect. "I got caught in the rain. That's all."

He glanced over my shoulder and out the window. "Understandable."

Alarm rose in my voice as I asked him, "What exactly did you and Jeremy talk about?"

And why couldn't I reach him?

Dawson pretended to pick a piece of fuzz from his slacks. "I'm not normally a kiss and tell kind of guy, you know that about me."

Suspicion hovered at the edges of my mind as I tilted my head in question. "Why are you telling me that?"

"I'm not even sure how, but somehow we ended up talking about that night you ran out on him and called me."

My nerves tingled as it became clear where he was going.

"I told him I was concerned about how confused you were that night and that I didn't mean to kiss you, it just happened."

Bile rose up my throat.

He didn't seem to notice. "But since I'd been through this type of thing with you before, he should be thankful I was there all night to stop you from reverting back to your old ways."

My mouth flattened. "That's not true."

He tilted his head to the side. "What part is a lie?"

Out of nowhere my mind wandered back to that New Year's Eve so long ago that I let Jeremy go. It was the same day I met Dawson at the old fort.

Tears burned my eyes but I held them back. Dawson had helped me but why was he twisting everything now? None of it was a lie, but the way he phrased it wasn't the truth either. I didn't want to hurt him but I had to tell him the truth. "Dawson, I felt sorry for you."

His jaw tightened. "No, you needed me and that's why you called me. You still need me, Phoebe, that's why I had to tell him the truth."

My head jerked up. "What are you talking about?"

He was so eerily calm. "That I knew everything about the two of you, down to the intimate details of your summer affair so long ago. How you lied to him all those years ago. Kept your identity a secret because you knew he couldn't take it. I had to laugh about it though—about a worthless guy thinking he could have a girl like you. Then or now. He has to know he's not enough for you. Come on, Phoebe, you sought me out the day after you first saw him again and fell asleep on my couch."

My jaw dropped. "It wasn't like that."

He slowly rose to his feet and circled my desk, where he proceeded to lean against the edge. "I looked into his past, like you asked me to, you know."

I frowned. "I never asked you to do that."

"Not directly, but since you asked me to look into his parents, I thought I should look into him too."

I steadied myself by gripping the arms of the chair. "You knew when you left my father's apartment that day, I already knew who the Trumans were. You didn't have to look any further."

He ignored me and gazed out the window. "I found out all kinds of interesting things. Not just sex club exploitations either. He has a juvenile record and has gotten himself into trouble concerning some illegal business matters as well. Makes you wonder what the son of the man who your father helped put away is really doing with you. Why he surfaced after five years. Doesn't it?"

I narrowed my eyes at him. "No, Dawson. It doesn't."

He shrugged. "It did me. I had to wonder just what he wanted with you."

"Dawson," I warned.

"Did you know about his past?"

I lifted my chin, feeling defensive. "Yes, I did."

"Well, anyway, we got off track. Jeremy called me here to give me that"— he pointed to the envelope on my desk—"and thought I should know how you felt about it. Pretty funny. Don't you think?"

I shook my head vehemently.

Dawson flashed his teeth at me. "Come on, you have to see the irony in it. He's spent what, a total of maybe three months with you? I've known you for five years, and yet he thought he should tell me how you felt. Like I wouldn't have already figured out why you didn't send me a prospectus. Like I didn't know you were worried I'd say yes even if I didn't think the plan was solid."

I gripped the prospectus toward me in a protective way, not sure why.

Dawson's eyes shifted to the white envelope. "You weren't wrong, Phoebe."

I swallowed, my nerves frazzled. Jeremy must have been listening to my conversation with Logan this morning.

"Jeremy also thought I should know he felt the plan was a concrete path to revitalization for the Saint. He even walked me through the material."

Concern drummed in my core.

"I'm sorry but it took all I had not to laugh. Some good-for-nothing son of a con artist thinks he knows what's best for your company? He thinks his opinion means anything to me?"

I sucked in a breath. "Dawson, I think that's enough."

He reached for the envelope but I jerked it away and stuffed it back in the drawer. "You see, Phoebe, I'd do anything for you. I've told you that. And to his credit, his presentation was very convincing. So much so, I almost said yes immediately. But then I had to wonder . . ." He let the words drift.

Ice formed in my belly. "Dawson, why are you acting like this?"

"Like what?"

"Where is Jeremy?" I asked in a raised voice.

He jerked his thumb over his shoulder. "Oh, he left."

I popped up, feeling panicky. "Where did he go?" I asked in a softer voice.

Dawson shrugged. "I don't know but if he took my offer, he left town."

My knees felt weak as I circled around my desk to sit in one of the chairs on the other side. "What offer?"

He glanced over his shoulder at me.

I was trembling. "What did you do, Dawson?"

He huffed. "What was best for you."

I rubbed my palms on my jeans. "What was that?"

Dawson strode around the desk and took a seat next to me. "I told him that if he disappeared from your life, for good this time, I'd not only fund your entire project and save your family's legacy but I'd also fund his Jet Set expansion as well, in whichever city he decided to move to next."

My eyes darted to his in shock. "Why would you do that?"

"For you. To protect you from him."

Tears pricked my eyes. "He wouldn't take money from you."

He tilted his head. "You don't think so?"

I shook my head vehemently. *Jeremy would never do that.*

"Phoebe, you know I love you, and I'll take you back as soon as you're ready."

I wanted to slap him. "He didn't leave me and I don't love you. You know that."

He heaved a heavy sigh. "I don't think you know what you want. Since the day we met, he's always been in the back of your mind, clouding your judgment."

"No, Dawson, that's not true," I screamed.

"It is. You'll see. You just have to take a step back and see him for what he is. If I'm wrong, then I'm sure he'll be at home waiting for you. If I'm not, he's taken off to find the next city for Jet Set."

I reached across my desk and grabbed my cell. Dawson kept talking but I wasn't listening to him anymore. I had to find Jeremy. I called him again. No answer. I called again and again. No answer.

"Well?"

I was shaking my head, trying to block out his words.

"Put your phone down so we can talk. I'll give you the money you need to save TSC right now, Phoebe."

I turned to him, anger swelling inside me. "I don't know who you are anymore."

"I'm who you turned me into," he laughed sardonically.

"No."

"Yes. You asked me to wait for you. You told me you needed a break. And then on the day that was supposed to be our wedding, you go home with the guy you cried on my shoulder about for so long. I'm who you made me."

I gaped at him. "I never want to see you again."

He took my arm. "Phoebe, you don't mean that."

I ran out and left him in my office.

He called after me. "Don't tell me you'd give it all up for *love.*"

All I could think was *yes, yes I would.*

The last words I heard him say were, "If you change your mind, you can call me."

I rushed to the elevator and down to the lobby. I was clutching my phone in my hand, willing it to ring.

In the cab, I left message after message—Jeremy's phone was now going directly to voice mail. When I got to his loft, he wasn't there. I searched upstairs and all I saw was the screen saver staring back at me from his computer. It was the photo he had texted to himself the night we went to the garage with Jamie and Lindsay. That seemed like a lifetime ago. There was no sign of him anywhere. In fact, I wouldn't have known he'd even been back if the mail hadn't been tossed across the counter. I looked through it since I didn't know what to do next and found an opened letter from the correctional institution in Butner. It was a notice of his father's parole hearing set for next month.

But there was nothing else.

Frantically, I called Jamie. "I need you," I said.

"Where are you?"

"I'm at Jeremy's loft."

"I'll be right there."

But I knew I was too late—Jeremy had left me again.

I could feel it.

And just like that, I was lost again.

CHAPTER 29

Lost Again

He had disappeared.

Friday, Saturday, Sunday, and even Monday went by in a haze.

I stayed with Jamie and Lindsay and I'm not sure I ever got out of bed. I checked my phone every hour, but there were no calls from Jeremy. I ignored all the others.

Jeremy had indeed just vanished. Whether it was out of anger or greed, I didn't know. Jamie tried to reach him but it was obvious by then he'd turned his phone off. Jamie had even gone over to the loft a few times, but there was no sign of him.

He was gone.

On Monday night, a familiar voice whispered in my ear. "Come on, St. Claire, I'm taking you home."

It was Lily and I threw my arms around her.

"You look like shit," she said.

I started to cry.

"Hey, come on now, I'm only kidding. You're beautiful. You know that."

I cried only harder, burying my head in her neck.

"Just let her stay here." Jamie's voice was soft.

"No, she has to get up."

I shook my head. "I can't. I've failed the company, and my parents."

"No, darling, no, you haven't. TSC has been faltering for years. If anything you saved it. Without your improvements to daily operations, it would be worthless."

"Mom?" I asked.

"Yes, I'm here."

"You don't hate me?"

"Oh God no. I love you, you know that."

"But what will you do for money?"

"Oh Phoebe darling, I'm a survivor. I'll be fine. I've put the house on the market and I'll find a place and wait for your father to return."

She was stronger than I thought.

"And I'll help any way I can." It was Mrs. Bardot.

"So will we." The voices came in unison.

I sat up and looked around. The room was filled with everyone I loved— Poppy, Jamie, Lindsay, Logan, Lily, Emmy, Mrs. Bardot, and even Danny.

"Danny, what are you doing here?"

He shrugged. "I came home early for the holidays," he said, but I knew he had really come for me.

But why?

Alarm traveled through my body. "What's going on? Why are you all here?"

My mother cleared her throat and came to sit next to me on the bed. She took my hand.

Panic replaced alarm and tore through me. "Tell me. Is it Jeremy?"

She shook her head. "No one has heard from him," she said grimly. "But something has happened."

"What?" I cried.

"As of this morning, we no longer own controlling shares of TSC."

I stared at her. "How? Why? Who?" One-word questions were all I could manage.

She shook her head. "The shares have diluted so much over the past months, and we've had to sell so much. It wasn't anyone's fault. It just happened."

"Who owns controlling interest?" It didn't really matter; the company was near worthless at this point.

She seemed hesitant to answer me.

"Mom?"

She sighed. "Hunter traced the transactions and found twelve smaller companies that had been buying up shares. They were funneled through a single holding company though."

"Who was it?" I asked, wondering why anyone would want controlling interest of a going nowhere company.

"The name of the company is J Truman."

My stomach wrenched. "Jeremy's father? How? He's still in prison."

Tears were now streaming down my mother's face. "This J Truman isn't Justin, it's Jeremy."

"No, no, he'd never do that."

My mother's expression was filled with anguish. "Hunter verified everything. It was him."

"No," I shrieked. "No!"

I grabbed my phone and called Jeremy. It still went to voice mail. This time I left a message. A simple one: "Why?"

I knew why though.

To distract me and take over my company.

But he hadn't foreseen the sex club leak and that's what ruined his plan. That's why he took Dawson's offer?

Of course.

I had just blinded myself to what I must have known down deep was the truth—he came back to use me.

To get his revenge on my father.

I jumped out of bed and ran to the bathroom.

How could I be so stupid?

My phone was still in my hand when it beeped. It was a message from Jeremy. It read:

Him: Believe in me.

Believe in him?

Believe in him!

He answers me now, when he knows I'm doubting him and with that message. Is he kidding me? Enraged, I threw my phone across the small room and screamed.

Bastard!

There was a soft knock on the door. "Phoebe. Are you okay?" My mother came in. "Come on, come home with me."

I nodded. I needed my mother and she was here for me. I realized it was the first time she probably knew I needed her and I wept for my own stupidity.

Over the next two days, I awoke in my childhood bed but refused to get up. All of my friends stopped by, sat with me, tried to comfort me, and tried to get me up, but I couldn't move.

I felt lost, completely broken, like my heart had been ripped from my chest. Jeremy still hadn't returned, as far as I knew anyway.

And I shouldn't have cared—but I did.

Where was he?

I still loved him. I didn't want to, but I did.

I started to doubt what was right before my eyes. What we had was real. I knew it except all the evidence pointed to him wanting to take over TSC.

A pang of guilt flashed through me. Where the hell was he? I wanted him to face me in person. Suddenly I knew one person who could tell me and I swallowed my dislike for her and grabbed my phone.

The number wasn't hard to find.

"Jet Set Miami." Kat's voice hadn't changed. It still made my skin crawl.

I cleared my throat. "Kat?"

"Yes," she said.

"This is Phoebe."

Silence.

"Phoebe St. Claire," I clarified.

"Yes, I know who it is. What do you want?" The coldness in her words didn't hinder my mission.

"I'm worried about Jeremy. Do you know where he is?"

Her laugh echoed through the phone line. "Are you kidding me?"

The phone slipped in my suddenly sweaty palm. "No. I need to talk to him."

She gave a huff. "I suggest you give Richie Rich a ring and let him enlighten you."

I drew in an angry breath. "Kat, if you're referring to Dawson, I'm not on speaking terms with him."

That shut her up.

"Kat?"

"For fuck's sake, don't tell me you didn't take his offer?"

"No, I didn't."

"Why wouldn't you have taken the money?" Kat said in a low, hard voice. "Jeremy doesn't have the kind of money you are looking for from investors. And Dawson was the only way to stop your empire from collapsing."

So she'd talked to Jeremy. "Please, tell me where he is. I need to see him."

"Did you not hear me?"

"I don't care about the money right now. I need to talk to Jeremy."

"Listen Phoebe, I'm going to give you some advice. Leave him alone. It's better for each of you," she said, and then hung up.

I clutched my phone.

Where are you, Jeremy?

Late Thursday night my mother came in my room with a concerned look on her face.

"What is it?" I asked, pulling the covers under my chin.

"A board meeting has been called for tomorrow and we both have to be there."

I nodded.

"There's something else. Starwood Hotels contacted Hunter. They are interested in buying TSC."

"Mom, no. We can't sell."

"Well, as of right now, it's not our decision. But I want to tell you, he worked out a tremendous deal. Starwood would take possession of all US hotels, except for the two in the city; those would remain under TSC and Starwood will change the name of all the hotels and let us keep ours."

"Why would they do that?"

"Because those were the terms we worked out."

"We?"

"Yes, I joined efforts with Hunter this week. I should have been helping you all along. I'm so sorry I haven't."

"But still, why would Starwood agree to those terms?"

"Because they see the value of the chain. The value you have built."

I smiled for the first time in a week.

"Now, we have to convince the majority of the new shareholders this is the right decision for TSC."

My smile faded.

"We're not sure who is going to show up tomorrow. So don't look so grim.

J Truman is a holding company, which means the actual shareholders of the stocks need to attend the vote. And hopefully those people will have level heads on their shoulders and see the benefit of selling. It's a fair price and they stand to make a good deal of money."

"Have you talked to Dad?" I asked hoarsely.

She nodded. "He's on board. He helped Hunter and me come up with the terms. He wanted you to have a part of the legacy to hold on to—it was his idea to carve the New York hotels out of the deal."

Then I started to cry.

I lost our family legacy.

I did that.

"No tears. You have to be strong."

I nodded. I knew I did.

"And you have to take a shower," my mother quipped.

I laughed as she hugged me.

She stayed with me, fell asleep in my bed stroking my hair. She hadn't done that since I was ten. I wondered then if I just hadn't seen that she was always there for me but I never let her know I needed her.

As she lay beside me, I couldn't help but wonder if life takes us on a path for a reason . . . and if sometimes where you landed was right where you were always supposed to be.

I didn't remember my dreams that night, but whatever they were I knew it wasn't of ruby red lips. They must have been peaceful, because when I awoke Friday morning, it was with a renewed outlook.

I'd spent so much of my life feeling lost. Seeking freedom from the name I was born with, when if I had just embraced it all along, I might have seen how very strong I really was. It wasn't money that defined who I was, it was me. Just me.

And I wasn't weak.

Not anymore anyway.

I was going to fight for what was mine.

On more than one front.

With a clear head, I jumped out of bed and took an extra-long shower, and then I got ready for my day with a vengeance. I pulled on the pencil skirt my mother had lent me and then buttoned the sheer blouse, which would thankfully be covered by what I discovered was a tight-fitting jacket. Normally I didn't wear such constrictive clothing but I felt powerful in the suit nonetheless. Still, when I slipped on her red-soled Louboutins, I had to fight the urge to kick them off.

I looked every bit like my mother.

Then I realized, maybe that wasn't so bad.

The board meeting wasn't until eleven, so my mother said she'd meet me there. I could see the pride in her eyes as I left for work that morning.

Was she always my biggest supporter and I just hadn't seen it?

None of us had spoken of Dawson, but everyone knew about what happened. Jamie had told them. As far as I was concerned, Dawson was out of my life.

But unlike Dawson, Jeremy, although gone, was still very much in my heart. I'd spent so much time thinking about everything and once my temper had cooled, I refused to believe he'd really abandoned me. But where was he? Why was he ignoring my calls and messages? I didn't want to believe he'd done what everyone said he had. But something had happened. I'd seen it that last night we'd spent together. He'd turned me off.

I didn't know why.

But I wanted him to explain it.

However, today I had to focus on work and then, after the board meeting, I was going to find Jeremy and put it all out there.

Even if he was done with me, he owed me an explanation if nothing else.

The office was practically empty when I arrived but as I was walking down the hallway, I felt a strange familiar presence stir in my belly. I couldn't shake it. When I passed by the boardroom, something compelled me to glance in.

My body trembled with way too many emotions to bear and the air whooshed from my lungs.

It was him.

Jeremy McQueen.

His back was to me, but I'd know him anywhere. Long, lean, and confident, he stood glancing out the floor-to-ceiling window that overlooked the park. My body tingled and I cursed my reaction but I couldn't prevent it. I still loved him with reckless abandon.

He turned and as his eyes flashed to mine, he smiled at me. Not in a rueful, or devilish, or charming, or even lustful way. It was that look of love I'd seen whenever he was watching me and didn't know I was looking.

The room started to spin. I eased my way back and dug into my palms with my nails to keep myself from falling into his lustful haze.

He strode toward me. "I did it." He beamed.

My heart sank with his vile admission and I couldn't prevent the anger I'd been holding back from flooding my body. Was he seriously bragging about taking over TSC? Had my faith in him been that misguided? My throat tightened as I tried to speak but nothing came out. My hands shook so badly, my fingers couldn't even keep hold of the straps of my purse. I don't know what came over me but before I knew it, I was slamming my fists against his chest. "How could you," I cried. "How could you?"

He caught my wrists and looked genuinely confused. "What is the matter with you?"

I sighed and my voice lost its strength as I spoke. "What's the matter with me? You used me to steal my company to satisfy your own perverted sense of revenge."

Jeremy dropped my wrists and pain arrested his features. "No," he spat.

Everything about his gorgeous face was suddenly wrong and I couldn't bear it. "I thought you loved me. But all you wanted to do was distract me so you could take everything from me while my father was away."

He visibly paled right before me. "Stop right there. Don't say things you'll regret. Sit down. We need to talk."

"There is nothing left to talk about."

Jeremy let out an exaggerated exhale and reached for me.

I flinched and jerked away.

Slowly turning his head, his jaw tightened as he spoke. "How about you let me explain," he tried again.

Exhaling shakily, I courageously stepped toward him. "What exactly do you want to explain? How you've been convincing companies to buy stock in TSC for over a year? Or how you manipulated me right under my nose and now you control my worthless company?" Bile rose in my throat with each and every bitter word.

Everything about him went hard, rigid, and he was shaking his head in disbelief. "I'm not who you think I am. I thought you already knew that."

"Then who are you?" I cried.

He didn't answer. He'd disconnected from me completely.

I'd seen that blank, cold look before.

I shuddered at what that meant.

Jeremy didn't deny anything I'd said though, and that made me want to grab him and spin him around, I was so mad. "Tell me, why? Why?"

Clamping his jaw, he glared at me.

"Tell me, Jeremy, did you ever really love me?"

His eyes turned cold, black.

Goading him, because anger pushed me to do it, and honestly my broken heart didn't know what else to do, I went on. "What, nothing else to say now that the truth is out?"

"Fuck you!" he growled.

I flinched. "You already have," I said, the fight in me gone.

He drew in a deep breath. "I'm sorry, I shouldn't have said that."

I had to look away from him or I'd cave. I knew I would.

"All you had to do was believe in me," he muttered.

My body was trembling.

He didn't seem to care what state I was in as he walked toward the door.

I threw my hands up in the air. "Sure, do what you do best—walk away."

Then he stopped.

I noticed something on the table. It was an envelope with a red ribbon around it.

He tapped it with his fingers but didn't turn around. "This is what I've been doing all week—contrary to what you choose to believe, I wanted to help you. The note I left you explained everything. I thought that would be enough." He laughed a little. "I guess I was wrong. I guess Dawson's hold on you was stronger than I wanted to believe. My mistake. It won't happen again."

Shaking my head, tears in my eyes, I snapped. "I have to know one thing. Why did you turn me off that last night? Why not see your plan through and marry me? You didn't know the news would break the next day and ruin everything."

He turned toward me and his eyes flashed with that same emptiness I'd seen that last night. "The only thing I ever wanted from you was for you to believe in me."

With that he walked out the door. His steps were slow and seemed to falter but that could have been what I wanted to see. I was trembling after all and my sight was blurry from the tears left unspilled. I didn't know what note he was referring to but there were no words that could erase what he'd done.

Closing my eyes, I blocked out the image of his back as he took those final steps to the elevator. I couldn't bear to see him get in it. He had already taken everything from me and yet it took all I had not to run to him and beg him to stay.

I was a stupid, stupid girl.

The elevator door closed and my eyes snapped open. As soon as he was gone so was my composure. My knees weakened and I crumpled to the floor like a rag doll. Minutes passed as I tried to pull myself together. I grabbed the table and rose to my feet before I reached for the envelope.

What was inside? The details of how he was going to break TSC apart and sell off the pieces? I didn't need to see that. I wanted to tear it up. Yet, I couldn't resist opening it.

My heart was in my throat as I crossed the room. With shaky fingers, I pulled the ribbon and opened the thick envelope. What I found was nothing like I had expected to see. It was filled with TSC stock certificates. I flipped through them, there were twelve of them with varying amounts of shares, all owned by different companies, and each signed—and not just signed but signed over to me.

I froze, my muscles clenching and going stiff. I didn't understand. If Jeremy wanted to steal TSC from me so badly, why was he signing the shares back over to me?

I had to find out what the hell was going on.

Hunter was getting off the phone when I barged into his office. He glanced up and his face looked pale. "Phoebe, I was just coming to find you. You're not going to believe this."

Anxious, I waved the envelope in front of him. "No, you're not going to believe this."

Hunter, though, was lost in some kind of state of shock. "The shell company, J Truman, is administered by Dawson Vanderbilt, not Jeremy McQueen."

His words echoed in my head. I felt dizzy and I had to sit down. The last of my emotional strength collapsed right there in his office. I could have been a rag doll I was so limp. "Dawson?"

"I'm sorry, Phoebe."

"What do you mean? You told me it was Jeremy." My voice sounded bleak. Barely able to get the words out.

"I know. I'm so sorry. I was wrong. J Truman is a Vanderbilt Brokerage holding company. It seems that over the past year they have brokered most of the stock purchases and more recently they have funneled all of stock we released through J Truman to the purchasing companies. My guess is the purchases were made on Dawson's recommendation."

My face felt numb but somehow I managed to move my lips and ask, "How did you find that out?"

Hunter flipped through a stack of papers. "I have a friend over at the SEC and I called him yesterday. I asked him to look into the recent stock purchases. I was hoping, in some offhanded way, they wouldn't be one hundred percent legit and I could use that against Jeremy as leverage to buy them back. I don't get it though, why would Dawson want me to think it was Jeremy?"

Everything suddenly clicked into place. It wasn't Jeremy at all who had been using TSC's vulnerability—it was Dawson. But for what? Some kind of leverage to keep me?

Tears scalded my skin as they slid down my face. "No, not you, me," I whispered.

I felt sick. The look on Jeremy's face as he turned to leave was already haunting me. I'd let him down by not believing in him.

I really was a stupid, stupid girl.

Hunter shook his head slowly. "I'm sorry. When I saw the stock agreements that had been faxed to me, I assumed you requested them. Jeremy Truman signed them all and I just assumed J Truman, the shell company, belonged to him. But here," Hunter handed me some of the papers he had in front of him. "They were never even faxed. Someone put them here and with everything going on, I just never noticed."

"Dawson must have done it," I said hoarsely.

Oh God.

What had I done?

I shoved the papers back in Hunter's hands. "I have to go."

"You can't. The board meeting will start soon."

I handed him the envelope I was still holding in my other hand. "Look inside. Somehow Jeremy bought the shares back and he is gifting them over to me. My guess is there's enough shares in there to give us back control."

Hunter started pulling the certificates out. "He must have gone to each company. How did he manage to convince them to sell?"

I gave a sad shrug. "I don't know but I have to find him. Take the deal with Starwood. My mother will be here if you need her. I'll call you later."

I hurried as fast as I could, sprinting to the elevator, and then running toward the street. Hugh had parked out front and just as my mother was getting out of the car, I hopped in.

"Where are you going?" Poppy asked.

"Find Hunter. He'll explain everything," I shouted as I closed the door.

"I have to get to Jeremy's loft as fast as you can," I told Hugh.

He got a gleam in his eye as he jerked into traffic. I pulled my phone from my purse and called Jeremy. It didn't go immediately to voice mail, but he also didn't answer. I hung up and texted him.

> Me: I am so sorry. Please . . . you have to forgive me.

I waited for a reply.

But none came.

My throat tightened. My mouth was completely dry. My body felt numb. I had done just what Dawson wanted me to do—believed the worst about Jeremy.

Traffic was ridiculous and it seemed to take years before I got to Jeremy's loft. I told Hugh to go. If Jeremy wasn't there, I was going to wait, and I didn't care for how long. I knocked and when there was no answer, I used my key.

As soon as I walked in, I was surprised. He was there. I could see him from the foyer. He was sitting on the sofa with his head down.

"Jeremy," I said softly.

He didn't answer me.

I dropped everything in my hands and went to him. "Jeremy, talk to me," I pleaded.

He looked up. His face was gaunt and his eyes had shadows under them. In my fury, I hadn't noticed any of that at my office but he looked utterly exhausted.

"I'm sorry." I dropped to my knees and took his hands. "You have to forgive me."

He just shook his head.

"Jeremy," I cried.

"Don't," he said.

"I love you."

"It doesn't matter." His voice was broken.

"We can get through this."

He shook his head. "No. This has to end. We can't keep doing this to each other. You're right—what we have is toxic. We're just not good for each other."

"Don't say that. You don't mean it!"

"I do."

"You don't." My voice rose.

"You believed the worst in me. I can't keep doing this."

"I said I was sorry."

His eyes gleamed, like he was listening but not hearing what I was saying. My throat got even tighter. "I didn't know, Jeremy. I didn't know Dawson had done this."

"It doesn't matter anymore." His tone was bitter.

"It does!"

His eyes were flat. "Don't you get it? That's what makes it even worse. You really thought I could do something like that to you. I was worried you'd be upset but . . ." His words trailed off. "Dawson wanted you to believe I could hurt you and you did. He was right, he knew better than me. He told me he did. I told him no, I knew you, and you would never believe a story like that. But you did."

"No, not in my heart I didn't."

He looked at me. "Phoebe. It's over."

I reached for his face. "No, don't say that."

He stood up. "I called Jamie. He's coming to pick you up."

I tried to pull him back down to me. "Don't leave," I begged.

"I have to, for both of us."

"But we can work through this."

I looked up and saw a single tear in his eye. "Good-bye, Phoebe," he said as he walked toward the door.

I scurried off the floor and ran to the door, blocking his way.

He stopped a cautious distance from me. "Don't make this worse. I'm going to leave and give you time to get your things together."

I shook my head. "I'm not going to let you go."

"It's not your choice."

I stepped closer. "No, but it's not only yours either."

"Why are you doing this?" Jeremy's anger came to the surface again.

I tried to put my arms around his neck. "Because I love you too much to lose you again over this."

He shoved me away. "You should have thought about that before you believed I'd betray you for money or revenge or whatever the fuck sick reason you believed."

"I'm so sorry," I pleaded.

His eyes, those intense blue eyes, blazed at me. "Not going to cut it this time around, sweetheart."

"Don't call me that. Don't act like you're okay with this," I screamed in his face.

"I tried to do this nicely."

"Tell me you want to live your life without me."

He closed his eyes. "I think it's better if we're not together." His tone was softer now.

"That's not what I asked. Look me in the eyes and tell me you want to live your life without me."

His eyes fluttered and his mouth opened, but he said nothing.

I reached for him again. "If you can't do that, then you owe it to us to stay here and talk through this. You might be right, we might not be good for each other, but we have to talk before we can decide that."

He stepped closer to me. "Why are you making this so much harder than it has to be?"

My heart stopped. "Because I love you, like I've never loved anyone in my life and I can't lose you. Not again. I was a mess without you this week. I never even—"

His hands went to my hips as I spoke and his intense blue eyes filled with anguish. Unexpectedly, the door opened and I had to move to avoid getting hit. I also had dislodged myself from Jeremy's grip.

"Hey, man," Jamie said to Jeremy. "I didn't think you'd still be here."

Jeremy looked at me with sadness looming in his eyes. "I'm sorry but I just can't."

"No," I screamed. "No."

He looked at Jamie. "I was just leaving."

My mouth dropped and tears filled my eyes. "Jeremy," I cried.

Jamie's gaze landed on me.

Jeremy stopped at the door and looked back at me. "I really think it's best this way, for both of us," he said hoarsely and then he closed the door.

I fell to the floor, my legs no longer able to hold me up. My body felt numb. He had done what he told me he'd never do—he left me.

Jamie collapsed beside me and pulled me into his arms.

"I ruined everything," I cried.

"Phoebs, talk to me. Tell me what happened."

We sat on the floor and I told him everything. How I was led to believe a lie and it was my fault that I didn't trust Jeremy.

I should have believed in him—in our love.

After a long while, I couldn't cry anymore. I just sat there, words coming from my mouth in a monotone that made no sense.

Jamie suddenly pulled me to my feet. "Let's go. What do you want me to get of yours?"

"Nothing," I said.

"Are you sure?"

I nodded. "They're only things. I don't care about them. I care about him. I want him."

All I could think about was how much I wanted him.

Everything that happened after that was a blur. Jamie had a car waiting outside. When we got in, I wasn't sure if he'd gone to work yet or not, but I was grateful he was there for me. If not, I would have never left and nothing good would come out of another confrontation with Jeremy so soon.

But I wasn't giving up.

Not this time.

I looked around and thought—I'd be back.

When I looked at Jamie, he was looking at me. "It will be okay. I would have Lindsay spend the day with you, but she and my mother left early this morning for a spa day and won't be back until late tonight."

"Lindsay and your mother?"

He gave me a slight smile. "Yeah, my dad came back a few days ago and my mother had a complete change of heart."

I grabbed his hand. "I'm so happy for you."

He squeezed it back. "But don't worry. Christmas in the Hamptons is still on."

I started to cry again at the thought of the holidays without Jeremy.

Jamie winced. "Where's my fucking head. I'm such an asshole."

"It's okay," I said and leaned my head against the window.

We drove the rest of the way to my apartment in silence.

The traffic was light and when we got to my place, I got out and turned back to him. "I think I need to go in alone."

"Are you sure? At least let me walk you up."

"No, I need to be alone."

"Lindsay and I can bring dinner over."

I shook my head no. "Honestly, I just need some time alone."

"I'll call you then."

"You don't have to check on me."

"Yes, I do."

"Okay," I conceded.

I was in a state of shock as I walked through the lobby.

Had that all really just happened?

"Miss St. Claire, Miss St. Claire," Jack called.

I turned around.

Jack was holding up an envelope. "A messenger brought this by last week but you haven't been home since. I was given strict instructions this was only to go into your hands by me or I would have slipped it under your door."

The note.

With trembling fingers, I took it. "Thank you, Jack."

"Are you all right?" he asked.

I nodded.

As soon as I walked into my apartment, I shoved off my mother's suit jacket and sat down to open the note. It read:

Phoebe,
    By the time you read this, I'll be gone but unlike the last time, I'll be back for you.
    I have some things to take care of and there are some things you should know. First and foremost, Dawson was behind the sex club

leak to Page Six. He's been following me and I'm not certain, but he might have someone monitoring my calls. I met with him this morning and my suspicions peaked when he knew about the sex tape, and a number of other things only you and I would know about, like your father's car.

More important, I fear he's trying to take over TSC and make it look like me.

That's why I am going to seek the advice of my father concerning my next steps. Listen, Dawson has made some threats to expose TSC's vulnerability if I don't stay away from you. So I think it's best if we don't talk until I get back. I don't want him to know what I'm doing and I'm not sure to what extent he's done.

Right now Dawson needs to think he's won so that he'll back off from whatever he's up to. Let him believe that. I have to figure out what to do to help you. It's my fault you weren't able to secure the investors for Sinners.

I'll make this right and be back as soon as possible. We have a lot to work out when I return. I'm sorry for the way I treated you last night and this morning. I just need you to believe in me.

Jeremy

Heartbroken, I fell back onto the sofa and clutched the note to my aching chest. Everything I needed to know was written on this one page. Why hadn't I found the strength to come home like Jeremy assumed I would have? He saw me as a strong, confident woman who wouldn't let a man bring her down, when in reality I was a weak girl who didn't know who she was because she'd spent so much time trying to be who she wasn't.

I blanched at the ugly truth—it wasn't jealousy that tore us apart; it was lack of faith when the heart mattered most.

Mistrust was just so toxic.

Stupid, stupid girl.

CHAPTER 30

Not Again

The Rainbow Room.

That's where I ended up.

Feeling like I might suffocate if I stayed in my apartment one more minute, I needed air and headed to Central Park. But when I couldn't bear the bitter wind on my face any longer, somehow I ended up in Rockefeller Center.

There's a big glass Nintendo store there that's been around for years but I had never set foot inside. Today I did. I just wanted to see what it was like.

Afterward, I thought I'd stop in Dean & Deluca, but to my surprise it was no longer located on the corner where I remembered it. Instead I stood near the rink and watched as people twirled around on the ice.

Even immersed in a crowd of people, I had never felt so alone. Tourists milled around drinking their drinks and talking about their day, all the while oblivious to my efforts at trying to figure them out. What made them tick? Love, lust, greed, passion, or need?

Actually the truth was that I no longer cared.

Twice, I'd lost the love of my life and that was enough for a lifetime. With a cleansing inhale, I sipped my fourth gin martini and stood and stared at the view of Manhattan laid out beneath me. Millions of shimmering lights blanketed the city that never slept. And behind one of those itty-bitty lights was the love of my life.

I shut my eyes and imagined everything that had happened over the past weeks playing out differently. And that Jeremy and I were out on one of our subway roulette excursions having fun.

I know he'd never been to the SixtyFive Bar at the Rainbow Room. I'd told him I wanted us to go. He needed to see this spectacular panoramic view that wrapped around the terrace. At night, there was nothing like it.

And tonight as I took it in, I let myself pretend for a few short minutes that he was here. It felt good to imagine him behind me, his hands on my hips, his breath on my neck, pulling me close as we took in the impressive view.

"Jesus Christ! What are you doing out here?" a familiar voice grumbled from behind me as an arm hooked me and set me on my feet.

My eyes snapped open. I hadn't noticed I'd acted recklessly and hoisted myself up. "Logan," I answered, surprised to see him.

He took my elbow and dragged me inside. "It's fucking freezing out there and you're wearing practically nothing. What were you thinking?"

I glanced down at my mother's sheer blouse and my lack of camisole beneath it. It was cream and the black bra I'd worn under it was lit up like a neon sign. "I left my jacket somewhere, but have no idea where," I giggled.

Logan grabbed my hand. "Come on. I'm taking you home."

I pointed my finger at him. "Oh no, no, no, no. I'm not going back there tonight."

"Are you drunk?"

I swayed in my mother's shoes as I pinched my fingers together. "I might have had a little too much."

He shook his head. "Jamie told me what happened. I'm sorry. You should have called one of us instead of going out alone."

I thrust my empty glass at him. "Now that you're here, how about you join me."

Logan grabbed my hand. "I'd love to have a drink with you. Come back to my place and I'll break out my finest whiskey."

Sly. He was a sly devil. Really good-looking guy. With hair the color of wet sand that always spiked forward and hazel eyes that sometimes looked brown, sometimes green, he reminded me of that guy from *Gossip Girl*, the one whose father went to jail for embezzlement. Tonight though, he looked especially attractive in his gray tailored suit and unusually smooth face.

I glanced around the room. "What will your date think?"

He huffed in annoyance. "My grandfather just left. I met him here for dinner to discuss some issues he's having with me."

I raised a curious brow. "Care to discuss? I know all about trust-fund issues." I winked.

I wasn't interested in him romantically and he wasn't interested in me. We'd been playing this cat and mouse game since that summer in the Hamptons when we shared a house. It was after that summer I began to notice he never attached himself to anyone and being my once naturally curious self about human emotions, I wondered why he never had a woman at his side.

He crossed his arms over his chest. "No. But I won't drill you or tear you to pieces for going out if you promise to never do this again."

While I wanted to argue, he was right. It was time to face it. I'd done something stupid and I knew I wouldn't be doing it again. I pouted nonetheless. "I promise."

He smirked. "Good. Now walk with me or I'm carrying you out of here, Phoebe. Your choice."

Indignation had me walking. "When did you get such a long stick up your ass?"

The elevator was only a few steps away and he pressed the button. "You shouldn't be out drinking alone at night."

Sobering, I shook myself out of my stupidity and gave a little huff. "Yes, you're right. We already agreed on that. It's just been a really rough day."

"I'm here if you want to talk about it."

Feeling the need to hug someone, I wrapped my arms around him and as soon as I did, the ache in my chest intensified and I couldn't stop myself from crying into his shoulder. "Why? Why didn't I believe in him?"

Logan stiffly wrapped his arms around me in return. He wasn't a hugger or someone you sought out when you needed comfort. He was tough, and strong, and protective, but the gushy stuff wasn't for him. I knew this was killing him. "How about I take you over to Jamie's?" he asked.

I glanced at my watch and snorted in the most unladylike way. "It's early still and he and his mother just mended fences. It's probably family game night and I'd hate to intrude."

He smirked. "Right. I think that ended years ago. But in case it hasn't, I don't think he'll mind."

"But I do."

"Then my place it is."

I shrugged. Logan's was fine but I just couldn't face Jamie and his lectures right now.

The last of the fallen leaves scattered across the pavement in the wind. Logan's place was a ritzy, white-glove building directly across the street from the Metropolitan Museum of Art. His grandfather owned the building and had insisted that Logan live there. Logan, of course, hadn't been the one to tell me that. He never told anyone anything. His grandfather's housekeeper's sister was Lily's manicurist and around here, that's how news traveled fast. Sad as it sounded, it was true.

Surprisingly, Logan wasn't that bad at taking care of a drunk. He made me drink two glasses of water, down a couple of Advil, and then tucked me into a bed in his spare bedroom. In the dark, I struggled with what had happened today.

But I must have fallen asleep because the next thing I knew the sun was coming up and I awoke with a stark realization.

It was my wedding day.

Or it was supposed to have been anyway.

It felt like a common theme in my life.

But this time, the sadness I felt was almost debilitating. The hole in my heart seemed to have grown bigger and deeper overnight. My stomach knotted as I let myself be engulfed by my grief.

Emotionally, I was a wreck. How was I going to recover from this?

Squinting, I looked outside at that great big ball of yellow fire and out of nowhere, a well of hope billowed up through me. Maybe, just maybe Jeremy would remember what today was too and when he did, he'd want to contact me. The thought had me jumping up and cursing this damn pencil skirt, which was hindering my movement.

I'd left my cell phone home and needed to get to it. Sliding on the red-toed devils, which were officially never gracing my feet again, I clumsily made my way into Logan's kitchen. There was a note on the counter telling me he'd gone for a run and would grab coffees. I wrote on the bottom of it—*Thank you for last night but I had to get home.*

My phone had no messages.

There were no notes.

The doorman said no one had stopped by.

Alone, I walked into my bathroom, my hope slowly melting away with each step. My face was swollen and puffy as I looked in the mirror. Not really caring, I stripped out of the clothes I planned to burn as soon as I lit my next fire and took a deep breath. I could do this—move forward. With a little bit of hope that what we had was real, I could.

With the water steaming hot, I stepped in and cleaned myself up as best I could with the mood I was in. Still, I wanted to look presentable in case Jeremy came by. I went with black leggings and a long cream sweater that had a deep V. I usually wore a turtleneck under it but today I slid on one of Jeremy's white undershirts he'd left in the drawer I'd given him.

I breathed in his scent and I knew I'd never wash it. Dressed, my hair back in a ponytail, I sat on my sofa next to my cell phone and waited, and waited, and waited.

By three, sadness started to wreck me and I called him. No answer. By seven a deep sadness consumed me and I called him again. No answer. By nine, sadness crippled me and I called him yet again. Still, no answer.

I stared down at my damn phone. Today was the day I was supposed to marry Jeremy. I was to be his and him mine. That would have happened if my own lack of trust hadn't ruined everything. And with that hard, cold truth, what should have been the happiest day of my life was very likely one of the worst.

Tears clogged my throat as I tried to muster up the strength to go out but I couldn't even do that. So I fell asleep crying because he never called, never texted, or never reached out in any way.

The familiar sharp stinging in my throat woke me up the next day. Those damn red lips wouldn't leave me alone while I slept. I knew he didn't leave me for Avery—or for anyone else—but the possibility that he might turn to her now was haunting me.

With a deep hole in my heart that I was certain would never heal, I heaved myself out of bed and slithered to the sofa, where my cell phone was beeping with unanswered calls.

Hope glimmered in my heart as I pushed the white button and my notifications scrolled through the screen. Too many to go through between Facebook notifications, work e-mails, personal e-mails, and texts, so I went directly to my phone icon and hit the missed calls button. Lily had called three times, Jamie twice, my mother once, and even Logan, but no Jeremy.

A beep alerted me to an incoming text but before I read it I hit the messages button to check for any that might be from him. None. The text was from Lily.

Lily: I'll be back as soon as I can. And please call me before you look at Page Six.

Dread roiled in my belly as I ignored her request and grabbed for my laptop. I clicked in the address bar and typed PageSix.com. Immediately, the air seemed to expel from my lungs.

There were two photos side by side. One of Jeremy and Avery standing beside an older-looking man with glasses and a hat whom I'd never met but seen many times and the other of just the man himself. The caption read: *Elvis Costello plays Whitney Museum's good-bye gala.*

I read the short accompanying article: "Elvis Costello played hit after hit at the Whitney Museum's final gala at its Breuer building before it moves downtown. Museum director said the new Whitney would open in the spring of 2015. Accompanying board of directors member, Avery Lake, admitted she wept earlier from nostalgia, but then found Weinberg's excitement infectious. Lake dazzled in a gown by designer and Whitney vice president Pamella Roland. When asked whose arm she's been seen on lately, her lips were sealed."

Looking closer at the photo, I noticed he wasn't touching her in any way. Not that that meant anything but it made me feel better. Still, seeing that photo of the two of them hurt.

I felt like I was spinning, falling, going down that rabbit hole I refused to land in again. I'd been there, done that, and thank you very much but I didn't want a redo.

Whether Jeremy ended up in Avery's bed or not, I had to see him, to at least let him know that I never really gave up on him.

Stalkerlike qualities or not, I was going to find him and profess my love to him.

With shaking hands I found myself outside his door less than an hour later. I rang the bell. Waited. No answer. I knocked. Waited. No answer. I considered using my key but I knew it was wrong and besides, if he'd changed his locks already, finding that out would really kill me. So instead, I waited outside his door for three hours.

When hopelessness set in, I knew it was time to leave. But before I did, I pulled out the dried flower I'd saved all those years ago and left it with the note I'd written just before I left earlier and leaned it against his door. The note read:

Jeremy,
You gave this to me the first time we met on the beach so long ago.
I've kept it with me as a reminder of the way our relationship began. I'm
leaving it with you in hopes it reminds you of what we once shared.
I will always love you,
Phoebe X

Outside, on the streets of Tribeca, the air was frigid. No snow had fallen but it was coming. I could feel it in the air.

Ducking into a coffee shop to warm up, I sat down with my latte and called Jamie. He'd called me over and over and it was time I returned his calls. Besides, I was certain Logan would have ratted on me about the other night and I welcomed the ass-whipping he'd be giving me.

"Phoebs?"

"Yeah, it's me," I said.

"What the fuck? Do you think you could call me back?" he muttered.

"I'm sorry," I sighed.

"No, I am. I know you're having a rough time."

My cup warmed my hands as I leaned against my phone cradled to my ear. "Hey, I need to know, have you talked to Jeremy?"

"No Phoebs, I haven't. He won't pick up."

"I'm worried about him. He doesn't really have anyone here to turn to."

And I didn't think he was turning to Avery.

I didn't.

Jamie cleared his throat. "Yeah, I know. I've been trying but no luck."

I sipped my drink. "Okay."

"Hey, you know I'm here if you need me. Right?"

That made me smile. "I know. Just make sure you keep Jeremy close if he needs you. I won't be upset."

"Yeah, sure. No problem."

Laughter from the table beside me bubbled up. "Where are you?" Jamie asked.

"I'm out having coffee right now, just clearing my head. But I'll call you later, okay?"

"I love you, Phoebs."

I exhaled a breath. "I love you too." I hung up and scrolled through my calls and hit one of the recent ongoing calls.

"Jet Set Miami," the familiar voice answered.

"Kat, it's Phoebe again," I said tentatively.

Silence.

Uneasiness stuck in my throat. "I don't want to keep you but I wanted to—" *I wanted to what?* I paused, not sure exactly what I was doing. I wanted to make sure Jeremy was okay but telling that to Kat didn't make any sense.

"Hey, listen, Phoebe. I know I'm some sort of link to Jeremy for you and I don't mind you calling me but I haven't talked to him."

My hands were trembling. "Really?"

She sighed. "Yeah, he's shut me out."

I rubbed my palms on my pants. "I'm worried about him to be honest."

"I am too." She sounded choked up.

"Well, you have my number if anything comes up."

"Yeah, and Phoebe . . ."

"Yes," I said.

"I'm sorry things didn't work out," she said as she hung up.

Those damn tears scalded my cheeks. "Yeah, me too."

Monday rolled around like a slap in the face and I couldn't believe I had to go in to work. I'd tried to contact Jeremy again but he still didn't return my calls.

He needed time.

Time heals all wounds.

I had to believe it—otherwise I would wither away.

But then Monday passed and Tuesday came, and days later I'd still heard nothing from him. The only sighting of him had been that damn picture with Avery. It had been a week and nothing. That's when realization finally hit. I really, truly had lost him. It was the Hamptons, all over again.

And it was time to accept that truth.

He'd left and wasn't coming back.

The dawning was brutal and I felt so alone. It was early morning, but I picked up the phone anyway and made a call I should have made a week ago.

"Mom," I cried.

We'd talked earlier in the week but I wasn't ready to go through everything that had happened. It was still too raw. But in this dire time of need, I finally told her everything I hadn't been able to admit over the last week. I'd never leaned on my mother before but I did now. I told her what had happened five years ago all the way up until last Friday and she listened without judgment.

"Phoebe," she said before we hung up.

"Yes."

"Don't lose faith in him. He needs someone to believe in him for who he is. If you stay strong and just do that, I know he'll come around."

Her words were like a hand reaching into my chest and squeezing my heart. I hadn't done that, and that's why he left me. My tears fell anew as I dragged myself out of bed to start yet another day without him.

I called him another time and left another message that said, "I love you." I called after I took a shower but this time said, "I should have believed in you." I did it again before I left for work and said, "I love you and I believe in you." And again after I got home but this time as I spoke to his voice mail, I felt the finality of it all and after I'd hung up, I sat on my couch and typed out one final message.

Me: I will believe in you until my dying days.

Just as I set my phone down, it rang. "Hello?" I answered anxiously without looking at who it was.

"Hey, Lindsay and I are bringing dinner over and you can't say no."

"Jamie," I sighed. "I won't be good company."

Jamie huffed, "If you think we're friends for the company, I might need to enlighten you on what a pain in the ass you are."

I glowered at his words but felt the corners of my mouth tip up nonetheless. "See you soon," I conceded.

"You know I love you," he said, and hung up.

Yeah, if I hadn't known it before, I did now—I was surrounded by people who cared about me.

CHAPTER 31

That's What Friends Are For

There's this little thing called self-preservation that I felt compelled to embrace.

It was early afternoon and I had come home before lunch. I just wasn't feeling well and couldn't make it through an entire day. Things at work were on autopilot now, as the sell-off was in place, and we were at a standstill until it was complete.

I had just lain back on the couch when someone knocked. I knew who it was because there were only a handful of people the doorman would let up without calling me, and even fewer that weren't working.

"Come in," I called.

Lily poked her head in. "Good, you're home. I went to your office first and they told me you went home sick. Did you hear the news?"

I sat up, surprised she was back and happy because I'd missed her. "Depends on which news you're referring to."

"Lars. His picture is all over the news. He was taken in for questioning when cops pulled him over and found Rohypnol in his possession."

"So he did slip that to me," I said, not entirely surprised.

Lily was carrying a big bag of food in her hands. "That would be my guess. Rumor has it, he's been doing this since college but none of his victims will come forward, so he's going to be let go."

"Why would he do that?"

I just didn't get it.

"People do things for all kinds of crazy reasons."

She had a point.

I heaved a heavy sigh of relief that I hadn't been one of his victims but I felt bad for those who had been.

"You look like shit, by the way. Have you eaten?"

I shook my head.

She set the bag down. "Soup and crackers for lunch."

I rolled over. "I'm not hungry."

She pulled me up. "I know, but you have to eat anyway."

The note was beneath me and I pulled it out.

"What's that?"

"The destruction of my relationship," I sighed.

"Let me see," she said.

I handed it to her. I'd told her about it on the phone. Why she needed to see it firsthand, I didn't know.

She sat down next to me and began to cry as she read it, and in response, the tears flowed from my eyes as well.

Damn it. I was trying to be strong.

When she was finished, she turned to me. "You know it's not over."

I slanted her a look through blurry vision. "If the fact that he won't have anything to do with me isn't enough, that picture should have enlightened you."

She shrugged. "It doesn't mean anything." She looked sympathetic. "You just have to give him some time."

I sighed. "That's what I thought yesterday, and the day before that, and the day before that one, and so on. But then this morning, I realized time isn't going to fix anything. In fact, time will only make things worse."

"It hasn't been that long."

I scowled. "It took five years the first time. I'll be old and gray this time around." It was the first time I was brutally honest with myself. There wasn't going to be another *this time around*.

"You don't know that."

I looked at my optimistic friend. "Yes, I do. This isn't *Pretty Woman*. Jeremy's not going to stride in here and carry me off into the sunset. He doesn't want to see me. Ever again. He made that very clear."

"It's only been a week. How many times have I done things that hurt Preston? It never stopped him from trying to get me back."

I gave her a little smile. "He's not Preston."

"No, he's not." Her voice had a chill to it.

I jerked my head up and looked more closely at her. Her mascara was smudged and she had circles under her eyes. "What's going on with you two?"

She batted her hand. "We'll talk about it later."

A pang of guilt flashed through me. "No, tell me now."

She raised a bowl of the soup. "If you eat, I'll tell you."

I took the bowl and lifted the lid. "Crab bisque?"

She nodded.

I reached for a spoon.

She grabbed the other soup and kicked her shoes off.

I did the same.

Lily sat Indian style next to me and inhaled a deep breath. "So, it turned out Preston was having anatomical problems."

My eyes widened. Jeremy was right.

"And, for some reason, he . . . stirred, only if he saw me, well, you know."

I almost choked on my spoonful of bisque. "He got a hard-on if he saw you kissing another girl?"

She dipped her spoon in her own soup. "Yes, anatomically speaking, it seemed he was only able to become erect when the pressure was off him to perform."

"Cut the therapist lingo, Lily, and tell me what's going on."

She fixed me with a look that said she was trying. "Well, obviously we couldn't keep inviting women into our bedroom to jump-start him. I mean we could but it would really take the fun out of spontaneity, not to mention frequency would suffer."

I shook my head.

With a slight shrug of one shoulder, she said, "Hey, I'm just being honest."

I blew on my soup. "Okay, so?"

"So, we went to talk to a sex therapist and after listening to us, he explained to us that my domineering ways were emasculating to Preston and he suggested that I give up some of my control."

I pursed my lips. "Makes sense."

She huffed. "Well, if Preston knew how to take control it would."

I bit back my laugher. "So that didn't work."

She shook her head. "Nope. The therapist then suggested we try things Preston's way for a prescribed period of time."

I set my soup down. "Wait, the therapist wanted you to keep kissing girls?"

"Yes, it was the control Preston needed over our relationship is how he described it." She uncrossed her legs. "So that's what we did."

"And you found women who were happy with just a kiss?" I asked cautiously.

She pointed to my soup. "Eat."

I picked it up and stirred it with my spoon.

"It was Paris after all, and although the women would more than likely have left after just a kiss, I allowed them to stay and go further because it turned Preston on."

"How much further?"

"At first, just fondling. We kissed. They touched me. I touched them. And Preston got it up. But after a few nights, that wasn't enough."

I inhaled, curious where this was going.

"He needed to see more."

"What did the therapist say about that?"

She bit her lip. "We didn't tell him that part."

"Why not?"

"It was too embarrassing."

"Okay, so what happened?"

She set her own soup bowl down. "He wanted me to let the other women, you know."

I did know. I cleared my throat. "Did you?"

"No. I told him I couldn't do that and he let the idea die for a bit and we spent the next couple of nights trying the exercises the therapist gave us."

I opened a package of crackers. "How'd that work?"

Lily rolled her eyes. "Not very well. It's just not in his nature to be the dominant one. That's why I had to take that role on in the first place. We both ended up extremely frustrated. He kept going down to the bar, and I kept pulling out my vibrator."

Cracker crumbs fell on my lap as I bit into one. "And?"

"A couple of nights ago, when I was already in bed, he brought a young thing up to our suite and into my room. She was pretty, but young, like twenty-one young."

"I get it, she was young and pretty."

Lily nodded her head. "I looked at him and his eyes pleaded with me and I thought, what the hell. I could do this for love. So, I let her kiss me, and then I let her slip my nightgown off and play with my breasts like I knew Preston liked. But this time, I undressed her. Preston watched us and I could see his excitement. After she was naked, the thrill in his eyes made me curious, so I invited him over."

I tried not to gasp but I couldn't help it.

She ignored me. "Once he undressed, there was no mistaking his desire. He was rock hard and it made me wonder."

She puffed a breath that blew her bangs and left me anticipating just what exactly she wondered about.

"He joined us and I backed off, and he never even noticed, he was so into this girl. I realized then, I was the problem—not his anatomy, not us, but me. It wasn't me kissing girls that turned him on. It was the other girls. So I ended things for real this time."

I put my food down and hugged her. "I'm so sorry."

She shrugged off my hug. "You know what, I'm okay. It was time—there had been too many breakups and reconciliations. If we truly loved each other, we'd have been in it for the long haul from the start."

Out of nowhere, I started to cry.

"Hey, there are no parallels here. None at all. Jeremy and Preston are completely different men."

I shook my head, and then really started to fall apart. "It was my fault. I believed the worst in him. How could I not have trusted him?"

She pulled me in for a hug this time. "You were manipulated."

I laid my head on her shoulder. "I'm not sure he sees it that way. And anyway, excuses don't matter. I should have believed in him."

She sighed. "You never know."

I closed my eyes.

Maybe.

Maybe someday they would matter, but not today. He was too hurt to see anything but that. I knew that. He had yet to respond to me in any way.

It wrecked me.

Turned my heart inside out and upside down but I had to move forward.

"So Dawson," she said.

Annoyance took hold of me at his name. "I never want to see him again."

"Are you going to press charges?"

"No, Hunter says there was nothing illegal done except the false signatures and Jeremy would have to pursue that legal battle. Dawson knew how to get my attention because he knew my weaknesses. He wanted me back and thought showing me Jeremy was devious would do that."

She scoffed. "It kind of backfired."

"Did it?" I let my words trail off, too exhausted to discuss Dawson any further.

After a few minutes, I looked up. Lily must have felt the same. She had let her head tip back and had fallen asleep. I followed suit and closed my eyes too. I just needed to shut it all out.

How could I have done those things to him?

A knock at my door woke me up.

"Come in," I yelled and sat up.

"Hello, hello." It was Mrs. Bardot.

"Not so loud." Lily rubbed her head.

"You're not hungover," I reminded her.

"No, but I still have jet lag."

Mrs. Bardot set down a couple of bottles of wine. "I thought it might be time for cocktail hour. And it just so happens, Gidget, it's the best cure for jet lag."

Lily popped up. She was used to her nickname. "I'll get the glasses."

I stretched and looked around. It was dark out. I glanced at my watch. It was six thirty. Jamie and Lindsay would be here soon with dinner.

Lily returned with a wine opener and three glasses. She set them next to the now cold soups.

Mrs. Bardot, who despised clutter almost as much as Dawson, picked up the trash and I stood to help her, following her to the kitchen with the soup bowls. As I was pouring one down the drain, Jamie came in with Lindsay behind him, each carrying a bag full of food. Behind Lindsay came Danny, then Logan, and Emmy too.

"You have the most amazing friends, my dear," Mrs. Bardot whispered in my ear.

I looked at them all. "I do."

I had that to be thankful for.

"Where's Phoebs?" Jamie asked Lily.

She pointed over her shoulder.

He turned toward the kitchen. "Hey," he said with a smile. "I hope you don't mind, but I invited a few people."

"No, I don't mind at—"

I dropped the container in the sink.

My heart stopped beating.

My brain stopped processing any thoughts.

Behind Jamie stood another tall figure.

I tilted my head to be certain it was him.

He looked tired.

He looked worn.

He looked amazing.

Jeremy walked toward me with trepidation in his intense blue eyes.

I didn't care.

I ran as fast as I could around the counter and launched myself at him. My legs wrapped around his waist and my arms snaked around his neck. My pulse sped up as he gripped me back in return, holding me as tightly as I was holding him.

Was I dreaming?

After a few moments, I pulled back to look at him. I just had to make sure he was real.

He was.

And he looked beautiful.

"Hi," I breathed.

"Hi," he said back with a quirk of his lips.

I flushed under his intense gaze and for some reason, I felt so nervous in his presence that I had to avert my eyes from his lustful stare. That's when I noticed everyone was watching us.

I didn't care.

My mother had come in too, and surprised to see her, I waved to her.

She waved back. "I hope you don't mind, but Jeremy invited me."

"No," I answered in astonishment and refocused on the man in question. "What are you doing here?" My voice was still so breathy.

He took my face in his hands. "I promised you once that I'd never leave, and I don't go back on my promises."

I blinked back tears. "But what I did—it was unforgiveable."

He shook his head. "Not true. Nothing between two people who love each other should be unforgiveable."

I started to cry in front of everyone.

Jeremy's hands moved to the back of my head and he pulled me to him. "Shh . . . don't cry. I'm sorry I didn't come back sooner."

I couldn't stop myself.

"Can we talk?" he whispered in my ear.

Shivers chased down my spine at the feel of his breath on my skin. I never thought I'd feel it again.

I nodded toward my room in a motion that indicated he should take us there. I wasn't getting down and I wasn't letting go of him for one minute, not ever. Not if I had anything to say about it, that is.

"Excuse us," he said to everyone.

Lily clasped her hands together. "See, your prince came for you."

Logan gave me a smile like I'd never seen from him before.

And Jamie pretended to choke and then joked, "Don't mind us out here listening."

My mother huffed in her take-charge way. "Let's get dinner on the table." Her voice was stern and she directed her comment to Jamie, who now looked petrified.

While things carried on without us, I put my hands on Jeremy's face and stared at his mouth.

Those lips.

I loved them.

I loved him.

I couldn't wait another moment to feel his lips against mine. "I'm so sorry. I love you," I breathed into his mouth.

He kicked the door closed behind us, and crashed his mouth to mine.

I stopped kissing him just long enough to manage "Lock the door."

Jeremy set me down and reached behind him, pressing the button. He was breathing hard when he pulled away to look into my eyes. "I love you too."

Music started to play from the other room and I was thankful to whoever was smart enough to turn it on.

But I wouldn't have cared about them overhearing us enough to stop, not even my mother

Well, maybe her.

It's just—I had missed him desperately.

And I wanted him.

All of him.

Right there.

Right now.

I needed to show him how much I loved him.

Pushing against each other, our bodies began to gravitate toward the bed. It was a painful few small steps at a time, as we were focused on other things, like never losing contact with one another's mouths.

Every part of my body was pressed against his when he pulled away. "We should talk."

I had a hard time finding my voice. "Yes, we should."

Jeremy captured my mouth again, hard enough to bruise my lips.

I didn't care.

I loved it.

My hands were on his chest and I could feel how fast his heart was racing. His hands were on my backside now, squeezing. Our attraction hadn't been squelched by our weeks apart or the horrible things we'd done to each other. It was still between us, blazing hotter than ever. We were gasoline and fire, one touch and we went up in flames

Suddenly, Jeremy stopped, as if just realizing we weren't actually talking. "Why didn't you take the deal the Dawson offered you?" he asked.

His question stunned me. "Because it meant giving you up."

Jeremy stared at me another moment before asking, "Did Dawson spend the night with you that night you were at your father's penthouse?"

Air swooshed from my lungs and I found it hard to breathe. I was afraid. Afraid he'd come to see me, only to leave me when I told him the truth. Meekly, I took his face in my hands and answered, "He did but on a separate couch."

Jeremy flinched. "Did you kiss him?"

With caressing hands, I found his face and cradled it. "He kissed me, but I didn't want him to."

His stance was filled with tension. "You're certain?"

I stroked his cheek. "I am."

His eyes closed. "And his face. That was you?"

"Yes."

The tension eased from his body. "That's all I need to know."

Jeremy always made things so simple between us.

Why couldn't I do the same?

I was going to work on that.

My mouth moved close to his again. "I only want you."

His lips parted and a growl-like noise escaped from his throat. "That's good to hear since you're mine."

That was fine by me.

I took in a deep breath. *My turn.* "What about Avery?"

He hesitated.

My stomach churned.

"You're referring to that goddamned picture?"

I closed my eyes to brace myself.

His lips were at my ear. "I'm sorry for that. I stopped in the event to talk to Weinstein, and Weinstein only. She cornered me and dragged me in front of the press. I promise you it will be the last time she does that."

Satisfaction raced through my veins and then his mouth slammed against mine and he took it with a possessiveness that made my stomach flutter. When we paused between kisses for air, I pushed his jacket off and removed his shirt, in a frantic need to let him claim me.

With his torso bare, Jeremy nudged his knee between my legs. Hardness assaulted me and I whimpered. Bemused, he tilted my chin to look at him. His smile was unabashed and his rakish good looks threw me off kilter. With his hands at my hips, I didn't have to worry about falling though. He was there to keep me steady.

He always had been.

I wished I'd seen it.

The words weren't meant to be spoken now, not in the heat of passion, but I had to know. "What changed your mind?"

Without hesitation, he answered, "Your mother."

"Poppy?" I blinked in surprise.

He nodded. "And my mother too."

"Your mother?" I said in even greater surprise.

"And myself."

"You?"

Jeremy's fingers drifted upward and lifted my sweatshirt over my head, letting it fall to the floor.

My heart was racing as I stared up into the intense blue pools of his eyes. "Tell me?"

His eyes were bright with emotion as he confessed, "Let's just say I decided to break the cycle. I'm not proud of my own behavior pattern—turning my back and running isn't how I want to live my life."

I understood that. There was nothing I could say in response. I'd hurt him immensely. Full of emotion, I managed to ask, "What did my mother say? What did your mother say?"

His answer wasn't immediate. His hands drifted to the elastic band of my sweatpants and he tugged them down without effort. I, in turn, stepped out of them so as not to trip. I was left wearing nothing special beneath my sloppy clothes but he looked at me with an appreciation that caused goose bumps to erupt up and down my arms.

It wasn't until he lowered his head to sprinkle soft kisses up my neck that he answered, "A lot of things."

Exhaling, I tried to ease the nervous tension this conversation had created.

His lips were at my ear. "What's going on in that head of yours?"

I was torn between needing him and wanting to know what on earth my mother could have done to change Jeremy's mind. "Later," I panted at the same time my fingers crept down the muscles of his chest and found that V I loved so much.

He groaned ferociously in my ear and a riot of butterflies swarmed in my belly as desire pumped through me in even cycles, over and over, as I undid his fly.

"Hold on a second." Jeremy stopped to toe his boots off and shake out of his jeans. He wore nothing beneath them and a rush of excitement raced through me.

Within moments, his lips were back on mine and then suddenly, the back of my legs hit the mattress and I fell to the bed.

He didn't falter as his palms caged me in and he hovered above me.

And then, I swear I felt the earth move when he gave me that smile, the one that said just what I thought it did—that he really, really loved me. I couldn't control my reaction. My heart went bang, bang in my chest. With trembling hands, I pressed at his chest lightly and said, "I need to know why you changed your mind. You were so set. You said we were finished."

He gave me a sobering nod and dropped down beside me. Looking at each other, we both paused in the intimate moment. We had to. Grabbing a blanket I covered us and prepared for possibly the most important conversation we'd ever have.

Raised on one elbow, Jeremy started drawing heart shapes on top of it right over my stomach. He did that all the time and I realized then, it was subconscious. As his mouth opened, everything about him changed. Not in a bad way but in a way that opened him up, and I felt like, for the first time, he was going to let me see all of him. He looked down at me. "Unexpectedly, your mother was pounding at my door before the sun had even officially risen this morning."

I gulped and gave him a sheepish look. She must have gone there as soon as we hung up this morning.

He winked, letting me know it was okay she had paid him a visit. "She thought it was important I know you never went home last week, which meant you never got my note." His eyes shifted to somewhere over my head. "But honestly, I didn't give a rat's ass about that note anymore."

The harshness in his tone caused me to shift and twist so we were facing each other. I wanted to look into his eyes, not up at him.

He watched me intently. "I'm sorry but I want to be honest with you."

I nodded, ignoring the wave of emotion climbing up my throat.

"When that was clear, she moved on to inform me that Hunter had convinced you both that I was the one who purchased the shares because of a forged signature."

I breathed him in and listened to what had led him back to me.

His eyes were on me, pinning me, making me even more anxious. "She wanted to make sure I knew that."

"But knowing those things didn't change your mind about us, did they?" I could barely speak through my nervousness.

He slowly shook his head. "No, they didn't. I was still licking my wounds."

I swallowed as I waited to hear what had brought him back to me.

"Your mother is a smart woman. No one should underestimate her."

I nodded, in complete agreement. I'd learned a lot about her as of late.

"She knew what it was that had triggered my reaction. No one has ever really understood me and honestly, I don't think I ever fully understood myself. And yet, this woman, who by all accounts I should have hated but at the same owed so much to, managed it."

I bit my lip.

He shook his head in wonder. "She somehow knew that if I could only understand the truth, I'd believe more in myself and then I wouldn't have this deep-rooted desperation for other people to believe in me."

My heart was torn between anguish over my own recklessness of not identifying that need and swelling with pride over his admission of what he needed to be whole. I reached for him and squeezed his hand. "The truth?" I asked, not sure what that was.

He nodded. "I've wanted to know about my father, my mother, my parents since I found out about Justin. I never understood why my mother didn't believe in me enough to tell me the truth about our family."

Guilt tore through me. Believe in him. That's what this was about. That's what that night was about. And I failed, more than once.

He shook his head as if reading my mind. "Turns out, I needed to believe in myself. My mother's choices weren't mine. And whether or not she believed in me enough to know I could handle it, that was her burden, not mine."

My hand let go of his to wipe away a tear sliding down my cheek but he did it for me and the tenderness was almost too much.

With a shaky breath, he continued, "Your mother talked to me about my parents and what they were like when I was a baby. No one had ever shared that with me. I was wanted. They loved me. I could see it in the photos I had never seen before."

"Photos?"

Jeremy leaned forward and nudged my elbow. "I guess we'd met a few times before when we were three."

My lips turned up. "I wonder if you looked at me then with those bedroom eyes."

He huffed out a wicked laugh. "I'm certain I did. You rocked a onesie like no other baby I knew."

Admiration rooted within me. In the midst of all this sadness, he could still find humor.

Only him.

Jeremy's eyes seemed to cloud over with sadness and he went on. "Your mother wanted me to know how much my parents really loved each other and how sad she was that they were torn apart. I knew there was a message in there somewhere but honestly, I didn't quite get it at the time. And after she left, I spent the rest of the morning analyzing what she'd said. And I was pretty sure she was trying to tell me not to give up on someone I loved like my mother had on my father."

I swallowed. "My mother said those things?"

He gave me a knowing nod. "Yes."

I was momentarily stunned while at the same time touched.

He went on. "That's not all she did though. Early this afternoon, there was a knock on my door. Imagine my surprise when I opened it to see my mother standing there. Poppy had called her and asked her to come see me. I guess she told her"—he rolled his eyes—"that I was at a crossroads and it was time to open up to me. And so she did. I couldn't believe it but she was standing there ready to tell me all the things she never could."

My heart pricked. "That must have hurt."

He leaned over and kissed my forehead. "Yeah, it wasn't a walk in the park, especially when she admitted she wished she'd made different choices, which was why she finally told me about my father. As I listened to her tell me he was a good man who made a very poor choice, and in turn, so had she, it made me realize I didn't want to wait twenty-five years to be with the one person who makes me feel complete. My mother abandoned my father because of his misdeeds and lived her life regretting it. I won't make that mistake. Like I said, I'm breaking my own poor behavioral pattern. I decided to run after you, not away from you."

Moved, I turned my head to sweetly brush my lips against his.

Jeremy took advantage of how close I was and rolled on top of me but he didn't kiss me. Instead he gazed down at me and continued our conversation. "Look, I know Hunter was trying to manage things as best he could. But I also knew that Dawson was manipulating TSC's financial situation. I just had no idea how far he was willing to go with you. I never thought he'd jeopardize his relationship with you just to try to extract me from your life."

Obviously Jamie or my mother had fully filled him in. Thoughts of how Dawson had morphed into someone I didn't even know began to surface, but I pushed them away and glanced up at Jeremy. "I still don't understand how you managed to save the company."

He gave a huff of laughter. "I spent the week buying your shares back. Traveling from company to company to convince them to sell the shares back they had purchased under Dawson's advice."

"How were you able to do that?"

His lips twisted. "It's amazing how three little words will make anyone listen."

I gave him a confused look.

He returned that look with a wicked grin. "*Pending SEC investigation* will make anyone pale."

My jaw dropped. "You didn't."

"Yeah, I did. And if that didn't work I was going to let it leak that there was an impending defamation legal suit on the horizon. Which I was more than happy to see through if I had to."

I tenderly brushed some hair from his eyes. "But Jeremy, even with the stock price so low, that had to cost you a fortune."

He shrugged. "It did drain me. But so what? It just means expansion of Jet Set will take longer than I anticipated."

My heart took a dive so far, I wondered if it had fallen out of my chest. I'd pay him back. I had to. Somehow, I'd find a way to do it.

"Even I have to admit, I looked guilty. I guess what I'm trying to say is I'm not so sure I wouldn't have believed what was right before my eyes either. The evidence was pretty convincing, as was my behavior. Between my omissions about who my father was and then the car, even I would have had doubts. But in here"—he pointed to his chest—"I wanted to believe you'd see past that."

My eyes stung with unshed tears. "If I could go back in time and do it all over again, I would. I can't tell you how deeply sorry I am."

He shook his head. "That's just it, I can't blame you. I could have found a way to get in touch with you. Even Kat told me to."

"Kat?"

He cleared his throat, knowing he was tiptoeing on a sore subject. "Yeah, she told me about your calls."

I shrugged. "I had nothing to lose and I was worried about you."

Smugness lurked in his eyes. "She told me."

I gave him a little shove. "You're never doing that again."

His smile was warm.

"Can I ask why you didn't get in touch with me?"

His face fell. We were each on an elbow and face-to-face with our hands resting on my hip. "I can admit I have a bit of a dark side. And that asshole lurking inside of me was still pissed at you for the accusations you made about the car."

I extended my elbow and rose farther up. "But I apologized for my poor reaction."

He nodded and let go of my fingers. "I know and I'm sorry I didn't accept your apology when you came to me. But I do now."

Feeling brave, I asked the question I needed to know the answer to. "Would you have come after me if I hadn't shown up at your door that night?"

Jeremy's face grew grim. "I want to tell you yes. I really do, but in truth, I don't know."

I tensed, worried what our future held. "Jeremy, the night of the video launch, you said you were going to call me later. Was that true?"

He took our hands and brought them to his heart. "Yes, it was. And I can promise you, from this day forward I will never let you walk away from me and I will never walk away from you. I don't care what it takes, we will stay together and work things out. I want you. I need you. You mean everything to me."

I saw everything I needed to see in his eyes but it was his forgiveness I wanted the most. And it was there, along with so many other emotions. "I'm sorry. I'm so sorry for not believing in you. I shouldn't have doubted you. And I promise it will never happen again. Never."

He pulled back. "I didn't make any of it easy. I should have been up front and honest with you from the start. From now on, no more mistrusting, no more hiding things we think will hurt, nothing but honesty."

I nodded in agreement. "Nothing but honesty—forever."

He stared down at me. "I don't want to be without you again."

"You won't be. I won't let you be, even if you try."

His smirk was wicked. "I love it when you try to sound forceful."

I bit my lip. "And I love it when you let me."

Jeremy smoothed the hair from my face and whispered, "I love you."

I leaned into his touch and whispered back, "And I love you."

With those words, I knew all the hurt, the betrayal, the lies, and the mistrust—they were behind us.

They had to be.

Seriousness loomed over us as we stared at one other, forgiving each other's sins in silence and expressing our love at the same time. Jeremy's elbows were beside my head and when his breath stirred, mine caught, and then we were breathing in tandem.

Somehow, the still moment led to a tangle of arms and legs and lips and hands.

Jeremy's fingers were working their way to the back of my bra and as soon as he unhooked it, he moved his hands down to slide my panties off.

I tingled from head to toe as my body melded into the mattress. "Are we done talking?" I panted.

He kissed me, soft, tender, long, and slow.

And I had my answer.

Jeremy was a complex guy. He was sometimes brooding, always charming, and at times he could be suave and debonair. But after today, I saw more. I saw a man raw and naked. I saw a man who didn't understand himself and struggled at times in his efforts. I saw a man so much like me that I finally understood what it was that each of us was attracted to in the other.

As cliché as it sounds—we completed each other.

We had been bare to each other many times, but today we were completely naked in a way we'd never been.

With what felt like drugged euphoria, I looked at him and had an uncontrollable urge to feel him everywhere—his chest, his abs, and down farther. I wanted to touch every square inch of him.

I couldn't get enough.

He, like me, seemed to want to feel all of me.

We touched and kissed until we were breathless, and when his lips slipped down my neck and he sucked my skin between his teeth, I threw my head back.

And when he repeated the action over my nipple, down my navel, and then on my clit, I lost my mind. The moan that escaped my lips was one I couldn't contain. I arched beneath him as he repeated the sensuous assault over and over. My hands went to his mussed head of hair and I wove my fingers through it. Pressing him to me, keeping his mouth just where I needed it, I finally let myself go.

Sensations ripped through my body and I cried out, "Oh God, Jeremy. I love you."

He reached up and put his fingers in my mouth to quiet me. I sucked on them as I came over and over. He didn't stop until he'd drained every ounce of pleasure from me. Even still, I pulled him toward me with the hair I had gripped on to.

"Did you like that?" he asked, and I heard the smile in his voice.

He knew I did.

And then he covered me with his body. All of him blanketed all of me.

It was perfect.

My hands pushed down to his cock. There was no room between us for me to stroke him, so I gripped him.

He made a small, helpless noise.

I wanted to hear it again so I slid my grip up and down as far as I could.

He made the same noise, this time louder.

My stomach flip-flopped and my excitement spun all around me.

He buried his face in my neck as he eased inside me.

We looked into each other's eyes as he slowly moved above me.

It felt so good.

Suddenly, he flipped us over so I was on top of him. "I have to be able to touch you."

"Oh God," I called out as he fondled my breasts.

His hands drifted to my hips, and then around to that spot he liked to caress.

I leaned down to give him better access and gripped his shoulders. I moved up and down slowly.

"Fuck, that feels so good," he groaned.

I kept it up.

Slow and steady.

His other hand found my clit and he caressed it along with that sensitive spot. Done together, the individual feelings sent chills down my spine.

The pressure behind me was tantalizing and I wanted more.

"Take me there," I whispered.

His face contorted as pleasure overtook him. "Not today. But someday."

He thrust upward and put both his hands on my clit. As he worked circles with his fingers, I began to lose my mind and forget about any other kind of penetration except what I was experiencing. A moan involuntarily escaped my lips. I tried not to be loud, but I lost all control.

He started moving, and then I took over.

I rose on my knees and gently slid down. I was in no hurry.

"Oh fuck," he groaned.

I did it again and his groans grew even louder. He was making noises I'd never heard and the whole thing was mind-blowing.

What we had together was mind-blowing.

I had been lost.

I had been found.

I had been lost again.

And now I had him—forever.

I knew that.

My toes curled as the pleasure wove its way between us. As I started to orgasm, waves of bliss riveted through me, and I could tell they were ripping through him at the same time.

I covered his mouth.

He covered mine.

And we both came violently as our connection grew ever stronger.

It was pleasure.

It was lust.

It was passion and desire.

But most of all, it was love.

I collapsed on top of him and he held me for the longest time. I knew there were people out there waiting for us, I knew there was no mistaking what we'd done in here, and I knew I was going to walk out there with the biggest grin on my face.

I didn't care. They would forgive us for it.

I wanted to be with this man forever. I smiled at him through lowered lids as my body attempted to recover.

Warmth spread through me like a wildfire when he brushed his lips to mine and said those three little words I thought I'd never hear from him again. "I love you."

Giddy, my reply was easy. "I love you, too."

With his fingers, he brushed my lips. "I don't ever want these lips to touch anyone's but mine ever again."

I kissed him and answered with absolute certainty, "They won't. They belong to you."

He made a noise that caused my heart to flutter.

As I lifted up with my elbows on his chest, I couldn't restrain my flood of emotions. "Promise me we'll never be apart again," I said.

He rolled us over. "We won't be, I promise."

I looked up at him and knew then exactly what I wanted. "Do you still want to marry me?"

He stared down for the longest while and a pang of anxiety pinged through me. "Yeah, of course I do," he finally answered.

I bit down nervously on my lip.

"What?"

I took a deep breath and went for it. "I know it's a week late, but can we get married tomorrow?" I asked. The words came out of my mouth so fast, I'm not sure he could understand them.

He blinked.

Was he confused?

Did he really not understand me?

My pulse raced. "Jeremy?"

His eyes flared in surprise. "Do you still want to?"

Relieved, I answered honestly. "Yes. Yes. Yes. Yes, I want to marry you as soon as possible."

Jeremy jumped up and looked around the room in a panic.

I sat up, worried. "What are you doing?"

He shoved his legs into his jeans and tossed me my clothes. "Get dressed. We have to get out there and see if Jamie can extend the permits."

Needing something fresh to wear, I got out of bed and opened one of my drawers.

Jeremy hopped on one foot as he tried to put his socks on while standing up. "What time is it?"

I turned to glance at him as he fumbled with his phone in his pocket. "I'm not sure."

His nervousness surprised me. "We have to get to Tiffany's before it closes."

Pretending not to notice his flustered state, I stood there quietly watching him. His long, lean body moved about with nervous energy I'd never seen before. He was always so calm, cool, and collected. I found his behavior utterly charming.

"It's seven thirty. Do you think it's already closed?"

I turned around, trying to tame my grin.

His lips tickled the skin behind my ear. "What do you think?"

"I think they close at seven," I said with a slight laugh I was trying desperately to conceal.

"Why is that funny?"

I kept giggling.

Jeremy gripped my hips. "What are you doing?"

"Getting dressed." I had to bite my lip to stop the laughter from bubbling out.

He slapped my bare behind. "No you're not. Could you hurry up?" he said and then turned me around.

While selecting some skimpy undergarments, I couldn't contain my glee and some small giggles escaped my throat.

I heard him clear his throat and slowly turned around.

Our eyes met and then his narrowed ever so slightly. "Why are you laughing?"

I bit my lip. "Because you're utterly adorable when you're nervous."

"Pffft . . . I'm not nervous." He waved a hand.

I stepped into the pair of clean panties I was holding and pulled the matching bra over my head. "If it's about Tiffany's, I bet Jamie can make one magic call and get us in just—"

Jeremy pounced so quickly and buried his face in my neck before I could finish. "Okay, so maybe I'm just a little nervous but you're brilliant."

I stopped laughing and my heart began to pound.

His mouth was on me.

Tongue.

Teeth.

Lips.

I wanted even more.

When he lifted his head to look at me, his lips glistened. My gaze fell to his smooth, bare chest. It was muscled and he had a hint of a six-pack, but he wasn't overly defined. I found him to be hotter than hell.

But then, I always had.

His mouth found mine and he backed me up against the dresser. He pressed against me and fit his leg between mine. Our breathing intensified until suddenly he hissed in my mouth, "We can't. We have to get out there."

Breathless and a bit dazed, I didn't really want to take the time to figure out what to put on so I quickly looked in my closet and found a jersey dress that I hadn't worn in a long time.

It was old but comfortable and presentable.

It would do.

I hoped not to have to stay in it long.

"Do you think they'll know?" I asked.

He threw me a wicked grin. "You were a little loud."

I slapped my hand to my mouth. "Oh God, my mother and Mrs. Bardot are out there."

Jeremy's hand slipped into mine. "At least they'll sleep soundly knowing you're satisfied."

I tugged at him and eyed his bare chest. "Are you going out there like that?"

The boyish grin that presented on his face melted me. "So okay, I'm more than a little nervous," he said as he slipped his T-shirt on.

Hungrily, I watched him. When he finished I purred, "And by the way, you more than satisfy me."

"Good," he said smugly, his nervousness seemingly gone as he eased down to kiss me—again.

All mouth.

And tongue.

And a little teeth.

I was almost panting when he pulled away.

"Come on." He grinned. "We're in a hurry. We have a wedding to plan in less than twelve hours."

My heart was pounding. He walked forward. I walked backward. We were in sync.

I was really going to be his wife.

He glanced at me with a slight impatience that made me laugh.

But I was already on my way. "I'm coming. I can't help it if you distracted me."

With his hand on the knob, he paused and looked over his shoulder. "You know, our life together is going to be great. I'm going to make sure our days are full of distractions. I want you breathless and screaming my name for the next fifty years. And I promise you—I will make you happy."

Pleased with his confession, I leaned forward. "Just kiss me."

"Yes, ma'am."

I giggled as soft, wet lips met mine in a passionate kiss.

Once we broke away, tears of joy welled in my eyes as he opened the door. I couldn't wait to get married. I wanted to be joined to him for eternity. We'd had our ups and downs and learned from our mistakes and I know we came out stronger because of them in the end.

As Jeremy stepped out into the living room, I marveled at how unfazed I was that my life was about to change. I'd always been wary of the whole *happily-ever-after* thing. I just never saw myself actually having one, but suddenly now I did. I saw it all—everything bright that my future with Jeremy held.

It was alive inside me.

For the first time ever in my life—I saw my perfect ending. He was right in front of me. My heart swelled as I watched how well Jeremy interacted with everyone I loved. And right now, in this very moment, I knew without a doubt, he would make me the happiest woman on earth.

How could he not—I already was.

And it was freeing.

The Hamptons

JEREMY MCQUEEN

Everyone has a dark side.

A part of ourselves that we are not proud of. Something that at times is hard to suppress. And I hate to admit it—but I'm no different. The good news is, I've tamed it. The bad news is, I have room for improvement.

I've come a long way.

There was a time in my life when I was nothing but a selfish fuck. I did what I wanted, acted how I pleased, without regard to who got hurt. That was who I was. I felt cheated and didn't know what to do with that emotion. I was brooding. I was moody. I thought the world owed me. I'll own it—most of the time, I was a prick.

And all because of the chip I had on my shoulder—I hated people with money. Couldn't stand to be around them. They made my skin crawl and my temper flare.

It was the Lucifer in me.

When Phoebe turned her back on me that summer, I felt like I'd been there before. My life was full of people turning their backs on me—my father, my mother. Was that what I had to look forward to my whole life? Well, I couldn't live with that. So I let her go. Yet, something inside me urged me not to and once I'd licked my wounds, I went after her.

She had lied to me about who she was.

Did she think that little of me?

I couldn't handle that. Knowing she was one of them was one thing, but her complete disbelief in me opened an onslaught of emotion I couldn't turn off. That wound was too deep and I left her without a second thought.

Yet everything in my life changed after that. I was surprised at how lost I felt without her. I wanted her back. I even started to wonder if it mattered that she'd lied, that she hadn't believed in me. But that dark side inside me knew it did. So I let her go and set out to prove my worth.

The years went by and my pride, my ego, my insecurities, and our entwined past kept me away from her. After a while, I wasn't staying away because she had money, or she grew up privileged, I'd let that go. It was more that she hadn't trusted me enough to believe I could overcome the lie.

Then I opened my own business and entered the same world she lived in, and it was then I realized there weren't two worlds—there was just one. There was no line in the sand. We were all the same. Maybe it was maturity, maybe not. But the lie she had told to separate her from her world wasn't as severe as it once was and I actually understood why she'd done it.

I saw who I was.

I didn't really like what I saw.

After that, everything was one push and pull after another. My mother. My father. My need to be more. And maybe even subconsciously my need to see her. It all shoved me to the breaking point. I had to get out of Miami and I knew just where I was going. The years had taken their toll though and even after I arrived, I never really planned to see her again. When I did, the pent-up anger I had locked away eased its way out and the sting seemed to lessen. The lies didn't hurt so much. Yet still, I kept my distance. I feared she'd open up something inside me I'd closed long ago—my heart.

I had work to do.

I had something to accomplish. Goals I needed to reach. I couldn't have that. But then she needed me, and I couldn't stay away. The moment I came in contact with her, the minute she said my name—I knew she had to be mine.

Strange how easy forgiveness can be if you just let it happen. Even after she thought the worst of me, in the back of my mind I was determined to show her who I was. After all, I was partly to blame. I should have come clean from the start.

But that's what life is all about, isn't it.

Live and learn.

In the end, it wasn't easy but we overcame the sins of the fathers, the sins of our past, and she became more than just mine.

She became my lover.

My friend.

My wife.

She's a part of who I am and I never plan on losing her.

My goals in life haven't changed, just their priorities. First in line, is to always make her happy. And first on the agenda, as promised, was to take care of the living arrangements. Which I did—very well, I might add.

Poppy sold her house and took Phoebe's apartment on Park Avenue, where she planned to live with Chandler after his release. And in the meantime, Mrs. Bardot was keeping her busy.

It eased Phoebe's mind to know the two women she loved so much had each other.

As for Phoebe and me, we have two homes.

The first is our permanent residence on the Upper East Side. It's a four-story brownstone located at 169 East Seventy-first Street. And it isn't just any brownstone either. The iconic forest green doors are a dead giveaway to any Holly Golightly fan, or so Phoebe says. It's the place the Audrey Hepburn's fictional character from *Breakfast at Tiffany's* lived.

I would never have said I was a lucky man, but with Phoebe in my life, I am. I found the place by accident the day it went on the market and bought it on the spot. It has four bedrooms, five bathrooms, an enclosed solarium, three wood-burning fireplaces, and even a backyard.

Fucking perfect.

The second is our summer home in the Hamptons. It's an older two-story house with a wraparound porch and a white picket fence Phoebe insisted we install.

It's the house Phoebe rented that summer we met. The owner, Mr. Charleston, hadn't been able to sell it with the real estate crash and had been renting it out for the last five years. Phoebe mentioned many times how much she loved it. When I called him and asked if he'd be interested in unloading it, he jumped at the chance.

The house isn't crazy big.

It isn't new.

And it isn't located in the socialite epicenter of South Hampton either.

But Phoebe and I don't care about any of that. What we care about is the unobstructed view of the Atlantic, the white sandy beach, and being together.

That first time I left her, I was young and immature. She'd lied to me and I felt wounded. I wasn't sure I could ever recover from the duplicity and it wasn't until I was actually standing in front of her that I realized I already had. She was whom I craved, needed, wanted, and seeing her made me realize nothing else mattered.

The second time I left her, I was wrecked. I had to cool off but once I did, I knew I wouldn't survive without her. Her mother and mine might have given me the boost I needed, but I'm pretty certain I would have come around—this time. The need to find out if there was a chance for us would have eaten away at me.

There hasn't been a day that has passed that I haven't wanted to go after Dawson for what he did and what he tried to do. But Phoebe begged me to stay clear of him. Still, the need lurked within me every day until karma made its appearance. Recently, Page Six published an article about the new *it* couple, Avery Lake and Dawson Vanderbilt, and I thought, *fuck me very much*, the two of them doomed to each other for eternity might be just enough satisfaction for me to bear the wrongs.

Might be.

As I drove up to our summer home, I couldn't help but grin. The white Porsche I gave her for her birthday last week remained where I parked it, the windows of the house were thrown open to let in the afternoon sun and the ocean breeze, and soft music played from inside.

I got out of my car and hurried up the stairs I still needed to fix. Moving quickly still, I flung the rickety old screen door open and yelled, "I'm home."

Phoebe rushed to the top of the stairs. She had pinned fresh flowers in her hair and her eyes sparkled with excitement and anticipation. She twisted her butterfly ring the way she always did when she was nervous. "How'd it go?"

I tried to look grim, but I couldn't do it. So instead, I grinned like a motherfucker. "It's ours."

She came flying down the stairs, her small belly looking sexier by the day.

"Slow down, the baby's going to think he's on a ride at Coney Island."

She threw her arms around me. "She likes it when I move fast."

I raised a brow.

Phoebe, being Phoebe, countered.

With the previous stress of the takeover attempt on TSC and the instability between her and me, Phoebe neglected to take her birth control. And although we hadn't yet discussed having a family before we found out we were pregnant, we were both excited about the news. Since then, we've decided we want a big family.

Being an only child will do that to you.

"When do we take over?" she asked excitedly.

My gaze fell to her body. "Can I get a kiss before we talk business?"

She still didn't like to mix business with pleasure.

Her mouth parted and she swiped her tongue along her lower lip. "No. You have to pretend we're at the office."

I stepped closer.

I could feel the heat rising between us.

With a huff of laughter, I told her the way it is. "I'll pretend to be anywhere you want but that won't change what I want to do to you."

She took a step back. "Jeremy, I'm serious. If we can't work together here during the week without distractions, then we'll have to stay in the city and drive out on the weekends."

My fingers swept down her bare arms. "I thought you liked it when I distracted you?"

Phoebe attempted to tug her hand from mine, but not hard enough. "I do. I mean I don't. You know what I mean."

I tried not to laugh at her as she tugged again and I freed my hold on her. "Can you explain that to me?"

She put her hands on her hips. "Tell me when we take over Finale."

I shook my head and stared at the woman I couldn't believe I got to call my wife.

Jamie pulled it off and we got married as planned with heaters surrounding the lower portion of Bethesda Terrace. Once Starwood took ownership of all the hotels except the two in New York City, the money from the sale went to Poppy, and Phoebe took ownership of the two remaining hotels. Instead of following through with Sinners, we did something better. We consolidated the hotels into Jet Set New York.

And business was booming because of it. In fact, the money I'd laid out to buy the shares back had been recouped.

Jet Set headquarters now resides in the former TSC office space and Hunter has taken the helm as CFO. Jet Set Miami, Jet Set New York, and the soon to be launched Jet Set Hamptons are run by both Phoebe and myself.

I took her hand from her hip—the one with the two-and-a-half-karat heart-shaped Tiffany ring that she selected in less than fifteen minutes. She said I always drew hearts on her skin with my fingertip and that was the shape ring she wanted.

With a genuine smile, I looked at her. "July first," I whispered.

She smiled back and rested her hands on my hip. The baby wasn't due until the end of August, and I knew she wanted to be able to help with the launch of Jet Set Hamptons so I did the best I could to drive the deal forward. Her arms circled me and her fingers slipped inside my waistband.

My cock twitched. "I tried for sooner, but it was a no go."

"It's perfect," she said, pressing her fingers into my skin.

I think she was happy.

I drew in a breath that quickly became a gasp as her fingers slid down a little. "Good, on to the next order of business."

"What would that be?" Her words came out scratchy and hoarse.

My lips fell on hers and I kissed her with everything I had. Just as the passion started to flare, I pulled back and let my gaze fall to her body.

She was flushed from head to toe.

I liked getting her all stoked and then making her wait.

Taking my time, I followed every curve from her neck to her toes. "You can't dress like this during work hours if you don't want me to be distracted."

She shifted her hips a little. "You said you wanted to go out for a swim before my mother and Mrs. Bardot arrived, so I got ready."

Ahhh, she liked to make me wait too.

I was having none of that. I had to move things along. My hands skimmed down her body. "That reminds me, Jamie called. He and Lindsay are coming for dinner too."

She pushed herself into me. "Oh good. I can't wait to see them."

This was probably not the best time to sneak this in but I had to. "And Kat will be here this weekend to review Miami operations."

She narrowed her gaze. "As in here, here?"

I nodded and narrowed my eyes at her. "Yep, that's what I said. She's coming here, as in her feet will be on this very floor."

Phoebe made a fierce noise.

"Did you just growl?" I had to ask.

Her mouth dropped open. "I did no such thing. I just can't believe you invited her to stay with us."

My lips quirked up. "Admit you growled."

She shook her head.

"Would you rather I fly down to Miami?" A few days ago, the doctor had told Phoebe she shouldn't travel too far at this late stage of her pregnancy.

Phoebe made that noise again.

At this point, I decided it was probably best if I dropped it. She and Kat would find their way one of these days. I bent my head to brush my lips over the exposed skin of her shoulder. "You should probably know, bikinis, covered up or not, will always distract me."

She smiled brightly. "I know that."

She was so easily distracted lately.

I bit down on her shoulder. "Then why did you scold me?"

She moaned a little. "Because it's fun."

I ran my hands up and down her dress. It was tight and skimmed all her curves as well as her protruding belly. "I have something much more fun it mind."

Her fingers traced my erection. "Swimming?"

I tried to laugh, but it came out more like a groan. "No, not swimming. Not now anyway."

She looked down at her belly. "Too bad, she likes it when we swim."

I took a step forward and nudged Phoebe toward the stairs. She took one step back. I took one step forward. "That's because he's going to be an Olympic swimmer."

She giggled. "Holly could go for the gold too, you know."

I eased her down onto the third step. "Holly, huh . . . I like it."

She smiled at me. "You do?"

I took her wrists and pinned them above her head. "I do, but there's no way we're calling the baby Fred if it's a boy."

She lifted her head to kiss me and then said, "I was thinking Truman."

I looked at her. "Are you serious?"

She nodded and tears welled in her eyes.

The fun faded away as the moment turned intimate.

I captured her mouth with mine.

God, I loved her.

Names had played a strange role in our relationship.

Saint.

St. Claire.

McQueen.

Truman.

And up until that moment, I hadn't given them much thought. But it struck me then, was a name who you were?

I had grown up Jeremy McQueen.

Would my life have been different if I had grown up Jeremy Truman?

I'd never know.

But as I looked at my wife, the mother of my child, I knew it was time to let that hostility go.

Whether the baby was a he or she, it didn't matter. What mattered was the love that surrounded him or her.

My mother had raised me in the environment she thought was best. My father had respected her wishes. And when I'd gone to see him, he helped me with a vigor that made me feel like he cared about me. I owed it to my child to allow as much love into his or her life as humanly possible.

I sat beside Phoebe, not certain how she'd react to what I was about to say. "I think we should invite my parents to visit."

My father had been released on early parole and was staying with my mother. I wasn't sure what their relationship entailed, and up until that point, I hadn't cared. Our families were tangled, messy, and complicated, but Phoebe and I were grown-ups and what had happened when we were young wasn't our burden to bear.

She took my hand and rubbed it over her belly. "I think that's a wonderful idea."

I looked at her with adoring eyes.

I always had.

And I always would.

I shifted my body so that I was hovering over her as I pulled her clothes off. When she was naked, I stared at her. "Beautiful," I said.

She liked when I called her that. She said it made her feel sexy.

She was sexy.

My hand went behind her head to cradle it, and I pulled her toward me. Her fingers sifted through my hair. Then I finally let my mouth cover hers, nibbling at her lip before I plunged my tongue inside.

Her moan vibrated against my lips as she kissed me back.

I knew the weight of her body as it crushed over mine.

The feel of her skin.

The way she tasted.

How much she liked me to lick her orgasm.

What she sounded like when she came.

I knew what she feared.

What she loved.

I knew what her favorite color was.

I knew what she liked and what she didn't.

And she knew all the same things about me.

Phoebe once referred to our relationship as toxic, and at one point I did the same. But without the feeling that the toxicity of our relationship was draining the life and energy from it, we never would have been compelled to expel the poison that was driving us apart.

Jealousy.

Mistrust.

Fear.

Uncertainty.

They live in everyone.

But Phoebe and I worked together and drove those toxic elements from our relationship.

Love and lust, in equal, healthy doses—now that's all that remains.

ACKNOWLEDGMENTS

My infinite thanks go to:

Amy Tannenbaum of the Jane Rotrosen Agency, who pushes me with each book and always has my best interests at heart. Thank you for being more than willing to talk to me anytime, about anything. Amy, you are such an amazing person and I couldn't be more grateful to have you as my literary agent.

Kerry Donovan of Penguin for always finding ways to make what I write so much better. I couldn't respect your outlook on romance any more than I do.

Penguin and the team at New American Library, for so eagerly and enthusiastically taking on each book as if it is my first and for your willingness to work with me on even the smallest of details. I really appreciate all of you.

Katy Evans, Mary Tatar, Kim Anderson Bias, and Jody O Fraleigh. Thank you for all your help, input, and for your friendships—all of which I truly value.

Hang Le, your ability to help me bring my words to life through teaser images astonishes me every time.

In addition, I would also like to thank everyone who read this book and provided me with their feedback.

All of the bloggers who have become my friends—you're all so amazing and I cannot possibly put into words the amount of gratitude I have for each and every one of you!

And finally, my love and gratitude to my family—to my husband of twenty years who became Mr. Mom while continuing to go to work every day; to my children who not only took on roles that I for many years had always done—laundry, grocery shopping, cleaning—but always asked how the book was coming and actually beamed to their friends when telling them their mom wrote a book.

And finally—a giant thank-you to all of you.

And don't miss *The 27 Club*, an unforgettable
new stand-alone romance from Kim Karr! Available now.
Continue reading for a preview.

The 27 Club

Janis Joplin. Kurt Cobain. Amy Winehouse. Zachary Flowers. I always
knew my brilliant brother would one day be listed among the great ar-
tistic minds of our time. I just didn't know he would join the list of ex-
ceptional talents who left us too young, too soon.

I was always the calm one, the perfect foil to his freewheeling wild spirit.
But since his death shortly after his twenty-seventh birthday, I'd found
myself adrift and directionless.

I knew it was time to face my destiny, and I was ready to yield. But then
I met Nate, Zachary's best friend. Only he could help me put the pieces
together, fill in the blanks that Zachary left behind. I needed him to
answer my questions—and I wanted him for more. He awakened in me
a sensuality that had never been explored, never satisfied. Nate's presence controlled me, his touch seared me, and it was up to me to convince him that he was brought into my life for a reason. . . .

CHAPTER 1

Out of My Head

October 2006

In the darkness, it looks more like Pandora's Box than a place where an artist once lived. Nestled between two houses, each the size of an arena and both lit up like football fields, this much smaller home sits dark and alone—no movement from within, no cars in the driveway, no one living inside.

The picture that appears through the rain doesn't seem to reflect any part of him. But something of my brother has to be here. Even just a small piece left behind for me to catch a glimpse of.

A rush of melancholy hits fast.

My throat tightens.

I can't breathe.

Sweat forms on my brow, even though the car is cool.

This isn't one of my asthma attacks—this is grief rearing its ugly head. The grief I tried to deal with at home in all those therapy sessions. The grief I know I have to accept. But just like accepting my destiny—I'm having a hard time doing this.

Destiny—that hidden power that controls fate. Even though it's a path I don't want to be on, I'm not certain I can stray from it.

It owns me—I don't own it.

My fate might very well be inevitable, just as my brother's was.

I've almost come to accept that.

Almost.

Taking a deep, calming breath, I close my eyes, demanding my fear stay at bay.

I'm stronger than this.

Yet in the darkness, I don't feel stronger.

My mind swirls with sadness and I quickly snap my eyes open, hoping to eradicate this feeling of dread. My eyes flutter for a moment before I'm finally able to lean forward and take a closer look.

With the illumination of the car's headlights, I stare through the windshield at the house I've stayed away from for far too long.

And in this moment, everything about the property comes to life. It's a work of art—as if my brother painted the picture for me to help ease my fears, like he did when we were kids.

It's there, the small part of him left behind for me to see. Not his body turned to ash, not the marker at the cemetery bearing his name, but a piece of who he was during the life he led here.

The green bricks of the driveway show his funky edge; the triangle-shaped sailcloth carport demonstrates his love for the abstract; and the house's tropical-modern design with its Spanish-style roof is in itself a work of art worthy of being hung on a gallery wall.

Yes, I can see it now.

I can see him living here.

Happy with the life he led before he died.

Just what I was hoping for.

As I sink back down, the worn leather seat seems to swallow me whole as sorrow mixes with relief and rivets through every vein in my body.

Not what I imagined, but the longer I look, the more I can see him living here.

It's perfect.

It's him.

Suddenly, I'm stuck between the dreamlike state I've been in, refusing to accept the truth, and the reality of my situation. The finality renders me immobile—I'm here but he's not, and all I can do is sit motionless.

"You did say 302 South Coconut Lane?" the driver asks over his shoulder.

My eyes meet his in the mirror. "Yes, this is the right place. Just give me a moment, please."

With trembling fingers, I reach for the handle and attempt to gather the courage to at least open the door. I just don't know if I can do this. I'd have thought the passing of time would have made it easier, but maybe it hasn't been long enough.

The driver clears his throat, sensing my apprehension. "Do you want me to take you somewhere else?"

I hand him my credit card. "No, this is what I came to Miami for."

With a signature on the driver's iPhone, I'm ready. I pull the strap of my overnight bag onto my shoulder and step out. Water sloshes everywhere, but I stop for a minute and look up to the heavens.

Moments pass.

Seconds.

Minutes.

I have no idea.

Once I've gathered my courage and strength, I shift my gaze back down and notice the balcony. It's too dark for me to tell, but I can't imagine it wasn't built for framing some kind of beautiful picture, something worth looking at.

Water fills my eyes and my tears mix with the rain, as the idea of Zach sketching from there comes to mind.

The driver hands me my suitcase and shuts my door before hopping back in the car.

At that moment, the sky seems to open up, and before I can button my coat, I'm soaked.

Hurrying forward, I stop at the white metal gate. With a slight push, I'm walking into a tropical paradise. Trees line the walkway and a natural stone wall protects the area. The pathway leads to a few stairs with a glass door at the top of them.

Walking slowly, very slowly now that I've shielded myself from the rain, I'm at the bottom of the stairs way too soon.

I'm not ready for this.

Feeling like a lost girl, one who is waiting for her brother to take her hand and guide her to the playground to swing, I can't help but wish that he were here beside me.

With a breath in and out, the smell of salt in the air assaults my senses. The ocean must be very close. I wonder if the sand that surrounds it is anything like the sand at the beach Mimi took Zach and me to every summer.

God, how we loved going there.

We'd walk on the pier, swim in the lake, ride the carousel, and eat Abbott's famous custard. There was a beach closer to where we lived in Canandaigua,

New York, but it didn't have an Abbott's. Zach loved the black raspberry ice cream so much that he'd get two.

"I need to stock up until next year," he'd say.

It was so rare that anything made him happy, and I bet Mimi would have bought him a hundred ice-cream cones if only his happiness would have lasted.

Tires squealing onto the main road jar me from my memories.

On shaky legs, I take the stairs slowly. I reach for the keys Zach accidentally left at home when he visited at Christmas. He left his whole keychain. I would have mailed it, but I didn't find it for months and by then he had had new keys made.

I remember the day Zach told me he had bought a house. I was so glad he was doing well, that he was happy.

Finally, I had thought.

It takes me a few more seconds to gather the courage to unlock the door. The first key I insert doesn't work; neither does the second, nor the third.

A gust of warm wind whips around my black raincoat and blows up the nylon like a tent—a sign of the impending tropical storm that the driver mentioned before I tuned everything else out.

Nervousness and impatience blend as I wonder who I'll call if I can't get in. Zach's friend Nate would be a good start. Over the years, we've talked on the phone if he was around when I'd call my brother. He also called me right after Zach's death. He told me he would take care of everything until I could make it down here. And we've e-mailed quite a few times over the past seven weeks. In fact, I e-mailed him just before I boarded the plane this afternoon, telling him I was coming. But last I checked he hadn't responded yet.

I'm surprised.

He's always responded immediately to my previous messages. It may seem odd, but I feel like I know him well, even though we've never met.

The rain comes down harder and I look around for where my brother might have hidden a spare.

The terra cotta planter off to the right seems like the perfect location, but when I try to lift it, I can't. The palm tree inside is much heavier than I thought.

With nowhere else popping out as a place to hide an extra, I wonder if I should call and ask the driver to return. But before I do, I try the keys again—this time turning a few of them the other way.

To my shock and surprise one finally works. My stomach flips as the door easily swings open and I'm launched into darkness and the loud sound of beeping.

Shit, the alarm. I hadn't thought of that.

Should I try the same code Zach used on all his accounts?

That should work.

With the flip of a switch, a long narrow hallway presents itself. I find the alarm pad behind the door and press 0515, my birthday.

It doesn't work.

I press 0815, his birthday.

It doesn't work either.

What else?

The name of the gallery he worked for maybe? Nate's father's gallery.

What was it? Yes, Wanderlust.

I type the numbers corresponding to the letters and holy shit, the beeping ceases. I can't believe it. After all this drama, my nerves are finally starting to settle.

Once my bags are tucked inside the door, I glance down the hall.

Hardwood floors seem to run for miles until they end at the underside of an open-air staircase. With small steps I walk until I've reached the end and I'm standing at the perimeter of a large living room. My attention goes immediately to the windows and doors—they are everywhere. The entire back of the house is sliding doors with windows above them.

The night and the rain don't allow me to see anything beyond five feet, but I can make out palm trees, lots and lots of them. They sway back and forth through all the glass.

A beautiful picture.

Looking up, the high ceilings and large glass windows make the palms feel like they are part of the room. The two sparkling crystal chandeliers catch my eye—they are beautiful, but so unlike my brother. He always went for the shabby chic look. Modernism was never his thing.

Another hallway across the way mimics the one I'm standing in, and a fireplace sits in the corner. A large black leather couch, glass coffee table, and giant TV complete the room. I'm actually surprised by the sparse décor. It doesn't seem to be Zach's style at all, but maybe it came furnished.

I circle around the stairs to the landing and come face-to-face with a black plaster, life-size statue of a woman. It's definitely something Zach would have been drawn to—mysterious, sad.

It seems out of place in this space.

Surveying the rest of the room, I see a square kitchen in the center of the living area that separates the two hallways. The high-gloss black countertops match the stairs. Walking around them, I notice the kitchen looks perfect—like it's never been used. I quickly walk in and open the refrigerator—water, beer, wine, and nothing else. I guess Nate cleaned it out.

Following the hallway of windows that ends with a closed door, I turn the knob and squeeze my eyes shut, not opening them for what seems like hours. When I do, I'm standing in the entrance of what must have been his office. Computers, printers, and papers cover a large desk. Odd—I would have expected an easel and art supplies. And the walls should be covered with his sketches, not watercolors in ornate frames.

His studio must be elsewhere in the house.

I shut the door knowing I'll be spending time in there later going through all his papers.

Another door opens into the garage. I glance around—a few fishing poles, a basketball, football, and Frisbee, nothing else. The thought of Zach fishing or playing ball makes me smile, because aside from our yearly beach trip, he very rarely spent time outdoors—it just wasn't his thing.

Across from the garage is another door. When I open it, the switch on the wall does nothing. The brightness of the hall casts a sliver of light, and all I can see is an empty room with a bed in the middle of it.

With a turn of my flip-flops, I head back to the living area and the stairs. The entire space lacks anything personal, except the statue. Something about the statue speaks to me, but why I have no idea. It doesn't feel like it belongs, but it does—like the way Zach always felt.

With each step, I increasingly start to wonder if I should have just hired someone to do this and had the boxes shipped home.

This is so much harder than I imagined.

The stairs are sleek, so I take them slowly. When I reach the top, I pause and look around. It's an empty loft with two doors; one must go to the balcony, the other is open and leads to a huge bedroom. It too is white, no color at all.

So strange.

In the middle of the room is a large mattress with a wooden bedframe and metal bars inset in the headboard. The sheets are rumpled—the only evidence in the entire house that someone lives here—no, *lived* here.

With my hands clenched to my heart, I draw in a breath and attempt to push away my tears. I've cried for far too many weeks already. I'm trying to be strong. That is what he would have wanted.

I find myself once more searching for a piece of my brother, but again there's nothing. But then a small crystal dish on the dresser draws my attention.

Once I see what it holds, I can't stop the flow of tears from my eyes as I approach it. With wavy vision I pinch the small diamond that Zach wore so proudly in his ear.

Memories flood me once again.

"Please, Mimi, please. I really want one," Zach begged over and over.

"No, Zachary. There's nothing but trouble that can come out of that," Mimi *would say.*

It felt like the conversation took place every day for almost a year. But Zach didn't let up. He begged our grandmother to let him get an earring. She always refused. Over and over and over he asked and she said no. Then on his fifteenth birthday he came home from being out with Mimi sporting this very diamond. My grandmother finally gave in, probably feeling it was better than the fights, the drugs, and his all-encompassing need to rebel against everything.

The other metal in the bowl belonged to him as well—all his forms of self-expression. His lip ring, ear gauges, the circles with a ball hanging from them, most of which he acquired after he turned eighteen and no longer needed Mimi's permission.

These things in my hand were all a part of my brother.

He was a rebel.

Funny thing is that I always thought he was a rebel without a cause. I used to laugh about that, but today it makes me sad.

I remove my wet coat and shoes, circling around the rest of the room looking for pieces of him.

Nothing.

Nothing that was any part of him, not anything to define who he was.

But I know who he was.

He was my older brother.

He was my best friend.

He was a good man who didn't always make the right choices but had the best intentions.

Sadness lingers, as I think that I no longer have to wonder about him or worry about him. Now all that's left is for me to miss him, but I already miss him so much.

I'm alone.

Growing up, we only had each other—and our grandmother too. Our grandfather died before my grandmother gave birth to our mother, so Mimi knew single parenting well. She was amazing. She taught us everything she could, told us anything we wanted to know, but she refused to talk about the club. Mimi said she didn't believe in that old family legend.

Too bad destiny isn't something you can choose to believe in—it just happens.

Now, it's become more than a legend. It took him dying for me to believe. My constant reminder is the fact that Zach is also dead—he, like my grandfather and my mother, will forever be twenty-seven.

The question is: will I be joining my ancestors at the same young age?

Is that my destiny?

I hope not—but how could it not be?

I set the dish down and emotion overtakes me, the magnitude of my losses and my short life becoming all too real.

I collapse on the bed.

If I die at twenty-seven, will I have even lived a small part of my life?

Did my grandfather? Did my mother? Did my brother?

My head spins and I find myself back at that place I can't seem to crawl out of—I feel like screaming, but I can't because the idea of yelling seems like too much work when all I can think about is myself being next.

I yank off my wet T-shirt and shorts and bury my head under his pillow, wanting to block out that small voice telling me to push through this. I thought coming here would give me hope that life is worth the chance of what might or might not happen, but the sterility of my brother's home, the lack of anything he was surrounding me, stirs an uneasiness I can't seem to shake.

I feel like I'm already dying.

I've felt like this for many weeks.

Validation of a life worth living and dying young for was what I hoped to find by coming here. But instead all there is is a reflection of what I see when I look in the mirror—emptiness.

I close my eyes, wishing for all of this to be nothing more than a dream. But I know my first impression was right—I've opened Pandora's box.

Photo by Studio One to One Photography

Kim Karr lives in Florida with her husband and four kids. She's always had a love for books and recently decided to embrace one of her biggest passions—writing.